AFTER

AFTER

amy efaw

Viking

VIKING
Published by Penguin Group
Penguin Group (USA) Inc., 345 Hudson Street, New York, New York 10014, U.S.A.
Penguin Group (Canada), 90 Eglinton Avenue East, Suite 700, Toronto, Ontario, Canada M4P 2Y3
(a division of Pearson Penguin Canada Inc.)
Penguin Books Ltd, 80 Strand, London WC2R 0RL, England
Penguin Ireland, 25 St Stephen's Green, Dublin 2, Ireland (a division of Penguin Books Ltd)
Penguin Group (Australia), 250 Camberwell Road, Camberwell, Victoria 3124, Australia
(a division of Pearson Australia Group Pty Ltd)
Penguin Books India Pvt Ltd, 11 Community Centre, Panchsheel Park, New Delhi – 110 017, India
Penguin Group (NZ), 67 Apollo Drive, Rosedale, North Shore 0745, Auckland, New Zealand
(a division of Pearson New Zealand Ltd.)
Penguin Books (South Africa) (Pty) Ltd, 24 Sturdee Avenue, Rosebank,
Johannesburg 2196, South Africa

Penguin Books Ltd, Registered Offices: 80 Strand, London WC2R 0RL, England

First published in 2009 by Viking, a member of Penguin Group (USA) Inc.

5   7   9   10   8   6   4

Copyright © Amy Efaw, 2009
All rights reserved

"Waves" copyright © Connie K. Walle, quoted by permission of Connie K. Walle.
"Treasure This Moment" copyright © W.J. "Bill" Richstein, quoted by permission of Connie K. Walle.
"Happiness Waits" copyright © Ree Ivan, quoted by permission of Connie K. Walle.

LIBRARY OF CONGRESS CATALOGING-IN-PUBLICATION DATA IS AVAILABLE
ISBN: 978-0-670-01183-4

Printed in U.S.A.
Set in Berkeley Oldstyle
Book design by Nancy Brennan

PUBLISHER'S NOTE
This is a work of fiction. Names, characters, places, and incidents either are the product
of the author's imagination or are used fictitiously.

To "Baby Nick" and "Baby Vaughn,"
and to the countless babies who were never found
and have no names

AND

To the girls at Remann Hall

"Can a mother forget the baby at her breast
and have no compassion on the child she has borne?"

AFTER

chapter one

The TV's on, some lame morning show. The reception's lousy, and the sound's off. But Devon isn't really watching, anyway. More like staring blankly at the screen, the figures passing before her eyes in pantomime, signifying nothing.

She is lying there on the couch, a blanket tightly wrapped around her. Her body drained, her mind empty. She hears drizzle brush the windows, a steady, soothing sound. The gray morning has seeped through the miniblinds into the room. But she doesn't mind. Somehow, to her, the gloominess feels right. Perfect.

Her eyelids droop slowly. Then close.

Keys rattle outside.

Her eyes snap open. She blinks, confused. Her arms, legs, stomach jitter from the sudden sound. She feels shaky and cold and sick. She just might puke.

"Damn it!"

A voice. Somebody's there! Devon jerks her head to look behind her, toward the door. Her body tenses. One heartbeat. Two.

"Oh, that's it! I have . . . *had* it!"

But then . . . Devon breathes again, collapses back into the couch. It's only her mom's voice, talking to herself. And accompanying the voice is the familiar sound of struggle, that fighting against the dead bolt because her mom's last boyfriend kicked the door in. Their landlord did the repair—a shoddy job—and the door's never been right since.

"I'm . . . not paying . . . that shyster . . . another buck . . . till he gets his worthless . . . *butt* . . . up here . . . and fixes this door. I mean it! Not . . . one . . . more . . . miserable . . . buck!"

The thought that she should help her mom with the door vaguely drifts through Devon's mind. It's easier to work from the inside. Then another thought—that she should get off the couch, escape to her room—comes, too. But she just can't seem to make her body move.

"Yeah, I'll tell him where he can put his—"

The door bursts open, slams shut.

"Devon?"

Devon pulls her blanket tighter around herself.

"You're not at school?"

Devon doesn't answer. She's turned her eyes back to the TV. Back on the grinning faces.

"Devon? Hey . . ." Her mom yanks the cord on the miniblind nearest the door. Gray light eclipses the dimness and stretches for the darker corners of the room. "You okay?"

Clunk-plunk—Devon's mom has kicked off her shoes. Devon hears her mom heading her way, hears the muted footfalls across the stained carpet. It's not far to go, only about five steps from the door to the couch. In seconds, Devon senses her mom bending over her, feels that blonde hair pricking her face. Breathes in that mixture of dampness and cheap perfume, cigarettes and spearmint gum that makes up her mom's smell. Her mom had promised Devon that she had quit smoking "weeks and weeks ago." But here's the proof—she'd lied. Again.

"Come on, Dev—I slave away all night long and see my daughter for the first time in days, and there's not even one little 'hello'? Or something?" She waits a moment. "Not feeling good, hon?" She slaps an icy hand across Devon's forehead and holds it there briefly, considering. Then she shrugs. "Well, staying home's just not like you, Dev. But it's really nice you're here."

Devon turns her dark eyes upward to look at her mom, still leaning over her. Devon manages a smile, a faint one. Then shrinks away, deeper into the couch.

Satisfied somehow, her mom stands. "Sheeze. What a miserable night." She sighs loudly, slumping into the ratty recliner—the sole contribution that last boyfriend had made to the place and left behind when he'd split. "I'm telling you, one of these days? I'm quitting graveyard. You'll see. . . ."

Her mom blabs away about work, rehashing all the mundane drama from her night job at Safeway, but Devon isn't comprehending much. Can't hold on to the words. She keeps her eyes fixed on the TV, on the soundless Regis and Kelly miming a coffee taste-test—Starbucks, Peet's, Millstone, Seattle's Best—with open-mouth laughter, lips moving, eyes flirty, teasing each other.

Devon's mom gets up abruptly, startling Devon. Devon's eyes follow as her mom heads for the kitchen, still talking. "Oh, so get this—this morning. I step off the bus, right? And this place is like absolutely crazy. Ambulances, red lights flashing, everything. All these people just standing around . . . "

Devon's mind struggles to keep pace with her mom's mouth. She can feel herself slipping away again, but she makes the effort to stick with her. She forces her eyes open, focusing them back on the TV—needing something to anchor her to the conscious world. A commercial flickers across the screen. Four women are playing tennis; the sun is bright in some warm place.

"So, of course I've got to know what the big deal is, right?"

Devon can hear the faucet running in the kitchen now, the banging open of a cabinet. *Making Ovaltine*, Devon thinks. Half water, half milk—like always. Her mom's "sleepy time" snack.

"So I see one of them. You know, in plainclothes? You can tell what he is by the haircut. So obvious. Do they even think they're fooling anyone? But not bad-looking by the way—"

The TV is pushing some health club now, a ponytailed woman with a huge smile and great abs kickboxes—kick, punch, jab.

"—putting up that yellow tape stuff around that garbage can out back. Not the one where we dump our trash, but the other one. The big one. You know, farther down the alley . . ."

Her mom's voice cuts in and out. From far away, then very, very close. Dead air in between. Like a cell phone conversation with a bad signal.

" . . . I go up to him . . . ask what's going on . . ."

The microwave beeps. Devon flinches. She hears the door to the microwave open then, hears it shut. Hears her mom stir in the Ovaltine, a spoon clinking against the sides of a mug.

"You won't believe this, Devon."

Devon thinks of the swirling brown milk. Swirling . . . swirling . . . a vortex of brown, swirling milk. She fights the dizziness . . . closes her eyes.

"You just won't believe what they found in the trash."

Trash. Devon feels a vague anxiety slice through her mind. Trash . . . something about that word . . . And the thought seeps away.

"Poor helpless thing. Thrown out like last night's pizza crusts . . ."

Pizza? How has the conversation turned to "pizza"? Devon's mind is still way back somewhere with some not-so-bad-looking guy and Ovaltine. And trash. Her body feels so heavy. So cold . . .

"But I didn't get to see it because—check this out—it was still alive! They'd already rushed it to the hospital."

Pizza at the hospital? Devon's eyes are mere slits now, and they watch vacantly as her mom approaches from the kitchen. She's being careful with her mug, stepping delicately all the way back to the recliner. She stops at the couch, peers at Devon again. Brings her mug to her lips and slurps.

Please, Mom. Just go away. Leave me here alone. So tired . . .

"The weird thing is, we probably know the person that did it. We've probably passed that person a million times on the way to the laundry or something. Or on the bus. That person probably looks one hundred percent normal, too. Creepy. There are so many freaking weirdos around. You just have no idea. They come through the checkout at the Safeway all night long. . . . "

Silence is what finally jars Devon alert, a complete void of noise. Devon shifts under her blanket, turning to look over at her mom. She's kicked back in the recliner now, her empty mug on the floor, carelessly dropped and rolled over on its side. Devon can see the ring of chocolate on the inside.

Her mom catches her eye and says, "Oh, this is just great, Dev. Don't you think? We can have some quality family time today. You should get sick more often." She laughs, then waits for Devon to say something.

Devon turns back to the TV

"Well, I'm not all that tired yet. I've got a couple of hours of unwinding to do before I can even *think* about crawling into bed." She pauses. "So, what do you want to do?" She pauses again. "We could get a movie. I could make popcorn. We haven't done that in a long time. That would be fun, huh? A movie and popcorn?"

Her mom's voice is so hopeful and eager that Devon cringes at the thought of ruining it. Her mom, wanting to spend time with her. Only her. But Devon, she doesn't want to watch a movie. Or eat popcorn. Or do anything. Not today.

Her mom is quiet for a long moment. Or maybe it's way longer than that; Devon's not at all sure. Maybe it's many long moments strung together. Maybe Devon unwittingly fell asleep.

"Well, you're mighty chatty today." Her mom's voice has suddenly changed. Hopeful and eager are gone. Sarcasm has replaced them, a hint of hurt lurking underneath. But Devon can't fix things now. "You know . . . *fine*. If you're just going to lie there like a rock, let's at least turn up the volume."

Her mom rocks out of the recliner, glaring down at Devon on the couch. "I mean, I'd like *some* kind of a conversation here. I really don't think that's too much to ask. You're not lying there *dying* or anything. . . ."

Devon closes her eyes.

"And I'm going to put on *my* show. I can't stand these idiots. Where's that damn remote?"

Someone knocks on the door. Three loud raps.

Devon's eyes fly open, dart toward the door.

Her mom huffs and stomps over to answer it. "Ever think that maybe people are *sleeping* right now?"

She wrestles with the dead bolt. She yanks the door open. "Yeah?"

Devon shudders, buries her face under her blanket. Only her dark eyes and black hair, damp and matted, are exposed.

"Well!" Devon watches her mom do this little head toss, left then right. "Hey, guys!" Her tone is 100 percent altered now. Higher. All flirty. Just like that.

Devon can't make out who's out there, who her mom's so excited to be talking to. A shape of a person is all.

"The alley out back, right?" Devon's mom casually leans up against the doorframe, one hand on her hip. "I asked you what was going on, remember?" She cocks her head to one side. "You were putting that tape out there?" She flips her long blonde hair behind one shoulder. "That yellow stuff?"

Yellow . . . yellow. The color of Devon's mom's hair. The color of a sun break through the flat gray clouds. Of a lemon drop. Devon allows her eyes to droop closed for a moment.

"You remember *me*, too. Don't you?" Devon's mom giggles. "Oh, yeah, you do; I can see it in your eyes. . . ."

"Yes, ma'am. I, uh, seem to remember speaking with you earlier. . . . "

A voice other than her mom's. A stronger, deeper voice.

It's a man her mom is talking to. Of course.

"But now, for why I'm banging on your door at this early—"

"Bang, bang, bang." Devon's mom laughs. "I thought you only do that with your . . . um . . . *gun.*"

"—uh, yeah." He clears his throat.

Devon feels herself relax. It's just her mom, turning on the "charm." But as usual, way too strong. And cheap. It only attracts one kind—losers.

"Sorry to be bothering you, ma'am," the man goes on, "but this should only take a second. Let me introduce myself. I'm—"

Devon allows the grogginess to settle over her mind. Her eyes, directed at the door, start to glaze over.

"Ron." Devon's mom nudges the door open a little wider with her toe. "And you said you're Bruce, right? So, it's Ron and Bruce. And *I'm* Jennifer Davenport. Come on now, write it down in that little book you got there, Ron. And listen—take as many seconds as you need. Seconds, minutes, hours. For you, I got *all* day."

Devon opens one eye. Why doesn't her mom just take down those guys' numbers and make them go away?

"I like that attitude," the male voice says. "Anyway, we're just out here canvassing the area, trying to find out anything we can about—"

"Yeah, what a sicko." Devon's mom's voice turns pouty. She pulls at a long strand of hair and twirls it around and around her finger. Her long red nail pokes out of the blondness. "Poor little thing."

"We're just wondering if you've seen or heard anything unusual this morning."

The fog in Devon's brain is thick and heavy now. Through that one open eye, she watches her mom. Watches her mouth—open, close, smile. Her fluttering hands, the long red nails. Her bare feet, playing with the door. That little black snake tattoo slithering around her anklebone.

"I just got off the bus . . . made a beeline for you . . . a man with some answers . . . Ron . . . wish I could help you . . . maybe my daughter . . ."

At "daughter" Devon stiffens, both eyes suddenly sharp. Why is she being pulled into this conversation? She can see that the door's yawning open now, and her mom is nodding in her direction. Her voice bends funny, like she's standing at the far end of a tunnel, trying to relay a message. Devon concentrates hard, picks out the words.

"She's been around all morning. Home sick." Leaning close to the man, her mom whispers conspiratorially, "Or so she says."

"Really. Hey, that's great, ma'am. Mind if I talk to her?"

"I'm *not* a 'ma'am,' Ron," Devon's mom says, making a small move sideways. "Stop calling me that. Please! I'm not *that* old!"

"My apologies." The man steps into the apartment. His eyes do a quick scan of the room. Then they lock on Devon.

Devon watches the man move past her mom, taking the five steps from the door to the couch in about three. She can now see the other person her mom was talking with—another man, but this one is wearing a uniform. Familiar: dark blue, gold badge. He hangs back, near the door.

Devon's mom trails in behind the first man. She's all smiles, like she knows she's got the winning hand and the next play is hers. "Please ignore the mess, Ron. Devon's the typical teenager—no help at all. . . ."

The man is bending over Devon now: She breathes in his smell—clean, like soap. And he's smiling at her. "Hey there. You're Devon, right?"

Devon looks up at him. His words come out muffled. Like he's speaking to her underwater. She can feel her body tense. She squints.

"I'm Police Detective Ron Woods. How you doing?"

Devon's head feels strange. She shakes it, looks at the man closely.

She sees that he's got some surfer-boy blond hair, cut short. Brown eyes. Tan face. Wearing some kind of thick fleece jacket from REI or something. What did her mom say earlier? That she'd met some guy outside who wasn't bad-looking? Devon focuses on his smile. It's his best feature—nice teeth. Nice and white.

The man squats down to Devon's level and puts out his hand, doing that routine greeting thing. He waits a second for Devon to take it, then drops his hand, unshook. "Feeling kinda crummy today, huh?"

Devon just stares at him, her eyes dark and unblinking. She can't process why he's there, exactly. Why he's looking at her. Is he just being Mr. Polite before he makes his move on her mom? Pretending he actually likes kids or something? Devon's seen that routine before. Plenty of times.

"Devon!" Her mom is beside the man now, and her smile is gone. "Sit up and show some respect! What are you trying to do, embarrass me?" Angry lines crease her face, but she makes a fake, nervous laugh. "Come on, answer him! He's a *police officer*, for God's sake!"

Police officer. Devon's eyes widen as the words register. Her eyes flit to the man near the door, the one in dark blue. Two police officers.

"Hey! Are you listening to me?"

Devon can't move, can barely breathe.

"*Well?*" Her mom steps forward, flicks this quick, embarrassed glance at the man, then glares back down at Devon. "Hey,

I don't care how sick you are"—her mom reaches down—"there's no excuse for—" Her mom snatches the blanket. It flips up and away, like a flag blowing in the wind.

Her mom jerks back. "Oh . . . my . . . God," she whispers. The anger melts from her face. Her eyes are huge, her mouth open. "Oh my . . ."

The man sucks in his breath, hard.

Suddenly, Devon is very awake. Her eyes dart from his face to her mom's. From her mom's to his. Back and forth. The two faces are so different—one male, one female. One tan with light stubble, one pale with an end-of-the-day makeup residue. But the expressions are identical.

Devon draws her knees up and presses her hands down, between her legs, covering herself.

Her fingertips touch the fabric of her soccer sweats, and something else. Something warm. Sticky-slimy. And wet. Very wet.

She looks down to where her hands are.

And for the first time all morning she feels panic. Real-life, heart-pounding, want-to-run panic.

They see it. They see it all.

They see the blood.

Her eyes zip around the room, frantic, looking for something, anything. A way out. A place to hide.

And she's screaming. "Give it back!" Devon reaches out for her mom, fingers desperately grasping for that blanket. "Give me the blanket, Mom! *Please!*" Devon crawls across the couch, crawls across the pillow she was lying on, the now wet and sticky pillow she had hoped would absorb all the mess. She collapses, still reaching. Reaching. Now feebly reaching. The pain in her gut is intense. Tears slide down her cheeks, trickle into her mouth.

Her arm drops to the floor. "I'm sorry, Mom," she whimpers. "I'm so sorry. . . ."

The man's head whips around toward the door. Toward the other officer waiting there. "An ambulance," he shouts. "Now!"

Devon can hear the crackle of a radio.

"No! No way! What are you thinking?" Her mom's voice is hysterical. "Are you . . . do you think she—" She lashes out at the man. Wild arms flailing, red nails clawing. "Look! She's just home from school today. She's sick. She is *not* pregnant! Okay? She doesn't even have a boyfriend!"

Boyfriend. His face, his eyes with those long eyelashes too pretty for a guy's, materialize in her mind. His lips. She shakes it all back and away, deep inside. "No! Mom, don't!" Devon's voice is weak, quivering. She pushes herself up. "Please—"

"Don't you think I'd know if my own daughter's pregnant? What kind of mother wouldn't know her own daughter's pregnant? What kind of mother . . . she's so responsible . . . Do you hear me? *Are you even goddamn listening to me?*"

Devon quickly turns to the man. She wants him to understand. It's so simple, really. If he can understand, then maybe he'll go away. Her mom will stop screaming, and then both of them could go to sleep, finally get some rest. "I just had . . . a really . . . bloody . . . period," Devon stammers.

The man is nodding at her. He does understand.

"I . . . I didn't know what to do!" Devon continues, her voice growing earnest. "I tried . . . but the tampons, they couldn't stop it . . . way too much blood. I haven't had one in forever. . . . Please . . . "

"No! Get out of here!" Devon's mom lunges at the man, grabbing his shoulders from behind, her long nails digging into his jacket. "Get the hell out of here! Are you *hearing* me?"

The other man, the one in the uniform, appears suddenly, pulling Devon's mom off of the first man. Lifting her up from under the arms, he drags her far away from him and Devon and the mess on the couch.

"Don't . . . you . . . touch me!"

"Mom . . . I'm sorry . . . " Devon whispers. "Don't be mad."

"I'm going to report you! You . . . I'm going to press charges!" Devon's mom is raging from a distance now; she's in the kitchen, shrieking and throwing things. "I know my rights! *I said, get your filthy hands off me!*"

Devon squeezes her eyes shut, moves trembling fingers up to rub at her temples. *Water*, she thinks, *I need water.* She hadn't drunk for hours. Hadn't drunk all night.

"Devon," the man says. "Devon? Will you look at me? Hey, right here."

Devon opens her dark eyes, looks at him.

The man gently pulls her hands away from her head. "That's a girl." Then he cups Devon's face in his hands. They're big, strong hands. He leans closer. His eyes are intense, reaching deep into hers. "Okay, now, listen to me. Calm down and listen. Can you do that for me?"

His voice is steady. Soothing. Like the rain. Devon feels a wave of heat wash over her body. She closes her eyes again, then opens them. Everything's outlined in silvery white. Hyper-bright.

"This is important, okay? Concentrate on what I'm saying to you. . . ."

Devon tries to do what he said, tries to concentrate, but she can feel herself slipping under, losing him. Metallic flecks flurry around the corners of her vision, closing in. She hears her mom, shrill and sharp, still screaming . . . something about reports. About a boss.

"'You have the right to remain silent. Anything you say or do may be used against you in a court of law. You have the right to an attorney. . . .'"

The man's words flow over her. She feels apart from it all—his words, her mom's hysteria, her pounding heart. She watches his lips move. His nice, white teeth. She breathes in and out. . . .

And her world goes black.

chapter two

THE WHEELS OF the gurney hit the pavement, and Devon is jarred awake. The heavy ambulance doors slam, startling her. She opens her eyes, a flash of sunlight burns her retinas, blinding her for an instant. Then, slowly, a face emerges from the blankness, sort of floating above her. It's a young man's face—dark short hair, dark eyes. Those eyes are on her, watching.

"She's coming around." Devon hears him say this to someone other than herself. "Let's move."

The wheels scrape across concrete and the gurney rocks, though Devon isn't fully conscious of anything—the gurney beneath her or the ambulance parked nearby. She is only aware of those dark eyes above her and a vague knowledge of moving forward through a shady courtyard. And a tremendous sleepiness pressing through her.

Sliding glass doors open, drawing her attention. She raises her head slightly, peers down the length of her body toward her feet. She notices the other person there then, the other person who the dark-eyed man had just spoken to, another man with his back to her. He's guiding them forward through the sliding glass doors and into a hallway. White and cool and bright.

The man speaks over his shoulder to the dark-eyed man. "Where do they want her—trauma side or OB? Did they say?"

Before the dark-eyed man supplies an answer a woman appears at Devon's side, and the gurney stops. She's wearing sky blue scrubs and one of those doctor things around her neck—a stethoscope—and a frown, an irritated, weary one. The skin of her face is that permanent sort of gray from being too tired too often.

Quick talking shoots back and forth between the woman and the dark-eyed man like the give and go on the soccer field before a goal.

"She's fifteen," the dark-eyed man says. "Adolescent pediatrics?"

"But she's hemorrhaged."

"Right, they don't normally handle that—"

Devon can't keep up. She drops her head, rests her cheek on her shoulder.

And that is when she sees them. Black straps, three of them. One across her chest, pinning her arms to her sides. Another across her thighs. The last one across her shins, near her ankles.

Thoughts start to pull together in Devon's mind, and an uneasiness creeps over her.

The woman points behind herself, down a hallway to the left. "One of the OB exam rooms around the corner on the end. I'll call Dr. Klein to examine her."

The gurney rolls again, away from the sliding glass doors. On the right sits a large blue desk with phones and monitors and people bustling, people in scrubs—green, blue, white, multicolored. On the left the gurney passes partitions, curtains from ceiling to floor separating them. Inside one, Devon glimpses a woman sitting in a chair, holding a wad of gauze to her head, crying.

Devon turns her eyes away, looks instead at her own arm. A clear tube is there, jabbed into her wrist and taped in place. She follows the tube upward to where it ends at a small bag of clear liquid, hanging from a metal hook way above her head. Almost level with the man's dark eyes.

Something clicks in Devon's mind, and she knows exactly where she is. She's watched hundreds of scenes just like this one from her spot on the couch at home. People scurrying, wearing scrubs, stethoscopes around their necks, charts under their arms, tension in the air.

Panic spikes through Devon's brain, panic so startling she can't contain it. *They'll know. All of them, they'll know!* She whips her head from side to side, bucking against the straps holding her down. "NO!" she hears her own voice yelling. "No! Let me out of here!"

The gurney rolls faster. It makes an abrupt right turn, rushes down another hall. The man at Devon's feet is running. The dark-eyed man looks down at Devon once, his eyes wide with alarm.

"I want out of here! Take me home!"

The gurney flies through a doorway and halts abruptly. The dark-eyed man yells at the other man to slam down the brakes. Then he leans over Devon, panting softly. "You've got to calm down," she hears him say. "You need help, and we're here to do that. We're not going to hurt you. . . . "

"No!" Devon squirms under the straps. "Let me out!"

A squat woman in light green scrubs rushes into the room, a

taller one in white right on her heels. One of them yanks a green curtain across the door, then each takes a side of the gurney.

Devon is trapped, bodies on all sides.

"Don't touch me!" Devon kicks, struggling to free her feet so she can run. "Let me go! I want to go home!" A sharp pain rips through her, deep between her legs and across her gut. She opens her mouth and gasps with the sheer violence of it, and for one long heart-stopping moment she's absolutely silent.

Then her scream rolls out of the room and floods the hallway outside.

"That's enough of that!" the tall woman in white shouts into Devon's face.

This woman is serious; she's someone important, Devon can tell. Devon bites down on her lip, cutting off her scream.

"You need to get control of yourself," the woman continues, pulling back from Devon slightly, her voice a little less harsh. "You are accomplishing nothing with your behavior. Except, perhaps, arousing my ire." The woman nods at the other in green, then turns her full attention back on Devon. "Now. I know this is a little scary, so we're going to give you a mild sedative to help you relax."

Devon shrinks into the gurney; her eyes shift to the woman in green moving closer. Between the woman's plump hands is a long needle, pointed upward. A tiny spray squirts from its tip.

"No," Devon whimpers. "No . . ."

The woman in green smiles down at Devon. Her face is round and pleasant featured, but her eyes are wary. "I'm not sticking *you*, sweetie. This goes directly into the IV." She disappears behind Devon, reaching for the clear bag above her. "You're going to feel amazing in a few seconds."

Almost immediately, a coolness snakes up Devon's arm, then across her chest. She wilts into the gurney, the pain in her groin, the fear in her mind, melting away.

The woman in white seats herself on a stool, leans toward Devon. She lets out a small puff of breath. "Much better, huh?"

Devon says nothing, just stares at the woman, sort of mesmerized by her, by her glasses in particular—tiny rectangles of thick black plastic. Tacky on some people, but on this woman, they work. The white she is wearing, Devon realizes, is actually a white lab coat over layers of stuff—a black sweater and a white blouse under that—as if she had bundled up for the snow, which is rarely necessary along Puget Sound unless you are skiing at Snoqualmie Pass or climbing Mount Rainier. This woman has an interesting, intelligent face—not young and not old. And her blonde hair is pulled back into a hastily formed ponytail, escaped wisps falling everywhere.

"Well, just so you know who you're dealing with," the woman says, "I'm Dr. Klein."

Devon says nothing.

The woman in green moves around from behind Devon. "And I'm Cheryl. Nurse." Cheryl bends down and removes the straps holding Devon to the gurney. "Now that you're all nice and quiet, I think we can get rid of these." She smiles down at Devon, as if to add, Right? But instead she only says, "They were necessary for your transportation over here in the ambulance."

"We're going to take your vital signs next," Dr. Klein says then. "That would be your blood pressure, pulse, and temperature."

"You've had a physical before, haven't you?" Cheryl moves to Devon's left, holding up a blood pressure gauge and carefully straps it around Devon's biceps. "For school or sports or something?"

Devon nods slowly, watching Cheryl work. She feels the band tighten, squeezing, her pulse pumping hard against the pressure. Her brain feels tingly. Devon shuts her eyes and stops her mind from traveling back to that last physical, the one she had back in September for soccer.

"Well, good," Cheryl says. "Then this is nothing you haven't seen before."

There's a space of quiet between them, then Dr. Klein says, "So. What happened today?"

Devon doesn't respond right away. Then she shakes her head and whispers, "Nothing."

"Nothing," Dr. Klein repeats, letting the word sort of marinate in the silence. She takes a deep breath. "Well, that's not what I heard."

Devon opens her eyes. She feels the fear building back up inside her despite the artificial calm from the sedative. *What has she heard?* The nurse sticks a thermometer in Devon's ear, but Devon shrugs it away before it beeps.

"I've heard," Dr. Klein says steadily, "that you've lost a *lot* of blood." She indicates somewhere below Devon's waist. "No, I can *see* that you've lost a lot of blood. Your blood pressure is dangerously low, your pulse is dangerously accelerated. We don't know about your temperature, because you didn't allow us take it just now, but your skin feels hot to the touch and clammy. You passed out before the paramedics even arrived at your house." Dr. Klein raises her eyebrows, little curves above those thick black rectangles. "That's not 'nothing.' You are in bad shape, Devon."

Devon? How does she know her name? Devon's heart hammers in her chest, echoes through her ears.

"The blood seems to be coming from your vaginal area." Dr. Klein pauses. "Can you tell me about that?"

Devon's eyes dart around the room, looking for the two men who'd brought her to this place. They are nowhere. The man with the dark eyes, he left her. She looks over toward the door, toward the green curtain pulled across it. And her mom? *Where is she?*

"Devon?" Dr. Klein presses. "Can you help me out here? Shed some light on this for me?"

Devon shakes her head fast. "No. I . . . don't . . . can't . . ."

Dr. Klein presses her lips together. "Okay." She reaches into a pocket of her white coat and *thwaps* a latex glove over each hand. "Cheryl and I"—Dr. Klein stands and Cheryl moves closer—"are going to pull your sweatpants off now." Dr. Klein nods at Cheryl quickly. "Very carefully—"

Two sets of hands reach for Devon's waistband.

"No! Please!" Devon is breathing hard and fast. "I don't want—"

"I'm just going to take a little peek to see what's going on—"

"No!" Devon pushes herself up on her elbows, pulling her legs in protectively. "Don't touch me. . . . Don't . . . "

"We're not going to hurt you, Devon," Dr. Klein says, sliding around the gurney to Devon's right side. "We just need to look—"

"No! You can't . . . you can't make me do this. . . ."

Dr. Klein leans closer. "Listen to me, Devon. You are in an examination room at Tacoma General Hospital's ER. You were brought here in an ambulance. I am Dr. Laura Klein, the physician on duty. I don't care about *why* you're here. I don't care about what part you may or may not have played in being here. That's history. It's done, it's over, and no one can change it. All *I* care about is your health. And you're in very dangerous shape right now, in danger of possibly *bleeding* to death. Do you hear what I'm telling you?"

Cheryl steps closer to Devon, rubs her back softly.

Dr. Klein adjusts her glasses. "And I'll be damned before I'm going to have some foolish girl die under my care. I want to be able to go home tonight and crawl under my blankies and sleep well. So, don't make this harder on yourself—or *me*—than it needs to be."

Devon hugs her legs to her chest, her arms shaking. She can feel the needle from the IV tugging at her wrist. "You can't make me do this," Devon whispers.

"Now, I want you to lie back down," Dr. Klein says, ignoring Devon's protest, "and Cheryl and I are going to remove your pants—"

Cheryl gently unwraps Devon's arms from around her legs and slowly pushes her down onto her back. Dr. Klein steps forward, reaches for the waistband of Devon's sweats.

"No . . . doctor . . . " Devon pleads. "I want to go home." Devon reaches down and clutches the elastic waistband with her fingers.

"Don't do this," Dr. Klein says. "Don't make this ugly."

Cheryl plucks Devon's fingers from the waistband. At the same time, Dr. Klein tugs the sweatpants down over Devon's thighs, off her legs.

"Okay, I'm going to remove your underpants now." Dr. Klein nods at Cheryl. "I'll have to cut them off."

Cheryl hands Dr. Klein a small pair of scissors, and Devon hears two quick snips. Devon squeezes her eyes shut as the doctor pulls away the soaked fabric and carefully pushes Devon's knees apart, spreading her thighs.

Devon is too weak—too sore—down there to resist much. She turns her face into her shoulder, whimpering softly.

"You're doing fine," Dr. Klein says, lowering herself to the stool at the foot of the gurney again. "Now I'm just going to take a quick look."

Dr. Klein's rubbered fingers gently probe toward Devon's private place, spread its skin apart.

Devon bites her lip.

"Oh," Dr. Klein says suddenly. "The umbilical cord. It's still here, Cheryl." She takes a deep breath. "She's shoved it up inside herself."

"So, the placenta hasn't been delivered," Cheryl states matter-of-factly.

Devon raises her head, her heart pounding. *What?* She looks between Cheryl and Dr. Klein. They are staring at each other, both thinking hard.

What! What do they see?

"We've got to get her to the Birthing Center's OR immediately," Dr. Klein tells Cheryl, her voice tense.

"Yes," Cheryl agrees.

Birth Center? Oh, God! No!

"Devon"—Dr. Klein is standing now, leaning forward— "we're going to move you—"

Devon shakes her head. "No."

"You have something inside of you that we have to remove or you could die—"

"No!" Devon screams, pulling her naked legs toward herself.

"Devon! We know you've just delivered a baby—"

"NO!"

And with her thighs, Devon thrusts up and out.

Devon's right knee connects solidly with Dr. Klein's face.

The black rectangular glasses clatter to the floor.

chapter three

TWO POLICE OFFICERS lock Devon in the back of a squad car that smells of sweat and filth and stale cigarette smoke.

But first they handcuffed her. They walked into the hospital room where she'd lived for the past three days, sitting under the sheets with the two white pillows supporting her back. Devon noticed how they wouldn't look directly into her eyes when they told her to stand, cuffing her right there beside the bed. Matt Lauer was left giggling with some sitcom star on the TV in the corner of the room when they escorted Devon down the quiet hallway with all the nurses watching.

The squad car drives the two blocks up Martin Luther King Way and turns left. Devon knows the street; during the off-season she'd sometimes jog this very route coming out of Wright Park. From her seat, she can hear the dispatcher over the police radio, a sudden static spurt before the voice. The two police officers sit up front, sipping coffee from Styrofoam cups.

Devon looks out the window. The sky is a flat, brooding gray. Familiar buildings pass. Farley's Florist. The Dollar Store. The Salvation Army Thrift Store. Sunriser Restaurant. Jason Lee Middle School, newly remodeled and pretty now. The sight always surprises Devon, even though it's been a long time since it's changed.

A sign outside a church proclaims:

LOVE

IS GOD'S WILL

IN ACTION

Love. Devon feels empty and numb and a little sorry for herself. She looks down at her hands, cuffed together on her lap, and waits for the ride to be over.

The squad car stops at red lights and crosses intersections, then turns right, up a short hill that leads to the juvenile detention center at Remann Hall—a complex of squat white buildings not far, Devon realizes, from the Morgan Family YMCA, where she had learned to swim when she was four. Unlike today, her mom had been with her then. Standing there in the waist-deep water, making sure that Devon wouldn't sink when the teacher wanted her to float. Singing along with Devon and the class the "I'm a Little Teapot Short and Stout" song that ended every lesson.

The squad car stops in a parking space. The police officer who'd been riding shotgun heads for the nearest building. The one behind the wheel cuts the ignition, then moves around the car to open Devon's door for her. Devon stares at him standing there, remembering the only other guy who had ever opened a car door for her.

Last summer. The sky was bright blue mirroring the water, the sun warm. A perfect day. He had smiled down at her; he'd had That Look in his eyes—warm and eager and a little bit vulnerable. When he'd look at her in that way, and smile that tilted smile, her body would tingle with an electric tension that robbed her breath away.

That was then. And now?

Now she is here.

The police officer is waiting. "Come on, miss," he says. "Time to get out."

Devon nods, swings her legs to the outside. Stands. Waits for the officer to close the car door. Follows slowly behind as he strides toward the building his partner just entered. He turns back to Devon, notices her slight limp and takes her elbow as they continue to cross the asphalt.

Devon says, "Thank you," because she knows it's the expected response, and because she's relieved for his support. Her pelvis feels so unstable it scares her—a throbbing, leaking hollowness between her legs.

But the soreness doesn't worry her much. She's done soccer tournaments where she'd played back-to-back games in summer heat without ever being subbed out. Lead thighs, aching tightness through the calves and ankles and feet, bruises on shoulders and ribs are all part of the game, consequences that Devon has come to expect, sometimes lasting for days afterward.

Devon knows the soreness always goes away . . . eventually.

And even what happened to her That Night. That nightmare. The sweat, the intense pressure, the haggard uncontrolled breathing, the involuntary shaking, the gruesome ripping— Devon halts the images, actually squeezes her eyes shut to stop them. What she went through those lonely hours—while outside her bathroom window nighttime slowly turned to day— was more physical, more excruciating, than anything she had ever experienced. When she lay on the cool linoleum covered with her own gore—after it was over and done—she knew she'd feel it later. But even then, she realized the pain wouldn't last forever.

The blood, however, is something altogether different. Something unexpected. The constant seeping through thick hospital-issued sanitary pads and disposable underwear, the sickening sweet smell of it. She'd hated asking the nurses to bring her fresh things, afraid of the avoiding eyes and tight nods some of them had given her when she finally brought herself to do it. Devon can't help but suspect that all the blood must be a sort of never-ending punishment—some kind of twisted reminder—for what had happened to her That Night.

The police officer opens the door they'd been moving toward, waits for Devon to step inside.

The other officer is already there, leaning up against a counter, relating information to a frizzy-haired woman behind a desk, a shield of bulletproof glass between them.

"But you should already have the police report," the police officer is saying to the woman through the glass. "She's been at Tacoma General the past three days. They just released her to us about a half hour ago."

Devon can't make out much of the woman's response because of the glass. And anyway, the other police officer is nudging her toward a long wooden bench backed against a line of windows with a view of the parking lot.

"Sit," he tells her, then drops to the bench himself, crossing his arms, as if expecting a laborious wait.

Devon stops at the window. A white minivan so dirty it looks gray creeps by. The woman behind the wheel hunches forward, her nose nearly touching the windshield—peering left, then right—like she's lost.

Devon turns away and eases herself down onto the bench. She feels a strange pulling on her breasts as she bends, a definite tenderness that she hadn't felt before. One of the nurses had told her this would happen, that it was a normal part of the postpartum process. Her body only doing what it's designed to do.

"Her discharge papers? Yeah, I got them right here," the police officer is saying to the frizzy-haired woman as he pushes a file through a slot in the glass. "Uh, no. They said they'd forward her medical records later on."

Devon drops her head, fixes her eyes on the scuffed floor without actually seeing it. She hears the police officer's voice, still talking to the woman, without really processing his words. Devon's straight black hair falls across her face, but she doesn't brush it aside. She's careful to think of nothing; she just waits, waits to carry out the next action required of her here.

Finally, the police officer turns from the woman behind the glass. He says something. Hesitates. Then says it again.

Then yells, "*Hell-o!*"

Devon jerks, looks up. That police officer—he's talking to her. Staring at her, impatient.

"Sorry," she whispers.

He continues to study her. "This is your first time here. Isn't it, kid?"

Devon swallows, nods her head. "Yes."

"Yeah. Well. Piece of advice? Stay alert. You can't be zoning around in la-la land here. You gotta know what's going on every minute."

Devon nods again. "I'm sorry."

The police officer is still watching her. Devon looks down at her hands. She doesn't like him watching her, afraid of what he thinks he sees.

"All right then," he says finally. "You need to step over here now. This lady has a couple questions for you before you go inside and finish getting inprocessed."

Devon pushes herself off the bench and walks up to the glass, her stomach twitching. Questions. What do they want to know? What will they make her say? A woman had come to talk to her at the hospital, but Devon had said nothing. Devon holds her hands in front of her because of the cuffs.

The frizzy-haired woman observes Devon's approach without much interest, then asks for her name, date of birth, address, and next of kin. Is she currently taking any medication?

Devon answers all of the questions completely.

The woman types everything into her computer, raising her eyebrows slightly at Devon's middle name. "Devon *Sky* Davenport," she repeats. "Sky? *S-k-y?*"

"Yes," Devon says, addressing the back of the computer monitor now rather than the woman's face directly. "*S-k-y.* As in"—she swallows—"as in, 'the sky's the limit.'"

But Devon doesn't volunteer any further explanation, doesn't explain to the woman the story behind the name. That, in fact, "the sky's the limit" is how Devon's mom has always defined Devon and her supposed potential in life. Her mom would say it when Devon brought home a flawless report card or when Devon received a stellar postseason evaluation from her coach or when a complete stranger commented on Devon's exceptional manners or after the Latest Loser packed his stuff and walked out. "You'll be Somebody for both of us," her mom would say.

Not anymore, Mom. Everything's changed. Now, for me, "the sky" isn't anything but flat and gray and too far away to ever reach. She takes a deep breath. *If you were here with me, you'd see it for yourself.*

But her mom isn't here. She hasn't come to see Devon at all. Those long hours Devon spent alone between the bleach-white sheets, watching the door to her hospital room and hoping her mom would cross the threshold. It never happened; she never came.

Devon closes her eyes, bites her lip to stop the trembling. She won't cry in front of this woman. No—she won't cry in front of anyone.

"All right, Sky Girl," the woman says, "I'm going to have you come inside now. You've got a court appointment at one this afternoon, and we've got a number of things to get accomplished before then."

Devon nods, suddenly exhausted.

She walks through the door the woman's opened for her.

"Davenport, Devon," calls out a petite woman with frosty blonde hair, short and stiff with hairspray in that wispy, windblown look.

Devon hears her name, and an adrenaline jolt jazzes her heart. Her eyes lock on the woman, but Devon doesn't answer, doesn't move. She'd taken a shower during Intake, but sweat pricks anew along her still-damp hairline, across her upper lip. Under her arms.

This is it. Her name being called. It nails her to this place.

The woman scans the line of molded plastic seats against the wall. Eleven kids sit there with their hands uncuffed and waiting to get called into court. They are all dressed alike in their stiff polyester jumpsuits with leg irons pinching their ankles, white tube socks, and cheap rubber slides. The girls wear orange and the guys wear blue, and Devon in her own orange jumpsuit is sitting right there with them, third plastic seat from the end.

"Uh . . . " The woman checks her clipboard again, just to make sure. "Davenport?" She looks uncertainly at the guard sitting at a desk behind her.

Devon knows she's now bordering on disrespect, but she can't make herself respond. And how should she respond, anyway? Raise her hand, like she would in honors world history when Ms. Guggenheim is standing up front, wanting the date the Magna Carta was signed?

Devon swallows; her spit is paste. The kids beside her—the guy with the dreads and long scar crossing his face, the girl with her completely shaved head and piercing blue eyes—do not look the types who'd ever raise their hands in class. Or, for that matter, even *go* to class.

And this woman, as small as she is, scares Devon. She has this sort of authoritative aura about her and a hard-looking face. From the moment the guard with the Motorola on his hip led Devon from the inprocessing area to this room and told her to wait for her name to be called, Devon has watched this woman. She's been coming in and out a door at intervals with that clipboard she's holding, calling jumpsuited kids forth. None looked thrilled to be following her, and none came back through the door after they had. The makings for a teen scream summer thriller.

The woman crosses her arms, the clipboard hugged to her chest, annoyance gathering in her eyes.

Devon could run. She could just jump up and sprint out of there. But how far would she get? Not very—the leg irons locked around her ankles and the throb deep between her legs and the guard who's posted near the door with the handcuffs clipped to his back belt loop and the other one who's sitting at the desk near the front and the maze of hallways that brought her here would all conspire together and prevent it.

The other kids fidget in their plastic seats, start looking around.

Devon finally raises her hand halfway. "Here," she whispers.

The woman studies Devon, humorless. "Oh, okay," she finally says. "I get it—you forgot your name . . . *temporarily*. Nice."

Devon shakes her head, No.

Someone off to Devon's right—maybe the guy with the dreads—laughs under his breath.

Devon stares down at the woman's feet, careful to see nothing else. Black wedge sandals, an intricate design of thin straps weaving around her feet and toes. Devon had wanted some like them herself; the memory is there suddenly. How she'd once lingered at the display at Nordstrom's, touched the smooth leather. Imagining them on her feet, she'd picked up each sandal, feeling its feather weight. But they'd been expensive. She couldn't buy them herself because she had to save up every dollar of her babysitting money to offset Regional camp fees and the never-ending need for that new pair of keeper gloves. And she hadn't wanted to set her mom up just to have to say no, so she never asked.

Kait, her best friend then, had stood there at the shoe display with her. She'd prodded Devon to buy them. "Trust me, Dev," she'd said, "you'll *definitely* regret not getting them. You'll look back and wish that you did." Devon pushes the memory out of her mind; that was before the two of them had slowly drifted apart. Devon hasn't allowed herself to dwell on the specifics for a long time now. Can't really remember the details anyway. And then Kait wrote that letter, and everything got ruined.

"Well?" The woman sticks her clipboard under her arm, her tone beyond irritated now. "Come on, then, Davenport. You're up."

Devon slowly pushes herself to her feet, wincing slightly. Sitting all this time has made her body stiff—her pelvis, her hips, even her back aches. But especially her breasts; they throb like she's just absorbed a corner kick full in the chest.

Devon feels the woman's eyes on her. Does she guess? About why she's here? Is it written on that clipboard of hers? Devon stands a little straighter, keeps her eyes on the floor in front of her.

The woman turns and moves toward the door.

Devon follows. The chain of her leg irons *ching, ching, ching*s between her feet behind the soft slap of the woman's sandals.

The woman opens the door. Devon steps inside.

A waft of stale air, then a hushed ambience, flows over her. The door closes softly behind her.

It's the courtroom, but it doesn't look anything like Devon had expected. This seems much smaller than anything she'd seen on TV. Up front is the judge's bench. It's a two-level, terraced wood structure. On the top level sits the judge, wearing a black robe. Two cylindrical white pillars sandwich him, one on each side, and the U.S. and Washington state flags stand tall behind him. On the lower level below the judge, two women sit facing each other and tip-tap on computers, their flat screens back to back. Three rectangular tables are perfectly spaced across the width of the room before the judge. People sit behind those tables, their backs to Devon. A uniformed officer is stationed in the corner of the room, covered in partial shadow.

The woman with the clipboard slips off to the right, sitting in a chair near the door. And Devon is left standing at the threshold alone.

Devon stares at the judge, unsure of what else to do.

The judge's hair is short and dark, his features lean. He is briskly sorting through a stack of papers before him. After a moment, he lifts his eyes, trains them on Devon. They are intense and commanding and seem to look right down into her, down into her mind. Like he can read what's there.

A shiver runs through her, and Devon shifts her eyes away to the gold nameplate on the front of the raised wood structure:

HON. STEPHEN V. SAYNISCH

Her judge.

A light sweat breaks across Devon's body, and her hands tremble. *This is for real.* She wipes her hands along the sides of her legs. A smattering of coughing and throat clearings comes from somewhere off to her left, and she jerks her eyes in the direction. A small window is there, and through that window she can see a long crowded bench along the back wall. The gallery. She yanks her eyes away, looks back at the judge. People are there in the gallery, watching her. Just like in all those courtroom dramas on TV, people are sitting back there and thinking things about her—terrible, imagined things.

And her mom. Is her mom sitting there with them?

Devon feels dizzy, light-headed. Queasy.

A loud, staccato whisper. "Hey!"

Devon's eyes snap straight ahead toward the sound, toward a man sitting behind the table closest to her.

He's glaring over his shoulder—over his reading glasses—at her.

"Sit!" he whisper-hisses, his index finger pointing at the chair on his right.

Devon quickly shuffles forward, lowers herself into the chair, her heart thumping in her chest. She places her hands on her lap and folds them carefully.

"I'm your lawyer," the man whispers into her ear. "At least for today. We'll talk later."

Devon nods because her mouth is too dry to trust with her voice. But her lawyer has already turned away from her, his attention directed at the piece of paper in his hands. Devon wets her lips and observes him cautiously out of the corner of her eye.

His hair is sparse—the few tufts rooted between his receding hairline and his bald spot fluff up like the crest of some exotic bird. His dark suit is wrinkled, the shoulders lightly dusted with dandruff. As he scans the paper, his lips move, silently forming the words he sees.

Nothing like what Devon expected a lawyer to look like. Nothing like those lawyers on TV. He's sort of shabby. And old.

But then she feels a twinge of guilt. After all, he's her lawyer. He's going to get her home today, away from this place. Right? Yes. Definitely, yes.

"Just keep your mouth shut unless I say otherwise," Devon's lawyer whispers without looking at her. "If the judge asks you something"—he jabs his finger on the piece of laminated paper taped to the tabletop in front of her—"you have two choices."

Devon looks down. Two sentences in bold black scream:

"Yes, Your Honor."
"No, Your Honor."

Devon swallows and nods again.

"State versus Devon Davenport, number zero zero, dash eight, dash seven five seven nine four, dash one."

Devon turns toward the new voice. Only a few feet to the left of her lawyer, behind his own table in the middle of the room, sits a young man speaking into a microphone. He wears a dark suit and power red tie and seems nervous by the way his leg shakes up and down under the table as he reads from the file before him. Looking across him, Devon can see the third table over on the far left side of the room. Behind it two women hunch over a stack of papers, their heads close—pointing at this, nodding at that.

Her lawyer pokes her with his elbow, and Devon jerks upright. She glances at him apologetically.

"Sit up," he whispers again. "When the prosecutor speaks, act like you care."

"Your Honor," the young man in the red tie—the prosecutor, apparently— is saying, "the respondent is before the court today for an arraignment—"

Respondent? Wait. Didn't her lawyer just say that man was the prosecutor? Or is that her—the "respondent"? Devon wants to ask, but her lawyer is so busy, rifling through a cardboard box of folders on the table before him. Red. Green. Blue. Yellow. He pulls out a yellow. Opens it. Leafs through it.

The young man drones on. Devon looks down at her hands in her lap, at her fingertips, specifically. They are gray. From the fingerprinting. Earlier today, the frizzy-haired woman behind the bulletproof glass had uncuffed Devon's wrists before snipping off the hospital wristband and replacing it with another, similar band for Remann Hall. Then she held Devon's hands.

Had rolled each fingertip over the cool black ink, had stamped each onto a white card until all the little boxes had been filled with her prints. Devon couldn't get the ink off completely, not even when she'd scrubbed her hair in the shower afterward.

Devon shoves her fingers under her thighs, hiding them. The humiliation of the inprocessing is still so raw. Fingerprints were only the beginning. Then came the mug shot. The strip search. The lice check. The shower. A different woman—one with short gray hair—had watched from the corner of the bath- room as Devon stood naked before her, the water trickling over her shoulders, down her back.

The woman had, at least, turned her eyes when Devon dried herself. But afterward, the woman had spotted the blood smeared on the rough towel, the small pinkish puddles on the tile floor.

"I take it you're pleading Not Guilty to this." Her lawyer is looking at her, frowning over his glasses.

Devon looks back at him blankly.

"Pay attention," he whispers again, harsher this time. "I'm talking about the charges just read against you."

Charges? Devon blinks. *Charges against me?* What had just been said about her? How could she have missed that? All the other people—in the gallery, behind the computers, sitting at the tables—had heard it. But she—The Respondent—had not.

Her lawyer sighs heavily and turns back to the yellow folder, visibly displeased. "Generally, at this point in the process," he says, speaking directly into the folder, "we plead Not Guilty. Once we get a chance to talk, things may change."

Devon nods, but her lawyer doesn't see it. Doesn't even check back to see if she understood. *Doesn't he care?* He licks his index finger, flips to the next page in the folder. Shouldn't he talk to her *now*? Ask the judge for a time-out or something and then take a few minutes to get to know her? Explain these charges to her? Or, at the very least, look at her? Why won't he *look* at her?

The red-tied prosecutor suddenly stands, starts moving toward Devon's table. She feels herself shrink back.

"Due to the age of the respondent," he says, slapping down papers in front of Devon's lawyer, "which is two months short of sixteen, and the severity of the charges"—he walks toward the judge's bench and hands a duplicate copy to one of the women typing at her computer, who in turn passes it up to the judge—"the state requests declination of jurisdiction to the adult criminal court."

Adult criminal court? Stillness blankets the courtroom, and Devon feels panic churning inside of her again. Clothing rustles behind her, someone sniffs, then a faint whispering. What does this mean? Criminal court. *Criminal?* Oh, God. They think she's a *criminal.*

Devon's lawyer snatches up the papers and whips through them, shaking his head, muttering.

Devon's eyes dart from her lawyer to the judge to the prosecutor with the red tie. The prosecutor returns to his seat, hands folded on the table, also watching the judge.

The judge finally surfaces from the papers. "Sounds reasonable." He squints across at Devon's lawyer. "Defense?"

Devon watches as her lawyer slowly stands, his face still in the papers, shaking his head.

"Your Honor," her lawyer starts, his tone incredulous. "*Clearly* the State has not reviewed the respondent's file." He pointedly opens the yellow folder. "She has no prior arrests. And she's maintained an exemplary school record." He starts pulling papers out of the folder, one by one. Makes a show of reading details from each and then dropping them—*flutter, flutter*—before they finally rest on the table. "No disciplinary problems . . . exceptional grades . . . participates in school athletics . . . honors classes . . . tutors fellow students." He looks up at the judge. "Your Honor, she's as clean as you or I—"

"However, she *is* currently charged with a crime, a number of *felonies* in fact. Correct, Counsel?" The judge looks annoyed. "You *have* received a copy of the charge sheet? *Yes?*"

Devon's lawyer stares back at the judge, saying nothing for a moment. Then, "'Innocent until proven guilty,' Your Honor. We must look at the respondent *prior* to the charges. Her record is spotless. *Zero* priors. How often do you see *that* in this courtroom? Her record screams rehabilitative potential, and at the very least she deserves the chance to demonstrate this potential with a hearing. She and respondents like her are the very reason the juvenile system was created."

The prosecutor disagrees. It goes back and forth for a time, the young man and Devon's lawyer both making speeches with big words, waving their hands all around. Devon tries to stick with them, but their words are too unfamiliar, her body too tired, the voices too buzzing, blending together. The small courtroom, squeezing her in, making her feel trapped. Caged. Her forehead sinks into her hand, her eyelids droop closed.

Is she really the person sitting here? Is she really wearing this orange polyester jumpsuit with the chains between her feet? Is there really a judge in a black robe presiding over all these people? It's all so surreal. Just this morning, Devon had awoken to a nurse with a breakfast tray of scrambled eggs and toasted English muffins, packaged apple jelly and butter on the side. The nurse had gone over the discharge instructions with Devon then, absently smoothed her hair, petted her, like she was some little lost child.

How could it have come to this so quickly? How could it have come to this at all?

"All right," the judge breaks in. "Probation, please weigh in here."

One of the women from the table on the far side of the room clears her throat and starts to speak. And she's saying, "Jennifer Davenport, the respondent's mother."

Her mom. Devon sits straighter in her seat, her heart beating fast.

So, *is* her mom somewhere in this courtroom? Maybe she's been here all along, silently willing Devon to turn around and look at her, to see her sitting there in the gallery supporting her. Maybe she'll stand up right now and beg the judge to let her daughter come home, promising that this time she'll take good care of her. Really good care of her.

The woman across the room is still talking. Devon listens as the woman explains to the judge and both lawyers and the uniformed officer stationed in the corner and the women typing at their computers and the woman with the clipboard sitting near the door and the people watching from the gallery that Devon's mom is currently "unavailable."

That Jennifer Davenport, the respondent's mother, has failed to report to the police for questioning.

That Jennifer Davenport, the respondent's mother, has not turned up at either place of her employment—the Safeway at the intersection of 25th Street and Proctor or her bartending job at Katie Downs on Ruston Way.

That Jennifer Davenport, the respondent's mother, has not returned voice mails left on her cell phone.

That Jennifer Davenport, the respondent's mother, has apparently vacated her residence at Kingston Manor Apartments. That at this point in time, it is unknown whether she has done so temporarily or permanently.

"And," the woman finishes, "she is not present in the court today, Your Honor."

The woman says all this with no emotion, so matter-of-factly, like it's no big deal. Like it's expected.

Devon crosses her arms in front of her aching chest, hugging herself against the hurt and disappointment and guilt. She puts her head down on the table.

All Devon can think is her mom's disappeared. Again.

But this time, it's Because of Me.

Devon's throat tightens. That look on her mom's face that morning, the shock and disbelief. That look that said she was going to bolt. It's right there all over again, filling Devon's mind, refusing to be shoved away.

Devon never should have hoped for anything else. She should have known her mom wouldn't come to be here with her today.

Her lawyer kicks her foot—"I said, *sit up!*"—and Devon snaps alert. She drops her arms to her sides.

And then something truly horrible happens.

Devon's breasts suddenly feel like they're being stabbed with a hundred pins, like they're two huge pincushions. Like something is wringing them, hard.

The nurse who had brought breakfast this morning had said this would happen. "Don't be scared. You'll need to bind yourself. Get an Ace bandage. Or a really tight sports bra. And ice, lots of ice."

Devon gasps with the shock of it, the pain of it.

All eyes lock on her.

All eyes watch as her jumpsuit changes.

Two wet, warm circles form where her breasts touch the fabric, and spread.

Milk. My milk. Oh, God, why?

And Devon starts to cry.

AETER

chapter four

THE GAVEL BANGS, and a guard ushers Devon out of the courtroom.

Devon's face is down, hidden by the straight black strands falling across it like a widow's veil. She watches only the gray, industrial carpet under her feet as she moves forward, her arms crossed tightly in front of her to hide her chest. She can feel the dampness there against the heels of her clenched fists—the cool, tacky dampness.

What had just happened in there? Everything was chaos at the end.

Her lawyer had rushed a whisper in her ear, a whisper that Devon hadn't fully heard. She'd been distracted, desperately pressing her fists into her breasts to stem that warm and sticky oozing. But she was miserably unsuccessful, just as she had been unsuccessful That Night when she could no more control her body than she could stop each ticking second. That Night when this nightmare had begun.

"We'll talk," her lawyer had said. "Very soon." Devon had looked directly at him then. She'd needed some sort of connection. But he'd quickly turned away from her to straighten his stack of papers, smacking them on the tabletop one or two extra times to give himself something to do until the guard appeared and led Devon away.

"Hold up a sec," the guard tells Devon now that they are in the quiet hallway outside the courtroom. He squats before Devon to unlock her leg irons and remove them. "It's Devon, right?" He looks up at her. "Devon Davenport?"

Devon nods.

He smiles as he straightens, awkwardly holding the leg irons in one hand. "Well, now it'll be easier to walk at least." He has dark, honest eyes that Devon trusts. His gaze drops for a moment to Devon's tightly crossed arms.

Devon looks down at her feet.

"Hey," he says. "I know it isn't exactly easy in there. Especially the first time."

Devon nods quickly. She's anxious to get moving, to reach the next appointed place.

"All right," he says. "Ready?"

"Yes," Devon whispers.

"Then let's go." He slowly leads her away from the courtroom and through the hallway, a maze of white walls and olive green doors and gray carpet. When they finally stop, it's inside a small and narrow room, a large closet actually, with shelves of folded things: blankets and sheets and pillows. The guard selects some of each and tightly rolls a blanket around it all. Devon allows her eyes to look around as the guard busies himself with collecting these things. She notices a shelf with jumpsuits, both blue and orange, and another with white tube socks and undershirts and rust-colored slides. Yet another holds white towels, just like the one she'd used to dry her body this morning. Rough and white and thin.

The shower. Her nakedness. The blood, diluted pink from the tepid water dripping down her legs.

Devon feels herself shake with the memory, and she hates herself for it. Hates her lack of control over her own body. Her lack of control, period. She hugs herself tighter.

The guard is watching Devon now. He had just said something and is waiting for her to respond.

Devon feels his eyes on her and looks up quickly. "I'm sorry?" she whispers. "I didn't hear—"

"Your bedding. The residents here carry it to their unit themselves. So . . . "

Devon hesitates a moment, studying the unwieldy bundle in the guard's arms. Doesn't he know why she's here? Hasn't he heard what had happened? About the kind of physical condition she's in? No, not completely, she decides. He'd never ask her to carry all that by herself if he knew. She feels a tiny flutter of relief.

"Oh." Devon clears her throat. "Okay. Sure." She turns away from him slightly, so he won't see the front of her jumpsuit, and carefully unwraps one arm from across her chest and then the other and reaches for the bundle.

When the transfer is done, when she's clasping the bedding to her chest, she feels safer somehow. All those layers hiding her, protecting her, giving her a definite purpose. She will carry her bedding until she's told to stop. She will not drop any of it, and she will not complain, no matter how far she must carry it or how heavy it becomes.

"Okay, then," he says. "Let's move along."

Devon feels a sudden warmth gush between her legs then, feels it spread across the lining of her underwear, deep into the thick maxi pad the gray-haired guard had handed her after the shower. Panic grips her gut. Devon's never prayed much, but she tosses one up now, a small one: *Please, God, don't let it show on the outside. Please.*

"Ready to roll?"

Devon nods and, ignoring the cramping across her abdomen, follows the guard through the maze of white walls and gray carpet.

They stand side by side, Devon and the guard, facing a metal door. The guard had pushed a buzzer, and they are waiting for the door to open.

"Unit D," he says, filling the stiff silence between them. "We call it Delta Pod, though. It's that police phonetic alphabet thing." Short silence. Then, "Eight pods total in Remann Hall, Alpha through Hotel—that's, uh, *A* through *H*—but only one is female. At least most of the time. It all depends on the number of girls we get at any given time."

Devon says nothing, but she wonders at the word *pod*, at what it means. Is it *pod* as in "peas in a pod"? Or *pod* as in iPod? Or *pod* as in the groups that whales travel within as they swim the wide open ocean beyond Puget Sound? She'd witnessed the free beauty of the whales once, on one of those orca whale watching tours out of Seattle. Her mom's boyfriend at the time had made a big deal about paying for it, the guy who'd owned that used car dealership on South Tacoma Way. The one who'd snorted when he'd laughed and squeezed Devon's mom in an obnoxious way when he'd thought Devon wasn't watching.

But then a low buzzer sounds, and the memory evaporates because the guard's pushing open the heavy door and they are stepping forward through it.

The door locks—*CLANK*—behind them.

A heavy, metallic, final sound.

Devon and the guard are inside a bright entryway, white walls on either side with closed olive doors. Underfoot is white vinyl tile, polished so it shines. Devon can see her own distorted reflection there, a faint orange smear topped with a black smudge for hair. She jerks her eyes from the image.

The smell here is similar to the hospital's: disinfectant masking stale air with an underlying hint of cafeteria food—something beefy, like stew.

Straight ahead, the entryway opens into a large room. From it comes the sound of voices and movement. Sounds that fill Devon with dread.

Together Devon and the guard move forward, toward the noise.

Devon clutches her bedding tighter. Her arms ache from its weight, and her pelvis throbs. The bedding slips slightly, and she makes the readjustment. She is intent on directing her eyes in front of herself and in front of herself only, straying nowhere else.

Devon follows behind the guard as he veers toward a large desk just inside the vast room. A woman with a blonde ponytail is sitting behind it. She looks up briefly and smiles. Her smile is quick and bright.

"Hey, Joey," she says.

"Hey," he says back. "This is Devon Davenport. Just back from court."

"Wow," she says, reaching for a clipboard. "That rhymed. Impressive."

"I try."

The two guards exchange information, and in that space of time Devon allows herself a furtive look around, her eyes snatching up the details.

A huge, bright room. Four white walls, but irregularly shaped. A warped trapezoid.

A high ceiling, like in a gym.

That ubiquitous gray carpet with a sort of white vinyl tile sidewalk bordering the entire room.

The two longest—and adjacent—walls display perfectly spaced olive green doors, each labeled separately in white: D-1 to D-16. The cells probably, Devon thinks.

She feels herself shudder at the thought, then quickly flicks her eyes away toward the wall consisting entirely of glass with a door to a small outdoor courtyard.

The opening to the entryway from which she and the guard have just come takes up about half of the last side of the room. The other half is a wall housing three olive green doors. The doors have individual labels, stenciled in white on top of each doorframe: SHOWER ROOM. LAUNDRY. CONFERENCE ROOM.

This could be a freshly painted rec room in a Boys and Girls Club. A place she'd known well, one that wasn't frightening. A place where she'd played Foosball and Ping-Pong with the other little kids after school while her mom worked. A place where Devon had first learned soccer, inside on the floor of a basketball court.

And the noise she hears is reminiscent of a Boys and Girls Club, too.

The noise.

She takes a breath, forces herself to look toward the noise.

Toward the two round plastic tables situated off center in the irregularly shaped room.

Her heart hesitates, then pounds. The scene, like cigarette smoke in a small room, squeezes Devon's lungs.

Girls.

Girls playing cards. Girls scribbling on paper. Girls laughing and talking or sitting alone.

Girls roughly Devon's age.

Girls in orange jumpsuits. Like hers.

Pod, her mind whispers. *Like peas in a pod. And you, you are here with them.*

One or two girls look Devon's way, curious. Another glances up, then says something to the girl beside her, who giggles. Another raises her hand and waves.

Devon looks away, to the desk the woman guard is sitting behind. It is solid and impersonal and somehow reminds Devon of the reference desk at Main Library.

Those girls aren't anything like me, Devon tells herself. *They've done something bad, really bad, to end up here.* The scariest kind of girl is in this place, the kind she'd give a wide berth to while jogging in Wright Park or step away from while waiting for the bus. The kind the police drag out of Stadium High in the middle of class.

She doesn't belong here. Her thoughts turn desperate, grasping for supporting evidence. Her report cards are immaculate, certainly very unlike any of these girls'. Unfamiliar teachers recognize her in the halls and smile. Fellow students shout over the clamor to commend her latest performance in the goal: "Go, Tigers!" Strangers call her to babysit. She tutors fellow students in Spanish, gives young aspiring goalkeepers individual training sessions. Referees kids' rec soccer games, keeps the parents on the sidelines in control and civilized. Don't these people here realize this? Can't they see it? She's not anything like them.

She has to get out. Today. She must get out today.

"You need to leave your bedding here."

Devon looks up blankly, the voice yanking her from her thoughts. She slowly comes to realize that the woman guard had just said something to her, and the man guard is no longer there. Where did he go?

"I . . . I'm sorry," Devon stammers. "I . . . didn't hear you."

"No." The woman gives Devon an exasperated smile. "No, you weren't *listening*. What I said was: 'You need to leave your bedding here.'"

"Oh." Devon almost smiles with relief. She's not staying after all! "Because I won't need them."

The woman eyes Devon quizzically. "No," she says slowly, drawing out the word. "Because you haven't been assessed by Mental Health yet. That's usually one of the very first things we do here at Remann Hall after Intake, but the priority today was getting you into court. So, you can just drop your stuff right here, and I'll take you to your cell."

Devon stares at the woman, confused. She doesn't get the connection between Mental Health and a pillow and blankets, why she must relinquish them if she's going to remain here. She squeezes her bedding harder, takes a step backward.

The woman cocks her head, a frown creasing the space between her eyebrows. "Um, I think I just told you to drop your bedding here? You cannot take it with you. This is for your own safety, Devon, until Mental Health determines differently."

The room quiets.

Devon can feel eyes, many eyes, from the tables behind her slowly homing in. Devon squeezes her own shut, feels her lips tremble. She just can't do what this woman is asking of her. Not here. Not with all those girls watching. They'll see her, they'll see her jumpsuit. And then they'll all know.

Devon shakes her head.

"Okay." The woman sighs. "I don't think you quite get how things work around here. It goes like this: I tell you to do something, and you do it. End of discussion. Now, let's try this one last time. Please drop your bedding, right *here* and right *now*, and then I will take you to your cell."

Devon's arms quiver, from all the squeezing and the fear. The woman is obviously prepared to mete out punishment if Devon doesn't comply. Devon can't imagine what that punishment might be, but how could it be worse than what she's just been asked to do? But still . . . she is unaccustomed to punishment or authority-figure disapproval. She is unaccustomed to confrontation. Except with an opposing player near her goal, but that skill has no crossover application in a place like this.

"Can't I"—Devon takes in a shaky breath and swallows— "couldn't I just . . . when I get to . . . my cell? Please? I promise—"

"No," the woman interrupts. "And I'm losing patience, fast."

Devon looks at the woman while she's looking back at Devon. Devon knows she has no choice now. She relaxes her arms. The bedding tumbles to her feet in a heap.

The woman lifts her chin with an expression of self-satisfaction. Her eyes travel from Devon's face, down to her chest, and stop. She takes a small intake of breath, whispers, "Oh."

Devon's face burns. She looks at the floor.

For a moment Devon and the woman remain like that.

The room stills around them.

The woman quickly steers Devon toward the back wall of perfectly spaced olive doors. They must pass the two round plastic tables, all the eyes quietly tracking them. The woman does her best to shield Devon, but those eyes, like the ones in the courtroom, are sharp. They don't miss the wetness of Devon's clothes, dark and ringed like massive armpit sweat, except freakishly misplaced.

Whispers erupt. Soft at first, then urgent. A muffled giggle.

Devon's hair prickles, pulls away from her scalp. They are discussing her and laughing. Somehow Devon's legs function, move her across the room.

"Hey! What's up with her boobs?"

The woman guard stops at one of the olive doors. D-12 is stenciled in white on the doorframe above it.

The woman releases Devon and unlocks the door. Devon counts breaths until the heavy door is pulled open, anxious to escape the eyes and finally hide. The woman moves aside, allowing Devon to pass.

Devon steps forward, peers in.

Light gray cinder block walls. Dark gray cement floor with a drain in the center. Stainless steel toilet and sink in the far corner. Blue plastic rectangular block against one wall—the bed, she guesses, because of the thin rubberized mattress that's tossed over it. Three narrow slats of frosted plastic on the far wall, allowing three faint horizontal shafts of sunlight into the space. The faint reek of urine.

A tiny, walled-in cage.

Devon turns to the woman. This can't be real. She opens her mouth to say something, to plead.

The woman nudges Devon forward. "This is your cell."

Devon stumbles inside.

The woman follows behind. She indicates the three fixtures. "Bed. Sink. Toilet. And that's about it for an orientation." She looks at Devon. "I'm going to allow you to keep the mattress, only because I'll be monitoring you every five minutes. *However*, if I determine that you're not using it appropriately, out it goes. Mental Health should be by to talk to you soon." She pauses. "You have any questions for me?"

Devon says nothing, her eyes locked on the stainless steel toilet in the corner. Horrifying. She can't do this.

"Okay, great." The woman nods her head. "Well, once Mental Health talks to you, you'll get a booklet that spells out all the rules and regulations for this place. You'll be tested on it sometime tomorrow. We do this so everyone's on the same page and knows exactly what to expect here." She hesitates, clearing her throat. When she speaks again, she's perceptively talking faster. "One final thing. I'm very sorry, but I have to ask you to remove your bra."

Bra? Devon fires the woman a look of shock, crosses her arms over her chest.

"It's for your own safety until Mental Health talks to you."

Devon feels her throat tighten, and she closes her eyes. She is so tired, so miserable, so utterly worn down.

"Look." The woman guard clears her throat again. "I don't . . . I won't give details, but bras can be used for dangerous purposes. As can blankets and sheets and even mattresses, the reason I had you leave your bedding outside." She pauses. "So, please. Let's just get this over with. Your bra?"

Wearing bras is dangerous? Devon's mind spins back before she can stop it. His lips on her face, leaving soft kisses on the tip of her nose, across her closed eyes. Her throat. She sighs, throws her head back, and his lips travel down the length of her neck. Tremors sizzle through her spine. His hands move gently down her back. Reaching under her shirt—slowly, cautiously— his fingertips touching her skin, an icy electricity. Unhooking the clasp . . .

Devon shakes her head, pushing the memory away. No, when bras come *off*, that's when things get dangerous.

She opens her eyes. The woman guard's hand is out, waiting.

Devon presses her lips together and slowly turns away. Reaching behind her back, Devon shakily works the clasp from the outside through her jumpsuit and the undershirt beneath. Under her collar, she loops a thumb under one strap and shrugs it off her shoulder, then loops and shrugs the other strap before pulling the bra off entirely and out one sleeve. Her breasts are heavy and sore and only reluctantly surrender their damp fabric, finally slapping painfully against her chest.

Devon balls up the bra in her fist.

The tears are building again, so close and ready to roll. She breathes deeply. Keep it down. Don't break now. She grabs her breasts then because she must; they are hard and hot, that prickling again. The warmth wets the jumpsuit between her fingers, trickles down her ribs.

Devon turns quickly, thrusts the bra into the woman's hand,

not meeting her eyes. "It's wet"—A small sob squeaks from her throat. "It's so gross. I'm . . . sorry." She covers her face with her hands.

"Oh, listen." The woman's voice turns gentle now. "Don't be." She pats Devon softly on the shoulder as Devon sniffs and gasps with her effort to force the tears down. "I'll get it washed in the meantime. Okay? And bring you a clean jumpsuit." The woman pauses, her hand lingering on Devon's shoulder. "Everything's going to be okay. I know it doesn't seem like it now, but eventually it will. I promise."

Devon's resolve is caving with that woman's simple gesture. Her body shudders with the strain of keeping it all contained: the shame, the pain, the watching eyes, the secret whispers, the end the end the very end of everything.

Just go! Devon's mind screams. *Please just go and leave me alone!*

One last squeeze on the shoulder, then the woman's feet step away, brush across the cement floor.

"Oh." The woman turns back momentarily. "I almost forgot: welcome to Delta."

The door clanks shut.

That sound again.

Heavy. Metallic. Final.

Devon stands with her face in her hands for a long time. Then she curls up on the rubberized mattress, turns toward the wall.

chapter five

"Devon?"

Devon opens her eyes, squints at who's peering at her from her opened door. The voice belongs to a woman, someone unfamiliar. Light streams from behind this woman and into the dark cell, washing her out, so all Devon sees is a faceless shadow of a shape.

A dream. Devon closes her eyes, draws herself into a tight ball.

"Devon." The voice again, more persistent. "Devon, my name is Dr. Bacon. I'd like to talk to you for a few minutes. Would that be okay?"

Devon's eyes snap open. She's awake and cold. She sits up abruptly, looks around. Her back is slick with sweat, her undershirt sticks to it. A sweat that would fit if she were on a field with a ball, newly clipped grass under her cleats. But she's not. She's inside a tiny cell with a toilet in the corner and a cement floor. The sweat exists because of the rubberized mattress beneath her and under that, the molded plastic bed.

"Devon?"

Devon finally turns her eyes toward the woman at the door.

The woman steps out of the shadow. Devon can see her face and hair, one long braid that slips down her slender back to brush her waist. "Sorry I had to wake you," the woman says. "I know it's been a long, hard day. You must be exhausted." She twists to kick a jam under the door so it stays open, then carries a folding chair into the room, placing it the perfect distance from Devon—not too close, but not far away either. She rests her hands on the back of the chair and smiles, her eyes intent on Devon's face.

Devon likes the way this woman is dressed. Dark straight skirt that hits her ankles, three-quarter-sleeved tee, sports watch, hemp trail mocs. And that braid. Earthy, yet neat.

The woman is older than she seems; her hair is almost entirely gray.

"May I sit down, Devon?"

Devon scoots backward until her back hits the wall behind her. She pulls her legs into her chest. The front of her jumpsuit is stiff from the dried milk. Always leaking, then drying, and leaking again. She can smell it, too. An organic sort of sourness.

Finally Devon nods, Yes.

The woman sits, her hands folded loosely on her lap, and watches Devon with quiet eyes.

"I'm a doctor who works with the residents at Remann Hall," the woman starts. "A psychiatrist. And I'm here to talk with you for a few minutes and ask you some questions."

Devon stares at her knees.

"Devon, I know what happened. Why you're in Remann Hall."

Devon glances sharply at the woman. Her breath comes quick and fast.

"I know, for instance, that you recently had a baby, and that the baby was found in a garbage can behind your apartment."

Devon hugs her legs closer, hides her face in her knees. If

these things are true, why is her mind so blank? The pain, yes—she can remember that. But . . . the other . . . IT . . . She's shivery and sick to her stomach.

"And I suspect, Devon, that you are not feeling very good about yourself at the moment." She pauses. "That's why I'm here. That's why it's important that you try to talk to me now. About your feelings. About what you're thinking."

The woman waits a moment. Devon can feel her eyes on her, observing the bent head, the rigid shoulders, the long straight hair spread across her shins like a gauzy fan.

"There are many reasons why people do things like put their babies in garbage cans. The purpose of this visit is not to speculate on why *you* did that, or to determine your guilt or innocence. I'm not the police."

Devon holds herself very still. If she holds still, barely breathes, maybe the woman will leave.

"I'm simply here today to make sure that you're not going to do something to harm yourself. Do you think you can talk to me about that, Devon?"

Devon and the woman sit in silence. The woman shifts in her seat. The folding chair squeaks. Devon's pulse thumps across her temples.

The woman will not leave.

Devon feels the adrenaline in her chest, the pumping of her heart. It's the feeling of being in the goal when the striker gets a breakaway and is sprinting toward her with the ball. It's just between the two of them—a battle of skill and decision, 1 v 1. The perfect shot or the perfect save. She waits. On her toes, her body loose. Her arms out to the side, her palms facing out and ready, the net open behind her. Still she waits. Patient for that striker's touch. And then she goes, springing out of the box, cutting off the angle, diving for the ball, solid and real between her gloves.

This woman is waiting for Devon now. If Devon doesn't move, then Devon loses. If you don't come out of the goal but stay frozen on the line, the striker almost always scores.

This woman will not leave.

She isn't like the woman who had visited Devon every day at the hospital, the social worker with the scraggly hair and decades-old glasses who tried in vain to coax information out of Devon. Devon had stared straight ahead at the wall across from her bed, at the happy two-parent African American family depicted in watercolor there—the summer picnic with the lemonade and bright sunshine, the birds in the sky. Then, Devon had said nothing, and the woman went away.

If Devon tries that tactic again and says nothing, Devon suspects that this woman will simply wait her out until she does.

"I think so," Devon whispers at last. "I think I can talk . . . about that."

"Good," the woman says.

Something breaks inside of Devon then; the relief is palpable. "I've never done anything wrong in my life," she says softly into her knees. "I've never *ever* been in a place like this."

"Yes, I know."

"When"—Devon swallows—"when . . . can I . . . go home?"

The woman doesn't speak right away. "I can't answer that. It may be a long time."

Devon doesn't move.

"Does this scare you, Devon?"

She thinks about the day she's just had: court, the girls outside of her room, the eyes, the hot humiliation, the fear. Days and days, untold days, like this. She takes in a shaky breath. "Yes."

The woman nods. "Does it scare you so much that you'd hurt yourself in order to escape it?"

Devon considers the question. She thinks about the times when she'd been scared, even terrified. She'd known many of those times. But her mom always came home, eventually. Or the shouting in the next room would stop—with a slammed door or tear-filled promises or the boyfriend moving out. Even That Night—the pain, it had finally faded.

Nothing had been as harrowing as That Night. Many thoughts had passed through Devon's mind then, but hurting herself was not among them.

"No," Devon answers, her throat so tight she barely gets the words out. "I won't hurt myself."

"I'm glad," the woman says and, leaning forward, gently touches Devon's hand. "I'm so glad to hear that, Devon."

Devon raises her eyes to the woman.

And wishes, truly wishes, that she could say the same herself.

Because hurting herself would be so much easier.

chapter six

A metallic snap, like the bolt of a gun, locking into place. Devon shoots upright, her feet tangled up in her sheet. Her eyes jerk toward her door, the source of the sound.

Her heart hammers and her body's jittery from being woken up so abruptly. She looks around, takes stock of where she is. Cinder block walls. Cement floor. Stainless steel toilet in the corner. Heavy door, tagged with scratched obscenities and closed.

She's still here. It wasn't a dream.

She can smell herself, an intense combination of greasy hair and BO overlaid with the sick spiciness of soured milk and blood that had seeped through her clothing and dried. She'd never taken a shower last night, even though the psychiatrist had told her she could. At dinnertime, she'd gotten a fresh jumpsuit and undershirt along with her tray, but it hardly mattered now.

She pushes herself to the edge of her plastic bed, kicks off the sheet. Gloomy daylight hovers in the room, leaking through the three window slats over the stainless steel toilet. It could be morning, but she's not sure. Once the staff had given her back the bedding last night and she'd finally fallen asleep, she'd slept hard. Like the dead.

She hears noise coming from outside her room. She stiffens, straining her ears. Muffled voices. Movement.

The girls. Is she going to have to go out there now? Have them follow her with their eyes and wonder? Hear them whispering about her?

She sits very still, listening. Everything is reduced to her heartbeat and her breath and the indistinct sounds outside. No one is coming for her, she decides. She pushes herself off her bed and creeps toward the door, toward the slim rectangular window there, and peeks out.

The olive cell doors bordering the large room are opening. Girls in orange jumpsuits emerge from them. They slink to divergent corners of the room, like cats. One girl has a mop, another with a bucket joins her, and together they clean the vinyl tile. A black girl Windexes the glass door leading out to the courtyard. A tiny blonde stands before the control desk and talks to the staff there, but it's not the one from yesterday. This staff is older with dark skin and short dark hair.

Devon stands watching for a long time, careful to remain unseen. Some of the girls congregate around a cardboard box beside the control desk, pulling out large ziplock bags containing toiletries. They carry these bags back to their rooms, then return them to the box sometime later.

Everything appears calm and orderly, and this helps Devon relax. Take away the orange jumpsuits, and this could be a dorm at soccer camp—doing light chores, getting dressed, preparing for a day of scrimmages and skills.

Soon a male staff rolls a cart into the room from the entryway. The girls abandon their activities to line up and in turn retrieve a cafeteria tray from the cart. Each carries her tray, either to one of the two round plastic tables or back to her cell.

Breakfast. Devon's stomach groans as she watches the girls move their plastic sporks between their trays and their mouths. When was the last time she ate? Back in the hospital, she remembers. Scrambled eggs and English muffins. A lifetime ago.

She wishes now that she'd eaten the sloppy joes and potato salad the staff had brought her last night. Her stomach had been too jumpy to keep anything down. As the tray sat, the food turned cold and unappetizing, orange grease coagulated on ground beef.

Devon's back aches from standing in one place so long. And her bladder is stretched tight and throbs. She hasn't yet dared to use the toilet in the corner of the room—too gross. But she can't avoid it any longer. Not unless she wants to add urine to her already dreadful stench.

She turns from the door and shuffles the ten or so steps to the toilet on the other side of her room. Her pelvis is still stiff, and the place between her legs feels hollow and sore, and this amazes Devon. Will she ever feel all together again?

Devon pauses to scrutinize the toilet, a look of disgust on her face, which she catches in the tiny mirror at eye level above the toilet. It's very small and scratched, but she stares at it for a long moment.

Her present reflection fades and, in her mind, another materializes. A similar look of disgust on her face, but then the mirror before her was wide and the bathroom spacious and bright. And the look was directed at herself.

She had crept away from his bed, leaving him asleep across the jumbled sheets. She'd closed the bathroom door softly behind her. Standing naked before the mirror, she'd stared at the girl she saw there. At the disheveled hair and smeared mascara and lips that he'd kissed. Slowly shaking her head at the image in the mirror, the thought played over and over in her mind like a scratched track on a CD: *Why? Why did you do it? Why did you let it happen?* Then she'd turned away, covered her face with her hands, and cried. She would never again be the same person. She'd been irreversibly changed.

Devon backs away from the tiny scratched mirror now, rubs at her eyes to clear away the memory. When she drops her hands, she notices the toilet paper roll, stuck into the round cubby on the side of the stainless steel toilet. Her tight bladder reminds her of why she's standing there. She steels herself for the job, then pulls a length of the paper, folding it over, and then pulls another, meticulously covering every inch of the rimless seat. The toilet isn't as filthy as she'd feared; it's pretty clean, actually. But still, Devon won't take the chance of catching something gross, like lice. Or something worse, like an STD. Devon's seen the girls who use these toilets. They'd laughed at her. Yeah, they'd be the kind to have lice and STDs.

She unsnaps her jumpsuit, letting it fall to her ankles, then tugs down her underwear. Her thick maxi pad, badly needing replacement, sticks to her pubic hair, and she winces at the discomfort and the mess. She lowers herself to the seat and waits for the relief to come.

When she's finished, she sinks her forehead into the palms of her hands. *That wasn't so bad.* With her forearms pressed into her sore and heavy breasts, she remembers that she's still braless beneath her undershirt.

The door to her room scrapes open, and Devon jerks upright.

A short, slight woman, the staff from behind the control desk, steps through the doorway, holding a food tray in one hand.

The woman looks at Devon, and Devon yanks her jumpsuit up over her knees. Sweat breaks out everywhere.

"Caught you in the act, huh?" the woman says. "Don't think this is a first for me, okay? You girls need to get over yourselves."

Devon watches as the woman continues inside, shoving the crumpled sheet out of the way and placing the tray at the foot of Devon's bed. "This is your breakfast, but don't expect room service every day, okay? After today, you'll be coming out of your room like everybody else. We always keep the new residents in their rooms for twenty-four hours after Intake, okay? To get used to things. It's called Orientation Status. That's a rule, okay?"

From her mortifying spot on the toilet, Devon, in a funk of disbelief, observes the woman. She can't understand the woman's absolute disregard for her privacy, moving methodically as she does in her shapeless Seattle Mariners T-shirt and black Adidas sweatpants and speaking in that crusty lilting tone of hers with a hint of an accent that Devon can't place. She could be Mexican or Native American or even Indian, judging from her skin color and short black hair, straight and flat and shapeless on her head, and her chiseled facial features. She could be forty, or she could be sixty; Devon can't guess.

The woman glances around the room, nodding to herself, like she's doing a mental inspection. Then she turns her dark eyes on Devon. "My name is Henrietta, okay? You're going to be seeing a lot of me. Most of time I work nights, okay? But today, I have the day shift, too. Back-to-back shifts. So you better not mess with me, okay? I am not in a mood to be messed with."

Devon nods.

"Good." Henrietta also nods, satisfied that she'd gotten across whatever she'd intended to communicate. She drops a thin booklet on top of the food tray. "You need to read this, okay? If you have any questions, just ask. I make cell checks every fifteen minutes, okay? That means me looking into your window to make sure everything's all right. By lunchtime, you need to be ready for my test, okay?"

Devon nods again. "Okay," she whispers. She doesn't want to tell Henrietta that she'd already received the booklet from the staff woman last night, that it's stashed in the cubby under her bed. She'd fallen asleep memorizing it. That was before the doctor had shown up, waking her.

"And you need to pass it, okay? So don't blow it off." Henrietta studies Devon for a moment. Devon averts her eyes to the floor, feeling miserably uncomfortable under the woman's gaze, wishing that she would just move along and give her some privacy. And quit saying "okay?" every five seconds. How annoying. Devon shifts on her seat, her butt growing painfully numb.

"After you eat, you'll need to take a shower, okay?"

"Oh." That makes Devon feel better, something positive to look for. She glances up. "Okay. That would be . . . really great. Thank you."

"Thanking me makes no difference. It's a hygiene issue with you, okay?" Her voice turns scolding now. "Let me tell you, I would have made sure you got one last night, even if I had to drag you out of your cell myself." She clamps her mouth shut, says nothing further for a moment. "But we'll wait—okay?— until the other girls start school for the day. That way we won't be violating the twenty-four-hour rule of no contact with the other residents, okay? The shower is right across the common area. So it's just better if no one's around then, okay?"

School? They have school here? Well, whatever. She won't have to see the girls, at least not in the near future. And maybe not at all. She may be gone soon, hopefully before tomorrow ever comes. She'll be back at Stadium High School, sitting in her own classes. Turning in her critical analysis on *The Taming of the Shrew* that's due for Mr. Andrew at the end of the week. She'd already finished it two days after he'd assigned it.

The woman steps toward Devon. Her face is intent, almost like a hawk's on the hunt.

Devon shrinks back, her spine touching the cool stainless steel behind her.

The woman pulls a thick maxi pad out from somewhere and tosses it on Devon's lap.

Devon stares at it. She can feel heat crawling across her face.

"You have a meeting with your lawyer at ten."

Her lawyer? Devon feels her heart pick up, beating fast. Maybe she *is* leaving here. Soon. No, today! Is that the reason for the shower? So she can leave all fresh and clean?

Devon looks up, smiling slightly, her embarrassment momentarily forgotten. "Thank you."

But the door's clanked shut. Henrietta is already gone.

chapter seven

The first thing Henrietta says when Devon steps outside the shower room is, "Comb your hair." She shoves a black plastic comb into Devon's hand, then leads her to the door labeled CON-FERENCE ROOM, two doors down from the shower and directly across the common area from Devon's cell. "Let me tell you, first impressions are lasting impressions. You only get one, so make yours good." She opens the door and moves aside. "Okay?"

Devon takes a step inside and stops. Who she sees isn't who she'd pictured. This person isn't old and balding or wearing a shabby, dandruff-sprinkled suit or hunching over a stack of files, barely acknowledging her presence.

Instead, this person is a woman. And young. In a dark, per-fectly pressed suit, cream cuffs peeking out of her jacket sleeves. A tight, neat updo, almost like a beehive. Blonde hair, but not like her mom's fake blonde straight out of a box. This woman's hair is almost gold, with too many colors weaving through it and catching the light to be fake. Tiny, wire-framed glasses. And she's looking right at Devon.

Devon feels the teeth of the comb biting into the palm of her hand. She's acutely aware of her own sloppy appearance, her hair still wet from the shower, dripping onto the shoulders of her jumpsuit and leaving wet tracks.

This must be some mistake, Devon thinks. This isn't her law-yer. This person belongs in an episode of *Law & Order*, not here with her. Devon turns back, but Henrietta is gone. The door has clanked shut, probably locked.

"Devon?"

Devon turns back around. The woman half-stands, smiles, and offers her hand across the table. "Hi. I'm Dominique Barcell-lona, your attorney. You can call me 'Dom.' How are you doing today?"

Devon stares. She can detect a faint whiff of the heavy sweetness that clouds over the makeup counters at Nordstrom's. It's like what her mom sprays, thinking it will mask the ciga-rette smoke. Devon feels her heart twist, then harden, with the thought of her mom. Always hiding something and never pres-ent when Devon needs her. Devon frowns, looks at this coiffed woman with suspicious eyes: so, what is *she* hiding?

"Okay." The woman's voice has an edge to it now, but she keeps her lipsticked smile in place. "Mind sitting down?" She lowers her unshook hand slightly, indicating the stool across the table from her.

Devon realizes then that she had been rude; she hadn't tak-en this woman's hand and shaken it. So much for first impres-sions. She opens her mouth to apologize but then quickly shuts it. Why should she apologize? She'd been taken off guard, hadn't she? And this woman . . . Devon feels an uneasiness growing inside. What will this woman want from her anyway?

"We have a lot to discuss today and, unfortunately, not a whole lot of time in which to do it." The woman checks her thin watch on her wrist for emphasis. "So, we should get started right away."

Discuss? Devon doesn't move.

The woman frowns slightly, then her hand disappears behind her back, smoothing her skirt before sitting down herself. "Uh, is there a problem, Devon? You seem a little . . . confused."

Devon looks down at the comb in her hand, runs her thumb over its teeth. It tickles. "You're not a man," Devon whispers, then glances back up at her.

Something flicks in the woman's eyes, and her frown is replaced with a smile. "Your powers of observation are impressive." She laughs. "This *is* the twenty-first century. News flash: women have been attorneys for quite a while now, Devon." She clicks her tongue. "Wishing for a man to rescue you—not a great way to make friends."

Devon shifts her weight, uncertain what this woman had meant by that. *Friends? Right.* And wanting a man to rescue her? This has pushed a button. Devon rubs her thumb across the teeth of her comb again, hears the faint *prripp, prripp* it makes. She needs nobody—man *or* woman—to rescue her. Ever.

The woman waves toward the stool opposite her again. "Sit. Please."

Devon hesitates, but then moves to seat herself. Both the table and stool are bolted to the floor. It is the same type of table, Devon realizes, that the girls sit around in the common area—to eat on, to play cards on, to watch Devon from and laugh.

She feels itchy. She doesn't want to be here. Not in this room or at this table. Not sitting here at this predetermined distance from the bolted-down table, either, which can't be altered by either tipping back the stool or pulling it out a few inches. And definitely not with this strange woman, who makes dumb comments, thinking she's so smart. Who is so unprofessional that she wants Devon to call her by her first name, like they're "friends." Well, she won't.

"Okay." The woman lifts a brown accordion folder from the floor and drops it on the table, sounding like a slap between them.

Devon's eyes jerk to the folder. On it, a white label spells her last name DAVENPORT in black.

"Let's start at the beginning." The woman opens a yellow legal pad, readies her pen. "Why don't you tell me why you're here."

Devon's eyes stay on the folder. It isn't empty; she can see that. The band around it is stretched taut. So, why the question? Doesn't this Dom, this *attorney*, this *female* attorney, already know? It's all right there in front of her.

This irritates Devon. The inefficiency of it. The *insincerity* of it. She looks down at the comb, stares at it a moment, then pulls it through her damp hair, as if the woman isn't even there. The shampoo Henrietta had given her was cheap and greasy. The comb meets no resistance. Bits of water sprinkle her hand.

The silence lasts a long time. Devon finally peeks at the woman across from her. She's exactly as Devon had last seen her, pen poised over the yellow paper, watching her. "Well, why are *you* here?" Devon blurts at last.

Her voice was too loud, she thinks. Too aggressive, distrustful. She hadn't meant to sound like that exactly; she'd merely meant to sound disinterested and bored. But there it is, and she can't take it back.

"Excuse me?" The woman looks surprised to have been asked a question. "Why am *I* here?"

Devon looks away. "You aren't my lawyer. You weren't in the courtroom with me."

"Oh," the woman says, drawing the word out. "I see . . ."

Devon looks back at her.

The woman carefully places the pen on top of her legal pad, folds her hands in front of her. "You're thinking of Mr. Stevens. Well, he just happened to have the docket when you first appeared in court. Since then, the big guys who make the decisions at the Department of Assigned Counsel—where I work— sat down and discussed your case and basically decided that out of the, oh, eighty-plus attorneys who work there, I am best suited to represent you. But I had some input into that decision, too; I wanted your case. Does that answer your question?"

Devon doesn't say anything, she just stares back at the woman. Her voice is so cool, calm, measured. Not like Devon's own—so stumbling and emotive. And what the woman had just said, that she'd *wanted* her case. Why? And even that word: *case.* Like Devon is something to be studied. Something to be discussed and decided upon.

"I'll take that as a yes." The woman picks up her pen and taps it on her yellow legal pad. "Now. Do you understand what happened yesterday? In court, I mean."

Yesterday? Was that only yesterday? Devon closes her eyes. Her memory of those few minutes in the courtroom is disjointed. The judge. The attorneys. The impressive-sounding words. Her jumpsuit darkening with her own leaked milk. Her humiliating tears, right there in front of everyone.

The woman waits a respectful amount of time, then launches in. "Well, you were there for an arraignment. English translation:

to have the charges against you formally read. But the focus quickly changed because the prosecution—the lawyers representing the interests of the county, the ones trying to put you in jail—"

"I know what *prosecution* means," Devon whispers. She looks over at Dom quickly, guiltily. Why had she said that? So rude.

"Well, good. Then you must also know that the prosecution filed a motion requesting a hearing to determine whether you should be tried as a juvenile or as an adult. It's called a declination hearing, because the juvenile court would then be *declining* jurisdiction over your case. These hearings are actually mandatory with cases like yours. Class A felonies, that is. Now, the purpose for this hearing—"

Class A felonies. Devon turns away. She doesn't want to hear any of this. The criminals on TV deal with felonies, not her. She fixes her eyes on the wall to her left. White painted cinder block, like every other wall in this place.

"—is to determine your rehabilitative potential. But before we go into all that, I think we need to talk about your charges. Do you understand, and I mean *really* understand, what you're being charged with?"

Devon keeps her eyes on the wall. How many coats of paint did they have to slather on it for it to look so smooth and glossy? *A lot*, she decides. *Cinder block is pretty rough.*

"All righty then. I'll take that as a no." Out of the corner of her eye, Devon sees the woman reach for the brown DAVENPORT folder.

Were the walls always painted white? Had they ever tried a different color? Like fluorescent green, for instance, just to see how it looked? Because, if it were Devon's choice, she'd try fluorescent green. One of her keeper jerseys is that color. It always makes her stand out on the field, draws the ball toward her.

Her keeper jersey; she thinks of it now. The number 1 on its back. A lonely number. Only *one* goalkeeper on the field. Only *one* player who guards the net. Only *one* who stands strong and alone behind the other ten players on the field. No place to hide, no way to disappear.

The woman pulls off the rubber band holding the DAVENPORT folder together. It expands as the woman opens it, displaying pocket after pocket, papers tucked into each. The woman pulls out a sheet, looks it over briefly, then slides it across the table toward Devon.

Devon's eyes are disloyal; they shift from the wall to the paper all on their own. The woman's hand is holding it there, her slim fingers with short neat nails. The polish matches her lipstick. Something Devon's mom would have approved of. Something Devon couldn't care less about. Keepers' hands are meant to catch balls, not look pretty.

The woman pulls her hand away, leaving the paper, stark and white, before Devon. "This is called a charge sheet. And on it, your charges."

Devon directs her eyes back to the wall.

"Devon," she says sharply. "Look at me."

Devon presses her lips together, slowly turns her eyes toward the woman. Devon realizes now that she's sitting on her own hands, death-gripping the sides of the plastic seat under her thighs. The comb is gone, dropped. She hadn't heard it fall. Sweat dampens her armpits, even though the room is cool.

The woman's eyes are locked with Devon's. "Your charges,"

she says again. "Attempted Murder in the First Degree."

Devon feels her thighs tighten, quiver. Somehow she had managed to avoid hearing any of this in the courtroom.

"Abandonment of a Dependent Person in the Second Degree." She pauses, gauging Devon's reaction. "Criminal Mistreatment in the Second Degree, and Assault in the Third Degree. That makes four charges, total."

Murder? *Murder?* And there were others, too. Abandonment. Mistreatment. Assault. A whole horrible list. This is what they think she's done?

But how? How did she do these things? She can't remember any of it.

"The assault charge, according to the police report, occurred once you had arrived at the hospital, when you resisted the medical personnel's efforts to examine you."

Devon watches as the woman pulls other papers from a pocket in the brown folder. "I have the police reports here, along with all corresponding statements of witnesses and, of course, the statement from the victim of the assault herself, a, uh, Dr. Laura Klein."

Doctor. Black rectangular glasses. Blonde ponytail, wisps around the face. White lab coat. A knee comes up. A yell. People run from all directions, close in. Pin down arms, hold legs. Confusion. Flailing. A needle, sharp and cold.

Devon is shaking. She pulls her hands from under her legs and hugs herself to stop it.

That knee. Was that knee *Devon's* knee? It's all there now, right there; she sees it in her mind. So near and clear and vivid. She squeezes her eyes shut. The scene plays over and over. An unwanted memory. It didn't exist before, but now it's there. This woman, the one sitting across from her, placed it there. Pulled it out of some dark corner and dropped it in the light.

"As I'm sure you can guess," the woman is saying, "the attempted murder charge is categorized among the most serious of crimes, Devon, a Class A felony. The other three charges of abandonment, criminal mistreatment, and assault are all Class C felonies. My opinion? They're charging you with abandonment and criminal mistreatment—basically the same charge just worded differently, which I think is totally bogus, by the way, but that's something we'll deal with later. And the assault charge? Well, that's just really pushing it. Anyway, my feeling is that they're charging you with those other lesser offenses so that if the attempted murder charge doesn't stick, they can get you on something. But abandonment alone can get you up to five years in jail."

Five years? In jail? Devon's breathing picks up. Faster, faster. She looks behind her, toward the door. They can't put her in jail, can they? Not if she can't remember . . .

The woman continues to explain the legal definitions of abandonment and mistreatment, but Devon's mind is stuck on those five years. She does a mental fast-forward of herself five years from now, imagining her life. Twenty years old, almost twenty-one. In college. Walking across a campus—not just any campus, but UNC's or Santa Clara's or even U Dub's playing Division I soccer—a backpack over one shoulder, heading down to the field, visions of keeping for the national team dancing in her head. The World Cup and the Olympics further in the distance and still only a dream, but definitely something to work for. All gone, zapped, because of this.

No, not because of *this*. Because of IT.

But. She had heard them—hadn't she?—all those nurses at the hospital, whispering in the hallway? The baby's okay, they'd said. She's here at the hospital. Getting stronger. Healthy. Pretty, even. Strange sort of irony, isn't it? Both baby and mother in the same hospital at the very same time, but unable to see each other? Sad state of affairs. Oh yes, very sad. Very, very sad.

A tinge of relief slips through Devon's thoughts. The nurses called IT a "she." That means IT is alive. Not only alive, but healthy and pretty and strong.

So, they've got it all wrong. IT wasn't abandoned, IT was found. IT wasn't murdered; IT lived.

Devon feels her body relax. Her hands drop to her lap. Okay. She hadn't done anything, after all. They'll all realize that they'd made a huge mistake. They'll apologize, exchange the orange jumpsuit for the clothes her mom will bring for her when she finally comes, and this will all be far behind her.

Devon turns back to look confidently at the woman across from her. She'd been discussing her ideas on the various legal issues she plans to pursue but stops when she sees the look that Devon's given her, a look of smug triumph. "Don't think you're off the hook just because the baby lived, Devon."

The words are a slap. Devon's hands become fists in her lap.

"When someone attempts to commit a crime, the attempt is classified as if he or she had actually accomplished that crime. That's the way the law looks at it; the *intent* is what's important, not that some stroke of luck or act of God or whatever you want to call it made everything turn out all right in the end. Understand?"

How had this woman read her so thoroughly? Devon was always able to hide everything so well. It's her game face; she could pull it all in and never let it show. In the goal, or at home. She is impenetrable.

The woman places her hands flat on the table. "Am I getting through to you? 'Cause right now there's a baby found in a trash can behind your apartment who's linked to you, and the D.A. is charging you with attempted murder. That means you could conceivably go to jail . . . for life."

Life? A strangled sound involuntarily squeezes out of Devon's throat. *Life?* She turns away, faces the wall again. She can feel her lips quiver, the muscles in her face melt, her eyes sting. *Keep it under control*, she tells herself. *Don't cry. Stay solid. Stay hard.*

"Look, I don't think that's likely to happen, Devon, I really don't." The woman's voice softens somewhat. She reaches out and touches Devon lightly. "It was an attempt; no judge is likely to give the max for an attempt. Especially if you stay in the juvenile system. There's no such thing as life imprisonment in the juvenile system. The maximum time you'd get would be to the age of twenty-one." A slight pause. "That's why it's so important that we win this hearing coming up next week, so we can keep you in the juvenile system."

The woman's fingers feel heavy and far too warm.

"I just don't want you operating under some false sense of security. I want you to know up front what we're going against." The woman takes a breath in, lets it out. "And I'm sorry, but I'm just not getting the impression that you are facing up to any of this appropriately. I don't feel like you're taking your situation seriously."

Devon flings off the woman's hand, twists around to glare at her. "What, do you think I'm stupid or something?" She feels something ignite inside. "Do you think, even for one second, that I've *ever*, in my whole entire life, been in a place like this?" She narrows her eyes. "You don't know me; you don't know one thing about me. You don't have the first clue about what I do or do not take seriously. So, save the lecture." She stands up. Her voice actually shocks her, it's so icy, so mean. But she can't stop. "Just stick to the law part, okay? I'll handle the consoling Devon part."

The woman just sits there, her eyes on Devon. Devon is trembling, but still she holds the woman's stare. The silence between them is thick, the kind of thick that takes force to shatter, like a jackhammer.

Finally the woman pushes off her stool and slowly leans across the table. "Go ahead, Devon. Make me your enemy." She's speaking quietly with those measured tones of hers, but her words have heat to them. "Under the law, all you're entitled to is an *adequate* defense. That means the next time I technically have to see your sorry face is the next time we're planted in front of the judge. If that's what you want, then that will just have to be okay with me. But that's no way to win. And guess what, Devon? I *like* to win."

Devon can almost feel the woman's eyes searing into hers, shooting out little angry lasers.

"If you have any dreams in that head of yours that you hope to attain. If you've got any kinds of plans for your life besides rotting away in a place way worse than this, then I'd think you'd like to win, too. So realize this, Devon: I Am Your Future."

Devon feels herself deflate. She drops her eyes to the floor. She's not a mean, rude person. She's never even *thought* of treating anybody the way she'd just treated this woman. Not even her mom, who's more child than adult most of the time. Her mom, who still hasn't bothered to see what's become of her in the days that have passed. Her mom, who hasn't come to reach out and touch her and tell her that everything will be all right because she'll take care of it.

But this woman, this Ms. Barcellona, this *Dom*, has.

The woman straightens, starts packing her things. The yellow legal pad. The sheet with Devon's charges written on it. The DAVENPORT accordion file.

Devon feels a tugging. The words are right there.

The woman—Dom—bends to lift her briefcase from off the floor.

Devon could say nothing, just let her go. She clears her throat, mumbles, "Okay."

The woman stops, looks over at Devon. Her eyes are guarded. And annoyed, like she has several other more important matters to attend to and has no time for Devon and her games. "Okay? Is that what I just heard you say? 'Okay' what?"

Devon looks down at the table. How can she make this right? "I understand," Devon whispers. "You are my future. I don't want . . ." She looks back up at her and takes a deep breath. "I don't want to be enemies with you . . . Dom."

Dom considers this. "You going to cut the attitude?"

Devon nods.

"You're ready to work with me?"

Devon hesitates, afraid of what this "work" may require. But she has no choice, really. She nods again.

"Good." Dom smooths her skirt and sits back down on her stool. "I'm going to try to meet with you at least once more before the hearing. It's scheduled for April eighth—that's exactly a week from today. In the meantime, I want you to work on three things for me, okay?"

Devon doesn't say anything.

"O-*kay?*" Dom says again, louder.

"Okay," Devon says quickly. She meets Dom's eyes so Dom will know that she's sincere.

"First, I want you to participate in all scheduled activities here. That means attending school, eating with the other residents, doing chores. Anything that is required and anything that is offered, is mandatory for you. Second, get on the highest behavior status you can manage. You may not understand how it all works right now, but a staff member should explain the point system—"

"I read the booklet," Devon says, eager to demonstrate her ability to comply. "Last night."

"Okay, good. Staying on Regular status would be good. But working up to Privilege or especially Honor status before the hearing would be even better. The judge looks favorably upon 'model' residents. Third, I want you to work on a list of names, some people we can potentially call as witnesses to speak positively to your rehabilitative potential. Basically to say nice things about you, sort of like character witnesses: teachers, coaches, friends, employers."

A list of names? Of people to talk about her? Devon feels the panic rise. Impossible. She can't do that.

Dom is defining some legal concept, now, the *Kent* factors, which she's saying are eight specific criteria that judges must consider before sending a juvenile offender to the adult criminal court system. "Most of the factors are completely legal and fact based," she explains, "such as your age when you committed the offense, the nature of the offense—meaning, how serious it is—your previous criminal record, et cetera. We can't make much of an argument against those objective criteria; they are either true or they are false. But the area where we potentially can sway the judge is with the more subjective factors. So, that's where we'll need help from your character witnesses."

Devon watches as Dom flips to a page of her legal pad. "Here are some ideas. You're a soccer player. You play varsity for Stadium High School in the fall and a premier club pretty much throughout the year, correct? I think I've read that in your file. So, that makes potentially two different sets of coaches. And then you got selected for the Olympic Development Program last year. Could you explain to me what that—"

"No!" Devon is up, backing toward the door.

Dom looks at Devon, one carefully manicured eyebrow arching above her glasses. "No?"

Devon starts pacing. She'd rather stay here forever than hand a list of names over to Dom and then know that the people on that list would know everything about her, about IT. What would remain of her then? Not the person they thought she was.

She thinks about the charge sheet that Dom had tucked back into the DAVENPORT file. Murder. Abandonment. Mistreatment. Assault.

She thinks about her coach. The way he'd smile with undisguised admiration after a game where she'd made an amazing save. "You're crazy, Dev. You scare even *me*."

She thinks about her teachers. She thinks about her teammates, the kids at school. She thinks about Kait.

Once they hear what happened, even if untrue, there'd be

no admiration left. Devon would become someone to hate. To *fear* even.

"I'll do everything else, Dom. I promise! I'll be a perfect model inmate. Just . . . not that. Don't make me do a list. Please. I don't want anybody to know. . . ."

Dom puts the paper down, watches Devon for a long moment. "But, Devon," she says softly, "everybody *already* knows."

Devon stops pacing, looks back at her.

"Your story's been in all the papers. On the radio and TV. On YouTube, even. There's this reporter from the *News Tribune* who's very aggressively wanting to follow this thing from start to finish. She's contacted me several times already—she's e-mailed, left voice mails. She's stopped by my office, left messages—"

Everybody already knows? Devon feels her body go cold. The walls seem to close in on her, the painted white cinder block walls.

"That's definitely one thing that we're going to challenge, the use of your name in the media. I know it's not illegal, but that should not have been allowed. . . ."

Her name? In the media? Devon stumbles toward the table.

Dom's voice trails off.

Devon can't think or breathe. She collapses onto her stool, lays her head down on the table.

"I thought you knew, Devon, how huge this is." Dom quickly sifts through her DAVENPORT file, pulls papers out. "Here are copies of the newspaper articles, of what's been published so far. And copies of some of the police photos. I was going to wait to show these to you later, but . . ." She pushes the papers toward Devon. "Take these with you and read them, look them over. You really need to know what we're up against."

Devon doesn't lift her head.

The *News Tribune*. A reporter from the *News Tribune* had interviewed Devon once. She'd won the Golden Glove MVP award at State Cup last May, and the *News Tribune* wanted to tell the story. A photographer had spent forty-five minutes one day after school, posing Devon in the goal down at Stadium's field and snapping off pictures. They were set-up action shots, but they still looked cool. Her mom had cut out the article and slapped it into a frame from Wal-Mart. She'd hung her handiwork near the door to their apartment so no one with eyes would miss it.

Devon feels numb. Dead.

Everybody knows. Everybody. Everybody.

"Devon? Are you okay?" For the first time, Dom's voice sounds unsure.

Devon says nothing, not one word. She pushes herself up. She slides the papers toward herself. She slowly folds them into quarters. She closes her hand around them.

Devon lifts her face to Dom's.

Is she "okay"?

Will she ever, ever be okay?

chapter eight

Devon waits until she's back in her cell, back on her rubber-ized mattress and alone, to unfold what Dom had given her. Her hands are trembling. The paper rattles.

She takes a breath and looks down at the creased photocop-ies, black on white. Clean, perfect font forming words arranged in rows and columns with block margins.

So innocuous. It could be about anything. She quickly shuf-fles through them.

Then she sees the pictures.

A sharp pain slams into her chest, seizes her breath.

One of the couch—the blood-soaked cushions, the crum-pled blanket. And another of the bathroom—the blood smeared across the linoleum, a pile of soiled towels in the corner. And still another—a torn open trash bag, revealing the garbage con-tained within.

"Oh, God!" Devon pushes them away. The papers hit the ce-ment floor and fan out.

Devon can't breathe; she can't get enough air. She gasps like the salmon, just pulled from the Sound, as they flounder and flop beside the weekend fishermen along Ruston Way.

Devon shoves her fist into her mouth, bites down hard. Snot runs over her knuckles.

She wants to die. She truly wants to die. Because it's all there, right there on the floor. Right there in black and white.

Devon stares down, at the mess of paper there, for a long time. Her heart pumps fast.

Read them, look them over. You really need to know what we're up against. Dom's words. *I Am Your Future,* she'd said. *You're ready to work with me?*

Dom wants her to stand up and meet this straight on. Now. Not later. And Devon knows that Dom's right, she's absolutely right.

Devon struggles to get a grip. This is so unlike her, this meltdown. This is not how she operates. She's a pro at being calm when the entire world turns to complete chaos around her. In the goal or at home, she is the opposite of her mom, who lives in constant freak mode.

Devon is not like her mom. Right?

She is NOT like her mom!

Devon stares at the papers again, concentrates on them, the black on white. They are the ball sitting harmlessly on the grass before her. In milliseconds the striker's foot will send it hurtling toward her. But for now, it is nothing, harmless. It is just a ball. A round object with air inside.

She pulls her hand out of her mouth. She hugs herself, rocking forward and back on the edge of the bed.

Devon must take this. She must pick up the papers and look at them. Like facing a penalty kick, it's her job to deal with it. Even when she wasn't the player who caused the foul in the box.

Devon wipes her hands on the stiff polyester of her orange jumpsuit. She takes a deep breath, then pushes herself off the bed, reaches for the papers. She kneels on the floor and makes herself look at them.

The one with the trash bag is on top, and the bag is the first thing she sees—the black plastic torn and frayed—sort of framing the entire photograph. Her eyes move on to the other objects in the picture. The striped Tim's potato chip bag. The stripped toilet paper roll. The frozen juice container. The crumpled newspaper pages.

These objects are strangely familiar. Like artifacts from a place and time she's lived, but too long ago to clearly recall their specific connection to her. As her brain recognizes each object, one by one, she slowly starts to remember. And then, in a rush, she knows—she used those things. Those things were hers; she'd touched them all.

She'd touched them all That Night.

Before she can squelch them, her mind supplies the memories:

The Tim's chip bag: she'd finished off the chips with a microwaved hot dog and a stale bun for dinner, sitting on the couch, *The Simpsons* reruns playing across the screen, her chemistry homework open beside her.

The toilet paper roll: she'd had to rush to the bathroom, sharp diarrhea cramps rolling through her gut. She'd reached into the cabinet under the sink with her butt still over the seat, one hand fumbling for the new roll, the other clutching her stomach.

The frozen concentrate orange juice container: she'd made the juice before starting her chemistry homework—she was craving something sweet and cold and wet. She placed the frozen container in the sink and stood mesmerized as it thawed, the hot water a cascade pouring from the faucet.

The pages from the newspaper: she'd picked up the pile tossed on the floor outside her mom's bedroom door, the section with the personal ads lying on top, two prospects circled in black permanent marker.

That was her trash. She'd dropped it all into the Glad trash bag with the Quick-Tie, one by one.

And . . . the towels? The blood? The used tampons? The . . .

The images snap off. Stopped. Blank.

Her skin is pricked and cold. Each hair is erect, every nerve alive. She's panting as if she'd just done pressure training at goalie practice.

She grabs the papers, mashes them into a tight ball, hurls it to the floor. But a caption from one of the newspaper articles catches her eye:

MIRACLE BABY ANASTASIA RESURRECTED FROM CERTAIN DEATH
WHEN PLUCKED FROM A TRASH CAN EARLY YESTERDAY.

Certain death. Certain death. Her mind pounds out the rhythm the syllables create. Certain death. Plucked from a trash can. Plucked from her trash can—her toilet paper roll, her potato chip bag, her orange juice container. Stuffed into her Glad Quick-Tie trash bag. Her hands. Her.

That's why she's here. That's why she's sitting in this walled-in cage. Her black trash bag and what was inside of it. That's what all the charges are about.

She squeezes her head between her hands.

And heaves her breakfast into her lap.

chapter nine

The lock snaps open.

Devon jerks upright in her bed. Will she ever get used to that sound? That sound, which announces each new day?

She stands, shuffles to the toilet in the corner of her cell, relieves herself. The pad lining her underwear displays only a thin brownish streak this morning. Like the blood at the end of a period.

When she's finished, she goes to check outside her door. Like yesterday, the girls are moving around the room, preparing for the day.

This is the day Devon must join them. She must go out there, get a tray from off the food cart. Retrieve her bag of toiletries with the other girls and wash her face, brush her teeth. Go to school. Start working toward that Honor status so the judge will be impressed.

And that thought, her status and impressing the judge, reminds her that she has a job. Or at least, she thinks she might. Henrietta had assigned it to her yesterday afternoon.

"Since I had to clean up your mess today," she'd said, "you get to clean up after everyone else. Starting tomorrow. Okay?" Henrietta had said this after hosing the puke down the drain in Devon's cell. "What comes around, goes around." Then she'd handed Devon the unit rules test as promised and made Devon sit on the stainless steel toilet in the corner to take it while she herself proceeded to wipe down Devon's mattress and mop the cement floor with a strong disinfectant.

Devon feels some relief. She has a mission; she always does best with a task to perform. She now has a place to go and something specific to do when she steps outside her cell. She'll walk right up to the desk and the staff woman behind it and inquire about her job.

Devon turns to her bed, folds her one sheet and one blanket, first in half, then in half again, and once more in half before stacking them neatly at the foot of her bed as prescribed in the unit pamphlet. Devon places her pillow on top of the pile, then peers out her little cell window one last time. The path to the desk is clear, no girl in her way to step around. She takes a breath to center herself and pushes open the door.

"Good morning," the woman says when Devon gets there. She's unfamiliar, this woman. She's very tall and lanky with short dishwater blonde hair.

Devon nods back.

The woman waits for Devon to say something, to ask a question or register a complaint.

Devon clears her throat. "I'm new here. And I was told yesterday—I mean, Henrietta told me—that I have a job cleaning up? I'm just wondering what exactly it is that I have to do. Because I'd like to get started on it right away. If that's okay."

The woman says nothing for a moment, just looks at Devon with an amused expression on her face. "Well!" she finally says.

"This is new and refreshing. Someone *asking* me for a job? I seriously think this is a first."

Devon smiles to herself. One step closer to Honor.

The woman turns toward a white board on the wall behind her. A simple chart is there, chores listed in one vertical column—Laundry, Mop, Windows, Sink/Counter, Wipe Down, Trays/Trash—and first names in a second column beside it. The woman rubs off a name beside "Trays/Trash," picks up a dry-erase marker and writes "Devon" in its place.

This surprises Devon, that the woman knows her name already. Why does everyone here always have to know everything? Devon can feel her momentary burst of "take charge" confidence seeping away. What else does this woman know? Devon thinks of the crumpled papers stashed in the cubby under her bed. Has she seen the articles, too? Read them?

"Here you go," the woman says. "The girl who had Trays and Trash was released last night, so it's all yours. That means from now on, I expect it to get done by *you*. If it doesn't, you'll lose points, which will affect your status." She tells Devon the requirements for the job. After every meal, once all the girls have returned their trays to the food cart, Devon will stack the trays neatly. She'll then get a trash bag from the staff on duty and pick up any napkins, milk cartons, sporks, et cetera that were left around the room by accident. After that, she'll empty the trash in the bathroom and shower rooms. Finally, she will attach the trash bag to the hook on the food cart and wheel the cart to the door to the unit so that it can be taken away later.

"Pretty simple. Any questions?"

"No," Devon says, absently running one hand along the top

of the desk. "I don't think so." She sees a piece of paper taped there:

TOUCH THE CONSOLE

GET A 0!!!!

Devon snatches her hand back, looks at the woman guiltily. That rule wasn't in the pamphlet. She feels a jolt of panic—she doesn't know all the rules here. But she must. She must learn all the rules and perform them to perfection. It's her best shot of returning back to the real world, her real life.

"Don't be sorry for the things you didn't know anything about." The woman turns away to mark something on a clipboard. "But now you *do* know it, so don't let it happen again. Pretty simple." She points toward the floor beside the desk. "Now grab your toiletry bag out of that box. Your name's on one of them. Find it, use it, and bring it back when you're done."

Someone else is waiting to talk with the staff. In her peripheral vision, Devon can see a small, dark-haired girl bouncing up and down on her toes impatiently.

The woman shifts her eyes to the other girl then. Dismissing Devon.

After breakfast is over, the girls start to make their way to the classroom, one of the rooms off the entryway. Devon had managed to sit alone, in a corner, to eat a few bites of the toasted frozen waffle and mushy fruit cocktail. Beside her was a cart jammed with paperbacks, worn with use. Scanning the titles had given her something to do while the other girls moved around the room or did their chores or ate at the round tables. Only after most of them had cleared out did she move to collect the stray napkin, the stray spork.

Devon veers the cart with the trays and trash around the few girls loitering in the entryway outside the classroom. She stops the cart at the door to the unit, as she'd been instructed. The moment she'd entered through that door replays in her mind, and all the accompanying feelings—how she had felt clutching her bedding to hide her chest, stress churning in her stomach. That moment was not even two days ago. Her stomach still feels the same; that anxious feeling has never left her, not even in her sleep.

Devon peers through the door's small window to the hallway outside. Directly across is another unit, labeled UNIT C. Through the small window of the opposite door, she catches movement inside. Blue jumpsuits carrying breakfast trays to a cart, pushing and shoving and jostling each other. Boys.

"Mmmm. Nice, huh?" A voice whispers behind her.

Devon looks over her shoulder. A girl is there, standing a little too close, invading Devon's personal space. She's heavy-lidded, with only tiny dark slits for eyes, her brown hair twisted into two low braids held with rubber bands. Her face is too pale, even for the sunshine-challenged Northwest, with big, pouty lips.

"Yeah, well," the girl says, "as the saying goes, 'If you want to marry a prince, you'll have to kiss many frogs.' Compliments of my friend Anonymous. That, over there, is a pod *full* of frogs." She leans even closer, whispers, "Pucker up and get busy." She turns from Devon then, a crooked smile playing those lips as she saunters away and through the door to the classroom.

Devon takes a moment to steady herself; the girl had startled her, though Devon doesn't think she'd let it show on the outside, thankfully. And that thing about a prince. Hadn't Kait once said something to Devon about finding a prince, too? Devon pushes the thought away and follows after the girl toward the classroom.

"Time to zip the lips!" Devon hears a voice shouting over the loud girl chatter as she crosses the threshold. A woman rises from behind a cluttered desk at the front of the room. *Must be the teacher*, Devon thinks. She watches as the presumed teacher props herself on a tall stool beside the desk, a large whiteboard to her back. Waving Devon forward from where she had hesitated in the doorway, the teacher says, "Come on in. Take an empty seat." She scans the room and points. "That's a good one, over there."

Devon's eyes skim over the room's three rectangular tables and find the vacant seat indicated. It's beside the pale girl with the braids. The girl scoots her chair back to make room for Devon, presenting the seat to her with an open hand, her crooked smile creeping back onto her face. Devon feels sweat prickling all over her body.

"Hey!" The teacher turns back to the room of girls and raises her hand. "Ladies? Hello, ladies!"

Devon moves for her seat, careful to keep her face a mask. She does a quick scan as she moves: the three tables, including hers once she's there, will each hold five girls. She does the math—fifteen girls in all.

"Ladies, why am I raising my hand?"

The noise level in the room drops one notch, then two.

Devon reaches her place and sits down.

"Better." The teacher says. "Now—"

Devon feels eyes hitting her from all directions. What should she do with her hands? Place them on the table? Put them in her lap? She glances at the black girl sitting across from her. She's outright staring at Devon, sucking on her thumb. Devon looks quickly away. *Another option*, Devon thinks wryly, *place hands in mouth.*

"Uh, Ms. Coughran?" the thumb sucker across Devon's table blurts.

The teacher looks over at her. "Yes?"

Staring down at the tabletop, the girl says, "I just wanted to say that why you raise your hand is 'cuz you want us to be quiet."

A snort comes from somewhere in the room, and a "No duh" from another.

"You've got it," the teacher says. "Thank you, Destiny. Now—"

Devon chances another quick peek across the table at the girl who the teacher had called Destiny. She's sucking on that thumb again, her face unreadable. Her hair's twisted into tiny Rasta knots; it looks like she's wearing a wig of brown Cheetos sticking up everywhere, but cool. *Destiny*, Devon thinks. A curse, that name. Like her own middle name, "Sky." Devon's mother's dreams, compressed into three heavy letters.

"Okay," the teacher says, pulling up a clipboard from the desktop. "Roll call time. When I call your name, all I want from you is 'here.' Got it?"

Devon turns her eyes back on the teacher. She puts on a pair of funky reading glasses that had been hanging around her neck on a multicolored beaded chain.

"I'll start with me—Ms. Coughran—with whom most of

you are well acquainted." She smiles. "That's 'cough,' as in what you have when you're sick and 'run,' as in what you do when you're chased."

"Tee hee, Freak Woman." Devon hears the braid girl beside her scoff under her breath. "So funny, I forgot to laugh."

"Now, let's hear from the rest of you—Bella?"

"Here."

"Casie?"

"Here, Ms. Coughran."

"Destiny?"

Devon keeps her eyes on this Ms. Coughran as she goes down her list. Yet another person here with an indistinguishable ethnicity and age. But she looks too young to need reading glasses, Devon decides. She has this dark hair twisted up into some hair clips, and warm brown eyes. She wears hip clothes, but not pretentious or ridiculous for her age—a short jean jacket, boot-cut jeans, square-toed shoes, big sterling hoops in her ears. She makes a point to smile at every girl as she calls her name.

"Devon?"

Devon blinks, yanked back to reality.

Ms. Coughran is smiling at *her* now.

Devon's heart pounds. Okay, so what's the big deal? Calling roll happens the first day at any school. And sometimes every day, if you have study hall with Mr. Brugman (aka "Drugman"), who's never learned a single student's name in his twenty-two years at Stadium and is proud of it. Calling role is expected.

"Here." It comes out a sort of gasp, which Devon isn't satisfied with, so she clears her throat and repeats, "Here."

"I need your birth date, the last school you attended, and current grade. I don't have a copy of your school records yet, but

I'll put in a request for them today." Ms. Coughran has pulled a pencil from somewhere and is waiting for Devon to talk.

Everything in Devon's body is resisting this; the room is quiet, listening. What ever happened to the Right to Privacy? When the information comes out of Devon's mouth, it's fast and tinged with annoyance. "May fifth. Stadium High School. Sophomore."

"Thank you, Devon." Ms. Coughran turns back to her clipboard and resumes calling roll. "Evie?"

"Here."

"Grace?"

"Here."

"Haylee?"

"Stadium." Another whisper from beside her. The girl with the braids kicks Devon's chair and laughs softly. "What a crap heap. *Hate* that place." She leans close and whispers. "Bet *you* love it."

"Karma?"

"Oh! Right here, Ms. Coughran!" The girl with the braids straightens, her voice practically singing the words, pure sarcasm. Ms. Coughran pauses, watching Karma for a moment before moving on.

"Keesha?"

"Here."

"Lexie?"

Devon looks over at the girl with the braids. *Karma, huh?* Talk about a name setting someone up for failure. Their eyes meet. Karma smirks. When Devon doesn't look away, Karma makes a crude gesture with her tongue.

Karma's unfortunate name makes Devon think about her

own ridiculous one again. Take away the oppressive "Sky" part, and there's still the embarrassing "Devon Davenport." Her mom's subtle attempt to set Devon up to become a soap opera star. Or Broadway diva. Or fashion designer. Things that Devon's mom had always dreamed of one day becoming herself. Things that Devon would refuse to do even if held at gunpoint.

"And, finally, Tana."

"Here."

Ms. Coughran drops the clipboard onto her desk. "Okay." She pulls up a silver travel mug from the mess that's her desk and cups her hands around it. "Rule time."

"Snore," Karma murmurs beside Devon.

"We do this every morning so people new to the class know what's expected. And it also serves as a nice reminder for the rest of us. Because everyone needs reminders, don't we, ladies? Repetition aids learning."

Ms. Coughran goes through the rules and expectations. No curse words of any sort are allowed, including what she calls the three "s-words": *stupid*, *shut up*, and *sucks*. "Respect yourself and one another," she says. "Words hurt, and 'shut up' can be like a slap. Profanity is offensive and contributes to illiteracy. If you don't have anything nice to say, talk about the weather. Don't interrupt when others are talking, especially me. Don't discuss your charges, where you live, or anything else about your personal life on the outs with anyone in here. Unless the person who's asking is me." Ms. Coughran takes a sip from her travel mug. "Now let's talk about behavior."

Ms. Coughran goes over more rules, about not bringing court papers into the classroom or writing letters to boyfriends while in class or leaving the classroom without permission, the bathroom included. Devon half-listens, but mostly she allows herself to look around, to get the information she needs about the room through her eyes.

The small space resembles a kindergarten class, not anything close to what Devon had imagined "school" would look like here—if she'd allowed herself to think about it. Bright pictures cover the walls: watercolors of rain forests, tissue-paper American flags, pastel drawings of zebras, and crayoned coloring book pages of Disney's various princesses—Snow White, Cinderella, the Little Mermaid, Sleeping Beauty. The Disney display strikes Devon as very out of place, considering the kind of girl who goes to school here. Crammed bookshelves of different heights take up most of one entire wall. A long table across the back holds five turquoise desktop iMacs all in a row. Then there's the filing cabinets, plastic milk crates stuffed with art supplies, the TV and DVD player on a rolling cart, the overhead projector and globe and boom box, all stashed in the remaining available space. And, of course, Ms. Coughran's cluttered desk at the front beside the big whiteboard. Cozy chaos.

"Do not bring *anything* in here," Ms. Coughran is saying now. "No hygiene items, no combs, no cups. Nothing in your socks and nothing in your pockets. The only thing allowed in your pockets is lint."

Devon hears Karma groan beside her. "God!"

"Keep your hands to yourselves. And," Ms. Coughran says, "M.Y.O.B.—that's 'mind your own business.' That will take you far. Any questions?" She looks around the room. "Any answers?" She waits. "You ladies are all so good with the answers. I know there's at least one comment out there."

Devon looks around the room, too, but cautiously. The girls are all very busy watching their hands or the tabletops or the empty space in front of their faces.

"Nobody? Well, okay. Then let's hit it, people!" Ms. Coughran downs the rest of her drink and slams the mug on her desk. "Jenevra? Evie? You two pencil count and pass them out. Casie, get some paper and hand one piece to everyone. Please." Ms. Coughran turns her back to the class, faces the whiteboard. "Quickly, ladies."

Devon watches as two girls walk up to Ms. Coughran's desk and count pencils from a canister. The girl on the left, the one with the shaved head, moves like an athlete. Devon suddenly recognizes her; she's that girl Devon had seen her first day here, waiting on the plastic seats to go into court.

Ms. Coughran is writing a column of words down the whiteboard: *shadow, imagine, stars, twist.*

"You can kill someone with a pencil," Karma whispers in Devon's ear.

Devon doesn't respond in any way. Pretends like she didn't hear her. Or, even better, like she couldn't care less.

"There's lots of ways to do it." Karma laughs to herself. "Aren't you wondering why they're counting out those pencils oh so carefully?"

Devon says nothing.

"It's so when we break for lunch and they collect them back, they'll know how many they had in the first place. If the numbers don't match, we all get Lockdown and searched."

Karma's breath is hot, and Devon wants to shove her away. "Makes it very tough to kill someone around here. But"—she kicks Devon's chair—"it's still possible. Totally possible."

"Karma?"

Karma pulls back from Devon, her voice sweet again. "Yes, Ms. Coughran?"

Ms. Coughran is leaning against the stool now, her arms crossed. "You have something you want to share with everyone in the room?"

"Sure. I'm just explaining to . . . to . . . "—Karma snaps her fingers—". . . um . . ."

"Devon," Ms. Coughran says.

"Oh, yeah!" Karma says. "Sorry! I was just explaining to Devil—"

"*Devon*, Karma."

Laughter erupts around the room, some of the girls repeat it: Devil. DevilDevilDevil.

"Oops, gosh. So sorry, Ms. Coughran," Karma says. "I was just telling *her* why it is we count out the pencils."

"I'm sure you were," Ms. Coughran says. "But next time, let me do the explaining. All right?"

The noise in the room drops to quiet and still.

"*Absolutely*, Ms. Coughran. As my friend Anonymous always says, 'The less you say, the more you don't have to apologize.' It's good advice to put into practice."

Ms. Coughran holds Karma's gaze a long moment before turning back to the class. "Now, ladies," she says, "direct your eyeballs to the board." She tells the girls how they're to use the list of words in a poem, explaining that poems don't always have to rhyme. "We call it a poem, but it's really like a story, a story that ties together into one theme. Try to use as many of the words up here as you can, okay? If you can't do anything else with them, at least use each word in a sentence. And you can use any form of the word, in any order."

Devon looks up at the board.

Shadow

Imagine

Stars

Twist

Twilight

Courage

Sail

Clutter

Release

Diamonds

One girl raises her hand; she doesn't know what *twilight* means. Another wants to know if it's *sail* as in boat, or *sale* as like at a store when stuff's cheap.

Are these girls really that dumb? To not know the meaning of simple words? Devon sighs in exasperation.

Devon hears the sound of pencils rubbing across paper in the otherwise silent room. She has a piece of paper in front of her and a pencil, the eraser worn down flat. She sees Karma working beside her, her own pencil moving over her paper, her arm shielding her work from prying eyes.

Devon doesn't need an eraser because she can't write, not this assignment. She won't even pick up the pencil, hold it in her fingers. She doesn't like poetry, not anymore. Poetry makes her feel and remember too much, and she doesn't want to remember. Or feel. Not about poetry. Not about that night, that first night, with him.

Devon sits there in her seat and stares at the blank paper.

The moonlight is overhead, spilling onto the walkway and illuminating the poetry etched in concrete under their feet. The water ebbs and flows softly against the shore like a whisper, its frothy white foam a delicate lace.

"Really cool idea," he says, "whoever thought of doing this."

Devon looks at him. "Um, sorry. What?"

"The poetry." He points to the sidewalk.

"Oh. That. Yeah . . ."

They are quiet and shy, now that they've left the noise and distractions of the restaurant. It had been easy to talk then, to tell him about playing soccer and the music she liked, the concerts she'd been to, the movies she'd seen. Easy then to laugh at his jokes and nod and smile at all the appropriate times while he told her about Denver, where he lived with his mom, and the summers he'd spent in Tacoma visiting his dad, and playing baseball.

But now, in the quiet dark, with him walking beside her along Point Defiance, where the land gently juts into the Sound, she has nothing to say. It's one of those uncomfortable moments when two people are walking together, but not touching. When they aren't saying much, but the silence is not companionable. When they're trying to read the other's signals, trying to figure out what the other is thinking, feeling. The tension is there, the fluttering is there, the wanting to initiate *something* is there, but the fear of making the wrong move holds them back and to themselves.

Then he does the perfect thing; he begins reading the sidewalk poetry aloud.

wave no rest allowed
a tug-o-war pulling
between sun and moon
steadfast you hold
this slippery grip on life

They stare down at the words.

"Well." He grabs Devon's fingertips with his and laughs. "Isn't *that* an upper?"

But Devon doesn't say anything, not immediately. That last line about the slippery grip on life. That is so like her mom—always reaching for something, but that something is always slipping out from between her fingers. No matter how tightly she holds on, she'll always, always, lose it.

But that's not Devon. She has a grip. She knows what she wants and where she's going. Devon shakes her head. She doesn't want her mom's intrusion here.

Devon smiles up at him. "Yeah, losing your grip—not a good thing. A definite downer."

"How true. So much better to hold on." He suddenly grabs her hand then, fully encloses it with his. "Right? Nice and tight."

They laugh together, a little awkwardly, and move on. She steps slightly closer to him, lets her shoulder brush his arm as they walk hand in hand. Lets her hip bump his. Once. Then twice. Will he notice? And what will he think of her if he does? Does it matter? The night air breezing over them from the water is cool; she can feel the warmth of his body beside her through his clothes.

Oh, what is she *doing*?

They move forward, stopping at each poem as he reads them aloud. After some time, he drapes his arm loosely around her back, his fingers lightly touching her shoulder. They send tingles through her body, gentle electric waves. She feels herself lean into him.

"My turn," she says the next time they stop. "I'll read this one." She nudges him playfully. "You're being a poetry hog." Her voice is higher. A flirty girl voice. The one her mom uses when she's met a new guy she likes.

Devon clears her throat, first scanning the words so she won't stumble over them.

His hand drops down to her waist, and he pulls her closer, his thumb through her belt loop as together they study the poem in a brief silence.

"Defiance," he whispers, his lips soft against her ear. "I get it. As in 'Point Defiance'—where we're at right now. Cool play on words."

A shiver runs through her because to her, they are more than just a "cool play on words." But . . . how could she tell him this? That in this fragment of time, those words are so absolutely true and totally hers? She, standing here with the water and the moonlight and the warmth from his fingers pulsing through her. She, embraced by the shore, treasuring this moment. She, consciously throwing them away—all those little rules she'd carefully constructed to protect herself—just for this moment. She, walking in Defiance. In defiance of herself.

"Are you cold?" he asks. "Because you're trembling."

His hand is no longer around her waist; he is holding each of her hands in his, pulling her toward him.

She shakes her head and looks away, down to the pavement, her heart beating fast. The next poem is there, waiting. Like a fortune, pulled from a fortune cookie in a Chinese takeout, it says:

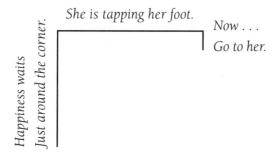

She is tapping her foot.

Now . . .
Go to her.

Happiness waits
Just around the corner.

She looks up at him. She is so afraid. But . . . his eyes, so beautiful and wanting her. He is leaning closer now, gently touching her chin, his fingertips tilting her face toward his. Then, he kisses her—sweet and soft and urgent.

She closes her eyes, shutting out the stars and moon and water lapping against the earth.

She lets the moment take over.

She obeys the poem.

And kisses him back.

"Can I be first to read mine?" The thumb sucker with the Rasta knots, Destiny, asks.

Devon shakes her head, tossing the memory away, far and away where it needs to stay. She wraps her arms around herself; the room is suddenly too chilly.

"Those who want to share, can," Ms. Coughran says. "I'm not going to force you. And yes, Destiny, you can go ahead."

But the ghost of the memory lingers in Devon's mind. His eyes. The way he watched her when she moved. His eyes, and the warm and happy way they made her feel inside. They started everything. But that night at Point Defiance, it hadn't been the very end of everything. Not yet.

Destiny stands, lifts the paper to hide her face, and reads in a fast monotone. "My mind/A twist of clutter. As I lie in bed—"

"Whoa!" Ms. Coughran says. "Sorry, but my hearing aid can't keep up with that. Can you please slow down and start again?"

Destiny nods and reads again, slower this time. "My mind/A twist of clutter/As I lie in bed imagining my life/I watch the shadows on the ceiling./Memories sail across my eyes./I need courage to see them./I fight with myself/But then I close my eyes to the twilight/And release myself to sleep."

Silence for a moment, and then the girls in the room actually clap. The sound makes Devon jump.

Devon glances across the table to Destiny, astonished. *She actually wrote that?* But Destiny is sitting again, looking down to where her paper now lays on the table. Her thumb is back in her mouth.

"Take that as a compliment, Destiny," Ms. Coughran says. "What do we say when we get a compliment?"

"Thank you," Destiny mumbles around her thumb.

"That was very nice," Ms. Coughran says. "I counted eight of the ten words. Am I wrong?" She looks around the room, but nobody responds. "I especially liked 'My mind a twist of clutter.' Isn't that so true? Particularly when you're lying in bed and things are weighing heavily on your mind? I'm sure all of us feel that way at times."

Devon can hear whispers popping here and there, but nobody says what they're thinking loud enough for the entire room to hear.

"Anyone else want to take a risk today and read theirs?"

"Me." The girl who counted pencils, the one with the shaved head, stands up.

"Okay, Jenevra," Ms. Coughran says. "Good. Read on."

Devon wonders at these girls. Why would they volunteer to read their poems aloud? It was a bearing of the soul, a letting down of the guard. Something Devon would never, *could* never, do again.

"I want diamonds, but they don't shine," the girl Jenevra starts. "I want to touch a star, but it's not mine./I want to find some courage, but I got lost./I want to sail in a boat, but it got froze with frost./I—"

Giggles erupt around the room.

Jenevra stops reading, looks up. "Yeah, that line really sucked—I mean *stank*." She smiles. "But I couldn't think of another word that rhymed with *lost*."

"Read on," Ms. Coughran says.

"I try to clean my clutter, but I make a bigger mess./I want to—"

"Hey!" Karma's whisper is in Devon's ear again, distracting her attention from Jenevra's poetry recitation. "You want to read mine, Devil? Even though I only used one of the words, I think it kicks ass." She thrusts her paper under Devon's face.

Devon looks down, can't help but read what's written there:

She can paint a lovely picture.
BUT . . .
This story has a <u>twist</u>.
Her paintbrush is a razor,
and her canvas is her wrist.

"So, what do you think?" Karma leans in closer. "Love it?"

Devon turns away, says nothing. *What a freak.*

Karma pulls her paper back, smirks. She whispers again, "Yeah, you *are* a devil. Deep down inside." She laughs softly. "So am I. So are all of us." She kicks Devon's chair. "Get over it."

chapter ten

The next day after breakfast, Ms. Coughran rolls the audio-visual cart out of her classroom and into the common area, where all the girls are waiting.

Devon raises her head. She's sitting on the floor, the book cart beside her; this has become her spot. It's where she eats her meals and spends her free time, little that there is, when she doesn't choose to retreat to her cell. This is her spot because it's the only place in the room that nobody else seeks out. She can remain invisible here, or at least out of the way, hiding behind the cover of a book.

"We're starting with P.E. today," Ms. Coughran says, ducking behind her AV cart. She grabs the plug to the DVD player, then pushes it into a socket on the wall behind her. She stands, sweeps a fallen strand from her face.

A few girls groan out their oppositions: "I hate P.E." and "Can't we do it tomorrow?" and "I got bad cramps, Ms. Coughran. Can I sit out?" A few express slightly more positive opinions. Like Jenevra, who yells, "Bring it on, baby!" But most say nothing, including Devon in her corner by the book cart.

"Hey!" Ms. Coughran says. "I don't want to hear your griping. It's already Thursday and only the first time we've done P.E.

all week. If it were up to me, we'd be doing this every single day. So, zip it."

"Let me pick!" Jenevra rushes up to Ms. Coughran.

"No! She picked last time!" someone yells. "It's not fair!"

Devon watches as two more girls run up to the cart, start rifling through the box of DVDs.

"Nope," Ms. Coughran says, "I'm picking." She wades through the girls and pulls the box up and away from them, balancing it on her hip. "Bye-bye now."

The girls slump away, mumbling. "You always make us do that boring yoga stuff," one of them says.

"Yeah, *Yoga for Dummies*. It's so dumb!"

"Okay, ladies," Ms. Coughran addresses the room. "Get into three rows, facing me. Come on, hustle up!" She selects a DVD and returns the box to the cart. "We've got other things on the horizon today."

The girls drag into the middle of the room, form three sloppy lines. Devon scans the group. Karma isn't there; she's nowhere in the room. Again. Devon hasn't seen her since they did poetry in class, yesterday morning. Right before lunch, Devon remembers, Karma had been called out of class. In the afternoon, she hadn't come back. And at dinner last night, Devon had overhead Jenevra telling some other girl that Karma was on Lockdown. Which, Devon's learned from the unit pamphlet, means solitary confinement in her cell for a staff-determined amount of time. Devon herself is locked down every night at eight, but that's only because of her current status—Regular—and the rules. Jenevra is on Privilege, so her bedtime is nine. And when Devon makes it up to Honor, she'll be allowed to stay up until ten. But last night, Jenevra made it sound like Karma was on Lockdown because of something she *did*.

"Let's move it, ladies!"

Devon pushes herself up off the floor, but first she dog-ears the page she's on and returns the book—some sci-fi about a kid who can access the Internet through a chip in his brain—to the cart. She takes a spot in the back row, on the end. Wonders if Karma is watching them all through her cell door's window.

Ms. Coughran slides her chosen DVD into the player and turns on the TV. Loud music bangs from the speakers. A large black guy with his hands wrapped like a boxer appears on the screen, shouting out enthusiasm. The girls start moving to his instructions. Some of them languidly wave their limbs around, going through the motions. Others are totally into it, especially Jenevra. She's connecting with the air in front of her like someone she wants dead is right there.

"That boxer guy is so *hot*!" some girl squeals.

"You're sick. The dude's, like, thirty or something."

Devon is bouncing on her toes, squinting toward the screen, trying to pick up the rhythm of the movements. Working her body feels good; when she sweats and her heart rate picks up, it'll be even better. She feels a gush between her legs then; it's warmed the pad lining her underwear. The blood still comes at times; this little bit, brought on by the bouncing, is nothing to worry about.

"Uh-uh, girl." Ms. Coughran appears at Devon's side, startling her. "Not you."

Devon stops bouncing and frowns at her.

"Two reasons. Number one: the doc hasn't cleared you for

exercising yet. And number two"—she points across the room toward the closed door of the conference room—"your attorney is here. She wants to talk to you."

Devon looks across the room to the closed door, and suddenly the pit of her gut drops. Dom wants that list. That list Devon has yet to write. That list that Devon hasn't even thought about. She'd been locked down in her cell for two full evenings with nothing to occupy her mind but staring at the gray walls around her and the back of the door. Obscenities and tags other girls had scratched there: JAC, KARTOON, BK-4-LIFE, CRIP. All that time and no list. Dom will be unhappy. No, Dom will be livid.

The music from the speakers blares. The girls have dropped to the ground for push-ups. No one is doing them correctly, Devon notes. *Head bobs aren't push-ups.*

"Devon?" Ms. Coughran says. "Did you hear me?"

Devon turns back to Ms. Coughran, says, "Okay." Because what are her options? She has none. She gives Ms. Coughran a little unsteady smile and walks across the common area toward the closed conference room door. Pausing there, she takes a breath, then turns the knob and enters.

Dom is sitting at the table again. This time her hair is down; it's stick straight and much longer than Devon would have guessed when Dom had worn her updo the other day. She wonders if Dom uses a hair straightener, or if her hair is like that naturally, like hers. Dom looks up when she hears the door—*Clank!*—behind Devon. Dom isn't wearing her tiny glasses, either.

"Hey, Devon," Dom says, pulling a hairband off her right wrist and drawing her hair back into a loose ponytail. "How did yesterday go? This is day four for you, right?"

Devon hovers near the door. This change in Dom's appearance is disconcerting. She liked the other Dom better, the tight and in-control Dom wearing a suit and glasses and the neat little beehive bun. Seeing her sitting there now in a sweatshirt two sizes too big and jeans with a loose ponytail makes her seem . . . erratic and unreliable, somehow. Why is everything so unpredictable here?

Devon walks over to the table and sits on one of the bolted-down stools across from Dom. She clears her throat. "Okay, I guess."

"No," Dom says. "You are not 'okay.' What's bothering you?"

Devon looks down at her hands. "I don't know . . . your hair?"

"You don't like my hair." It's a statement.

Devon looks up at Dom. She shouldn't have said anything. She should've just left it at "okay" and thrown her a convincing smile.

"What, you don't like the color? The style?" Dom squints at Devon, amused. "Or maybe it's not my hair at all that you dislike. Maybe it's just my ambience. Maybe it's that I've lost the glasses. Or the fact that I'm dressed like a total slob today. Am I getting warm?"

Devon says nothing. She doesn't like that Dom can glean these things about her so easily.

Dom shrugs. "Just a ploy to keep you on your toes. I wouldn't want you getting too comfortable."

Devon feels her body stiffen, her lips curling slightly.

Dom notices Devon's reaction. "Hey, I'm kidding! The days I don't go to court—and today's one of those days—I wear what I want. And in my opinion, comfort is key. When we met on

Tuesday, I'd just had a court appearance. The glasses, the hair, the suit—all part of the act. You have to look like a winner to *be* a winner. You must know a little about that, being the serious soccer player that you are."

Devon shrugs.

"You know the deal, right? Clean, sharp uniform, jersey tucked in. Socks pulled up, wrapped with color-coordinated electrical tape to keep those shin guards from sliding around. Clean cleats. Me in a suit? Same thing."

How does Dom know so much about soccer all of a sudden? Devon shifts on her seat, fiddles with her plastic security band, the one that the frizzy-haired woman had snapped on her wrist during Intake. Last name, first name, birth date. And then another number, her ID number. Eight digits. Like she's become that number, a breathing debit card.

The room is quiet for a moment.

"So, shall we move on?" Dom says. "How about that list. Got it for me?"

Still examining her wristband, Devon says, "I didn't . . . I don't have it with me."

"Not a problem." Dom pulls out her yellow legal pad and clicks open a pen. "I take great notes."

"Um, I didn't exactly . . . I mean I couldn't think of . . . I've been really tired. . . ." Devon's voice trails off.

"Okay." Dom lays the pen on the pad, centers it. "That *is* a problem, Devon. I thought we had an agreement. Remember? You were going to work with me."

Dom is tapping her fingers on the tabletop. Devon notices that her nails are clear today, no color.

"We have to be in court on Tuesday, Devon. That only gives

me"—Dom counts on her fingers—"four full days, and that's over a weekend, plus what's left of today, to prepare. Do I need to go over the importance of this hearing with you again? That its outcome will determine whether your case will be tried in adult or juvenile court?" She waits a moment, giving Devon the opportunity to say something. When she doesn't, Dom continues. "This is huge, Devon. It has nothing to do with your guilt or your innocence. At this hearing, nobody's dealing with that. But it has *everything* to do with your future."

"Yeah, I know. You already told me. I understand all that."

"Well, that's just great. But you see, Devon, without people who are willing to speak positively about you, to vouch for your character, to show that they care about you and your future, we'll lose this hearing. Plain and simple. And off you'll go to slug it out in the adult criminal system where you'll be looking at a maximum *life* sentence." Dom pauses. "Versus if you cooperate with me, follow my guidance, the max you'll see is five years. Where would you like to be five years from now, Devon?"

Devon looks down at her hands in her lap. Her throat aches. Dom doesn't get it. No one will speak positively about her. Nobody will care what happens to her, not now. Nobody, nobody, nobody.

Dom sighs loudly. "You are part of this process, Devon. A huge, gigantic part. I can only go with what I know about you, and most of that must come *from you*. Once I get this info, I can run with it. But I have to get it first. And, unfortunately, I'm not a mind reader."

Devon continues to watch her hands.

"Come on, Devon. Give me one name. Just one, and I can go from there." The silence stretches out between them. "You know," she finally says, "I should just walk out of this room. I really should."

Devon glances up at Dom. She's got her arms crossed. But her face is more thoughtful than angry, and this unnerves Devon. Some plan is forming behind those eyes.

"Okay—" Dom shakes her head. "I'll work this out, with or without your help. But I'll tell you this much, Devon: I'm not getting you. Why are you fighting this?"

Devon says nothing.

"I know this isn't easy. But, as they say, God helps those who help themselves, and right now you're not helping yourself. In fact, you're your biggest handicap. It's like you've decided that during one game—no, wait, in a *championship* game—you're going to go stand in the goal wearing a blindfold and think that you'll actually be able to stop all those balls from flying into your net. And I'm the coach, watching all this from the sidelines, and I just have to deal with it because you're the only keeper I have." Dom hesitates. "I can't bench you, Devon. You're it. You go into this blind, and you choose to lose."

Devon looks down at the floor. She kicks at one of the legs of the bolted-down table. "I don't want to fight this. I'm not really meaning to. I just . . . can't . . . I . . ." She looks up at Dom again. Should she tell her? That she can't remember? No, Dom won't believe it anyway.

Dom looks back at Devon. Finally, Dom shakes her head again. "Look, I don't have all day, so let's move on. The articles I gave you and the photos. Did you look at them, read them, at least?"

Devon can feel her stomach churning now. She swallows. "Yeah."

"And . . . when you did, you felt . . . you thought . . . what?"

Devon closes her eyes. She's so tired. "I don't know. I didn't really feel . . . anything."

Dom presses her lips together. "You're lying to me."

Devon checks back to Dom; when she speaks she hears her own voice shaking. *"I am not a liar."*

"Oh, no? Well, you are if you're saying that you looked at the photos of your apartment and the trash bag and felt nothing, Devon. That you read those articles about yourself and felt nothing? The pictures are pretty shocking, Devon. The *story* is shocking." Dom pulls her brown accordion file out of her briefcase and picks through it. "Okay, let's look at them together. Shall we?" She lays some sheets of paper on the table. Devon recognizes what they are—more copies of the articles and photos. She turns her eyes away.

"Okay, Devon. You saw the photo of the trash bag that the baby was found in. Let's start there. Talk to me. About what you can remember. There's a lot of evidence there, items I'll need specific information about. And the other police photos, too. We'll need to go over them, one by one. . . ."

Devon looks behind herself at the door. The walls of this small room are pressing in around her again. "I don't!"

"What do you mean, 'I don't'?"

"I mean"—she takes a breath—"I don't really remember anything."

"You don't remember anything about what?"

Devon doesn't answer.

"About the stuff in the pictures? About what you felt when you read the articles? The baby? What?"

Devon says nothing, just keeps watching the door behind her.

"You know, Devon, this little game you're playing? It's getting very old, very fast. And please turn around and look at me while we're talking. It's extremely rude what you're doing."

Devon slowly brings her head back to a general position where she could look at Dom if she wanted to. But she doesn't; she looks at the white cinder block wall behind Dom. "I'm not playing games, Dom. I just can't remember. I mean, I can remember some things, but then it . . . just . . . kind of, like, stops."

"Stops." Dom's tone is dubious.

"Yeah. It just kind of . . . shuts off." Devon meets Dom's eyes directly now. "I'm totally serious. It's like there's . . . nothing there."

Dom crosses her arms and shifts on her stool, squinting at Devon. She doesn't say anything for a moment. Devon can hear the pulsing music from the common room behind them. The thick walls muffle most of it.

"Did you mention this to Dr. Bacon? This 'not remembering' problem?"

"Um, who?"

"Dr. Bacon. The doctor who you spoke with at Intake? The one who asked you if you'd hurt yourself?"

"Oh." *The lady with the long gray braid.* But it wasn't at Intake; it was in her cell later that night. Devon frowns, shakes her head. "She didn't ask."

Dom presses her lips together, nods. Makes a note on her legal pad. Then, "Okay, then tell me what you *do* remember."

"About what? About that . . . That Night? Or . . . something else?" Devon brings a hand to her mouth, starts gnawing on her thumbnail. "Something before? Or after?"

"Just start talking, Devon. Start at the beginning, and I'll listen."

Devon takes in a big breath. She lets it out slowly. She hadn't come up with a list of names for Dom last night, but those hours of staring at the ceiling had provided a blank screen for her mind to fill, too tired to fight it.

She'd stared up at that ceiling. And she remembered.

"Okay," Devon says finally, her voice a whisper. "This is something I can remember."

The feeling is what wakes her.

It isn't like most other mornings, waking to the alarm screaming at her from the dresser. It's that feeling, that wave of nausea—that awful rising up from the bottom of her stomach to the back of her throat—that forces her out of her bed and propels her down the dim hall toward the bathroom. Had she remained curled under her sheets a second longer, she'd be sponging puke from her mattress and hauling her bedding to the laundry room for most of the morning.

Devon drops to the linoleum just in time, flings up the toilet lid, and grips the sides of the cold bowl. She doesn't think to pull her hair away from her mouth before she retches and retches, spewing orange vomit into the water, the splashlets spattering her black hair, her chin, even her cheeks and forehead, and the front of her oversized GIRLS HAVE MORE KICKS T-shirt she'd slept in. And the retching continues, the heaving continues, the gagging, even after she has nothing left inside herself, only the gut-rotting nausea, and a long strand of thick slobber swinging like a pendulum from her foul-tasting mouth.

Finally, Devon struggles to her feet. She stumbles to the sink, wipes her lips and chin with the back of one trembling hand while leaning on the counter for support with the other. She feels empty and weak. The sour stench of puke is everywhere, clinging to her skin, to her hair, to her T-shirt. As she reaches for the faucet, her reflection in the mirror stops her momentarily. Her face is so pale it seems to glow, the dark eyes staring back at her, large in their sockets, and she wonders for that second if the girl in that mirror could really be her. Because right now she feels like she should be dead.

She rinses out her mouth with water, swishing it around before spitting into the sink. Then she slowly brushes her teeth, the minty-flavored Crest with its pasty consistency causing another wave to rise in her throat. She closes her eyes with the effort to keep it down.

"Dev!"

Devon jumps, drops the toothbrush into the sink.

Her mom. Standing in the doorway, watching Devon, brows furrowed and worried. "You look *horrible*, hon."

Her mom is still dressed for work, that navy blue Safeway apron over her white blouse and blue bow tie. She glances at the toilet, then crinkles her nose as she moves around behind Devon to flush down what Devon hadn't.

Why is her mom home so early?

"Sheez, I *thought* I heard you in here. Gr-*oss!*" She quickly retreats back to the doorway, covering her nose with the palm of her hand. "Sorry, hon; you know the hard time I have with puke. . . ." She starts dry heaving then, takes another step backward, embarrassed. "I could *never* be a nurse. It's bad enough bartending. Are you sure you want to keep your appointment today?"

That's why she's home early. The appointment. Devon feels her pulse spike suddenly. She leans against the counter with both hands.

"I know I got off early to take you and all. But still, if you're sick, we could cancel it, no big deal—"

"No, Mom," Devon says quickly. "I'm fine." Devon tries to smile then, an attempt to give her statement credibility, because "fine" is not at all how she is feeling. In fact, besides feeling sick and weak, she's scared. Terrified, actually. Terrified of going to the doctor this morning, terrified of what he might find. But she must go to the doctor, she must get that physical, because she wants to play soccer. "Really. I had some tuna fish last night; I think it was bad or something. Or maybe the lettuce. Both had been in the fridge for a while." Devon feels dizzy suddenly. She takes a quick steadying breath before speaking again. "Plus, I've *got* to get that sports physical done. Our first game's tomorrow. Coach Mark said if I fail to bring the form back this afternoon, signed by a doctor, there's no way I can play—"

"What? You're his starting keeper. He wouldn't bench you for that. No way. He loves you! He wouldn't—"

Devon shakes her head no. She's bending over the sink, now, taking deep breaths. The effort it took for her to knock out that speech had nearly made her pass out. She hooks her hair behind her ears and picks up the red plastic container that holds her Neutrogena soap, lathers her hands. "Stop, Mom. Yeah, he would, even if it costs us a game. A rule is a rule. I'm lucky that he let me practice so long without it."

From her spot in the doorway, Devon's mom watches Devon wash her face. "Well, listen, Dev. I really hope you told him that it wasn't *my* fault your form's late. You told him that at least, didn't you? Because I know for a fact that I said I'd make you an appointment at least a zillion times. But you just kept putting it off and putting it off. And even on registration day, the school nurse had those slots to sign up to get the physical done with her, and you refused. That's how we did it last year, remember? And it would've only been twenty bucks. More convenient, too. I wouldn't have had to miss work—"

"Yeah, I told him, Mom."

"Oh." Devon's mom looks a little confused for a second, like she can't believe she'd just won an argument with Devon without actually arguing. "Okay. Well, don't go around eating rotten tuna anymore, okay? 'Cause I think I've got enough stuff going on right now without worrying about what you're eating. I mean, I don't want to have to quit my bartending job. Working Friday and Saturday nights at Katie Downs really brings in the bucks. And no way do I want to switch shifts at Safeway; the money's better on graveyard, and the work's way easier, and there are tons of people gunning for my slot. Plus, pretty soon I'll be taking those cosmetology classes in the afternoons. I'm going to register next week. I mean, I've got to think about *my* future, too, Devon. You know that. I can't be worrying about you all the time, hoping you're taking care of yourself, eating right. . . ."

Devon tunes her mom out. It's always the same blah blah blah—her various sacrifices, all her best years gone, all the things she could've done, not that she regrets any of it, but still. Devon finishes rinsing her face, buries it in a towel to dry her skin. The old rage starts bubbling to the surface, and for a second she forgets about how awful she feels. She thinks about what she wishes she could do right now. How she would look right at her mom, right into her eyes, and say, Um, who worries about *whom* around here? Who takes care of *whom*? But absorbing the blame is so much easier. And anyway, Devon's too wiped out to exert the kind of energy the subsequent conversation would take, so she just says, "Well, it's not just the tuna, Mom. I mean—" She takes a deep breath and busies herself with hanging up her towel then, because she knows what she's about to say isn't true. Yet. It isn't true *yet*. "I kind of started my period today, and my stomach's a little crampy from that."

"Oh." Devon's mom moves to stand beside Devon to peer in the mirror, checking out her own hair to ensure that the wiry strand sticking up isn't actually a rogue gray but a blonde highlight. "Well, in that case you better wear a pad today, even with a tampon. That'll kind of give the doc that subtle hint that he probably doesn't need to be poking and prodding around down there." She shrugs, rearranges a few strands of hair. "Saves a lot on embarrassment. For everybody." She smiles at Devon then, pats her shoulder. "Works every time. Oh, and take some Midol. It'll zap those cramps"—she snaps her fingers—"like *that*."

When her mom's gone, Devon looks back into the mirror.

Wear a pad today.

Thanks, Mom. Relief washes over her. Devon closes her eyes.

She's never felt so free from something in her life.

chapter eleven

DOM IS QUIET, just watching Devon. Pulling at her ponytail. Finally Dom clears her throat and speaks. "This was when again?"

"September," Devon says.

Dom slides her yellow legal pad toward herself. She picks up a pen, starts writing. "So, did you go?"

"To the appointment?"

Dom looks up from her legal pad. "That's what we're discussing here, Devon."

"Yeah. My mom took a quick shower and changed her clothes. And then we went."

"And this was your regular doctor?"

Devon doesn't say anything.

Dom taps her pen on her legal pad—*tap, tap, tap.* "Devon?"

"I don't really have a regular doctor." Devon shifts on her stool. "I don't really get sick, so it's no big deal. And with my mom's jobs, we don't have the greatest health care. We only go when we really have to."

"Okay, but you went that day. So, where did you go?"

Devon shrugs. "One of those walk-in clinic places. That's where we go when we *do* get sick or something. I went there only once before. I was twelve, I think. In sixth grade. I cut my finger.

I was trying to chop up a carrot." Devon looks down at her right index finger. She'd had a scar there for a long time; it's faded now. In the years since, she's jammed that finger more times than she can count, stopping goals. An ice pack and a couple of days off of soccer pretty much took care of it.

Dom returns to her legal pad, writes again. "Where was this clinic? Because I don't remember coming across anything about it in your file. Your medical records are pretty thin."

"Who knows? We took the bus."

Dom looks up again, frowns. "You don't know where you went? Come on, Devon. Don't play dumb with me."

Devon glares at her. "I wasn't paying attention, okay? I wasn't feeling very good. All I know is it was somewhere past Proctor on 26th Avenue or something. And it took, like, twenty minutes to get there." She crosses her arms. "Happier with that answer?"

"Okay, okay," Dom says. "Relax."

"Well, you're always accusing me of lying! I'm really sick of it."

"As you may recall, you haven't been entirely forthcoming thus far in our relationship. It's my job to question you, draw your story out, okay?" Dom opens the DAVENPORT file. "Hold on a sec; let's just see if I can find a record of that appointment."

"Fine, whatever." Devon stands, stretches her arms high over her head. She can no longer hear the music from the exercise video. She twists around, looks back at the door. Wonders where the girls are now.

Devon drops back on her stool, watches Dom as she sifts through her files. After a moment, she sighs, then folds her arms on the table and lays her head down on top of them to wait.

"Yes!" Dom says at last. "Got it."

Devon peeks up at Dom; she has pulled out a page. She looks it over briefly before shoving it across the table to Devon.

It's one of those generic sport physical forms, marked up with checks and illegible writing, and on the bottom a signature above a rubber-stamped address.

"Right there in your school records." Dom smiles, points to the rubber-stamped address at the bottom of the form. "This is where you went, in case you're wondering: the Urgent Care Center on North 26th Street—5702 North 26th Street, to be exact."

Devon feels that uneasiness creeping back over her. Records exist for everything.

"So, we've got the clinic's address. The doctor's name, not that I can actually *read* his or her name on it. Doctors' writing is the hardest to decipher for some reason—"

"*His* name," Devon mumbles.

Dom raises her eyebrows, surprised with Devon's contribution. "Okay. *His* name. Thank you. Now we're getting somewhere." Dom returns the sheet back to its place in her files. "So, ready? Tell me as many details about this appointment as you can."

Devon sits up, rests her face in her hands, rubs at her eyes. "What do you want to know?"

"How about start at the beginning? From when you first walked into the clinic."

Devon looks down at her wristband, pulls at it.

The waiting room is packed. Devon scans the room for an empty seat. There's only one; it's next to an old man with long, greasy gray hair and beard. He's digging under his fingernails with a paper clip.

Together, Devon and her mom walk up to the reception desk.

The woman behind the desk looks up. "Name?"

Her mom pokes Devon with her elbow.

Devon clears her throat. "Devon. Devon Davenport."

The woman consults a printed schedule. "At ten twenty?"

"Yes."

The woman crosses something off with a pencil, then hands a clipboard with papers to Devon over the counter. A cheap black pen is attached with string to the upper right-hand corner of the clipboard. "We don't have any information on record for you, Devon, so if you would, please fill out this new patient questionnaire—"

"But she's not a new patient," her mom says. "She's been here before. She'd cut her finger and needed stitches."

The woman smiles, forcing politeness. "She currently doesn't exist in our database. So, to us, she's new." She turns back to Devon. "When you're finished, dear, please bring this back up here to me." Then the woman turns back to Devon's mom. "Payment is due at the time of the appointment, ma'am. I'll need to make a copy of your insurance card—"

"Uh—" Her mom pushes Devon toward the waiting area. "Why don't you just go ahead and sit down and work on that? While I get this money thing figured out? 'Kay, hon?"

"Okay." Devon doesn't want to witness how her mom is going to dance around the payment issue anyway. She feels guilty enough as it is. She should've just gotten the physical at school during registration like she did last year. That was only twenty dollars. She could've paid for it herself out of her babysitting money.

She moves across the room to the one empty seat and sits down. Her body, every limb, feels drained, her brain foggy. The bearded man beside her has the predictable reek of cigarette smoke about him. She wraps herself tight in her sweatshirt and rests her head on her hand, the clipboard on her lap.

She skims the two pages of questions, then starts on answering them. Some of them are easy—does she smoke, drink alcohol, take recreational drugs? No, no, and no. Which medications is she taking currently? None. But the others, the ones about family health history, are not. Devon cannot answer questions about people she's never seen, never learned anything about. Her mom is the only relative Devon's ever known. She's from Spokane, was a high school cheerleader once. She'd left home one night when she was sixteen because she had gotten pregnant, and she never went back. That's all Devon knows. And her father? Devon doesn't even know his name. The one time her mom ever discussed him in any detail was on Devon's seventh birthday. She had said that Devon could ask one question about her father, and she'd answer it, and that would be Devon's birthday present. Devon had asked what her daddy looked like. "You have his exact eyes," her mom had said. "And his straight black hair. You have his face—its shape, the nose, the eyebrows. He was tall and very athletic. His hands were big. And that's all I'm going to say."

Devon looks up from the clipboard. Maybe her mom would know the answers to the heart problem, glaucoma, and cancer questions. But she is already occupied. She's found a seat near the window and a man about her age. She's smiling her big smile, moving her hands all around as she talks. Devon wouldn't want to interrupt the Potential Boyfriend flirt act, would she?

Devon completes the questionnaire the best she can. She brings it back to the woman at the reception desk.

"Thanks, dear," the woman says to her.

"I left some things blank. I'm sorry—"

"Oh, that's okay. You can go sit down again. We'll call you."

Devon slumps back down into her seat, rests her head on the wall behind her. She closes her eyes, takes slow breaths, tries to relax.

Sometime later, Devon hears her name. She sits up, looks around, momentarily confused about where she is and why. Had she been asleep? At the far end of the waiting room, a woman is standing with an open door behind her, smiling. She's wearing a green scrub jacket with multicolored dancing dinosaurs all over it. In her hands is a manila folder. "Devon?" she says again.

Devon feels a stab of adrenaline in her gut then, because she remembers where she is. She stands—her arms shaking as she pushes off the armrests. The room has cleared out, she realizes. Only a handful of people remain now, with plenty of open seats.

"That's me," Devon finally manages to say. "I'm Devon."

Her mom stands up, too, from the other side of the room. She's holding a magazine, her index finger marking her place. The man she was talking with is gone. She bends down to pick up her purse from off the floor, arranges the strap on her shoulder.

The woman at the door nods at Devon's mom. "You're going to tag along, Mom? Or—" The woman looks back at Devon then, raises her eyebrows, the gesture a question.

Or. Devon looks across the room. Her mom's eyes are wide and bright, so hopeful. She's twisting a strand of her long blonde hair around and around her index finger, watching Devon closely.

Does she want her mom to come in with her? She'd hear everything that is said then, hear the doctor's questions, hear Devon's answers to them. Devon isn't sure what all that will entail exactly, or even why she's become so anxious about this appointment. But what she does know is the embarrassment she'll feel, having her mom sitting in the room with her, seeing everything. Making her chatty remarks. But . . . that hopeful face. So pathetic.

Devon takes a deep breath, shrugs. "I guess, if you want to."

Devon's mom smiles at Devon, relieved. "Want to? What do you think? Of course!"

"Well then, ladies, right this way." The woman with the manila folder turns toward the door. Devon and her mom follow her through it.

The woman has Devon stand on the scale first, takes her height and weight. She annotates the information onto a form that's inside the manila folder. Then she has Devon sit down, takes her blood pressure and pulse and temperature. "Hmm," she says after reading the thermometer. "A hundred point three. You're running a low-grade fever. Feeling under the weather today?"

Devon shrugs. "I don't know. Kind of."

"And your blood pressure is a teensy bit high," the woman says as she writes into the manila folder. "Just a tad." She smiles at Devon. "Nervous?"

Devon tries to smile back. "Maybe a little."

"So," Devon's mom says, "what percentile is she in?"

The woman looks up. "Excuse me?"

"Her height and weight. What percentile—"

"Mom—" Devon starts.

The woman glances between Devon and her mom.

"What?" Devon's mom says. "It's a good thing to know, Devon. How you compare to other girls your age and everything. What's wrong with asking that?"

"Well . . . " The woman flips to the back of the folder, runs her fingers along a chart. "Five feet, eight and a half inches . . . a hundred and twenty-nine pounds. . . ." She looks up at Devon's mom. "She's in the ninetieth of height and fortieth in weight. Tall and slender." She smiles at Devon. "One of the lucky ones."

"She's already an inch taller than me," Devon's mom says. "Unbelievable. But the weight thing, well, I'm not saying." She winks at the woman. "I'm not fifteen anymore, dammit."

The woman laughs. "Weren't those the days? When we didn't worry about stepping on a scale."

Devon's mom plays with her hair again, frowns. "Yeah . . . it was . . ."

The woman leads Devon and her mom to an examination room, opens the door, pulls a fresh paper sheet across the exam table. She turns back toward the door, smiles at Devon and her mom one last time. "Have a seat. Dr. Katial will be in. It'll be just a few minutes." She closes the door quietly behind her.

"Well." Devon's mom drops into the chair near the door. She opens her magazine.

Devon paces the room. She steps over to a desk in the corner, picks up a pamphlet explaining juvenile diabetes, puts it down. She can feel her heart beating faster and faster, feel the adrenaline racing through her stomach. She leans against the desk, picks up a paperweight advertising some drug with a complicated name.

"I didn't appreciate *that* comment."

Devon looks up, relieved to have something occupy her mind for the moment. "What comment?"

"Oh, that weight comment. About stepping on the scale or whatever stupid thing she said. Obviously, she thinks that's something that I have to worry about."

Devon sighs. "Um, I don't think she was saying that at all."

Devon's mom is flipping through her magazine. "Well, maybe *she* has to worry about that. She could obviously drop ten pounds and not even notice. But she shouldn't project her own crap on me. I'm a size eight! I've never had a—"

"Mom! You're the one who made a big deal about not telling her your weight!"

Her mom stops flipping pages, holds up the magazine to show Devon a picture. "Now *that* is a gorgeous gown. Don't you think? Catherine Zeta-Jones is the most beautiful woman in the world. I don't think she could look ugly if she tried." She turns the magazine back around and starts flying through the pages again. "Or look old," she says, almost to herself. "Oh, I just love *In Style* magazine. They have the best articles."

Devon rolls her eyes—as if her mom actually *reads* them— and looks at the wall, at the watercolor hanging there. It's a landscape—a lake with a hazy impression of tall trees surrounding it and hills in the background, an early morning mist overhead. But in the middle of the silvery water, stands a large rock. A young child sits on that rock with her back turned, looking tiny and alone, the world so big around her.

A little rap on the door. Both Devon and her mom turn to look. A dark, lanky man pokes his head in. He looks foreign, Indian maybe. He wears a scowl on his face, carrying an air of sternness, even some irritation, with him; Devon can see this around his eyes, the way his brows furrow, how he holds his mouth. He knows how to dress and does so with care; Devon can see that even under his white doctor coat. The rich colors of his pressed shirt and khakis complement the olive tones of his skin.

"Well, come on in, doc!" Devon's mom says. "We don't bite."

He walks in, closes the door behind him. He looks down at Devon's mom, offers his hand. "I'm Dr. Katial."

"And I'm Jennifer," Devon's mom says, taking his hand. "Jennifer Davenport. And that's Devon over there, my daughter."

"Ah, yes. The patient." The doctor crosses the room to where Devon is still leaning against the desk, offers his hand to her. "Hello, Devon." He looks directly into her eyes as he shakes her hand. Devon can see then that he isn't really an angry person at all; his eyes are warm, like chocolate, and a little sad. Angry people don't have eyes like that. Devon looks down toward the floor.

"Why don't you jump up on the table," he says.

When Devon moves, he opens the manila folder on the desk and takes a seat.

Devon hops up on the table, leaves her feet dangling over the edge. She looks over at her mom; she's inspecting the French manicure she'd given herself. The magazine, Devon notices, she's stashed under her chair. Devon almost rolls her eyes again at that. What, is her mom hiding it? As if the doctor actually cares—or notices—that she reads vapid fashion magazines.

"So, we're doing a sports physical today." The doctor turns around to face the room, his legs crossed.

"Yes," Devon's mom quickly says. "But I'm also wondering

if . . . well, Devon's been getting her sports physical done with the school nurse, so it's been kind of a long time since she's been to a real doctor, you know, for a regular checkup with a real doctor, I mean. And—"

"How long?"

"Since, gosh, probably since she's been twelve or something. Maybe thirteen?"

Lie, Devon thinks. More like eleven. Summer after fifth grade. Her mom's friend Tiffany had said it was "criminal" to let Devon go so long without a checkup. "I'll take her myself," Tiffany had said, "if you don't."

"So, I was wondering—"

"Don't worry," the doctor says. "When we're done today, we'll have a pretty good picture of Devon's overall health."

Devon jiggles her left foot. The paper under her makes a crinkling sound.

"Well, she's superhealthy," Devon's mom says. "She hardly even gets colds. But the thing is, I'm just not sure where she's at with her shots. I think I've, maybe, misplaced her shot record. I got a notice from the school the other day. They said she's missing something, so . . ." She giggles nervously, combing through her blonde hair with her fingertips. "You must think I'm a terrible mother, Dr. Katial. No shot records, no checkups . . ."

The doctor smiles, shakes his head. "No, not at all." He stands, crosses the room to the door. "There's a database that maintains immunization information on everybody." He squeezes Devon's mom's shoulder as he passes her. "So, no worries."

The doctor sticks his head out the door, speaks to someone in the hall. Devon's mom draws her hair over to one shoulder, scoots around in her seat, crosses then recrosses her legs, arranging her little skirt just right.

The doctor closes the door, looks down at Devon's mom, gives her a small smile. "We'll have that in a few minutes."

"Wow," she says. "Technology. Amazing."

The doctor returns to his seat, focuses his attention back on Devon. "So, Devon, which sports do you play?"

Devon draws her hands up into her sweatshirt sleeves, clears her throat. "Soccer mostly."

"Mostly?" Devon's mom snorts. "More like *only*, Doctor. Soccer's her life."

The doctor nods. "Which position?"

"Keeper," Devon says. "I mean, goalie."

"That's a difficult position to play," he says. "You have to be mentally tough."

"I guess."

"She's probably the best keeper in the state for her age," Devon's mom says.

Devon shoots her a look, feels her face grow warm. "Mom—"

"Well, it's *true*, Devon."

"What else do you like to do, Devon?" the doctor asks. "What are your interests outside soccer?"

Devon thinks about this. She gives training sessions to little girls who hope to become good keepers like Devon one day. She referees kids' soccer games, too, on occasion. But that's still soccer. So, what *does* she do when she's not playing or practicing? She doesn't have much downtime. She studies hard. Takes long runs all over Tacoma. Sits in the empty apartment, watches cable until her brain aches. Boils up mac and cheese or ramen noodles for dinner. These things she can't tell this doctor, this man in his beautifully pressed clothes and solemn eyes. She sometimes walks the mile downhill to Main Library, though, to sit in its quiet comfort, a book, any book, in her hands. IMs her scattered soccer friends—from California, Nevada, Oregon, and Colorado, who she made at Regional camp over the past couple of summers—until some librarian kicks her off the public use computers. Hangs out at Kait's house sometimes, goes shopping with her at the Tacoma Mall.

"I like reading," Devon says finally. "I babysit a lot."

"And school? Are you a good student?"

"Yeah." Devon doesn't have to think how to answer this question. "I actually love school."

"Good girl. That'll get you far." The doctor stands. "Flip off your sweatshirt for me?"

Devon feels her heart speed up. Feels the heat from her face wash down her body, leaving a light sweat in its wake. She quickly pulls the sweatshirt over her head. She's thankful for the black tank she chose to wear under the sweatshirt. Otherwise, she'd be sitting here in her bra.

"I'm going to examine you now," the doctor says, crossing the room to the exam table, "starting from the top—your head— and working my way down. All right?"

Devon nods, swallows. "Sure."

"And if at any time you feel tenderness or discomfort, let me know. Okay?"

Devon nods again. "Okay."

"Okay. Just relax." The doctor puts his hands on Devon's head, presses her forehead with his thumbs, kneads her scalp. Devon closes her eyes. It's the luxurious feeling of getting her hair shampooed at the Gene Juarez Salon and Spa on her thirteenth birthday, the stylist's massaging fingers working the suds through her hair. No Supercuts coupon special that day. A complete spa treatment—facial, manicure, pedicure, a cut and style and highlights. Her mom was dating the salon's manager then; it was his special treat. He'd wanted Devon to like him.

"All right," the doctor says. "Now open your eyes." He pulls a small instrument from off the wall behind Devon, its coiled cord stretched taut. He flicks it on and tells Devon to track the light with her eyes—up and down, left then right. "And when did you last menstruate, Devon?"

Devon feels her body grow stiff. She jiggles her foot again, then glances at her mom. Her mom smiles back, gives a little wink.

"Keep following the light, Devon," the doctor says.

"Sorry." Devon jerks her eyes back. She clears her throat. "Uh, I just started it . . . my period . . . today, actually."

"And are you pretty regular?" The doctor pulls a second instrument from off the wall to peer into Devon's ears and nose. "It comes monthly?"

"Yeah." Devon nods. She thinks about the pad lining her underwear. "Pretty much."

"And about how long do they last? How many days?"

Devon swallows. "I don't know, four or five maybe?"

The doctor returns the instruments to their places on the wall. He has Devon open her mouth, suppresses her tongue with a wooden stick, checks her throat. He moves his hands to Devon's neck, feels the glands there. Then he pulls a stethoscope out of the pocket of his coat. "Okay," he says, putting the earpieces in. "I'm going to listen to your heart and lungs now. Just breathe normally." He holds the round metal piece in his hands for a moment to warm it before he reaches toward her.

Devon grasps the edge of the exam table, holds tight. Looks up at the ceiling. The doctor gently touches the metal piece just above her collarbone on one side, then the other, on her sternum, under her breasts. Devon holds her breath until he moves his hand away.

The doctor pauses to look at her. "Relax. Your heart sounds like machine gun fire."

"Okay," Devon whispers. "I'm sorry."

The doctor slips the metal piece under her tank top, touching places on her back. "Now, deep breath in . . . and let it out. Good. And again? Okay. Now hold it." Devon counts the seconds—one, two, three, four. "And let it out."

He steps back. "Lungs and heart sound good." He removes the stethoscope, returns it to his pocket.

"I told you she's healthy," Devon's mom says.

The doctor smiles over at her. "And so far, you're right." He looks back at Devon. "Now I'd like you to lie down. I'm going to poke around your abdomen for a minute. Just relax. And again, let me know if anything hurts."

The doctor presses her with his fingertips, under her ribs and along the top of her belly, moving from right to left. Devon studies the ceiling, her body going rigid even though he told her to relax. He moves vertically downward now, across her navel and toward her pelvis, then across from hip bone to hip bone, right to left. She sneaks a look at the doctor, watching his face out of the corner of her eye. He's staring straight at the wall, his lips pursed, concentrating, working methodically, his gentle touch inching across her. Then he frowns, troubled about something. "Tender here?"

Devon thinks she does feel something, but she shakes her head no. It's just a little twinge, she thinks. Probably because her stomach's so empty. Hunger pangs.

The doctor lifts her tank, touches her skin underneath, pressing the area near her navel again, moving downward toward her pubic bone. His fingertips are soft, his fingers long and cool; he must notice her clammy skin.

"I'm just going to unbutton your jeans now, take a little peek, and we'll be done. Okay?"

Devon nods, squeezes her eyes shut. She can feel his fingers work the buttons on her button-fly jeans. Her breaths come short and shallow, like little dog pants. When he pulls at the elastic on her underwear, she holds her breath. She can feel her own strong pulse in her neck. The doctor takes a quick peek at her private area, then buttons the top button of her fly. She lets the air out, watches the ceiling.

"All done," the doctor says. "I'll let you finish closing that up."

"Okay," she says, the word a squeak.

The doctor walks back to the desk, jots something down in the manila folder. Devon's hands are shaking as she buttons the rest of her fly. Her fingers can barely manage it.

"You can sit up now, Devon. And put your shirt back on."

She sits up. Her body is damp with sweat. She reaches for her sweatshirt, pulls it over her head. She wipes her forehead on her sleeve.

The doctor is sitting in the chair again with his hands folded in his lap and his legs crossed, watching her. "So, Devon, do you have any concerns about your health? Anything you'd like to discuss or ask?"

She swallows. He's watching her, those dark eyes staring right at her, waiting for her answer.

Why is he looking at her like that? Does he know—suspect—something?

She glances at her mom, shifts around on the table. She feels like she should say something, he expects her to. "Well, uh"—she clears her throat—"I've been kind of tired lately. But it's probably just because training is starting to ramp up—"

"Devon does extra practices in the fall with the boys her age at her soccer club," her mom says. "In addition to her high school practices. She's that good."

The doctor nods. "That's impressive, Devon. But are you more tired than you'd usually be during training, do you think?"

Devon shrugs.

He frowns slightly. "Anything else out of the ordinary you've noticed?"

Devon looks down at her hands.

"You did have a low-grade fever." He checks the manila folder. "One hundred point three."

Devon says nothing.

"Are you urinating more frequently?"

Devon looks up suddenly. "Yes," she says, surprising herself. Then she presses her lips together. Why is she saying anything at all? She was just going to get a quick physical and get out of here.

"How much more frequently? About how many times a day, would you say?"

Devon feels her heart pick up again, feels the palms of her

hands grow slick. She wipes them on her jeans. "Uh, I don't know. Maybe . . . ten? Twelve? I don't know."

"Hmm," the doctor says. "And for about how long have you noticed this going on?"

Devon swallows. This line of questioning makes her uneasy. "Since just before school started, maybe? So, about three weeks? It's just, like, I have to go after almost every class, that's all. But it's not a big deal, really."

The doctor turns to the manila folder, writes something down. Then he turns back around, watching Devon, thinking. "What about nausea? You've been feeling like throwing up lately?"

"She threw up this morning," Devon's mom says.

Devon glares over at her mom.

"But that's only because I ate something bad last night," Devon says quickly. "Some tuna, I think. Tuna salad. It's been in the refrigerator a really long time." Devon feels her eyes dart from the doctor's face to her mom's, then back to the doctor's.

Devon sees the doctor shift his eyes then, toward Devon's mom.

He looks back at Devon. He's quiet for a moment. Then he says, "You know, Devon, when young women get to be about your age—fourteen, fifteen, sixteen—they sometimes have personal issues they would like to discuss with their doctors. Questions they'd like to ask, issues they are worried about. And then there are a few personal questions their doctors may have for them." He smiles then. "That's sort of where we're at in the exam right now. Some girls like to have this conversation privately with their doctor. Others don't; they prefer to have a parent stay with them. It's totally up to you, Devon. Whatever makes you feel most comfortable." Then he waits, his dark eyes on Devon's face, his hands still folded neatly in his lap, his legs crossed.

Devon glances at her mom. She doesn't like either option; she'd rather just skip this part and go home. This wouldn't be happening if she'd kept her mouth shut.

"What Dr. Katial means, Devon," her mom says, "is I can step out for a minute if you want." She smiles at the doctor then, plays with her hair. "You know, we moms . . . We make everything so complicated, don't we?" She winks at him. "We're so obnoxious."

The doctor smiles at her. "Yes," he says. "At times, yes."

"Oh, so you think I'm obnoxious, huh?" Devon's mom's voice is higher, flirty. "That's not nice, Dr. Katial." She fake pouts. "Now you hurt my feelings."

He gives a little laugh, his face a shade darker. "In my professional opinion, Ms. Davenport, your feelings will recover." Then he turns his attention back on Devon.

"I—" Devon looks at the floor, wipes her hands on her jeans again. "Like, what kinds of questions?"

"More personal questions," the doctor says steadily.

Devon looks up at him, looks at him straight in the face. She feels anger then, intense hostility. It came on suddenly, inexplicably, just like that. "I'm not having sex, if that's what you want to know," she says, her voice shaking. "And I know all about birth control. I've had Sex Ed in school, you know. I'm a *sophomore*. So save the lecture." She crosses her arms, hugging herself at the waist. "I don't have a boyfriend anyway—"

"No, she doesn't," Devon's mom puts in quickly. "What's the matter with you, Devon? You're being very rude."

"So, is that it, Doctor?" Devon asks, her body trembling.

"'Cause I'm missing school right now. And I have a geometry test to take."

Dom is fiddling with her pen. Touching its tip to her yellow legal pad, then its clicker, then the tip again. "Okay, so then what happened?"

Devon shrugs. "He just kind of looked at me, said a bunch of stuff to smooth things over. Eventually, he said that he'd like to get a urine sample from me and see me back in about a week if I wasn't feeling better."

"Did he say why?"

"Because my fever and my throwing up and my peeing so much could all point to me maybe having some kind of infection or something. Urinary tract infection, I think he said. And he also wanted to make sure that nothing was going on with my electrolytes and . . . some other stuff. I forget what they're called—"

"Glucose levels, probably," Dom says. "Pretty standard tests."

"Yeah . . . whatever. Anyway, he said that you can get a lot of information from a person's urine. He said he wanted to rule out anything like diabetes. Stuff like that. I wasn't really listening."

"Okay, so you gave him that sample."

"No."

"No?" Dom leans forward. "Why not?"

Devon looks down at the tabletop, shrugs. "I couldn't go."

"Go?"

"To the bathroom. You know, *pee*?"

Dom frowns, leans back on her stool, her arms crossed. "Wait a minute, Devon. A girl who has to pee after every single class when she's at school, several times a day, suddenly can't go when her doctor asks her to in a cup?"

"He's *not* my doctor." Devon glares at Dom. "I just needed a sports physical. I never saw him before in my life, okay? And, plus, I'd just thrown up. Remember? I was probably dehydrated from that or something."

"Uh-huh." Dom eyes Devon suspiciously. "So, you're telling me you took the cup, went to the bathroom, sat on the toilet, tried really really *really* hard, and—darn it all—you just couldn't go. Not even one little drop."

"Yeah. Exactly."

"I'm not buying it, Devon."

"What, you think I didn't go on purpose?"

"Well." Dom raises an eyebrow. "You tell me."

Devon presses her lips together, says nothing.

"We'll explore that later. So, moving on. What next?"

"Well—" Devon takes a second to collect herself. She's all rattled inside. Why couldn't she pee? She had tried, hadn't she? Devon shakes her head, shoving the questions away. "So, anyway, the nurse told us to take the cup home and bring the sample back later. Like, the next day or something. She said we should keep it refrigerated until we brought it in."

"And did you? Bring back the sample?"

Devon looks down at her hands. "No."

"And why not?"

Devon says nothing, her eyes still on her hands. Why not? There was a reason, wasn't there?

"Your mom knew about this, right? That they wanted a urine sample from you?"

"Yeah, she was still sitting there in the room with me, remember? Plus, on our way out, he—the doctor—saw us leaving and told us again to bring it back as soon as possible. So, yeah, she definitely knew."

"Okay, so your mom understood that there was a possibility that you could have had a urinary tract infection or, even worse, something like diabetes, and she didn't make sure they got that sample?"

Devon shrugs. "He wasn't her type."

"What?"

Devon looks up at her. "You know, the doctor? He wasn't her type. He was too . . . refined. Had too much class. Was too smart. Basically, not a loser. I knew she'd never bother going back there just to bring in a cup of pee."

chapter twelve

A rap on her door, not the usual lock snapping, is what pulls Devon out of her sleep this morning. Her eyes spring open, check above her head at the window slats. Gray light, thick like fog, hangs there in the corner of her cell. A thought drifts through Devon's mind, *Too early to wake up.* Devon closes her eyes, throws an arm over them.

The rap again. Then the door scrapes open.

Devon sits up quickly. That staff person, Henrietta, stands in the opening. Devon can see the light from the common area bright behind her. Henrietta shields most of it.

"Time to wake up, okay?" Henrietta says. "Your lawyer wants to talk to you. People who say lawyers have it easy don't know any who work here. Okay?"

Dom's here? Again? It's been less than twenty-four hours, and she's back already. Devon bends to retrieve her rubber slides from the cubby under her bed. She won't stand on the floor, even in her socks, without them.

"You'll need this, okay?" Henrietta tosses Devon's toiletry bag on the bed. "Your lawyer won't appreciate morning breath hitting her from across the table." She looks around the cell then, nodding to herself. Inspecting, as always.

Devon glances around, too. Everything is in its place. Henrietta will have nothing to correct, thankfully.

"Come out when you're ready," Henrietta says at last. "I'll leave the door open. And don't take forever, okay? Your lawyer has other things to do today than to just sit around waiting for you. Okay?"

"Okay." Devon's voice is scratchy from sleep.

"I'll leave a note for the next shift, okay? So they'll hold a tray back from breakfast for you. If you're still with your lawyer by the time breakfast rolls around. Okay?"

"Okay, thank you."

Henrietta turns, scraping the door behind her. Leaves a crack for an opening; a sliver of light falls in an arc upon the cement floor.

Devon picks up her bedding, folds it before stacking it at the foot of her bed. Takes her toiletry bag to the corner of her cell where the stainless steel sink and toilet are waiting.

Dom looks up at Devon when the door clanks shut. This morning, she's wearing warm-ups. Devon notices Dom's damp hair, her ponytail hanging limply. Salt residue marking her temples, along her hairline. Her flushed face.

"Good morning, Devon." Dom smiles. "Sorry it's so early. I was at the Y, working out"—she unzips her warm-up top—"running on the treadmill and thinking over what we talked about yesterday. I do my best thinking when I'm running. I guess my mind is free to put things together. Excuse the sweatiness, but I just wanted to talk to you while it's all still fresh in my mind."

Devon pushes herself off the door she'd been leaning against.

"So," Dom says. "I have some questions. I hope you can help me out."

Devon raises her hands straight above her head in a long stretch. Yawns. "I'll try."

"Great." Dom pulls out her yellow legal pad and pen. "Let's revisit that doctor's appointment. The day you went to get your sports physical."

From where she stands, Devon can see writing on the legal pad. Things circled. Notes scribbled in the margins. It makes her feel strange inside. She knows Dom takes notes, has watched her do it. But still. Dom's been studying those notes, thinking them over. Generating more questions even while she's exercising. Devon hates questions. Questions require answers, and answers require reflection. Probing. Remembering. Hard, exhausting work. She hugs herself, her hands cradling her elbows.

"Why don't you sit down, Devon?" Dom opens her palm toward the stool across from her. "I don't know how long this will take."

Dom waits as Devon moves for the stool, sits down. "So, back to that doctor's appointment," Dom says. "Why do you think you reacted the way you did? When the doctor wanted to talk to you alone. To ask you more personal types of questions."

Devon shrugs. "He was annoying me. He wanted to know stuff that wasn't any of his business. And—"

"But you came to his office for an appointment, Devon. How is your health none of his business?"

"I was there for a *sports* physical. Nothing else. He didn't need to know any of that other stuff."

"What 'other stuff'? What did you think he'd ask you when he got you alone?"

Devon shifts around on her stool. "I don't know. He creeped me out, okay? I didn't want to be alone with him."

"But wait, Devon. Didn't you tell me—" Dom flips through her yellow legal pad until she finds what she's looking for. "Okay, didn't you say, and I quote: 'He wasn't her'—meaning, your mom's—'type. He was too refined, had too much class, was too smart. Basically, not a loser.'" Dom looks up at Devon. "I mean, those actually sound like some pretty positive descriptions. Don't you think? Creepy doesn't seem to fit."

Devon glances from Dom's face to the legal pad. Dom takes down *exact* quotes? Devon brings a hand to her mouth, chews on her thumbnail. "So what? He *was* creepy. Okay?"

"And, anyway, didn't he give you the option to have your mom stay in the room with you?" Dom looks down at her legal pad. "I think you mentioned that. . . ."

"Yeah. So what?"

"So, in that case you wouldn't have *had* to be alone with him, Devon, that's what. I'm thinking this excuse you're giving me? It's a bunch of crap." She pauses. "If you get tried in adult court, that's exactly what a jury will think, I can tell you that."

Devon looks at her thumbnail, gnawed down to the quick. She picks at the cuticle. She really shouldn't do this; a keeper's hands are too important to chew up, bit by bit.

"Which leads me back to my previous question: what did you think he'd ask you when he got you alone?"

"Nothing. I didn't think anything."

"Oh, really? Then why did you freak out and—"

Devon glares at her. "I didn't 'freak out,' Dom. I never 'freak out.'"

"Devon, you told me *yourself* that you started yelling at him. About you not having sex, and that you knew all about birth control, et cetera." Dom hesitates. "You know what that says to me? First, it says that you did, in fact, have an idea of what he might have asked you—questions involving sex. It also says that you were feeling very defensive about having to answer any such questions. Why else the attack? And, furthermore, you lied to him—"

"No, I didn't! I wasn't *having* sex, Dom."

"Okay, fine. That may be *technically* true; you were not *currently* sexually active. At least, that's the story you're telling me." Dom waits, lets the words stick.

Dom thinks she's lying again. What kind of person does she think Devon is? Her mom's clone? Sleeping with any guy who looks her way? Devon's eyes find an ink stain on the tabletop to examine. Is this a new table? Because she's never noticed the stain before. It's shaped like a stretched-out heart. Twisted and warped.

"Maybe your words were meant to deceive," Dom continues. "Maybe you wanted him to conclude that you've *never* been sexually active. You definitely wanted any further discussion of sex to end right then and there, that's obvious. You were pretty frantic about it. Why? That's what I'm trying to figure out here."

Devon traces the ink heart with her index finger. "Because it's embarrassing, talking about that stuff! To a man, especially. And I think that any other kid my age would feel the exact same way." Devon flicks her eyes toward Dom. "I bet *you* felt the same way when you were my age!"

Dom watches Devon trace the ink stain over and over for a moment without saying anything. Then she shrugs. "Okay, point taken. But . . . you were wearing a sanitary napkin. Why? You weren't having your period."

"Because, I told you, it's embarrassing. I didn't want him looking . . . down there."

"That's it, huh?"

Devon looks over at Dom. "Plus, my mom suggested that I—"

"So, you're the kind of girl who gets embarrassed easily, huh?" Dom raises an eyebrow. "So shy and innocent—"

"Yeah, maybe I am!" Devon jumps off her stool, starts pacing the room. "You think you're so smart. You think you know everything. Well, you *don't* know me!" She slams her back to the cinder block wall, hugs herself. "You know nothing about me. Not! A! Thing!"

Dom smacks the tabletop. "Okay, then *tell* me! If I'm missing something, Devon, *fill me in*! Because if I don't know it, the judge at the hearing on Tuesday won't know it. And the twelve people who may be sitting in the jury one day if this case goes to trial won't know it, either. But they will know the facts. And right now, the facts are all against you. Shall I list them?"

Devon drops her head back then, looks up at the ceiling, at the pattern its cracks make. Crisscrossed, like lines in a palm. The lines that hold a person's destiny.

"They'll know that you went to a doctor when you were approximately five weeks pregnant. They'll have heard that doctor's testimony. They'll know that he examined you, that he noticed you were wearing a sanitary napkin in your underwear, that you *told* him you had just started your period that very morning when you hadn't. They'll hear everything you told the doctor—about being fatigued, about your frequent urination problem, about being nauseous, how you threw up in the morning before you went to the appointment. By the way, all of these symptoms happen to be symptoms of pregnancy, and the jury will know that. The prosecution will have an expert testifying to *make absolutely sure* that the jury understands that. The jury will see the medical records, which state that you had a slight fever and high blood pressure. High blood pressure, by the way, is an indicator of extreme nervousness or stress. They'll know that you panicked when the doctor wanted to ask you some personal questions relating to your sexual activity. The doctor will testify that you refused to give him a urine sample during your appointment and that you did not follow his instructions to return a sample to his office or schedule a follow-up visit." Dom places her hands flat on the tabletop, pushes off her stool, and walks over to Devon, who still has her back to the wall. "So. How do you think that will play to the jury, Devon?"

Devon drops her head, looks down at her feet. "I don't know," she whispers.

"No? Well, let me help you out then." Dom puts her index finger under Devon's chin and raises her face so Devon is forced to look Dom directly in the eyes. "Those twelve people will draw the obvious conclusion. That you, Devon Sky Davenport, knew you were pregnant that morning—"

"No, Dom!" Devon squeezes her eyes shut. "I didn't—"

"That you did absolutely everything you could think of to hide this information from the doctor—"

"No! That's not true!"

"That you continued to hide this pregnancy for the next eight months—"

"No!"

"—and then, when the day finally came that you gave birth, you attempted to hide that evidence, too. You put that baby in a trash bag and tossed it in a garbage can and left it to *die*!"

Devon is trembling. Even her teeth chatter. She tries to jerk her head away, but Dom's finger is anchored there, too strong.

"These are steps, Devon. When you have steps, you have a plan. When you have a plan, you have what's called premeditation. Premeditation points to guilt. And guilt equals going to jail. For a long, long time." Dom pulls her finger away from Devon's chin and takes a step back. "That, right there, will be the prosecutor's argument." Dom crosses her arms. "And right now, even *I'm* buying it."

Devon's head drops. She wraps her arms around herself tighter, trying to control her shaking. Her breaths come rapid and ragged. "I didn't know any of that, Dom. I swear. I didn't know I was pregnant."

Dom throws her hands up. "When, Devon? When didn't you know you were pregnant? During the appointment? Because—"

"Ever!"

The word startles both Dom and Devon with its intensity. Dom takes another step back.

Devon swallows. "Okay? I didn't *ever* know I was pregnant, Dom. Not until . . . until That Night when . . . when . . . all that stuff happened."

"What 'stuff,' Devon? Huh? Quit hiding behind words." Dom yanks off her warm-up top, tosses it onto the floor. Puts her hands on her hips.

Devon says nothing. Just breathes. She feels something

coming, something dark and ominous sneaking out of some cubby in her mind. She shakes her head, flinging it back and away. Back to its shadow, its hiding place.

Dom takes in a deep breath, lets it out. She drops down onto the stool that Devon had just vacated. "So, you're saying that you didn't know you were pregnant until you gave birth. That's your story?" She closes her eyes. "You know, Devon, I'm sorry, but I'm just not convinced. And if I'm not convinced, well . . . it's pointless going over all that again."

Devon slides down the wall to the floor. She hugs herself into a tight little ball, her chin resting on her knees. "I think I was . . . *afraid* . . . that maybe . . . that I might be . . . pregnant," Devon finally says, the words a whisper.

"Okay," Dom says, pausing for Devon to continue, but she doesn't. "So, if you were afraid that you could be pregnant, Devon, that usually means sex was involved. Right?" Dom's voice is gentle now, her words creeping across the room to where Devon sits. "You know—a boy, a girl, together. You're a girl, so . . . can you tell me about this boy?"

Devon buries her face into her knees. *Please don't make me.* She's cold suddenly. The floor, the wall, is too cool. Her skin is moist, she realizes then. She's been sweating.

Dom stands, moves toward Devon, sits on the floor beside her. All very slow and cautious, like approaching a bird with a broken wing. "Was it rape, Devon?"

Devon shakes her head vigorously no.

Dom rests her head on the wall, looks up at the ceiling. "Okay. Then, it was . . . consensual?"

Devon starts to cry. Little sniffles, muffled by her knees.

Dom touches Devon's back, rubs it gently, little circular motions.

Finally, Devon raises her head, turns to look at Dom sitting beside her. "I think"—Devon's voice catches—"I'm ready. To tell you . . . about"—she sighs deeply—"about him."

"Then I'm ready to listen."

Devon rests her forehead on her knees and stays like that for a long time. When she finally starts, she's speaking to her lap. "So, last summer. I babysat these two little kids. Twins—a boy and a girl."

Dom waits. Then, "How old?"

"Three. I would take them down to the Tacoma Swim Club every morning to go swimming if the weather was nice. It wasn't far from their house, so we would walk down there. They'd always pick flowers out of people's yards even though I told them not to." Devon makes a small laugh. "They were—*are*—really cute kids."

Devon hears Dom take a long breath and let it out slowly. "Go on."

"Anyway, they'd swim and play around in the toddler pool, and I'd hang out on one of the lounge chairs and read and watch them. Sometimes I had to break up their fights. They fought a lot. Not bad fights or anything, just normal little-kid fights. Sometimes I played in the water with them. It just depended. We'd stay there until it was lunchtime, and then we'd go home."

Devon can sense Dom's growing impatience, feels her body restless beside her. "Good. Keep going."

"Well, one day," Devon says, "this guy was there. He was swimming laps in the big pool. They have lap swimming there before nine every day, and then they pull the lane lines out and have open swim for the kids. Anyway, his towel and stuff were on the chair next to mine, and when he came over to dry off, he saw the book I was reading—*The Kite Runner* by that Afghani guy. He told me he had read that book, too, for school; he thought it was awesome. But when they watched the movie in class afterward, he didn't think the director did the book justice. And then we started talking about all this other stuff, like for the entire time I was there. We really connected for some reason. But then I had to go because I needed to take the kids back home for lunch and their naps."

His eyes. Green with hazel flecks. Beautiful. Those too long lashes, wasted on a boy. His eyes had said more to Devon than any words his lips ever spoke.

Devon and Dom sit there in the quiet of the room for a moment. Then Dom clears her throat. "And this is the boy, Devon?"

Devon, her forehead still on her knees, nods yes.

"And how old is—or was—he?"

"A little older than me." Devon pauses. "He was going to be a junior. In high school." *He could drive.* But Devon doesn't add this.

"Okay, and can you tell me his name?"

"Do I have to?" Devon whispers.

"Yes."

"Why?"

Devon feels Dom's body grow tense beside her. "Because I'm your attorney, Devon. I have to know everything. Every single little thing."

"But he doesn't even live here. So why does it matter—"

Devon feels Dom looking at her. "What do you mean he doesn't live here?"

Devon hesitates, turns her face from her knees to look at Dom. Should she be saying any of this? What if Dom finds him, figures out where he is, and tells him? Devon doesn't think she'd survive that happening, having him know what happened. The trouble she's in. "I mean, he doesn't live in Tacoma. He lives in . . . in another state." *Colorado*, she thinks. Denver, specifically. But Devon doesn't say this. "He only comes here to visit his dad in the summers."

Dom nods slowly, narrows her eyes.

Devon can see something going on behind Dom's eyes, see her putting things together. Devon turns back to her knees, stares at the tops of them. At the outline of her kneecaps against the orange fabric of her jumpsuit, the sharp flatness of them.

"So when was the last time you saw him?"

Devon shrugs. As if she's trying to remember, to conjure up the answer. But it's there, the memory is right there, vivid and real.

The silent drive back, Devon looking out the passenger window, her forehead pressed against its cool glass. The geography they pass in the darkness—the shimmery water of the Sound, the moon shrouded with wispy clouds, the succession of glowing ovals slanted across the asphalt from the streetlamps. The shadows from the Japanese maples and rhododendrons stretching across the yards in front of cedar-shingled houses. They'd sat in the parking lot of her apartment complex when he'd stopped, both staring out into the night, he straight through the windshield and she through the passenger-side window. Each absorbed into their individual thoughts, the car idling.

"Do you want me to walk you up to your door?" he'd asked finally. These were the first words between them since she'd dressed back at his dad's condo, and he'd said them now with an awkward politeness.

Devon had shaken her head no, didn't look over at him. Then she slowly reached for the door handle, quietly opened the door, and stepped out into the night, filling her lungs with the cool air. Closed the door behind her and moved away from the car. She'd heard the sound of a window rolling down then, the passenger-side window, the window that still held the steamy imprint of her forehead.

"Devon."

She stopped then, looked back over her shoulder toward his voice. He was leaning forward across the front seat, looking at her through the open window. His eyes were shimmery, like the Sound reflecting moonlight, concerned and confused, his eyebrows crimped over them.

"Are you . . . okay?"

Devon dropped her head, looked at the gravel under her feet, swallowed down the ache in her throat, and shrugged. Then she faced forward again, her eyes focused on the stairwell, the stairwell that would take her to her apartment, to her empty apartment on the second floor and then to her room. She moved quickly—left foot, then right, then left. When she'd reached the first step, she heard the tires of his car crunch over the gravel, pulling away from her.

She looked back over her shoulder again, saw his right turn signal flashing. And then he was gone.

Devon feels the heaviness pressing into her now, the same heaviness she'd felt that last night with him. The feeling a mixture of disappointment, regret, dread, and a stubborn determination. And sadness. His eyes, bright with his own tears, the open pleading there. His voice holding the heaviness she'd felt.

"Was he there with you on the night of the birth?"

Dom. Another question. Always more questions.

"No," Devon says slowly. An image breaks free—lights too bright, her bathroom floor, the clutter and blood—streaks through her mind. She shoves it away. "No!" She swallows, then says softer, "No, he wasn't with me. I . . . I was alone. He'd gone back to . . . about a week later, he went back home because summer was over."

Dom frowns, puzzled. "A week later?"

Devon rubs at her eyes. "Yeah. A week later, after we'd . . . you know . . . " Her voice trails off. She squeezes her eyes shut to close off the new pictures in her head. How he'd held her, kissed her. The things he'd whispered as he touched her.

"Had sex," Dom finishes.

The words are a shock to hear, give Devon a jolt. So blunt and crude. Devon resists the urge to cover her ears.

"*Quit hiding behind words.*" Dom's words, Dom's voice, stern and annoyed and in her head. So Devon nods yes. Because isn't that what they did, after all—"had sex"? Two words: a verb tied to its object.

"So, how many times did you—the two of you—have sex, Devon?"

"Just that once," Devon says softly. "After that, he called and left messages, texted me, but I never answered them."

Devon sees herself then. Remembers sitting on her bed, her cell phone on her lap, staring at the caller ID—his caller ID—as it rang. Counting each successive ring, all five of them. Waiting through the pause as her voice message picked up, imagining the silly one Kait had left on it once and Devon had kept: "This is Devon's celly! It's time to leave your telly!" (Kait's girly giggle, then click). Then listening for her cell to make its obnoxious jingle—the indication that she'd just received a voice message—before finally putting it to her ear and hearing his recorded voice: "Devon? It's me again. Hey, we don't have to do anything, okay? I just want to see you. Please. I'm going back home in a couple days . . . Don't leave it like this." (His voice cracks.) "Call me? Please?"

Her hand, it could have grabbed the phone. Her thumb, it could have pressed the green Talk button. Her mouth, it could have formed the words to explain. Or say good-bye, to at least do that. But she just sat there, in her room, the blinds pulled tight. And her cell rang and rang, unanswered. The text messages came, one by one. And Devon never responded. Felt nothing.

"So, yeah." Devon stretches her legs out in front of her. "And then he went back home, I guess. And that was that. I never saw him again."

"So, you only had sex *one* time?" Dom asks.

"Yep." Devon takes in a long breath, blows it out. "The one and only time, ever, in my whole entire life."

Dom doesn't say anything for a moment. Then, "And that was . . . when?" Dom counts on her fingers, back from April. "July?"

The summer air, Devon remembers how its warmth had

felt on her skin that night. Watching the late sunset over Commencement Bay from the balcony of his dad's loft apartment—like fire spread across the water—and the stars' brightness poking through the darkening sky.

"The beginning of August, actually," Devon whispers. She remembers the date exactly—August eighth. But she doesn't tell Dom this.

"And did you—the two of you—use any kind of protection? A condom? Or—"

Devon turns to look at Dom, sharply. "No!"

"He didn't offer—"

"No! It wasn't like that. It just . . . happened. We didn't plan, we . . ." Devon looks back down at her knees, hugs herself. "I just don't . . . want to talk about it anymore."

Dom and Devon, they sit side by side, saying nothing for a while. Then Dom says, "So, *you* were the one who ended the relationship. Not him." She's silent again, thoughtful. "Why didn't you want to talk to him, Devon? See him again."

Devon swallows. "I couldn't. I wanted to forget I ever knew him, forget that anything ever happened."

"Why? Did he hurt you?"

"No! Because!" Devon jumps up, crosses the room, leans against the wall there, her back to Dom. "Because I made a promise."

"To whom, Devon?"

Devon's body starts to shake again. She feels the tears in the corners of her eyes, the achy lump in her throat swell. She drops her forehead to the wall, closes her eyes. "Myself." Her voice squeaks, her shoulders tremble.

"It's okay, Devon," Dom says. "It's okay."

"No, it's not! Because I promised myself every single day of my life. I *promised* myself, that I'd never end up like my mom. And when I . . . when I did *it* . . . with him . . . when I let it happen . . ." Devon's voice is thick, she feels it grating against the lump in her throat. "Oh, God! I was just like her."

Pictures churn in her brain, a jumble of morphing images. His arms. His muscles strong and safe, his hands gentle. His lips touching her face, her lips touching his. She lies back, pulls him over her. Their eyes, so much there. Their hearts beating, their breaths matching, only fabric between them. Her hands. Stroking his hair, his cheek, his back. Her eyes close then, her mind turns off. She lets herself fall away. Lets her body take over.

Devon bites the collar of her orange jumpsuit, feels it rough between her teeth. "Exactly like her." Her tears are rolling now, down her cheeks. She brushes her eyes against her shoulder, the motion quick and rough, leaving a wet spot there. "I hate her!"

There, she'd said it. The relief she feels saying those three words, it's there in her chest, opening a small space around her heart. Devon hates her mom for leaving her all those nights alone, lying tiny and afraid under her blankets, straining her ears for the sound of a key turning in the lock. Hates her mom for the times when that sound never came, when Devon was left to those solitary mornings, left to dress with clothes she'd pulled from the dirty clothes pile, left to pour Cap'n Crunch and skim milk into a bowl, then lock the door on the empty apartment. Left to walk to the bus stop alone so she wouldn't be late for school. Hates her mom for the times when Devon had tiptoed down the hall, needing her mommy to hug away a bad dream or a scary night sound and finding some man lying there, beside her mom in the bed, the sheets rising and falling with his breathing. Hates her mom for the crappy apartments, the police sirens waking her as they passed through the streets late at night, the eviction notices and shut-off utilities, the cigarette smoke that permeated everything, the frozen TV dinners and ramen noodles. Hates her mom for pushing Brian—the one good guy she ever dated—out of their lives. The man who'd read Devon stories and took her to the library. Who'd watched her soccer games and created that glow-in-the-dark solar system on her ceiling and came to the holiday program at school to hear her sing her one-line solo in *Winter Wonderland.* Hates her for having to be the person her mom wasn't, for her middle name "Sky."

For not being here for her now.

"I think everyone reacts against their parents," Dom is saying, "in one way or another."

Devon turns around. Dom's still sitting on the floor, her face contemplative and sad. Did Devon just tell Dom those things? Had she just opened up her mind and allowed all those memories to spill from her mouth?

"Yeah, I've had to deal with it, too, unfortunately. Not in the same way as you have, but it's that old parent expectation thing. It's why I'm here with you, actually, instead of with my dad in his big Seattle law firm." When Dom says those last four words— "big Seattle law firm"—her lips twist, and she makes a bitter laugh. But then she pushes off the floor and to her feet, rubs the back of her neck and shrugs. "It's just tough being someone's kid sometimes." She checks her watch. "Well, it's time. I've got somewhere else I need to be."

Devon watches Dom as she walks over to the table, starts gathering her papers and files together, places them neatly in her briefcase.

"I think we've made some real progress today." Dom looks over her shoulder at Devon, smiles. "Good job. Really, really great. I mean it. You've given me a lot to work with."

Devon looks down at her feet. She feels utterly wiped, suddenly. But also relieved, somehow. She envisions the rubberized mattress, her cell with the toilet in the corner. She could use a nap.

"I've arranged for a psychiatrist to talk with you this afternoon. I know it's a lot for one day, but she's agreed to testify for us as an expert witness at your hearing on Tuesday, and there's just no other time that she can fit in meeting with you. I think you may remember her—Dr. Bacon?"

The woman with the long gray braid. Devon nods yes.

"Can you please look at me, Devon?"

Devon looks up at Dom.

"I need you to be open with her. As open as you were with me just now, okay? The things you told me today, about your mom specifically, I am going to share with her—"

Devon frowns, opens her mouth to protest.

Dom puts her hand up. "Look, nothing that you're going to tell Dr. Bacon will surprise her. Believe me, she's seen everything. She's been dealing with families and their issues for a long time now. It is *very* important that you cooperate with her. I can't stress that enough. Do you understand?"

Devon nods, mumbles, "Okay."

"I mean it, Devon."

"*Okay.*"

"Okay, then." Dom picks up her warm-up top from the floor and puts it on. Zips her briefcase, arranges it on her shoulder. "Oh, and Devon?"

"Yeah?"

"You never told me his name, you know."

Devon pulls at her wristband. A flutter ignites in her gut. "I know."

"Well?"

Devon brings her thumb up to her mouth, but encloses it in her fist instead.

"Devon. If he's The Boy, then he's the father of the baby." She pauses, speaks softer. "Don't you think he has a right to know?"

Devon presses her lips together. Slowly meets Dom's eyes. Dom looks solid, like she could stand there all day if she must, even with that briefcase on her shoulder and places to go on her agenda and that shower to take. "Connor," Devon whispers.

Devon's heart made a little flutter when she'd said his name. After all this time, just his name on her lips, and her body reacts.

"Connor." Dom nods. "Okay . . . and does Connor have a *last* name?"

Devon shrugs, looks down at the floor.

"He does, but not today, right?" Dom sighs. "Okay, Devon. Baby steps. Just Connor. For now."

Dom puts her arm around Devon's back, gives her shoulder a little squeeze. "Come on. Time to go. I think your school's already started."

Devon feels herself lean into Dom as they walk toward

the conference room door. Dom reaches for its handle, pushes downward, popping the bolt. She holds the door open for Devon to step through first, taking a step back to let her pass.

"I'll be in touch soon," Dom says. She reaches out and gives Devon another light shoulder squeeze. "Have a good day, Devon."

Devon watches Dom walk away, round the corner toward the pod's entryway.

"You, too," Devon whispers.

chapter thirteen

DEVON approaches the classroom slowly; the door to it is open. From the entryway, she can already hear Ms. Coughran's voice from inside the room:

"Ladies! Why is it that when we change activities you think it's time to open your mouths? You want to do math facts for the entire day? Because I can definitely make that happen. . . ."

Devon stands in the doorway now, feels her heart speed up, under her arms grow moist. She hates walking into places late. Hates the moment when everybody stops what they're doing and looks at her. Her mom doesn't, though. She loves a grand entrance, loves it when people pause and take her all in.

Enough about her mom. She's not here. It's been exactly a week since Devon's last seen her, been almost five full days spent in this place, and she hasn't even bothered to call or leave a message. It doesn't matter what her mom would do.

Devon raps on the open door three soft times.

Ms. Coughran, perched on her stool, turns toward the door. She smiles over at Devon, waves her inside. "Just grab that empty seat"—her arm is extended, a finger indicating—"over there."

Devon turns her eyes, mentally connects the invisible dots between Ms. Coughran's finger and the assigned seat.

Karma is there, one seat away from the only empty seat at

that table, the only empty seat in the room, actually. Freshly sprung from Lockdown where she'd been for the past day and a half. And she's watching Devon from under her heavy lids, a slight smile twisting her lips.

Devon gets a sinking feeling inside, a draining sort of dread.

"You're just in time for our weekly health department's presentation," Ms. Coughran is saying. Then she addresses the room. "Did you hear that, ladies? We're having a guest speaker. Allison should be here any minute. So that means I expect your behavior to be . . ."

Devon takes a breath and starts moving toward the table, careful to keep her eyes focused on that task and nothing else. She purposefully doesn't acknowledge Karma's stare.

A small girl who Devon doesn't recognize is sitting beside Karma; she's between Karma and the open seat. The girl's hair is so blonde it looks white. Long and thin, like spider silk. Well, good. Devon won't be sitting right beside Karma, at least.

Karma whispers something in the small girl's ear, then gives her a shove. The girl quickly slides over, then ducks her head, long bangs veiling most of her face. Just as Devon arrives, Karma looks up, makes a big smile and pats the now empty seat beside her. "Right here, Dev," she whispers. "Saved you a seat. Ain't I sweet?"

Devon glances over at Ms. Coughran; she's busy with two girls at the front of the room, working out some kind of dispute. She hadn't witnessed the seat switch. Devon wonders what she would've done if she had. Send Karma back to Lockdown for the rest of the day? Devon pulls out the chair and sits. Puts her elbow on the table, rests her head in her hand. Turns her back to Karma.

The chatter in the room picks up now that Ms. Coughran's attention is diverted. A buzz of white noise.

Karma's mouth is suddenly near Devon's ear; Devon can feel her breath. "Miss me?"

Devon doesn't react at first. Then, "Not particularly."

"'Not particularly,'" Karma repeats in a fake British accent. She kicks the back leg of Devon's chair and laughs. "Yes, I pride myself on my rather vast vocabulary, *darling.*"

"Ladies!" Ms. Coughran yells at the room. "What is *up* with you today?" She stands, holding up her right hand, checking her watch on her left. The noise grinds down. Someone on the other side of the room spurts a sudden loud laugh, squeals, "Dang, girl!" Then, "Oops. Sorry, Ms. Coughran."

Ms. Coughran watches her own foot tapping the floor—*tap, ta-tap, tap*—waiting for complete silence. When she finally gets it, she looks up. "It seems that Allison is running behind. So, while we're waiting on her, let's have some *quiet* time—notice the emphasis on the word *quiet?*—thinking about your goals for today. I'm talking very short-term goals here, all right? They can be as simple as not losing any points today or eating your lunch without complaining about what it is."

"The only good thing is when we get pizza," someone says from another table. A small girl, black hair, cut short, little face with tiny features and wide dark eyes. An anime girl.

"Wow," Karma whispers to herself. "That was random."

"I didn't see a hand, Macee," Ms. Coughran says to the girl. "Please use it next time." She turns back to the room. "So, ladies, I want one goal you have for yourself. All right? Then I want a second goal involving a good deed you're going to do for some-one else. Again, it can be small. It can be as simple as a smile. It can be a compliment. Or it can be more significant, like helping someone with her chore. But you need to pick out a *specific* person and then come up with a *specific* deed. Understand?"

Jenevra raises her hand.

Ms. Coughran looks over at her. "Yes?"

"Can passing out the pencils count? 'Cause I already did that today for you. Actually, for all of us. Before we did that Sudoku stuff. Remember?"

"No," Ms. Coughran says. "It can't be something that somebody told you to do. You can't count the chores you've been assigned, ladies. It has to be something you come up with all on your own, out of the goodness of your heart—"

Karma snorts.

"But that was a good question, Jenevra. Thank you. Anyone else?"

Ms. Coughran looks around the room.

Karma kicks Devon's chair again. "Watch this," she whispers. Then she raises her arm.

"Okay," Ms. Coughran says. "Karma?"

"'You have two hands. One to help yourself, and the second to help others.' A wise saying from my good friend Anonymous, which I thought would inspire all of us to work really *extremely* hard on our goals today."

Ms. Coughran smiles. "Thank you, Karma, for that contribution. Anyone else have something to share?" Nobody says anything. "Okay. Let's see. . . . Karma. Since you seem so excited about the concept of serving others, why don't you show us how it's done? Please get some paper off the shelf for me and hand out one piece to everyone."

"*Absolutely*, Ms. Coughran." Karma stands, stretches both arms high over her head, then saunters over to a cluttered shelf, removes a small stack of white paper.

"I want these goals on paper, ladies," Ms. Coughran continues. "It'll seem more like a contract that way, and hopefully you'll, in turn, feel more obligated to actually follow through with them. If we have time, whoever would like to share her goals with the class may."

Karma takes her time passing out the paper, weaving around the three tables, saying "for you" to each girl as she hands one sheet to her. When Karma gives Devon hers, she leans over and whispers in Devon's ear, "You're welcome, *Devil*," then kicks her chair before moving on.

"Keep your feet to yourself, Karma," Ms. Coughran says.

"Ooops!" Karma slaps her hand up to her mouth. "So sorry! I guess I tripped?" She shrugs. "Well, as *they* always say, 'A stumble may prevent a fall.' And I know you wouldn't want me to fall, Ms. Coughran. Would you? You always have my best interests at heart." She throws her arms out. "So, it's all good! Right?"

"All right, Karma, just finish up."

Devon looks over at Ms. Coughran. She's back on her stool, twisting her funky beaded glasses chain around her index finger, watching. Devon's eyes meet hers. Devon can't read what Ms. Coughran is thinking, but she's definitely got something working in her mind. Devon quickly moves her eyes away, looks down at her blank paper.

When Karma's finished, she returns the remaining stack to the cluttered shelf, then drops into her seat beside Devon.

"Thank you, Karma," Ms. Coughran says. "Now, ladies, get

busy. *Quietly.* This is not a group project." Ms. Coughran retreats behind her desk, starts sorting through papers, tossing some of them into the trash can at her feet.

The room is surprisingly quiet; Ms. Coughran's paper shuffling is the most prominent sound. Devon glances around. Some girls are staring up at the ceiling, others down at their hands. A couple of the girls have put their heads down on the table, obviously sleeping or trying to. The white-haired girl Karma shoved is one of those. Devon checks on Karma out of the corner of her eye. She's drawing anarchy symbols, retracing them over and over, dark broad strokes slashing across her paper. Her thumbs are looped through holes torn near the cuffs of the long-sleeved white thermal shirt she's wearing under her jumpsuit, the fabric pulled tightly over her hands so only her fingers show.

Devon closes her eyes. She's so tired. That meeting with Dom, it was exhausting. She can feel that exhaustion deep inside her bones. How could merely sitting in a room wipe her out so thoroughly? But she hadn't been "merely sitting" at all. *We've made some real progress,* Dom had said. *We've.* Plural. Dom and Devon—like a team. Dom had smiled at her, too, told her she'd done a good job. *Really really great.*

And, just like that, Devon realizes she has a goal for the day: she'll try her very best to cooperate with the doctor. Dom had asked her to.

Devon feels a kick at her chair. Her eyes fly open.

"Wake up," Karma whispers. Then she leans in close, speaks directly into Devon's ear. "Why are *you* so happy, Smiley Face? Having a sweet little dream?"

This kicking thing is getting old. Devon turns her head slowly, coolly stares back at Karma. Devon's played this weary game before, but in a different form. It's what she's endured often enough before a penalty kick. The girl taking the kick trying to unnerve Devon, get in her head, so she'll screw up and let the ball into her net. But Karma doesn't have a ball to kick, and Devon doesn't have a net to protect. No acknowledged foul between them to atone for.

The two girls hold each other's eyes for a long moment. Devon feels Karma's animosity smoldering, reaching out from between those heavy lids to strike her. But then a light rap on the classroom door draws Karma's eyes away, breaks the bond, and Devon also turns to look.

A woman too tan for the Northwest, with dark hair curling loosely to her shoulders, strides into the classroom. She's wearing a tight black T-shirt and cargo shorts, black Keen sandals. She's a person who's spent a lot of time outdoors doing athletic things, Devon thinks. The woman tosses a canvas bag on the floor below the whiteboard, then faces the room.

Ms. Coughran plops the stack of papers she'd been sorting back onto her desk and stands. "Ladies, Allison has arrived!" She moves so she's beside the woman, drapes an arm around her shoulders.

Allison gives the class a twitchy smile, dimples peeking out at them from her cheeks before quickly hiding again. "Sorry I'm late—"

"Hey, you are one busy lady, Allison," Ms. Coughran says. "And you're here now, so no worries. All right, ladies! Place your papers under your seats, so they won't distract you. And that means right this second. Macee, collect back the pencils and count them, please. If you don't get exactly fifteen, be sure you tell Allison. And remember, I'll be back"—Ms. Coughran glares at the class—"popping in when you'll least expect me, so you better stay controlled in here. Got it?" With a quick wave to Allison, Ms. Coughran is out of there.

"Um, I'm Macee?" Macee says to Allison, jumping up. "Ms. Coughran said . . . about the pencils? So . . . um, yeah." She skitters around the tables then, grabbing pencils.

Allison nods, gives her twitchy smile to the class, then turns to the whiteboard. Starts writing numbers across it, equally spaced:

$$12 \quad 13 \quad 14 \quad 15 \quad 16 \quad 17 \quad 18 \quad 19 \quad 20 \quad 21$$

The chatter in the room picks up again.

Karma kicks Devon's chair.

Devon sighs loudly, exasperated.

"'All this death and destruction is because of one's construction.'" Karma recites, leaning toward Devon again. "Just some more wisdom from my faithful friend Anonymous." She unhooks a thumb from her cuff, pulls up the sleeve so her wrist is exposed, thrusts it under Devon's nose. "Some of us wear our scars on the outside."

Devon looks. A pattern of raised crisscrossed scars, some old and white, others more recent in various shades of pink or red. *Like the pattern of cracks on the conference room ceiling*, Devon thinks. Exposing the stress of the structure underneath its paint. She feels her stomach twist in on itself. She looks back up at Karma. She's unable to hide the shock on her face.

Karma smiles a victorious smile, delighted with Devon's response. "I'm told that the scars you *can't* see are the hardest to heal. So. Where are *yours*, Devil? Outside?" Karma yanks down her sleeve, rehooks her thumb. "Or *inside*?"

The woman, Allison, has cleared her throat. Devon turns away from Karma, focuses on the woman at the front of the room. Sees her give the class yet another twitchy smile.

Devon remembers Karma's poem then. She feels skaky inside. So it *did* mean something.

"As Ms. Coughran already mentioned, I'm Allison," the woman says over the voices. "I'm from the Health Department. Some of you have met me before; I think I recognize a few faces. . . ."

The girls continue talking to each other like Allison isn't standing up there at all.

"Hey!" Allison yells. "Excuse me? I'm conducting a class here. I'd appreciate it if you'd shut up and listen!"

That gets the girls' attention. Silence drops over the room. Macee is frozen in midmovement, bent over Ms. Coughran's desk, where she's counting the pencils she'd collected. Staring up at Allison, she whispers, "We're not supposed to say 'shut up.'"

"Well, okay, fine. Sorry." Allison clears her throat again. "But as I was *trying* to say, today's topic is Growing Up—"

Devon hears Karma scoff under her breath. "I was *born* grown up, hag."

"So, to start, people have certain expectations for you as you get older, right?" She looks around the room. "Meaning, the older you get, the older you're supposed to act. The more responsibility you're expected to take on. True?"

Nobody moves.

"But at the same time, as you grow older, don't *you* also have expectations for the people around you? Like gaining respect and autonomy from them?" She pauses. "*Autonomy* is just a big word for 'independence.'" She pauses again. "And sometimes, these two separate sets of expectations—what others expect from you, and what you expect from others—clash. Don't they? Causing some pretty big problems. Right?"

"Yeah. It's called adolescence, reject," Devon hears Karma whisper to herself. "Get some therapy, chicky; you'll get over it."

"These problems sometimes come in the form of prejudice or stereotypes." Allison looks around the room. "Are you all following me?"

"Uh, not really . . ." says some girl with curly blonde hair sitting at the far table.

"Okay, well . . . hopefully what I'm talking about will make more sense once we explore this together." Allison twitch-smiles. "So, let's start with prejudice. Have you ever been put down or called a derogatory name by an adult?"

The room is silent.

"*Derogatory* means 'offensive.'"

Still no response.

"Okay, well, one of my expectations for you guys right now? That you participate in the discussion. Me up here lecturing is going to get really boring fast—"

"Surprise! We've already reached that point," Karma mumbles to herself.

Again, nothing from the class.

"Okay, so how about this—have you ever been told that you're too young to understand something?"

Allison gets a reaction this time. Devon can hear whispering popping around the room.

"Or been made to feel that you're less intelligent than an adult? Maybe had an adult lie to you about something so obviously untrue, as if you'd be so stupid or naïve as to believe it?"

The whispering gets louder. Devon glances up at Allison, expecting her to shout again, but she doesn't. In fact, she looks relieved.

"Okay, so what about dress? Meaning, has an adult ever criticized your appearance or made negative comments about what you're wearing? Told you that you can't go out looking"—she makes little quotation marks with her fingers—"like that?"

Devon thinks about the questions Allison is posing, and she feels a strange void inside. Has she ever been told she's too young to understand something? No. Been made to feel less intelligent? No. With her mom, it's mostly been the opposite. The secret things Devon's mom had confessed to her, cried over, obsessed about. The advice her mom had sought from Devon, wanting reassurance and support. Devon would listen to her mom and would feel in this vague sort of way that, really, she *wasn't* quite smart enough or old enough or *something* to hear these things. To know what to say when the collection people called wanting the status of unpaid bills. To hear her mom retell the raunchy, age-inappropriate stories she'd overheard while bartending at Katie Downs. To cover for her mom, creating white lies to tell the Latest Loser that her mom wasn't around when she didn't want to talk to him. No, her mom rarely kept anything from Devon because of her youth.

"Has an adult ever invaded your personal privacy in any way? Like, read your diary? Or maybe listened in on your phone conversations? Monitored your e-mail or IMs or text messages?" Allison scans the room. "Does anyone have something they'd like to share? Because, really, I'm hearing a lot of whispering out there." She moves her hands around like she's stirring the air.

amy efaw ∽ 179

"Let's bring it out in the open so everyone can benefit from it."

"Well," someone finally says, "I'm *here* because of an invasion of my privacy." Devon turns to look over her shoulder at the speaker. A girl at the table behind her. Glasses, shoulder-length brown hair. Bad acne.

Devon tries to remember her name. Jean? Jan? Jamie? That one from last night after dinner, the one who'd lost the card game some of the girls were playing. The one who'd shoved Jenevra hard, then went screaming into her cell. Everyone got Lockdown for thirty minutes because of it.

"Okay," Allison says. "Go ahead. But, remember, let's keep things generic. No specific details, okay?"

"Okay," the girl says. "So, basically, I kinda keep a blog—I mean I *did* on the outs. And, basically, one of my friends' moms read something I posted on it that she didn't like, and, basically, she called the cops."

Allison nods. "Okay. But blogs are public, aren't they?" She glances around the room. "You put it out there because you *want* people to read what you write, correct? So I don't think you could call that an invasion of privacy exactly. Anyone else?"

Is it an invasion of privacy, Devon thinks, to be lying alone in the dark, hearing her mom's giggling in the bedroom down the hall with the Male Guest of the Moment? Or her mom asking Devon to help select which thong to buy off Victoria Secret's clearance table? Devon feels a tightening inside herself. It's definitely an invasion of something.

Karma stretches her arms high, throws her head back to look at the ceiling. "It's an invasion of privacy when after someone's"—Karma makes little quotation marks with her cuff-covered fingers—"*brother* comes to visit a resident here and the staff stops her on the way back to the pod and then forces her to open her mouth to check under her tongue and—oh my gosh, can you believe it?—they discover smack. I find that really annoying *and* unfair." Karma smiles at Allison. "Very prejudiced. Don't you think? That recently happened to a"—she makes little quotation marks again—"*friend* of mine."

Allison just frowns at her.

"Well, this one time my mom's boyfriend moved in with us." Jenevra is tilted way back in her chair, feet up on the tabletop. "She made me share my room with his kid. Kid as in *guy*. We were both fourteen, and we had to share the same *bed*! How about that?"

"Whoa!" someone yells. "That's messed up!"

Allison shakes her head. "I'm really very sorry about that. Wow."

"Whatever." Jenevra rubs her hand over her shaved head. "I kicked his ass. I mean *butt*. He slept in the bathtub after that."

"Yeah, well, when I was *thirteen*? My mom took me to the doctor? And had him do this check on me? To see if I was still a virgin!" someone says.

"Bet you weren't," Karma mutters to herself. She shifts around in her chair, restless.

"Well, my mom IM'd my friends and stuff pretending she was me!" another girl shouts, bouncing in her seat.

The examples come fast now, girls talking over each other, one upping each other.

"Okay, okay," Allison says, holding up her hands. "Those are all really good examples. But we should move on." She points to the whiteboard behind her. "So, I've written some numbers up here. These numbers represent years, all right? From age twelve to twenty-one. I'm starting at twelve because that's when most adults begin thinking you are less like children and more like something approaching adulthood. It's when you generally start gaining certain privileges and responsibilities. So, let's start listing some of those privileges and responsibilities up here under each year." She picks up a marker, uncaps it. "Age twelve?"

"Well, you can babysit when you're twelve," someone says.

"Good!" Allison writes "Babysitting" under the 12 column.

"And, also, you can take the city bus by yourself," someone else says. "And stay home alone."

Karma scoffs. "Did *that* when I was five."

So did I. Suddenly the room is there, in Devon's mind. The one with the toddler bed made up in pink piggy and yellow duckie sheets—she'd already outgrown both the bed and the sheets by then. But in the memory, Devon had stayed in that bed for hours, waiting. Finally sneaking out into the hallway when she had to pee so badly she was afraid she'd wet her panties. Everything quiet and still, the only sound was coming from the box fan propped in the kitchen window, a scrap of paper caught on one of its blades—*pflipp . . . pflipp . . . pflipp*—through the empty apartment. Her mom gone, disappeared for the entire weekend. The lure of the casinos and some guy with money drew her away. She'd left for work one Friday night and just didn't come home. "Sometimes grown-ups have to have a little fun, too," she'd explained to Devon when she had finally returned. "You weren't scared. Were you, hon?"

"It's still cheaper at the movies when you're twelve," another girl says.

"Good work!" Allison says. "Now. How about thirteen?"

"Well, you get into PG-13 movies."

"And you're a teenager."

"My mom let me wear makeup when I turned thirteen."

"You get your period."

"Shoot me!" Karma says to herself. "This is so lame." She thrusts her hand up in the air.

"Yes?" Allison looks over at Karma. "You have a comment?"

"Are you even kidding me? *Hell* no. I gotta go to the bath-room."

"We're not supposed to say 'hell,'" Macee says from the next table over.

"Yeah?" Karma looks over her shoulder at her. "Well, F.Y.I., *freak*, 'hell' is a hot spot destination. So, why don't you just go on down there and check it on out?"

"Uh, please watch your language and name-calling," Allison says. "You may go ahead and use the bathroom, but please come right—"

"Knock, knock!" A voice from the doorway. Then Ms. Coughran pokes her head into the room. "Excuse the interruption, but I must summon someone." She scans the room until her eyes land on Devon. Crooks her finger at her. "Devon, you are wanted in the conference room."

Devon stands up. Is this it? Dr. Bacon? Already? She feels her heart jerk.

Karma jumps up then, too. Kicks at Devon's feet, whispers, "Doesn't it feel good to be *wanted*?"

Devon moves toward the door. She feels closed in, can't wait to get out of this room so she can breathe. Too much Karma.

"And where are *you* going, Karma?" Ms. Coughran asks.

"Bathroom," Karma says sweetly, flashes her fake smile. "Miss Allison said I could."

Ms. Coughran steps aside, allowing the two girls passage through the door. Karma hip checks Devon as she pushes past her.

"Be good now, Karma," Ms. Coughran says.

Karma stops, abruptly spins around.

Devon almost slams right into her. Only her quick reflexes prevent it. But maybe she should have. Maybe she should've given Karma a good thunk, like she would on the field. That not-so-subtle warning to the other players that inside the goal box is her kingdom. That meeting her 1 v 1 in that particular place isn't going to be fun.

"I am *so* good, Ms. Coughran." But as Karma says this, her eyes are on Devon. "But not *you*," she whispers. "Or . . . did the *Devil* make you do it? Hmm? Is that it? Is that why you're here, Princess Perfect?" Smirking, she whips back around, saunters across the hall to the bathroom. She stops at the door, kicks it open, holds it there with her foot. "Oh, and Ms. Coughran? Just for future reference? I agree with my B.F.F., Anonymous, when she says: 'I'd rather be lucky than good.' Good is just so overrated. Bad girls have the most fun. Don't you agree, Devil?"

The door whisks shut behind her.

Devon just stands there, staring after Karma, at the closed bathroom door.

Ms. Coughran pats Devon on the shoulder.

Devon jumps.

"Hey, girl," Ms. Coughran says. "Don't let Karma get to you. She's just a button pusher. It's how she amuses herself. Next week, she'll be on to someone else. You'll see."

Maybe . . . But Devon doesn't quite agree; there's something more to it than that. Isn't there?

The thought vanishes because the door to the pod buzzes.

Devon turns as the door opens and the woman with the long braid steps through it. *Dr. Bacon.* She smiles at Devon, walks toward her.

"Hello, Devon," she says. She glances at Ms. Coughran. "Hello, Nadia."

"Well, howdy," Ms. Coughran says. "She's all yours. The conference room awaits."

"Thank you. And when Devon and I are finished, I'll need to see Macee."

"Okeydokey. I'll warn her." Ms. Coughran gives them a wink, says, "Later!" and heads into the classroom.

Dr. Bacon puts an arm around Devon then, gently leads her into the common area and toward the conference room. Leans forward so she can observe Devon's face. "So, how have you been? This is your fifth day here, isn't it?"

Devon nods. Yes, five long ones. She remembers her goal for the day then, the promise she made to Dom and to herself, though she didn't get it down on paper.

When they—Devon and the doctor—are both inside the conference room and the door clanks shut behind them, when the doctor's quiet eyes are across the table from her, waiting, Devon is ready to talk.

And she does.

"My middle name is Sky," Devon starts.

Dr. Bacon nods. "And how do you feel about that?"

chapter fourteen

when dinner comes, Devon takes her tray to her corner of the common area, near the book cart, to eat. Tonight it's lasagna; a reddish grease seeps out from between the noodles, pooling in the tray's depression designed for the main dish. Garlic bread, green beans—the grayish-green kind that comes in cans—and vanilla pudding, a dollop of that stiff, fake whipped cream on top.

Devon pushes her plastic spork out of its cellophane wrapper, takes a bite of the lasagna.

It doesn't touch her mom's, not even close. Lasagna is the only food her mom can make from scratch, and it is surprisingly good. "It's all in the ingredients," she'd say mysteriously when someone asked about the recipe. Devon's mom had learned how to make lasagna from her own mother—the grandma Devon's never met—in that "other" life, her pre-Devon life, in Spokane. And strangely, lasagna had become their special meal at every holiday, the closest thing Devon and her mom owned as a family tradition. As if, in that small way, her mom's long-abandoned family could be there with them. An unconscious presence.

Devon takes another bite, and a memory pushes forward into her mind. Last Thanksgiving. She hadn't eaten much that day, she remembers. She'd been feeling "fat" lately, the fly on her jeans becoming a struggle to zip, her hips and around the waist snug against the denim. So, she'd started wearing warm-ups more and more, for comfort. In fact, in this memory she's sitting at the Thanksgiving table in her soccer warm-ups, still damp from a run she'd taken earlier that afternoon. She hadn't felt like dressing for the occasion, or even cleaning up after her run, their only guest the Guy of the Moment. She had no desire to impress him.

"You could've at least taken a shower, Dev," her mom had hissed at her in the kitchen. "What's up with you? I mean, you could make an effort to be nice. Phil's a good guy. And besides that, I like him." She'd torn open a salad bag then and dumped its contents into a large mixing bowl. Sprinkled a package of salad toppers—sliced honey-roasted almonds—and shredded cheddar cheese over the lettuce. "Just put this on the table, okay? And grab the light Italian dressing, the good stuff by what's his name? That Newman guy? I've gotta check on the lasagna. It smells like it's burning."

When they were all seated at the table, the three of them, their plates covered with the salad and steaming stuff, Devon picked up her fork. Started pushing her food around.

"Wait up," Phil said suddenly. "Before we dig in, how about I say grace? You know, seeing as it's Thanksgiving and all? We probably should give thanks."

"I was just going to say that myself," Devon's mom said, pressing her hand over her heart. "Gosh! You read my mind, Phil! It's like we're the same person!" She was beaming across the table at him. Phil, who fancied himself a religious kind of guy. Phil, who'd insisted on taking Devon's mom to church on Sunday mornings, rarely the same one twice—at least on those

Sunday mornings that hadn't come too quickly on the heels of a rough Saturday night. Too skinny Phil, desperately trying to quell his receding hairline by globbing Rogaine on his exposed skin, but his balding head showing no visible change besides developing a bad case of dandruff.

Devon had rolled her eyes, less at Phil's request than at her mom's annoying fawning—and fake—behavior.

Devon's mom frowned. "Bow your head and close your eyes, Devon. Show respect to God."

And then Phil began in a slow, reverential tone, "Dear Lord, our thanks are on ya. Instead of turkey, we have lasagna—"

Devon peeked over at Phil. Was he even serious? But his eyes were tightly closed in concentration.

"Bless us this year, O Lord. That we shall see your gracious hand in all the good that we see therein. Amen."

"Amen!" Devon's mom had cheered. "That was so great, Phil. Thank you."

Okay, so what about all the bad stuff? Is God's gracious hand in that, too? Devon had wanted to ask Phil this but resumed pushing her food around her plate instead. Phil wasn't the kind to field such intricate theological questions. He'd just say something clichéd like, "All's we can do is take the good with the bad, Devon. The good with the bad."

Devon's mom smiled across the table at Phil. She lifted the jug of cheap wine, the table's centerpiece between the two flickering candlesticks, and poured Phil and herself each a glass.

By Christmas, Devon and her mom were eating their lasagna alone.

Devon takes another bite. She feels her stomach twist suddenly, squeezing out any appetite. She tosses her spork back onto the tray.

Devon wishes she'd quit thinking about her mom. At every turn, she's there. Especially her face That Morning. Always her face in Devon's mind, like the background on her cell phone—that face pops up whenever Devon's mind is idle. Realization breaking across that face, the realization that Devon wasn't who her mom thought she was. The face of someone whose dreams are shattering. But then Devon's guilt shifts to anger. So where is she? Huh? *Huh*? How could she just leave Devon here all alone? The last time her mom had seen Devon, she was bleeding and unconscious in their apartment. That was an entire week ago! Devon could be dead right now, for all her mom knew or cared. Devon spits the bite into the thin paper napkin. Drops it, crumpled, onto her tray.

Her mom's gone, end of story. She probably took off for good, never to return. Just like she did all those years ago when she left Spokane and her own mother and father. Devon just needs to stop obsessing about it, move on, and be done with it.

"So. The food's not good enough for you."

Devon looks up. It's Karma, standing before her.

"God! What a freaking snob." Karma plops down on the floor beside Devon, grabs up the tray. Snatches Devon's used spork and, without asking, starts shoveling in Devon's food.

Devon watches Karma eat without saying anything.

Karma devours everything but the vanilla pudding. She stretches out her legs then, kicks the tray away. The liquid from the green beans sloshes out of its depression, some onto the gray carpet.

Karma yawns, glances around the room surreptitiously. Then, with a swift snap, breaks off the end of the spork, the handled end. She tucks that piece into her bra, tosses the remainder onto the tray.

Devon shifts her eyes to the broken spork on the tray, its jagged edge. She thinks of Karma's crisscrossed arm, the raw gouges there. She checks back to Karma.

Karma's eyes narrow, challenging Devon.

Karma knows Devon's job, that she collects the sporks and napkins littering the room after each meal. Karma knows Devon could easily tell the staff about that broken spork.

And Devon *should* tell the staff about it. This information is definitely something they'd want. The memory of a TV documentary slips into her mind then, one that she once had watched from her solitary spot on the couch at home. A documentary about prison life. One of the wardens was displaying a shockingly huge stash of weapons confiscated from the inmates over a one-year period. Lethal implements made from ordinary things. Things like broken plastic sporks.

Is Karma making a weapon? Combined with a pencil—by attaching that jagged plastic shard to a pencil somehow, maybe with one of those rubber bands Karma uses to keep her braids together; it wouldn't be hard to do—she could stab someone. Karma had hinted at it the other day, hadn't she? *You can kill someone with a pencil*, she'd told Devon. *There's lots of ways to do it.*

She could stab me, Devon realizes suddenly. Devon thinks of Karma's scars, her impulsiveness. She could stab herself.

Devon would probably get extra points for reporting this. With those extra points, she might earn her way up to Honor before the hearing on Tuesday. The judge would be impressed. Dom would be pleased.

All these thoughts run through Devon's mind in an instant. Karma is still watching Devon, still challenging.

"Tattletale, tattletale," Karma sings softly, her voice taunting, "hanging by a"—she exaggerates a pause, as if she's searching for the correct word, then smirks—"*devil's* tail." Karma drops her head back, stretches her arms toward the ceiling unconcernedly. "Oh, don't you worry, Devil. *I* don't get off on trying to kill *other* people. Not *me*." She makes a point of glancing at Devon, then looks back up at the ceiling. "No, I just like having stuff around in case, you know, I need it." She breathes in deeply, lets it out slowly. "In case you didn't know, dead people don't bleed. If you can bleed—see it, feel it—then you know you're alive. It's irrefutable, undeniable proof. Sometimes I just need a little reminder." Karma turns to look at Devon then, straight into her eyes. "*I'm* alive. Are *you*, Devil?"

Devon says nothing. She doesn't break eye contact, though. Barely even blinks.

"But go ahead. You tell Staff Bitch"—Karma pats her chest where the plastic fragment is hidden—"and we all get Lockdown. Everybody gets an early night—not a prob; you like hanging out in your cell anyway, don't you? Reading all those stupid books and stuff?—and I get lots and lots of attention, which is always fun. They'll call down that Dr. Bacon freak job to work on me for a while, and, well, you know all about that, don't you?" Karma smiles at Devon, a saccharine one. "So, how was it, *Devil*? Huh?" Karma jabs Devon with an elbow. "You have a nice little heart-to-heart with the doc today? You cry to her about how much you miss your iPhone and your Abercrombie wardrobe? Your cute little convertible? Your itty-bitty doggy named Lulu? What kind is it, anyway? A Chihuahua? A rat that barks?"

Devon continues to say nothing, just holds Karma's eyes with her own. Is that who Karma thinks Devon is? The next candidate for *My Super Sweet 16*?

"Hey!" Karma snaps her fingers in Devon's face. "What, you don't like to talk? I'm not interesting enough? Huh? Not smart, like you?"

Silence between them, then Devon finally says, "So, you done with that?" She nods toward her near empty food tray, pleased she's kept her tone even and cool. Betraying nothing. Except, maybe, boredom.

Karma raises her eyebrows. "I don't know . . . *am* I?" She eyes Devon up and down, then finally pushes up off the ground. Bends over the tray, scoops the fake whipped cream off the pudding with an index finger. She checks back at Devon, licks her finger slowly, mock savoring the white fluff. She kicks the tray aside. "*Now* I am." She smirks at Devon, saunters away across the room. Devon watches her sidle up to Jenevra, give her a shove. Jenevra shoves her in return. They both laugh. Karma moves on, disappears into her cell.

And Devon understands what Karma wants.

She just wants someone to push back.

chapter fifteen

saturday mornings are different from weekday mornings. Devon senses this immediately. The door lock still jars everyone awake at seven thirty with its abrupt snap. The daily chores still await completion. The girls still stumble out of their cells, retrieve their hygiene bags from the box beside the control desk, and ready themselves for the day. But the mood in the unit is lighter. As if the fluorescent bulbs have all been brightened a notch, or a crisp breeze has been allowed into the room, freshening every-thing. As if a giant vacuum has been turned on, sucking most of the tension, stress, and tightness out of the air.

The girls are energized. They are talking louder, laughing, chasing around the room. Devon watches this from her spot beside the book cart. Like recess in elementary school, she thinks.

"My mom is coming today!" Macee, the tiny black-haired anime girl, skips around the room, announcing to everyone. "My mom is coming today! Today, today, today!"

Macee stops in front of Devon. "Hey, you," she says. "How come you're always sitting here? By yourself. You like books or something?"

Devon looks up at Macee. She's hopping from one foot to the other. Her jumpsuit is so oversized the crotch hangs halfway down her thighs with the pant legs rolled up, the fabric forming miniature inner tubes around her ankles.

Devon shrugs. "Yeah . . ."

"Then how come you're never actually reading them? You sit there with a book all the time, but mostly you're really just watching stuff."

Devon closes the book she's been reading—some teen fantasy about a girl disguised as a knight—and clears her throat. "Well, I read an entire book yesterday." She scans the book cart, finds the paperback she'd returned this morning, *Where the Red Fern Grows*. Points to it.

During the scheduled five o'clock Quiet Time in her cell last night, she'd started the book, later opting out of the evening Free Time in the common area—the supervised card games and letter writing and showering some of the other girls engaged in. She remained lying on her mattress in her cell reading, finishing the book just before the door's lock snapped shut and the lights went out. She'd stared up at her ceiling in the dark with the finished book open on her chest, quiet tears rolling off her face and down into her pillow, her throat tight and throbbing. She'd thrown her arm over her eyes. The tears were there because both dogs had died and because of the boy's empty sadness over losing them. The tears were there because she'd never had something—a dog or anything—that she had loved enough to mourn.

But Devon doesn't say any of this to Macee.

Macee shrugs. "Cool. I hate reading. Is your mom coming today?"

"No!" Devon's voice is harsh. Macee hops backward, her eyes widen.

Devon clears her throat again, softens her tone. "Sorry. I mean, no. I seriously doubt it."

"But it's visiting day."

"I know."

"Maybe she'll call." Macee glances over her shoulder, across the common room at the two pay phones hanging on the wall. "Or you could call *her*, you know. You're allowed. Just ask the staff."

Devon doesn't respond. She doesn't tell Macee that, apparently, her mom doesn't want to be reached. If she did, she'd have called Devon herself.

At ten thirty, after the chores are done and the Saturday cell inspection is complete, the staff on duty, a new one with spiky salt-and-pepper hair and a face that looks like it's seen way too many bad things in life, drags out the basketballs. She drops the mesh ball bag that contains them near the door that opens out into the courtyard.

"Listen up!" the staff announces to the common room in general. "I need one volunteer to Windex the glass. Double points. And it's open to anyone, not just Privilege and Honor statuses." She looks around. "When, and only when, the job gets done will any of you get to go out to the courtyard. So, let's cooperate. Any takers?"

Devon, hunkered down in her accustomed spot, considers this. She should volunteer. She could use the extra points. Those points could push her up a status. Devon feels her hand creep upward.

But the staff doesn't notice Devon in the corner. *"And*

whoever volunteers also gets first dibs on these." She kicks the bag of balls.

"Yo! I'll do it!" Jenevra says, jumping up from one of the round tables.

Devon slinks her hand back down.

Jenevra collects the Windex and paper towels from the staff, and Devon returns to her book.

"Hey, you! Devon!"

Devon looks up, slightly dazed from reading and surprised to hear her name. She blinks away the images her mind has created from the words on the pages—jousting knights and pageantry—and turns her head toward the voice.

Jenevra is standing at the open door to the courtyard, bouncing a basketball, two girls flanking her sides. All three are watching Devon.

"So, you want to play?" Jenevra asks. "Two on two?"

Devon stares back at the girls. She can feel the cool outside air breeze through the opened door. She hasn't been outdoors since . . . since she was brought to this place in the back of that squad car. How many days ago was that now? Six? One of the girls, the tall one with the short red hair—someone Devon doesn't remember ever seeing here before—smiles over at her. An encouragement.

Ms. Coughran's warning jumps into Devon's mind: *Not you, Devon . . . the doc hasn't cleared you for exercising yet.*

Devon shakes it away, clears her throat. "Sure." She dog-ears the page she's on, shoves the book back into its spot on the cart. She stands up uncertainly then, wipes her hands on the legs of her jumpsuit.

Jenevra fires the ball at Devon. On reflex, Devon's hands snap up. Catches it solidly.

Jenevra nods at her. "Good hands."

"Thanks." Devon bounces the ball once. Twice. Then follows the three girls out into the courtyard.

The game gets competitive fast. Jenevra and Devon against the other two. One of the girls—Devon now remembers her name—is Evie, and the other one, the new redhead, is Sam. All three girls definitely can play, especially Jenevra, who's brilliant. Her moves are fluid, her footwork quick, her shots accurate, even wearing that cumbersome jumpsuit and rubber slide sandals. The courtyard is imperfect for a serious game—too small, about half court sized and shaped hexagonally, the cement underfoot rough and uneven. The walls surrounding them enclose the game, so the girls slam into them again and again.

Devon is surprised that she can actually hang with them. Like soccer, she'd learned basketball basics during the years she spent after school at the Boys and Girls Club. But when the time came to choose, when Devon turned eleven in fifth grade— "You've gotta pick one sport, hon," her mom had said. "I'm not made of money, you know."—Devon chose soccer. Her height, athleticism, and having Jenevra as her partner are what keep her in the game now.

"Let's break a sec," Jenevra says after they'd played hard for about twenty minutes.

Sam drops the ball; it bounces, then rolls along the cement floor, finally stopping in a far corner. The girls lean against the glass wall overlooking the common area inside and catch their breaths. They don't say much. Devon is relieved that they've stopped playing; her inner thighs are shaky and sore from the

quick movements, and her crotch throbs. She may have over-
done it, just as Ms. Coughran had warned the other day, playing
so soon after. . . . But the sweat, it feels great. Her heart pumping, not from stress and fear for once, but from pure physical
exertion. Devon looks up the cinder block walls to the patch of
sky that's visible from the courtyard—a solid gray. No clouds,
no sunbreaks. She takes in a long, slow breath.

"You play much?" Devon hears Jenevra ask.

Silence.

Sam nudges Devon. "Hey. Dude. She's talking to you."

Devon looks over at Jenevra. Her shaved head, pale face,
intense blue eyes. Especially against the overcast day, those eyes
seem to glow, they're so blue. "Oh, sorry. Um, not really."

"She plays soccer," Evie says.

Devon turns to Evie, curiously. *How does she know that?*

"Yeah?" Jenevra wipes her forehead on her sleeve.

"Yeah," Evie says, "at Stadium." She looks over at Devon and
adds in explanation, "I go there. Junior."

Devon nods. "Oh."

"She's really good," Evie continues. "Starting varsity keeper as a freshman and everything. She even plays with the boys
sometimes."

"Cool." Jenevra stretches her neck, cracks it. "Whenever you
can kick a guy's ass, kick it hard."

Devon turns to study Evie closely. Does she know this
Evie? Seen her in Stadium's hallways? In class? She's ordinary-
looking—long dishwater hair, brown eyes, medium height.
But no—Devon has no idea who she is. There's that feeling in
her gut again, that queasy loss-of-appetite feeling. Devon's not

anonymous at all. These girls in here, some of them know her. From before. What else do they know about her?

And—she looks at the three girls in their orange jumpsuits and rubber slides, talking just like any other girls in any other place—why are they here?

"Well, I go to Foss," Sam says. "They're putting in a new track this summer. Hey, let's get some water. I'm dying."

"Right on." Jenevra pushes open the door into the pod.

A screeching from inside blows out to them.

The four girls stop, crowd in the doorway.

"What the—" Jenevra starts.

Devon leans over Jenevra's shoulder to get a better view. The screaming is Karma, though it took Devon a second to recognize who it was. The braids are gone, her long hair frizzed and clumped instead, as if she'd ripped out her rubber bands and just tore her braids apart. She's kicking at the doors, throwing herself against the walls.

"This fucking place! This fucked-up, fucking place!"

The spiky-haired staff rushes across the room at Karma, yelling. Two others—men—come flying into the common area from the pod's entryway.

The staff gets to Karma first, twists her from the wall and in one violent motion—her hand in Karma's hair, elbow jammed in Karma's spine—Karma is slammed to the floor, facedown. The two men drop down on either side of her, hold her flailing limbs. They snap plastic flexi-cuffs around her wrists behind her back.

The staff steps aside, breathing hard, shouts, "Lockdown! Everybody! You've got ten seconds! Now!"

Girls from all around the room drop what they're doing and hustle toward their cells, giving Karma and her attendants a wide berth.

Karma is kicking and squirming against her captors, her spewed obscene speech and sobs partially muffled by the floor. One of the men hauls her to her feet by use of her cuffed wrists, roughly pushes her toward her cell. "Cool it, Karma," he yells, giving her a hard shake. "Watch your mouth!" He gives her a sharp shove into her cell. "You relax, and the cuffs come off. Let's move. Now. Inside."

"Screw you," she hisses. "'The harder I fall, the higher I'll bounce,' Big Tough Guy! 'What doesn't kill me, makes me stronger.' Ever hear of Nietzsche? Huh? Ever hear of—"

"Let's go," Jenevra whispers. She, Evie, and Sam move forward into the pod. But Devon stays frozen in the doorway. The staff, how they slammed Karma around. Karma, how crazy she was acting.

Jenevra stops, turns around. Blue eyes lock on Devon. "Hey! Come on!" She jogs back to Devon, grabs her hand, pulling her into the common room. "What, this your first takedown or something?"

Devon says nothing, just lets Jenevra guide her through the common area.

Jenevra makes a sound, a sharp laugh. "Look, it's *Karma*. Okay? Believe me—this isn't *her* first. She probably just had a fight with her dad or something. He's some big CEO dickhead with, like, this parade of bitchy trophy wives. Karma was caught with drugs the other day, you know. He probably just came to give her crap. Stuff like this happens all the time during visiting hours."

"You two, move it!" the spiky-haired staff yells at Devon and Jenevra. "This ain't no promenade, do-si-do square dance, ladies! Get in your cells. When you hear the lock pop, you can come out. Until then, stay quiet."

"Well, see ya," Jenevra says. She drops Devon's hand, moves to her cell. Devon finds her own cell, D-12. Pulls open the door, steps inside.

The door locks—*clank*—behind her.

She slumps back against it, stares down at the floor for a long time.

Her heart won't stop hammering.

She closes her eyes.

Rushing feet, doors slamming. Indistinct voices. The sound of panic.

Devon opens her eyes. Looks around. Cool cement floor under her numb butt. Her back's to the door, her neck stiff. She rubs at her eyes. She must have been sleeping.

The commotion outside continues. Devon remembers now— Karma had freaked out earlier. They'd all been locked down because of it. The basketball game out in the courtyard, it ended.

The pod had been quiet for a long time after that.

Devon hears the static of a radio—the police kind.

She pushes off the floor. Her left foot is asleep. She stomps it, the sharp tingling making her wince. Turns to look out her cell door window.

The movement she'd heard out in the common area is from several staff rushing around. And two paramedics with a stretch-er between them. An orange-jumpsuited girl is strapped down on the stretcher, an IV bag swinging from a metal hook over her head. When the paramedics veer the stretcher toward the entry-way, they pass Devon's door, and Devon sees who the girl is.

Karma.

Her face is pale, and her eyes are closed, unnaturally serene. Her hair is wild, flattened against the thin pillow. There's blood on the orange jumpsuit, but most prominent is the blood soaked into the white thermal undershirt Karma always wears under-neath, its sleeves especially. Devon sees blood smears across the white linen of the stretcher.

The source of all the blood—Karma's arms.

Devon feels cold inside. *The spork!* Karma had used it.

"If you can bleed—see it, feel it—then you know you're alive."

The white thermal undershirt, stained red.

"I'm alive. Are you, Devil?"

Devon stumbles backward, away from her window. Feels the bile rise, burn in her throat. She should've told the staff. Why didn't she tell?

The stretcher. The IV bag swinging, a liquid-filled pendu-lum. The black straps securing Karma to the stretcher.

The black straps.

The black straps, they held Devon down once.

Devon had been on a stretcher, too.

The dark-eyed man. The bright lights of the emergency room.

The doctor with the rectangular glasses, layers of shirts un-der a white lab coat.

"I can see that you've lost a lot of blood . . . in danger of possibly bleeding to death."

Devon, too, had bled.

"If you can bleed . . . you're alive."

Devon shakes her head, tries to clear it, but the images come crashing now, fast and unstoppable.

Blood. Blood everywhere.

A piercing scream. Devon covers her ears with her hands.

She sits up. Looks down, between her legs.

A pulsing purple cord, tough and slick. Connecting them—Devon and IT. Clumsy fingers—Devon's hand—grasping. Somehow finding the clippers in the bathroom drawer. The toenail clippers. Trembling fingers, difficult to manipulate. The clippers, slippery, blood-smeared, clatter on the linoleum. Again. And again. The constant screaming. The pulsing cord, finally shredded and frayed. Spurting, an unchecked garden hose. Blood everywhere.

But Devon is free. Free from IT. Free and panting and shaking all over. Watching the miniature writhing limbs, the tiny opened mouth. The blood-spattered face.

"If you can bleed—see it, feel it . . ."

That ear-shattering scream, grating and unrelenting. *Shut up! Make it stop!* Devon frantic, spots the sink. Like a cradle, just to hold IT, contain IT for a moment. Until the black bag, billowing open and wide, finally swallows the scream.

Devon grabs her head, squeezes her temples with her palms. Hard. Harder. Her fingers clutch at her hair. But the image is still there: IT was alive—breathing and bleeding and screaming. And she—Devon—had scooped it all into a black trash bag and tied that bag tight.

POP! The lock on her cell door.

Devon starts, opens her eyes.

The door is ajar. The spiky-haired staff is standing there in the opening. Flushed and tense.

Devon is breathless. Her body dripping, sweat running down.

The staff gives Devon a quizzical look. "Your attorney is here to see you. In the conference room. Great timing, but what can you do?" She pauses, glances around the cell. "Is everything okay in here?"

Devon clears her throat, releases her hair, smoothes it down. "What . . . what happened to Karma? I, uh"—Devon takes a breath, trying to calm herself—"saw her from my window. The stretcher . . ."

The staff turns to look over her shoulder momentarily, as if imagining Devon's perspective, what she might have seen. She faces Devon again. "Just an incident in which Karma made the unfortunate choice to hurt herself. Now, if you please, cross the common area to the conference—"

"But she was bleeding." Devon brings a thumb up to her mouth, chews the nail. "A lot."

The staff nods. "You're right, she was. But your attorney is waiting for you, and I have—"

"Did she cut herself?"

The staff sighs with exasperation.

"She did, didn't she?"

"Stop." The staff raises her hand firmly. "Right now." She takes a breath. "I'm not at liberty to discuss the incident with you at this time. But later this afternoon, during our Saturday Pod Meeting, we'll discuss the incident at length with everyone. All right? But right now, you are required in the conference room." The staff pulls the door wide, steps aside, inviting Devon to pass.

Devon takes in a shaky breath, wipes her damp forehead on her sleeve. The horrific picture in her mind is still there, that last glimpse. The blood-speckled mass slumped inside the sink's basin. The tiny scrinched face, the struggling little fists. IT was alive. And still she held that bag firmly between her two hands, closed her eyes, and done it.

Devon feels her stomach lurch. She just can't see Dom right now. Devon looks at the staff. "Um, can you please tell her, my attorney, that I . . . I'm, uh, not feeling very good right now. I think I need to lie down—" She turns for her bed.

"No." The staff yanks Devon back by the arm. "No. One foot in front of the other. Now."

The staff's mouth is a stern straight line. Devon has no other choice. She thinks of Karma, throwing herself against the walls, shrieking profanities and sobbing. It would be effective. But no, Devon would never—*could* never—lose control of herself like that. She obediently steps out into the pod.

She slowly crosses the common area to the conference room.

When she reaches the door, she turns to look back over her shoulder.

The staff is watching her, her arms crossing her chest.

Devon grasps the handle and pushes down.

chapter sixteen

"Great timing, huh?"

Dom is sitting at the table, scribbling away on her legal pad. Today she's wearing black cycling shorts and a pink cycling jersey with a large yellow flower on the front and her hair in a loose ponytail. Her bike helmet, with black cycling gloves and sunglasses shoved inside of it, is tossed behind her stool in the far corner of the room.

Finally Dom looks up, pen in midstroke. "No response?"

Devon drags over to the stool opposite Dom, sits down. "Yeah, with all the stuff"—she waves a hand toward the door behind her—"that was going on just now . . . " Her voice trails off.

"It *was* kind of crazy out there."

Devon looks down at her hands. "I really don't want to be here right now, Dom. So, yeah. You're timing really isn't the greatest."

"Sorry to screw up your day," Dom says, her tone tinged with sarcasm. "But thanks for your honesty."

Devon jumps up. She's way too jittery, her mind too jumbled; planting herself on that stool isn't going to work right now. She stands awkwardly behind it. "So, you rode your bike here?"

"Doing my part for the environment, yes."

Devon looks over her shoulder toward the door behind her, then back to Dom. "Cool. You do that a lot? Ride your bike places?"

Dom sets her pen down, nice and centered, on her yellow legal pad. "I do, but I'm not here to discuss my preferred mode of transportation with you. Okay? I hate to constantly bring this up, but we have a hearing coming up in three days. That's why I'm here yet again. We have some new developments we need to cover—"

"That girl." Devon looks back at the door again. "Do you . . . know her?"

Dom looks confused for a moment. Then, "Oh, the girl on the stretcher? The one who was on her way out when I was coming in?"

Devon nods. She brings her thumb up to her mouth, gnaws. "No."

Devon starts pacing. "Well, she took the spork from my tray at dinner last night and broke the end off of it. I think she used it to cut herself."

Dom watches Devon, following her back and forth with those steady eyes.

"She was freaking out all over the place this morning. So, the staff slammed her to the ground and made all of us lockdown in our cells. Then a little later, an ambulance came. I saw them take her away on that stretcher. I was looking out my window. She had blood all over her."

Dom nods. "I'm sure seeing that was very upsetting for you."

Devon stops pacing, throws her arms out. "Did you even hear what I said, Dom? She used *my* spork, the part she broke off of it, to cut herself! I'm sure that's why she was bleeding so much. She must have done it in her cell during Lockdown. She—her name's Karma—she showed me her arms the other day. She had tons of scars from cutting herself." Devon backs into the corner of the room nearest the door, slides down to the floor. "I should've told the staff about the spork. I should've *said something!*"

"So, why didn't you?"

Devon shrugs. "I don't know. I guess I didn't want . . . I don't know."

Dom leans forward. "Are you friends with this Karma girl?"

Devon *friends* with Karma? Devon shakes her head. "No. No way. We talk sometimes. I guess. Mostly she just tries to get in my head."

"I see." Dom sits back again. "Well, Devon, one thing you have to learn? You can't control other people. Yeah, maybe you should've told the staff. But Karma makes her own choices. Just like you. Just like me." She pauses a moment, leans over sideways around the table to get a better view of Devon. "So, this is what's bothering you then? Because you seem very agitated today. More so than usual."

Devon draws her legs toward herself, rests her chin on her knees. Shrugs again.

"It's not your fault, Devon. Whatever Karma did, she did to herself." Dom stands, walks over to the stool Devon had only briefly occupied, sits on it herself so she's closer to Devon, can see her clearly.

Devon watches Dom. She's wearing those little cycling shoes, the kind that clip into the pedals. They make a *click-clack* sound against the cement floor as she moves.

"I don't know," Devon finally says. "When I saw Karma on

the stretcher, I just—" She hugs her legs tighter to herself. "I just started, you know, *remembering* . . . stuff."

Dom sits up straight. "Like what?"

A flash of memory. The dark-eyed man, looking down at her. The concern on his face. The bright lights of the emergency room, the rocking movement of the stretcher rolling across the floor. Devon's slow realization of why she was there, the panic rising inside of her.

"When I was on a stretcher," Devon says. "At the hospital." *And the blood in the bathroom. The blood . . . and IT.* Devon squeezes her eyes shut.

But she can feel a tugging in her mind. Questions inching forward, questions about IT.

Should she ask them—Where is IT now? *How* is IT?— because Dom, she might know.

Devon opens her mouth. "I . . . I was just . . ." She swallows, then lowers her head. She can't do it. "I don't want to talk about it."

Dom and Devon stay like that for some time—Dom watching Devon hug herself—both saying nothing.

Finally, Dom takes a deep breath. "Well, Devon, I can't upload your brain into mine. You know you're going to have to share these things with me—everything, not just the things you feel like sharing—hard as that's going to be. But right now, we need to talk specifically about Tuesday." She turns from Devon, picks up her pen and legal pad, leafs through it. "So. I met your soccer coach at Stadium yesterday. Mr. Dougherty—"

Devon's head shoots up. A jolt in her gut. "Coach Mark?"

Dom turns around, studies Devon for a moment. "Yes. I had

a good conversation with him. Talked to him for about an hour or so."

An hour? A lot of information can be discussed in an hour. Devon feels her throat constrict. Whispers, "What did he say?"

"Well, he thinks you are a very talented soccer player. One of the most talented he's ever had the privilege to coach." Dom checks her legal pad. "His words exactly."

Devon tries to force down the lump that's swelling in her throat. "Does he know about . . . about . . . you know. What happened?"

"Of course." Dom hesitates a moment, then, "Everyone does, Devon. I told you that before."

Devon drops her head back down on her knees.

"He said he's known you for a long time."

Devon nods. "Ever since I went competitive. I've played for him since I was eleven."

"So, in addition to being your high school coach, he's also been your club coach?"

Devon nods again.

"And that's, uh"—Dom glances at her legal pad—"for the Washington Premier Football Club? 'Football' meaning 'soccer,' right?"

"Yeah."

Dom doesn't say anything for a moment. Then, "A couple of things came up while we were talking, things I'd like—no *need*—to explore with you." Her voice turns stern suddenly. "And I want you to be one hundred percent open and honest with me about it. No playing dodgeball. Got it?" She looks back at her legal pad. "He said that you had gotten injured, and that the injury kept you out of soccer for most of the winter training and all of your spring club season thus far." Her voice takes on an edge. "This was news to me, of course."

Devon doesn't say anything. She places her hands flat on the floor, pushing against it.

"From about mid-January on is what he said. Is that right?"

"Yeah, I guess."

"You *guess*? Look, either this statement is right, or the statement is wrong. We're talking solid facts here. So, which is it?"

It happened about a week after winter break, Devon remembers. The drizzle was a little heavier that afternoon than the typical Tacoma winter day. Had been for days and days. The mist a thick spit, almost like it had some snow in it, coming down at a slant. The ground in front of the goal a slick, muddy mess. But they practiced anyway. In the Northwest, if you cancel practice for rain, you'd be canceling it almost every day. "We love the rain!" Coach Mark loved to yell on such days. "We love the mud! Love it more than your opponent hates it!"

"Yes." Devon takes a breath. "It's right."

"Really?" Dom's eyes narrow. "Funny how I didn't find any record of this injury anywhere in your medical files, Devon. So, why don't you just tell me about it now."

Devon shrugs, kicks off her rubber slides. Rakes the cement floor with her toes. She feels the rough bumps through her socks.

The memory is right there. She's with her club team, practicing at her club's field complex off River Road. The girls are preparing for a preseason showcase tournament in Southern California, only a few weeks away. This practice, Coach Mark is putting them through a simple crossing and finishing drill, one they've done countless times. The forward at the top of the box passes the ball to the midfielder who's making a run along the inside of the sideline toward the field's right-hand corner. She takes a touch, then crosses it back to the center of the goal box. The forward, running onto it, simply one-touches it into the net—that is, if the ball can get past Devon in the goal.

This particular time Kait, the team's top forward and, until recently, Devon's best friend, is running onto the cross that's coming from her right, Devon's left. It wasn't a great ball from Madi on the outside, Devon remembers thinking—not to feet and coming to a bounce just behind Kait at the six. But Kait handles the ball fine anyway, popping it up and half-volleying it when it's on its way down, and the ball blasts toward the goal's right corner, to Devon's left. Devon dives, arms outstretched, hands reaching for the ball, her body propelling parallel with the ground.

The ball's coming too fast, too wide. She does what she can now to tip the ball out and around the post, but at the last instant, the ball makes an unexpected curve. Devon's bottom hand, her left one, takes the full impact of the shot, forcing her arm back. She hits the ground; her left shoulder feels a violent wrenching there. She wants to get up for the second save, but the mud is too slick and she's sliding across the ground. Kait, she's still coming at a full sprint and crashing the goal. Devon rolls slightly onto her back, tries to slow herself. She hears the *swoosh* of the net behind her as the ball hits it. *Gave up a goal.* Her head, the back of it, slams into the post.

Darkness.

Devon opens her eyes slowly. She blinks away the rain. Above her teammates are crowding, anxious faces looking down at her. She catches a glimpse of Kait, standing off to the side with crossed arms, her lips pressed tight together. And Coach Mark, he's kneeling at her side, his mouth moving, his words unintelligible.

Slowly, her surroundings take shape, make sense. She's outside—gray sky, rain. Wet grass. Mud underneath. Cold. And her head—it throbs. She moves to swipe the rain from her face. A searing burn from her shoulder. She cries out.

"So," Dom says when Devon has finished telling her story, "did they call an ambulance?"

"Uh—" Devon blinks, shakes the memory from her mind. "No."

"Anyone take you to the emergency room?"

"No!" Devon stops, collects herself. "I mean, no. I didn't want to go there, to the hospital. I . . . after a couple of minutes, I felt fine. Really. Coach Mark ended practice early, and then he drove me home."

Dom nods. "Yeah, he told me that he was very worried about you. He wanted to make sure that you got home okay."

Devon remembers sitting in his Tahoe, the passenger seat. Resting her aching head against the window, holding her left arm close to her body, not saying anything. Watching the rain splat the glass, then slowly slide down. The windshield wipers swishing across the glass the only sound.

"So, your mom took you to a doctor later."

Devon shakes her head. "No . . . "

Dom frowns down at her legal pad. "But Mr. Dougherty said that you missed school the next day, and when you came back the following day, you told him that you had gotten a concussion and a shoulder subluxation—you had explained to him that your shoulder had sort of rolled along the edge of your socket and snapped back in place again—and that the doctor had said you wouldn't be able to practice for at least four to six weeks, mostly due to the concussion. And that you had to go to physical therapy three times a week for the next six weeks to strengthen the muscles around your shoulder's rotator cup." Dom raises her head, looks at Devon.

Devon shifts her eyes back down to her knees.

"So, you're telling me now that you *didn't* go to a doctor *at all*?"

Devon chews on her lip. Risks a glance up at Dom.

Dom is frowning. "Should I take that as a no? Because I wasn't able to dig up the medical records documenting any of this." She drums her fingers on the tabletop. "Did your mom know *anything*? About hitting your head and hurting your shoulder?"

"Well, when Coach Mark brought me home, my mom was still at work. I go to sleep way before she gets home most nights, and I went to sleep extra early that night because I wasn't feeling very good. And then, well, my mom was asleep when I got up in the morning. So . . ."

"But—" Dom looks up at the ceiling, gathering her thoughts. "Okay, so you *did* stay home that next day? Like your coach said?"

"Yeah, because I wasn't feeling that great. I was sore all over. My head was still hurting—I had this huge lump. I didn't feel like sitting in school all day."

"Okay. So when *did* you tell your mom?"

Devon picks up one of her rubber slides. Slips a hand into it. "I didn't."

"Why not?"

"I really didn't want to deal with it. She'd just obsess over nothing. Plus, going to the doctor's expensive! We don't have money to just—"

"Excuse me, but smashing your head into a goalpost and getting your shoulder knocked out is *nothing*? I think if your mom *hadn't* obsessed about it, I'd be concerned. And there are some things in this world worth spending money on, Devon. Okay? You didn't even give your mom the chance to make that choice!" Dom sighs with frustration. "You *robbed* her of an opportunity to finally make a good decision for you!"

Dom's comment stings. Devon slips her other hand into the second slide. Goalkeeping wearing these? Totally ridiculous.

The conference room is silent. Finally, Devon peeks up at Dom. She's on that stool with her jaw clenched, her cheeks flushed. Devon quickly returns her eyes to the slides on her hands.

"Didn't the school call your mom that day to report your absence?"

Devon shrugs. "My mom never asked me anything about it."

"I see." Dom's voice is pinched. "So, that stuff you told your coach. You just"—she flicks her hands out—"made it up?"

"Um." Devon clears her throat. "Not exactly."

She'd left the apartment that next morning before her mom got home from work. Walked the mile to the library, the main one downtown. A place to be until after her mom had slept and left for her cosmetology classes in the afternoon. She'd Googled around on a library computer, trying to figure out what had likely happened to her physically the previous afternoon. WebMD and some sports medicine sites, that's where she'd gotten the diagnosis—moderate concussion and shoulder subluxation—and the recommended treatment plan. Devon remembers how relieved she'd felt when she'd made this discovery, and how she hurriedly scribbled everything down on a piece of scrap paper a librarian had given her. When she'd walked home, she took a circuitous route, wandering all the way down to Commencement Bay. She'd stood there a long time, staring out at the horizon. The water looked beautiful and new. The fog had finally burned off after so many gloomy days. The sun was out, shining brightly. The air warm. She'd wished she'd had sunglasses. The glare on the water hurt her eyes.

Not anything like the last time she'd observed that particular view, the time when she'd watched a sunset with Connor from his dad's balcony.

"Why did you feel so relieved, Devon?"

Devon looks up at Dom. Had she actually told all of that to Dom? Yes, she must have.

"It seems to me that discovering that you might have sustained a concussion and had injured your shoulder pretty seriously, you'd definitely want to go see a doctor, just to check everything out. I'd think you'd be *worried*, not relieved."

Devon softly taps her two sandaled hands together. With Dom, there's always more questions. Questions, questions, questions. Never satisfied. Always digging for more.

"You want to know what I think, Devon? I think you were *afraid* to go to a doctor." Dom's tone is clipped. "I think all this crap about your mom freaking out and you not wanting to spend money is just that, *crap*."

Devon stops tapping the sandals together. She feels her hands grow slick against the rubber. She tosses the sandals down, rubs her hands on the legs of her jumpsuit.

"I mean at this point"—Dom checks down at her legal pad— "around mid-January, you'd be"—she counts on her fingers— "about five months pregnant." She turns back to Devon. Raises an eyebrow.

Devon looks away, shifts around. Her butt's numb, sitting in one position for so long.

"So, if you *had* gone to a doctor, he or she would've undoubtedly discovered that you were pregnant. At five months, women start to show—"

"No!" The word flies out of Devon's mouth. "No, I wasn't thinking that at all!"

"You didn't want a doctor seeing you. Be honest! You didn't want to take the chance—"

"No, you're wrong!"

Dom rolls her eyes. "Come *on*, Devon!"

"No! I mean it. I didn't think I was pregnant. I mean, I don't *think* that I thought I was. I . . . " Devon is rubbing her thighs faster and faster now. "I know that you probably don't believe me, but . . . it's so confusing! All I know is that I was sort of happy that I didn't have to practice for a while. That I was going to be able to take a break from it. From soccer, I mean."

"Uh-huh. And why would you be happy about that? I thought soccer was your *life*, Devon."

Devon glares at Dom. "Yeah? Well, how would you like to do something day after day for years and never get to take a break? Maybe I was getting sick of soccer! Ever think of that? I go to my varsity girls' practices. I go to the boys' practices. I go to my club practices. I play indoor soccer in the off-season. I do separate specialized goalkeeper training. I do camps and

3 v 3 tournaments all summer long. I was getting totally burned out. So . . . so, when I got hurt, I knew I had an excuse to stop for a while."

"So, that's it? You just needed a little vacation from soccer? Right before your team was going to travel out of state for a show-case tournament? Right before your club league season started? You'd just leave your team without their keeper?" Dom doesn't look convinced. "Okay, fine. Then let's go with that, shall we? Going to a doctor wouldn't have changed anything. The doctor would've undoubtedly made a similar diagnosis, done some tests, taken some X-rays, maybe an MRI, and you would've gotten your little vacation. Four to six weeks off. Maybe even more. End of story."

"Well, maybe they wouldn't have found anything wrong with me."

"Yeah." Dom makes a snide laugh. "Maybe they would've found *a lot* wrong with you."

Devon brings her thumb up to her mouth. Chews on it. "I . . . I didn't feel like I was that good anymore." Her voice is so soft, Devon isn't sure she's said anything at all. "I was playing really bad, Dom. I was feeling heavy and slow. My timing was to-tally off. And my jumping . . . toward the end of my high school season in November, I was having a hard time putting the balls over the crossbar. Those high balls would just roof me some-times. Coach Mark was starting to notice it, too. He kept getting on me to play faster. He kept yelling at me." The last sentence is a squeak. She takes a moment to pull herself together. "One time he screamed in front of everyone, 'Get the lead out of your ass, Davenport! You are totally ineffective back there!' He . . . he'd never said anything like that to me before. Ever." Devon covers her face with both hands. "So, I . . . I wanted to take some time off and work out on my own in the afternoons, take a month or whatever and get in really great shape before the season started. Work hard on my core and run. Jump rope." She drops her hand then, looks up at Dom. "I was going to come back before league started. That was my plan, Dom. I swear."

"And, according to all that extensive research you did on your injuries, you determined that it was perfectly safe to work out."

"The Web sites just said no contact sport activities. No heading the ball. Stuff like that."

"Uh-huh. And, so, did you? Work out?"

Devon nods. "Yes. Every day. Even on the weekends. I was running about thirty miles a week. And I even did those shoulder-strengthening exercises that I found on the Internet."

"Well, you never came back, did you?" Dom's voice is quiet now. "The girls' season for Washington state's premier league started at the end of February, and you never came back to practice, Devon. So, you didn't stick to your 'plan' after all."

Devon shakes her head, whispers, "I wasn't ready yet."

"Wasn't ready yet." Dom studies Devon for a long time. Devon can see all sorts of thoughts going on behind Dom's eyes. Dom's expression is one of intense dissatisfaction and suspicion.

Finally, Dom stands up. She slowly walks to the wall on the other side of the room opposite Devon. Leans against it and crosses her arms. Stares at the floor for a long time.

"What about friends?" Dom says at last. She looks over at Devon. "You never mention them. Except that one girl here in Detention, that Karma . . ."

"She's not my friend," Devon says quickly.

Dom cocks her head. "So, *do* you have friends? Anyone you feel close to, anyone who you'd be able to trust with your secrets? Your worries?"

Devon looks down at her knees again. "Yeah. Of course. Everybody has friends."

"No, I don't think that's always the case, Devon. Most people have lots of acquaintances, but acquaintances aren't *friends*. There's a difference."

Devon shakes her head. "Whatever. I already talked to Dr. Bacon about this stuff yesterday. Why do *we* have to talk about it again?"

"Because I want clarification, Devon. I have a specific purpose for the questions I ask, and Dr. Bacon has her own reasons for the questions *she* asks." Dom pauses. "Dr. Bacon has drawn the conclusion that you have two completely separate sets of kids who you interact with. You have a set of kids that you hang out with at school, and then you have your club soccer teammates. Is that correct?"

Not exactly. There's one girl who straddles both worlds of school and club soccer—Kait. But Devon doesn't want to go there with Dom right now, and she didn't mention Kait to Dr. Bacon, either.

Devon nods. "Yeah, pretty much. I told her that on my club team, most of us go to different high schools, so during practice is pretty much the only time we see each other. Most of them have no clue what I'm like at school."

"Are you a different sort of person at school than you are with your club team?"

Devon doesn't know how to answer that question, so she just shrugs.

"Your coach told me that you are a leader on the field," Dom says. "That your teammates really respect you and seem to like you a lot. So, what's the situation like with the kids who don't play soccer? The regular school kids. Do you have friends there, too?"

Devon draws her legs in closer, wraps her arms around them. She thinks about Dom's question. Does she have friends? Her number is programmed into a lot of people's cell phone contacts, so she gets plenty of texts, and she usually has kids to sit with at lunch. Some of them play on the varsity soccer team with her, and some don't. But she's never had anyone over to her apartment; Devon's mom just isn't around much and it would just be weird. And Devon doesn't like to waste time at the mall or the movies after school or on weekends very often; she's way too busy for that and doesn't have the money for it anyway. This arrangement has always seemed to be enough for Devon. Mostly, the people at school are her "friends" simply because they are there.

Except Kait. She was always more than just "there." The years of sleepovers at Kait's house—the prank calls and movie watching and music listening and whispering in the dark. But, well, Kait wasn't really speaking to Devon much anymore.

"I'm just not a big talker, I guess," Devon says at last. She raises her eyes to Dom. "I really don't like to talk about myself very much. So, when I'm around people at school, I sort of just sit there and listen. It's not that I'm shy or unpopular or anything. It's just that if I have something to say, I say it. Otherwise, I'm sort of just there. And I'm totally fine with that."

"But it's different when you're out there, playing soccer?"

"Yeah, because I definitely have things to say then. About

the game and what's happening on the field. From the goal, I can see the entire field."

"Okay," Dom says. "So, did you talk to *anyone* about Connor? About your relationship or how you felt about him? To a teammate or someone at school? Anyone at all?"

Devon shakes her head no.

But over the summer, Devon remembers, Kait had grown suspicious. "You're acting very strange, Dev," she'd teased in her silly singsong. Like always, they were coming off the field together, their afternoon practice finished. "You're being really secretive. You look like you are *glowing*." She'd grabbed Devon's cell then, right out of her backpack, ignoring the sweaty shin guards and gloves that smelled like roadkill. She clicked through Devon's call log. "So, what's this three-oh-three number? Hmm? Wow—it's in here a lot recently. Way more than *my* number even!" She looked over at Devon and grinned. "Could this possibly be a *love* interest? Could Devon the Untouchable have finally met her prince?"

Devon grabbed Kait's bag, then, and snatched her car keys. And they chased around the field, laughing and squirting each other with their water bottles until Coach Mark yelled, "That's it, Tweedledee and Tweedledum! Next practice, get here fifteen minutes early 'cause you're doing suicides. You two obviously have way too much energy!"

And Kait had yelled back, "So, which of us is Tweedle *Dumb*?"

Devon closes her eyes. No, she didn't even tell Kait about Connor.

"But your mom knew about him?" Dom says. "Right?"

"Nope."

"Your mom had no knowledge of your romantic involvement, having sex—"

"No way! I'd never, not in a million years, tell her that! I don't talk to my mom about *anything.*"

Devon stares back down at the floor again. She's so tired suddenly. So done with talking. Can't Dom see this?

"All right, let's push on to something else." Dom kicks at the floor with the toe of her cycling shoe, thinking. "The question I'm going to ask you now is one I've asked you before, but in a different way. The difference is subtle, but important. Before, we've discussed the fact that you were *afraid* that you *might* be pregnant because you'd had sex that one time with Connor. The context of that discussion revolved around your behavior during your September appointment with the doctor at the clinic, with Dr. Katial—how you reacted to his questions, your not returning the urine sample to his office, wearing the sanitary napkin in your underwear, et cetera. *This* question has to do with later circumstances, as time moved forward in your story. Did you ever notice anything specifically about your body that may have led you to believe that you were, in fact, pregnant? You've told me that you felt heavy and slow at soccer practice, that you noticed you weren't jumping as well. And that you were starting to wear baggier clothes because they felt more comfortable. Did you, at any time, suspect that you were pregnant, Devon?"

Devon thinks about Dom's question. Did she suspect? Did she?

Running up Carr Street, what game did she always play? She'd stand on the corner of 30th and Carr after running the three miles to get down there, staring up at the monster hill before her, as long and steep as any in San Fransisco. She'd check her watch. If she could make it up those six blocks from hell— from 30th Street to Yakima—in under two and a half minutes, then there wasn't anything "wrong" with her. If she failed to make her self-imposed time . . . But it was just a stupid game; she knew that nothing was "wrong" with her. It was just a way to motivate herself to bust her butt, to give herself a goal with consequences. And two and a half minutes was not a generous window of time. But she made it every time, sometimes with only seconds to spare. Her lungs would burn and her heart pound, and she'd bend over at the waist, feeling like she might puke when she was finished. Her stomach tight and throbbing.

Except once.

When she'd stopped her watch that one time, it read 2:36. She'd stared at the numbers, a cold sweat pricking her skin.

Just six seconds. It didn't mean anything. Right? Six seconds is basically four strides. One full breath cycle. A brief lapse of concentration. It probably happened when she'd sidestepped that walker with his unruly dog, straining at its leash.

And the air was thick that day, the temperature too warm for February. She hadn't slept well the night before, either, had kicked around in her sheets, worrying about a world geography project that was due at the end of the week. And she'd skipped lunch earlier that day to cut calories, skipped lunch every day that week, actually. She shouldn't have. Skipping lunch always made her weak. All of that together could easily account for those lost six seconds.

But still. She hadn't made the time. It could be a sign.

She jogged the remaining mile home. Pounded up the steps

to her apartment. Untied her shoe to retrieve the key she always attached to her shoelace when she went running.

She yanked open the door, slammed it shut. Closing off the light from the outside.

She stood in the doorway, catching her breath and thinking.

She dropped to the floor and hooked her feet under the couch. And did sit-up after sit-up until she'd done five hundred without stopping, falling back exhausted, panting up at the ceiling.

Trying so hard to squeeze down the lump that was her stomach.

To flatten it away.

"Devon? Come on. Please focus!"

Devon snaps her head up. Blinks, clearing her dim living room and that ratty couch away. "Sorry . . . I . . . "

"My question again: Did you ever suspect that you were pregnant?"

Devon shakes her head no. Just because she did a few sit-ups? It means nothing. She did sit-ups every day.

She thinks about what Dom mentioned, the clothes she'd worn. Baggy warm-ups mostly. Loose-fit jeans, oversized sweatshirts. Just because she dressed like a slob? She'd been so tired lately, all that extra running. Warm-ups were just easier. Ponytails so much simpler. Applying makeup just to sweat it off? Less grooming meant more time for sleep.

But there were other things, strange little rituals, and her mind creeps toward those things now. How she'd avoided ever entering her mom's bedroom. That antique full-length mirror was always there, the one her mom prominently displayed like artwork on the far wall between the two windows—ornate and condemning. She'd stopped taking baths, too, something she'd always loved to do with a book—she'd soak and stretch and soothe her overworked muscles. But at some point she'd started to opt for the quick five-minute shower, instead. She'd wash hurriedly—her hair and face, shoulders and arms, legs and feet. Her midsection—why bother? The water from the shower-head above, mixed with the soap and shampoo, rolled down her body and rinsed away her sweat adequately enough. She wouldn't ever touch her breasts—she had let him do that once. She wouldn't touch her belly, either, the skin around her navel. Because what if? Ridiculous question. But . . . what if there *was* something there, deep inside herself, and IT felt her fingertips? Thought that her touch meant she loved IT?

She'd been touched once. All that touch brought on was fear, disappointment, and self-disgust. And a profound loneliness.

"Devon." Dom's voice. Full of resigned weariness.

Devon feels the wet track that a tear has left as it slid down her cheek. She wipes it with the back of her hand. "Yeah?"

Dom and Devon watch each other from opposite walls for a long moment. Then Dom shakes her head. "Look, we're not accomplishing much of anything at the moment. We've just sort of run out of steam. I wanted to go over some more of what you discussed with Dr. Bacon yesterday, specifically the things you told her about your mom, but it's not all that crucial for us to talk about right now. So, I'll just see you on Tuesday morning, all right? Before the hearing. We'll go over some last-minute details then."

Devon looks back down at the floor. She doesn't want to disappoint Dom. All these things building in her head, they are so scary. Her throat just won't open to let them escape.

"You need to get some rest. I'll ask the staff to let you stay in your room for the remainder of the weekend. But if you think of anything—something you remember and want me to know, or think I'd want to know, or any little thing at all—write it down. And we'll talk about it on Tuesday morning."

Dom pushes herself off the wall then, walks across the room to where Devon is sitting, her cycling shoes click-clacking across the cement floor. She offers Devon a hand to help her up.

Devon places her hand in Dom's. Dom squeezes it.

"Please trust me, Devon," Dom says softly. "I know how independent you've always been. But you have to let go now. You just can't do this on your own anymore."

"I'm trying, Dom," Devon says. "I really am."

"Yes, I know." Dom pulls Devon to her feet. "But try *harder.*"

chapter seventeen

Devon bolts upright, awake.

The ghost of a dream fades from her mind like a cool mist in the morning. Only a vague unsettled feeling lingers now—one of being lost or stranded somewhere alone or of leaving some important task undone.

Devon lies back down, closes her eyes, tries to bring the dream back. But it's gone, stealing along with it any desire for sleep. Devon tosses a while under her wool blanket and sheet, her mind pushing toward places, toward uncomfortable things, where she doesn't want to go. Things like how totally alone she had been. The past months, all those messages on her cell phone from people at school or her team, messages that Devon had listened to, then immediately deleted, unreturned. The texts she'd read and ignored. The invites to various parties and snowboarding trips and concerts that she'd declined. The class-assigned group projects that Devon had opted to do by herself. The semester exam study sessions that Devon had turned down, choosing instead to sit at her desk at home while her classmates were meeting at Starbucks, shoving tables together and drinking Venti lattes and Frappuccinos with extra whip. The times Kait and the varsity team captain, Lucy, had offered to accompany Devon on her afternoon runs—"So you won't get lonely," Lucy had said. "No way," Kait had scoffed. "To kick your butt"—but Devon always finding some excuse to run alone. Going to sleep before her mom got home from work, or leaving the house early in the mornings when she'd worked nights, the few quick text messages the only communication between them: "Left wash in 3rd dryer. Pls bring up." "Some guy coming at 11 to fix toilet. Let him in." "Chinese takeout in the fridge. Drink milk. XOXOXO!" Hustling between classes, her head down to discourage eye contact and conversation. Most days opting to eat lunch hunched in one of the library carrels or not at all, choosing instead to spend the time crouched inside one of the bathroom stalls while skater girls giggled and smoked by the sinks.

Why had she pulled away from everyone and everything?

Eventually, the calls and texts trickled to nothing. The offers to run after school stopped. Nobody talked to her in the hallways during passing periods. The teachers quit trying to coax answers from her in class. Only her mom kept up an attempt to engage, but Devon was rarely around to satisfy it. And her coach, of course. The worried look in his eyes, the unasked questions hovering there. But Devon avoided him, too, darting into a classroom or bathroom when she saw him coming.

And then there was Kait, the most difficult to dodge. She'd taken Devon's detachment so personally. "What's wrong?" she'd text. "Are you mad at me?" "Where were you at lunch?" "Did I do something?" And when Devon didn't reply, Kait finally wrote that long, angst-filled letter and slid it through the slats of Devon's locker. Kait just didn't get it; she couldn't understand that Devon's need to be alone had nothing to do with her. Devon crumpled the letter and lobbed it in the trash, and when she'd turned around to leave, Kait was right there, watching. Her shocked expression changed from hurt to disbelief, then hardened into scorn.

Oh, God. Devon had been lonely, so terribly lonely, for so long. The kind of lonely that sears, that burrows its way deep inside a heart and throbs. Like a gnawing hunger.

She finally kicks off her bedding to disrupt the stream of disturbing thoughts coursing through her mind. She stands, the floor chilly under her bare feet, then goes to look out the window of her cell. Checks the clock over the control desk across the pod: 7:03. Still too early for Wake Up.

She sees Ms. Coughran standing out there beside the control desk, talking to the staff—one of the day shift staffs, the blonde ponytailed one with the big smile. Seeing Ms. Coughran reminds Devon that today is Monday. She'll have to go to class today, be around the girls again. The nearly two-day window of time that Dom dictated she stay alone in her cell—reading, sleeping, and trying to relax—is officially over.

Ms. Coughran must have detected movement from Devon's cell, because suddenly she turns her head and looks right at Devon. Raises a hand, waves.

Devon jumps back out of sight, but it's too late. The lock of her door pops, and she watches Ms. Coughran move determinedly toward her cell from across the common area.

Ms. Coughran pushes the door open a crack, sticks her head inside. "Hey, girl! Saw you peeking out your window. Awake already?"

"Yeah," Devon whispers. "I couldn't sleep for some reason." She turns back to her bed, retrieves her rubber slides from the cubby because the floor is too gross for bare feet.

"I hear you. I had the same problem this morning; that's why

I'm already here at this ungodly hour." Ms. Coughran hesitates, then takes a step into the cell and glances around briefly. "Well, this chance meeting is actually good, Devon. It gives me a couple secs to talk to you. I've been wanting to get you alone."

Devon feels a little wary. *Why alone?*

"So, you want to come out in the common area and sit at one of the tables with me?"

"Did I do something wrong?"

Ms. Coughran laughs. "Oh, no, no. Nothing like that. No, I finally got your school records on Friday afternoon and have been meaning to talk to you about them. That's all. No worries." She pushes the door wider and steps aside, an invite for Devon to step outside.

It's not like Devon will be able to sleep anyway. Her mind's too whirling and, besides, the time's too close to Wake Up. Still . . .

"But I didn't brush my teeth yet—"

Ms. Coughran waves her hand dismissively. "Trust me— your breath can't be worse than my husband's, and I deal with that daily."

Devon steps out of the cell, and together they walk to one of the round tables. Each takes a stool across from the other.

This is the first time that Devon's sat here at one of these tables. The table's the same kind as in the conference room, but this one displays no warped heart ink splot. The only marks are some initials and symbols scratched into the hard plastic. She runs her hands over the table surface, waiting.

"Well," Ms. Coughran starts. "Your report card tells me that you are quite the Little Miss Smarty-Pants."

Devon shrugs, feels her face heat up. "I guess."

"It doesn't surprise me. Even though you didn't open your mouth *one time* last week." She gives Devon's hand a playful slap. "You just have 'that look.' That 'smart look.'"

Devon jerks her head up.

Ms. Coughran smiles. "Surprised? We teachers aren't as oblivious as you kids might think. Not much flies under my radar. And *nothing* flies under yours. True? You watch every-thing."

Devon frowns. Ms. Coughran is yet another person here who has been analyzing her, thinking about what kind of person she might be.

"Just because you don't say much doesn't mean people don't notice you, Devon. It's actually the quiet ones who often draw the most attention. There's this constant whirlwind of motion and sound all around, and then there's the quiet one, the eye of the storm. Quiet tends to stand out here because it's so uncom-mon."

Devon looks down at her hands.

"So, thus far, what do you think about what we do in class? Boring? Too easy?"

Devon shrugs. "I don't know. It's okay."

"But not very challenging." Ms. Coughran waits a moment. Then, "I realize this, and it's a big concern for me. The work is aimed at about a seventh-grade level. Sometimes that's challeng-ing enough for some of these girls."

Ms. Coughran goes on about how many of the residents at Remann Hall have come from terribly chaotic backgrounds, how their schooling may have been inconsistent, many of them being transient kids or with too many problems going on in their lives for them to absorb academics. Kids living in crack houses with

strung out and abusive parents, who'd rather have them dealing and distributing than writing book reports and memorizing
multiplication tables.

"So, my idea of what I'd like to see happen," Ms. Coughran
says now, "is for you to come into the classroom after dinner
every night, during the time that's scheduled as Clean Up and
Quiet Time, and work on self-paced programs on the computers. I've got some good interactive math and science activities
that you could do. And we could come up with a writing project together, if that's something you'd like. That way, your academics won't suffer too much while you're here. How does that
sound?"

While you're here. How long does Ms. Coughran expect
Devon to stay in this place?

Devon pulls her eyes from the tabletop and looks up at Ms.
Coughran. She's smiling and eager. Similar to the look her mom
gets when she's suggested an activity they could do together.
This instinctively makes Devon feel stubborn inside, initially
makes her want to reject the idea immediately.

"The staff has been thinking of bumping you up to Honor
status. They're going to discuss it this morning, in fact, during
their meeting—"

"Really?" *Honor status.* This news excites Devon, and she
smiles back at Ms. Coughran then. Dom will be very happy.

Ms. Coughran nods. "Yes, really. So that would move your
bedtime up to ten, giving you lots of extra time. If you can get
into the classroom at, let's say, five thirty or so, you could potentially work for at least three hours every night, unless the staff
has some special activity planned. So, what do you think?"

The possibility of keeping her mind engaged interests Devon; those lame word searches and Sudoku puzzles that Ms. Coughran has been giving them to do in class are starting to get tedious. And having something to occupy her evenings besides scouring the book cart or hiding out in her cell. A legitimate excuse to avoid the other girls, keep to herself.

"Sure," Devon says. "It sounds really cool. Thanks."

"Great!" Ms. Coughran smiles bigger. "So, then there'll be three of you all together—"

Three of us? Devon shifts on her stool. The idea loses its appeal suddenly. She won't be by herself?

"—who I think would really benefit from this arrangement. You know Destiny, don't you? She's actually a very gifted writer—"

Devon remembers that Destiny had written a poem and read it aloud to the class. Ms. Coughran had seemed impressed with it, and all the girls had clapped.

"And then there's a girl who just came here this past Friday morning. I don't know if you've met her yet—Samantha?"

Sam, the tall one with the red hair? Devon nods. "Yeah, I played some basketball with a new girl on Saturday morning. At least, I think that's who you're talking about."

"Basketball, huh?" Ms. Coughran shakes her head disapprovingly. "I hope you didn't overdo it, Devon. Playing basketball."

Devon rolls her eyes. "No, I didn't overdo it. Anyway, we had to stop because—"

Karma. Kicking and screaming, the staff slamming her to the ground. The stretcher, the blood. It's all there, fresh.

Devon hadn't really allowed herself to think much about Karma. Not since talking to Dom that last time on Saturday afternoon. Devon feels sick inside all over again.

Ms. Coughran raises her eyebrows, prompts, "Because?"

"Karma," Devon whispers.

"Oh, yes." Ms. Coughran's expression darkens. Her smile is gone, a tired sadness replaces it. "So I heard." She sighs loudly. "But she's back now."

Back? Here? "But . . ." Devon takes a breath. "But . . . she was bleeding. She—"

POP! The bolts on all sixteen cells snap open.

Devon and Ms. Coughran jump.

Together their eyes jerk toward the clock over the control desk: 7:30.

"Whoa!" Ms. Coughran giggles embarrassedly, slapping her palm to her chest. "Not used to *that* sound."

"Neither am I," Devon says, laughing. "It scares me every single morning."

"Yeah, I bet." Ms. Coughran stretches to her feet, yawns. "Well, anyway. Yes, Karma is back. Got in from Tacoma General last night, safe and sound and ready to cause trouble." She winks at Devon, then checks her watch. "Well, I'll see you in the classroom in about an hour. I'm going to skip out of here and grab myself some java. I'm a java junkie, you know." She knocks on the tabletop. "Gotta keep that pep in my step." She waves lazily behind her back as she walks away.

Devon sits there at the table for a moment, sorting out how she feels. She's relieved that Karma is back; it probably means that Karma's pretty much okay. She thinks about Ms. Coughran's special class, explores the idea of maybe getting to know the other girls, Sam and Destiny, a little better. It's not a completely *horrible* thought, she finally decides. Sam seemed okay. And Destiny might be kind of strange with her thumb-sucking issue, but at least she's quiet.

The common area is growing noisy. The girls are stumbling out of their cells now, rubbing their eyes.

Devon looks around the room, scans the faces. Karma isn't out there. At least, not yet.

Devon takes a deep breath, lets it out. And goes to join the girls retrieving their toiletries from the box beside the control desk.

This morning, Ms. Coughran moves the class out to the common area. A woman is already there, waiting for them in a wheelchair.

Ms. Coughran directs the girls to form a semicircle on the floor before her.

Devon chooses a spot in the back, behind everyone. Like being in the goal with the view of the entire field in front of her, the ball's erratic movement and the player reactions. She wants everything clearly laid out in front of her now.

Someone drops down right beside her. Exasperated, Devon turns to see who it is.

Karma.

Devon sighs. *Well, at least she's recovered enough to attend class again. And be annoying.*

Karma gives Devon a jab with her elbow, leans in. "Miss me?"

Devon feels anger then, feels it rise inside of her fast. It's like nothing's changed. Like the Lockdown and blood smears and ambulance stretcher and broken spork didn't even happen.

Devon jabs Karma back, hard. Turns to her, eyes narrowed. Whispers, "Why did you do it?"

"Do what?" Karma lets a smile slowly crawl across her lips.

"*You* know. I should've told the staff about my spork. I was an idiot not to."

"Oh! You mean . . ." Karma unhooks her thumbs from the holes in her cuffs, yanks up a sleeve. ". . . *this*?" She reveals a forearm, wound with a gauzy bandage. Moves like she's going to unwrap it.

Devon turns her face away. "Don't bother."

"So you care?" Karma laughs. "I had no idea, Devil. I am *so* touched." She pulls her sleeve down again. "Like I already told you, *I* wear my scars on the outside."

"Aren't you special," Devon mumbles.

"Yeah, I am. Thanks for noticing! And here's some insight from my personal friend Anonymous: 'No pain, no gain.' Ever hear that? You should try it sometime—embrace the pain, *Devil*."

"Yeah, well, *you* should just get over yourself, Karma, and grow up. You know, everybody in this place doesn't need to be always dragged along for the ride every single time you're dealing with your own personal drama."

"Yeah?" Karma jabs Devon with her elbow again, harder. "Well, *um*, I don't remember asking *you* for advice. At least I *express* myself. At least I don't hide my scars where nobody can ever see them and pretend that I'm *oh so perfect*, like you do. So keep your advice"—she jabs Devon once more—"to *yourself*."

Devon closes her eyes. She should just ignore Karma, let this pass.

But she feels her head turn to Karma. Feels herself look

Karma right in the eye. Hears her voice say, "Do Not. Do That. Again. Did you hear me? 'Cause I *mean* it, Karma."

Devon holds Karma's eyes for a long moment.

Then Karma laughs. "Oh, I'm *so* afraid, Devil. Maybe I was wrong about you. Maybe you do express yourself, after all." But then she quickly lowers her eyes down to her hands. Hooks and rehooks her thumb through the hole in her sleeve.

"Okay, ladies!" Ms. Coughran shouts over the noise in the room. "Turn down the volume!" Once it dies down, she continues, "I'd like to introduce Paula. She's going to talk to us today. She's a neat lady, so please give her your undivided attention." She gives Paula a pat on the shoulder. "Paula, the floor is yours."

Paula tells the room all about herself, how she came to live in a wheelchair. She wasn't always like this, she says. She'd once been just like them, had friends, a boyfriend, limbs that worked. Paula has a storyteller's voice. It doesn't take too long before the girls get pulled in.

"But I made some really bad choices," Paula says. "Two specifically. The first was to drink at a party, and the second was to dive into a swimming pool at that party. Unfortunately for me, that pool was only four feet deep. I broke my neck."

"Damn," Devon hears Karma whisper to herself. "Shoulda 'looked before you leapt,' lady."

"Thinking back on that day," Paula says, "if I had been sober, my mind would've been clear and I would've, as they say, looked before I leapt." She laughs then.

Karma and Devon glance at each other, find each other's eyes. Karma raises an eyebrow at Devon, smiles slyly. Then quickly turns away.

"Those two choices, the drinking and the diving, they changed my life forever. I broke three vertebrae and became a paraplegic, paralyzed from the waist down. I was seventeen at the time."

Devon watches as the girls in front of her look at one another.

"She was drinking underage," Macee whispers loudly to the girl beside her, the one with the white spider-silk hair.

"Thanks for that brilliant observation," Karma mutters under her breath. "'A fool empties his head every time he opens his mouth.'"

"So," Paula continues, "I've got a question for you all. When you initially saw me here today, what was the first thing that you noticed?"

"Your wheelchair," Jenevra says immediately. She's sitting right up front.

Paula nods. "Not my hair color, or the color of my eyes. Or the shape of my body, or my age, or what I happen to be wearing. No, that's exactly right. People see this"—she taps the arm of her wheelchair with her fingertips—"and that's who I become to them—a wheelchair. And most of the time, they can't ever get past that to see the person who's actually sitting in it."

Devon looks closely at Paula then. She sees Paula's skinny, atrophied legs lying inside a pair of black warm-up pants. Her feet in a pair of Nike running shoes, her ankles twisting inward, each foot sitting lightly on a metal footrest. A black strap around her waist holding her into the chair. Devon looks up at Paula's face. She's probably about her mom's age, Devon guesses. Short brown hair cut in a bob. Brown eyes, light blue eye shadow swiped over the lids. Tiny silver hoop earrings. Smile lines around her eyes, her mouth. Now that Devon really looks at her, she realizes that Paula's actually pretty, in a very pleasant, even happy, sort of way.

"I may be physically handicapped. I may not be able to walk anymore. I may have trouble dressing myself. I may be forced to pee through a tube for the rest of my life. But that doesn't have to define who I am."

Paula smiles, looks around the semicircle slowly. "I have a life sentence," she says simply. "For the rest of my life, until the day I die, I'm more or less a prisoner in this chair. And I have that life sentence because I made some really stupid choices when I was young. I can't really blame anyone else for my predicament, can I? Because at the end of the day, it's me and the choices I've made. Now, most of you guys made some stupid choices, too. Haven't you? That's probably why you're sitting here today. But unlike me, you *don't* have life sentences. You're going to get out of here at some point with the chance to change the course you're on at this moment. Second chances are rare in life; I know this from personal experience. Please do not let your past choices handicap you like mine have. Don't let them define who you are going to become."

The room is silent.

Paula laughs self-consciously then. "Enough preaching for today, huh? Okay." She leans sideways, pulls up a duffel bag from off the floor beside her wheelchair, places it on her lap. She takes out a plastic model of a spinal cord and passes it around, handing it to Jenevra first. Paula talks specifically about her injury, shows exactly where her spine broke. What it feels like to be paralyzed. How long it took for her to recuperate, the painful physical therapy. She answers the girls' questions.

Macee asks Paula if she can move her arms.

"God!" Karma whispers to herself. "Does she even have a brain? The chick's only been using her arms all morning!" She pauses. "Here's the advice I have for you, Macee: 'Never miss a good chance to shut up.'"

Devon laughs despite herself. She glances over at Karma again. She's still looking down at her hands, but she's got a slight smile on her face.

Tension is still there between them, but . . . Devon leans toward Karma, whispers to her, "Yeah, but then she'd only remind *you* that we're not supposed to say 'shut up'!"

Karma gives Devon a shove, whispers back, "Hey! Ridiculing others is not allowed in this facility. Let's just get that straight right now."

"Fine, and neither is you pushing me," Devon says, shoving Karma back. "Remember?"

"Oh, I won't forget it, Devil. Not me."

They turn their attention back to Paula, then. She's talking about all the road races she's won in her wheelchair. She tells them of her current challenge, how she's now been training for the Portland Marathon, her first. That she's going to do it this October.

After Paula wraps up her presentation, Ms. Coughran herds the girls back into the classroom. She asks Destiny to give a sheet of paper to each person, Sam to count the pencils and hand them out.

The classroom is quiet. The girls seem unusually thoughtful.

"Now," Ms. Coughran says, "time to write about a bad decision *you've* made. It doesn't have to be the bad decision that landed you in here. All right? It doesn't have to be a 'big' bad decision. It can be something small. So, one paragraph on that. For the second paragraph, I want you to describe the consequences that followed this bad decision. Consequences for you, but also for any other people it may have affected. Because, remember, the choices you make don't just hurt you. People don't live in glass bubbles. Any questions?"

Ms. Coughran looks around the room. Nobody says anything.

"Let's attempt to learn something with this exercise. Really stretch ourselves. Think about Paula and all the wisdom she's gained through her unfortunate experience. When we're all done, those who want to share with the class may do so. All right? Hit it, people!"

Devon stares at her blank paper. She thinks about what Paula had said about having a life sentence. Paula hadn't done anything wrong, anything *criminal* at least, but still her life was ruined. Devon thinks about what Dom had said that first time the two of them had met in the conference room, how she had explained that Devon could get a life sentence if she were to be tried in adult court. Then Devon thinks about the hearing tomorrow, remembers how much is riding on it, feels a sharp jolt of panic in her gut. She shuts off the thought, forces herself to breathe evenly and slowly. The roiling in her stomach starts to subside.

The familiar sound of pencils scratching across paper surrounds her.

Devon glances up. Karma is there, sitting at the next table over, in a chair facing Devon. But she's staring intently down at her own blank paper, her hands in her lap. Devon wonders about this. No scrawled anarchy symbols? No smirk? No acting like she's asleep and bored?

Then Devon looks back down at her own paper. What should she write? Random memories flicker in her mind.

A soccer ball slipping between Devon's hands before the jarring thump of her body hitting the ground, the ball whipping into the net behind her as the roar of the parents rises from the sidelines. State Cup last year; in the final minutes of the game her split second of hesitation had caused a goal and, thereby, the loss of the championship game.

Or her mom smiling, holding what was then Devon's little-girl hand. The two of them, strolling together through the Metropolitan Market, Tacoma's most upscale grocery store, off of Proctor and 24th and across the street from the Safeway where she worked. Her mom had been in a happy mood then, pointing to the vegetables gloriously displayed and asking Devon to name them. But later, Devon had thrown up in the corridor right in front of the bathrooms. Her mom had been furious. "Couldn't you even make it into the bathroom? Now someone has to come with a mop and clean up your mess! Do you know how embarrassing this is for me?" Another bad decision and a day ruined. If only she'd told her mom earlier that her stomach hurt. If only she'd run a little faster to the bathroom.

Or playing floor hockey at the Boys and Girls Club, sticks slashing, the hard puck sailing. A boy had bullied Devon into playing goalie so he could be a forward and score. Moments later, the puck connected with her face, leaving a black eye. "You should've stood up for yourself!" her mom had yelled at her later. "Now look at you, going to school tomorrow all ugly with that eye. What kind of mother will they think I am? Huh? Your teachers will think I hit you or something. They might even call Child Protective Services!"

Or Karma grabbing the spork from Devon's tray, breaking off its end. And Devon not saying a word about it. Not telling the staff. Not snatching it out of Karma's hand. And Karma ended up with blood-soaked sleeves because of it.

Devon could write about any of those things. They'd be acceptable. The assignment complete.

But Ms. Coughran had told them to stretch themselves, to learn something. Other than the Karma incident, which still stings, the others would just be too easy.

Devon thinks about this morning, about what her mind was pushing her to examine, the thoughts so unsettling that they drove her to kick off her blankets and leave her bed to look out the window of her cell.

Being all alone. Why had she chosen it? Because it *had* been a choice, hadn't it? Yes. That choice had been hers. Every step of the way. She could have answered her cell, returned the texts. She could have joined her classmates at the coffee shop to study, even though more laughing and gossiping and checking out of guys would've happened than actual studying. She could have run with Kait and Lucy those afternoons, could have spoken to her coach instead of avoiding him. Could have talked to Kait or written her back instead of crumpling up that letter and tossing it in the trash. Could have waited up for her mom to come home from work instead of feigning sleep.

And what would've happened then? If she'd stayed connected instead of pulling away? What had she been so afraid of? What had she been hiding from? Or—something that even Karma seemed to sense on some level—what had she been hiding?

The past six months are a blur, one gray drizzly day blending into the indistinguishable next. Days of the TV blinking endlessly in the dim apartment, meals of cold cereal or SpaghettiOs eaten alone on the ratty couch. The English essays composed on the library computers, completed early. Timing her ascent up the monster hill on Carr Street. Lying in bed, not ready for sleep, instead staring up at the ceiling, watching the shadows lengthen until the room filled entirely with darkness. It had started slowly, the pulling away from everybody. And then her isolation became comfortable, then something she'd protected. She'd get annoyed, sometimes angry, if someone tried to interfere with it.

But it hadn't been a good thing, Devon knows this now. It's never good to be alone.

Devon picks up her pencil. Taps its pointed end on the paper, making a small gray dot on the whiteness.

So. Choosing isolation had been her decision. And its consequence?

She starts to write.

chapter eighteen

"You slept, I hope."

Dom doesn't glance up when she says it. She's got her Black-Berry grasped in her hands, her thumbs flicking over the keypad.

Devon takes the seat across from Dom. "Yeah, I guess."

"Good." Dom raises an index finger, a wait-a-second signal. "Hold on."

They are inside a small conference room outside the courtroom, one of four situated across from the row of molded plastic seats that are against the wall. The same row of seats where Devon had sat that very first day here, waiting for her first court appearance. That day, Devon hadn't even noticed the four olive-colored doors to these rooms.

Devon scans the small space. Empty except for the table between herself and Dom. This time, instead of an attached stool, Devon sits in a folding chair, one of four around the table. But the walls are still cinder block, coated with the white paint, and the floor is covered with that familiar gray carpet.

She feels like she's going to puke, her heart is pumping that jittery pregame adrenaline through her body and into her limbs. She feels sleepy, too. Such a strange dichotomy of emotions—stress and sleepiness.

She watches Dom work. Today she's wearing a tight French braid, a dark blue suit, and an off-white, crisp-collared blouse underneath. And when Dom lifts her face quickly to check her watch, Devon notes the tiny wire-framed glasses. Devon remembers the short discussion she'd had with Dom about appearances one of the first times they'd met: "You have to look like a winner to be a winner," Dom had said. A definite "Karma" saying. And a comment that would've earned Dom a Henrietta Nod of Approval. Dom certainly looks like a winner today, Devon thinks. Looks like she's ready to play tough, mix it up if necessary, and take her yellow card if called on it.

Devon's mind shifts to Henrietta, to what an odd person she is.

Henrietta apparently had worked swing shift last night; she'd been present in the pod this morning to rouse Devon well before Wake Up. Had tossed Devon a clean jumpsuit, folded stiff like cardboard, a bleach-white undershirt, and socks. "Appearances are everything, okay?" she'd said after her customary bobble-head glance around the room. "Even judges judge the covers of books. Okay? Don't think they don't." Then she launched into a speech about the necessity for Devon to groom carefully this morning, to look her very best. Later, she'd argued with the staff on duty while Devon stood before the control desk, Henrietta insisting that she be the staff designated to escort Devon through the maze of hallways to meet Dom here in the small conference room outside the courtroom. Walking side by side, she'd peppered Devon with random advice. "Sit up straight, okay? Look the judge right in the eyes when he speaks to you. You're going to be nervous, don't think that you're not. Okay? Don't chew on your fingers. Don't fiddle with your hair, okay? It's not a beauty contest in there." Though she'd meant well, Henrietta only managed to increase Devon's heart rate. Her comments, Devon realizes now with a small amount of amusement, were as similarly unhelpful as those her mom would make before Devon played in a "big" game, at least back when her mom used to come and watch consistently: "Don't forget to squeeze the ball when you catch it, hon. Remember to do that thing—what's it called? A dive?—when the ball is far off to the side. Don't forget to jump." She might as well have reminded Devon to breathe.

Finally, Dom places her BlackBerry down on the table, looks up. Fixes Devon with her eyes through those tiny wire-framed glasses. Her face is set. Not stressed or anxious, just intensely serious.

"Sorry about that." She flicks her BlackBerry, and it spins 180 degrees. "Too many irons in the fire today. So." She raises an eyebrow. "Ready for this?"

Devon swallows. "I think so."

Dom is quiet for a moment. Then, "This hearing will take the better part of the day. It might even bleed over to tomorrow. I *need* you to be ready for it, Devon. It'll be long and grueling. At times very boring. At times emotional. At *all* times, no matter what is said about you—whether it's something positive or something negative, even something that you may perceive to be a total lie—do not react. No laughing or smiling. No crying. And pay attention. At least, *act* like you're paying attention." Dom pulls a yellow legal pad out of her briefcase, a sharpened pencil. Hands them across the table to Devon. "These are for you. Take notes on what goes on in there; that'll help you to stay focused and engaged. If you have something you want me to know—something that you suddenly remember about a particular witness or some detail that you think I've missed—or if you have a question about anything that goes on, just jot it down on that paper and tap me discreetly to get my attention. You'll be like my legal assistant, kind of like my second-chair attorney. Sound good?"

Devon nods. A team. Devon and Dom together, a combined effort. Her heart is hammering again. "Am I going to have to say anything?"

"The judge may ask you the occasional question directly, which you will need to answer as best you can. But, no, I'm not going to put you on the stand."

"So I'll just be sitting there next to you?"

Dom nods.

"The whole time?"

"Yes."

Devon feels relief rolling over her and lets her breath out slowly. She'd been imagining herself up front like in all those courtroom scenes on TV, feeling exposed and vulnerable, the judge pedantically peering down at her from his bench. An antagonistic attorney firing questions at her while she bumbles to find a cogent answer, to make sense. All those people watching. But that's not going to happen. She'll remain at the table beside Dom during the whole ordeal, and her back will be to the gallery. The courtroom is small, she remembers. Not many people will be there anyway.

"For a court proceeding," Dom is saying now, "this hearing is actually going to be pretty informal. So, quickly, this is what's going to happen." She folds her hands on the table. "This is not an actual trial, but a hearing, so there will be no jury today. This is what's called 'judge alone,' because a judge will be making the decision today based on the law and the facts presented to him. Not a jury. Understand?"

Again, Devon feels some slight relief. She thinks back to that first time in court, eight days ago. The judge was intimidating, but not mean. There hadn't been a jury that day, either. Devon nods her head. "I understand."

"Okay, good. The prosecutor will put on his case first. Remember, he represents the State, society at large, so it's his job to show that it is in the State's best interest that you be tried in adult court. He'll attempt to convince the judge that the charges against you are of such a serious nature that the adult system will be best equipped to deal with you, and society will be that much safer. He'll bring in his witnesses to support this argument. The police officers who found you in your apartment, for example. The man who discovered the baby that morning. Maybe the emergency room doctor you kicked."

Devon jerks her eyes down to the table, feels her face grow warm. Why did she kick that doctor? She didn't have to do that. She concentrates on studying the tabletop. Not one scratched initial. Not one ink smudge.

"Then *I'll* get the chance to cross-examine each of the prosecutor's witnesses. It's my job to neutralize anything negative that those witnesses may have said, anything that I feel is harmful to our case." She pauses. "You still following me?"

"Yes." Devon looks up at her. "I am."

"Okay. After the prosecutor is done putting on all his witnesses, it's our turn. At that point, it's my job to show the judge that it's in the State's and your best interest for you to remain here and be tried as a juvenile. It's my job to get the judge to see you as a real person. To effectively do that, I'll bring in our witnesses—"

A jolt to her heart. "Who?" Devon practically yelps the word.

Dom stops, watches Devon for a moment. Devon can see her eyes soften behind those wire frames. "I know this is very scary for you, Devon, having to see these people today, to listen to what they have to say. But you need to know that each of the people whom I'm calling as witnesses is coming here only to say good things about you. They care a lot about you and your future." She pauses. "I've carefully selected a variety of people out of the many I've talked to over the past several days so that the judge can see the many sides that make up who you are."

Devon shifts on her stool impatiently. "Okay. But who are the witnesses?"

"Are you sure you want to know ahead of time?"

Devon nods. "Definitely."

"Not all of them will be here in person," Dom says. "Some of them have written letters to the court."

Devon nods again. "Okay."

"So, your coach, Mark Dougherty, is one who will be here."

Devon swallows. She suspected he'd be one, based on Dom's questions about him the other day. "Who else?"

"The judge needs to know how well you are adjusting to life here in Remann Hall. So, I have two people who will be able to specifically address that—the teacher here in Delta pod, Ms. Coughran, and one of the detention staff, Ms. Apodaca. Henrietta is probably how you'd know her, and she will be testifying. Ms. Coughran has written a letter."

Henrietta? This surprises Devon. What is she going to say? That Devon maintains her cell immaculately? Combs her hair thoroughly every morning? Wakes up easily when roused from a dead sleep?

"You've been assigned a probation officer, Devon. All youth who come before this court for any reason are assigned one. I don't know if you remember, but at your arraignment last week, she spoke briefly—"

"No," Devon says. "I don't remember her at all."

"Well, I'll point her out to you once we're in the courtroom. Anyway, she's prepared a risk assessment on you and will report her findings to the judge. And then Dr. Bacon will come to give her expert opinion based on the few sessions she's had with you."

Risk assessments? Expert opinions? These worry Devon. What have they concluded about her? But then she thinks, she's here, isn't she? What does she expect? That's what these people do here, don't they? Assess and analyze the kids who live here? Kids like Karma and Jenevra. Destiny. Macee. Sam.

Why would she, Devon Davenport, be exempt?

"The judge will also need to get a clear picture of who you were before the incident. So I've asked your school guidance counselor from Stadium High School, Rita Gonzales, to help explain that in a letter. In it, she's discussed your grades, test scores, school disciplinary record—which is sparkling clean of course—your extracurricular activities, et cetera."

Ms. Gonzales? Devon barely even knows her. She'd gone in to see Ms. Gonzales once, right at the start of second semester freshman year. Devon had been placed in AP history instead of freshman honors American history by mistake. "Computer glitch," Ms. Gonzales had said. "I'm sure you could hang with those juniors and seniors if you tried. You're smart enough. But then the senior boys would be asking you out to the prom. And you wouldn't want that." She winked. "Not yet." Her office had smelled like microwaved popcorn. On her desk she'd prominently displayed a light blue dish decorated with snowflakes that was filled mostly with Jolly Rancher wrappers, and a framed picture of two chubby-faced toddlers with round, dark eyes.

"Also, Debbie Evans will be here to testify," Dom says, "because of your babysitting job this past summer."

Debbie knows? Devon drops her head into her hands. *What does she think about me?* Looking back, does Debbie suspect that Devon had done something terrible to her twins all those hours she'd been alone with them?

"And"—Dom hesitates—"your mom."

The courtroom is silent. Up front, the judge's bench is empty.

Everything is laid out as it had been the last time Devon was here—three rectangular tables equally spaced across the room and facing the judge's bench, the two back-to-back computer screens below it, the two flags.

The only other person currently in the room is a uniformed policeman, casually reading the *Wall Street Journal*. Devon turns to look behind her. The long bench along the back wall is still there, but vacant.

"We're here a little early," Dom says, "so we'll be all situated and comfortable when everyone else arrives."

Comfortable? Will Devon be comfortable for one minute today? One second?

Dom walks over to the table on the far right, the one where

Devon had sat that first day beside the attorney with the sparse hair and dandruff-sprinkled suit. Dom places her briefcase on the table, unzips it. Pulls out the chair on the left.

Devon moves behind the chair on Dom's right, the one she'd taken last week. She'd cried in that chair. The laminated sheet is still taped to the table: Yes, Your Honor. No, Your Honor.

From a side door, a woman enters, drops a briefcase on the table on the far left-hand side of the courtroom. She smiles, calls over to Dom.

"I'll be right back. That woman over there is your probation officer, Ms. Gustafson." Dom gives Devon a quick pat on the back before moving across the courtroom.

Devon watches as two other women enter together through that same side door, take their places in the face-to-face chairs below the judge's bench. Turn on their computers. They talk quietly. One spins in her chair, around and around, back and forth, like Devon used to do in the beauty shops as a small child while her mom got her hair colored and styled. The other woman just sits in her own chair and laughs, shakes her head with amusement.

Next, a young man, who Devon recognizes as the prosecutor from last week, walks through the door. Devon can feel her stomach jitter as he marches up to the center table, plops his briefcase down on it.

All these briefcases in the room. Filled with papers. Papers about her.

The prosecutor turns toward Devon in his dark suit with faint pinstripes and bright blue tie. Nods at her quickly, then turns away to arrange his files, set them out just right. Devon notices that he's wearing one of those obnoxious earpieces. He checks his BlackBerry, tucks it back into the holster at his hip. He rolls his neck, shakes out his hands. Checks his BlackBerry again.

Devon feels awkward standing here, chewing on her thumbnail, waiting. She drops her hand with annoyance. When had she started this nail-biting habit? It needs to end.

More people are trickling in now, filing into the long bench at the back. Those sitting together talk in low voices, clear their throats. Cough. Turn off their cell phones.

Finally, Devon pulls out her chair, sits down. Carefully places her yellow legal pad and pencil on the table. Folds her hands in her lap. They're clammy so she wipes them on the legs of her jumpsuit, refolds them. She can feel all the eyes behind her, feel their gaze at the back of her head. At the back of her tight French braids—two identical cords of shiny black hair, the ends twisted with rubber bands and brushing her shoulders. Dom had fixed them in the little conference room before they'd left for the courtroom. The braids actually itch now with all those eyes on them. Devon resists the urge to unclasp her hands again and touch them. Resists the urge to look back at those people behind her.

Her mom might be there. Dom had said that last night her mom had finally returned all those messages Dom had left on her cell. Late last night. After midnight.

Devon stares down at the laminated paper, busies herself with reading what's there: Yes, Your Honor. No, Your Honor. Yes, Your Honor. No, Your Honor.

Finally Dom returns, chats in passing with the prosecutor in the pinstripes at the middle table. He says something and shrugs, then reaches up to remove his earpiece.

When Dom takes her seat, an amused expression lingers on her face. "Nice Bluetooth. I should've just let him keep it on. But, then, that wouldn't be playing nice, would it? The judge would've eaten him alive for wearing it in here, and he would've looked like a total fool." She checks her watch. "Speaking of the judge, we're just waiting on him to arrive. Should be any minute now." She leans over, looks closely at Devon, down at her tightly clasped hands, then back up into her face. "You doing okay?"

Devon nods.

"All rise!" a voice barks from the side door.

Dom nudges Devon, and everybody in the courtroom is on their feet. Complete silence descends.

The judge enters, his black robe trailing lightly behind him. The same judge as last time with his short military-style haircut. He mounts the steps to his bench, Devon can hear his feet hit as they make contact with each step. He takes his seat, then waves dismissively. Everybody moves to sit down again.

"Devon!" a sharp whisper from behind. "Hey!"

Devon jerks her head on reflex, scans the faces in the gallery behind her.

Her mom.

There, standing in the center of the long bench. Waving and smiling. Long red nails, big red lips. A new spaghetti-strapped sundress, too bright for the room, and ridiculously too summery for April in Tacoma. Her lips form the words, "Hi, hon. I'm here!"

Devon jerks back around, falls into her seat. She fills her lungs then, again and again. Way too fast. Silver sparkles flicker at the corners of her vision. She shakes her head. *Hold on. Don't pass out. Don't cry.*

She's been wanting her mom to be here all this time, hasn't she? And now that she actually is . . .

Dom places a hand on Devon's arm, gives it a gentle squeeze. "Just breathe," she whispers, "but slowly. Relax and breathe. And you'll be okay."

"This court is called to order," Judge Saynisch says. He clears his throat, shuffles the papers before him. "We're here today for a declination hearing in the case of State versus Davenport." He looks up, squints at the courtroom. "Is that your understanding, Counsel?"

"Yes, Your Honor," the prosecutor says quickly.

Dom nods. "Yes, Your Honor."

"All right, then," the judge says. "Let's get to it." He nods at the prosecutor. "Opening statement, Mr. Floyd? Keep it brief."

"Yes, Your Honor."

Devon snatches up her pencil, pulls her legal pad toward herself so she's ready. Her fingers are trembling.

She hadn't waved back. Her mom had waved and smiled at her, had finally shown up here to help her, and Devon hadn't responded. No smile or wave back. No nod. Nothing at all.

chapter nineteen

The first thing the prosecutor does is stand. The second is to make a speech. He tells the judge, "This case, Your Honor, is about the commission of society's most serious crime—murder—against society's most innocent, most *helpless*, victim. A victim who doesn't possess the physical strength to defend herself. A victim who lacks the ability to even plead for her own life. But this case is about much more than even that, Your Honor. It's about a breach of trust, the breaking of a bond. The most basic bond in the human experience—the bond between a child and her mother. This is a case, Your Honor, where the victim is a baby, and the perpetrator is her mother."

Devon glances over at Dom. She's sitting very still, listening, hands clasped over her opened yellow legal pad. When the prosecutor said that last line, Dom had pressed her lips together, picked up her pen.

The prosecutor goes on to discuss how egregious is the breaking of the maternal bond. He says, "Of all the people on the face of the earth, Your Honor, the one person this particular baby should have been able to count on to welcome her into the world, to keep her safe and protect her, was that person sitting right over there." He turns his face and eyes toward Devon. "But, instead, Your Honor, that person"—he extends his right arm with index finger elongated and pointing—"*that* person was trying to kill her." He pauses. "She scooped her tiny infant body into a black plastic trash bag, tied it off tightly, and tried to suffocate the life out of her."

The prosecutor goes on, explaining how Devon had hid her pregnancy, deceiving the people closest to her—her mother, her soccer coach, her teammates, her classmates. How she'd purposefully sought no prenatal care, and when confronted with the opportunity to actually discuss her pregnancy with a doctor, became hostile and uncooperative. How she began wearing baggy clothing to conceal her changing body and started skipping out on soccer practices once her body got too cumbersome to play anymore. And how she'd doggedly carried out the deception to the very end, when she gave birth to the baby alone in her apartment. And after it was over, how she'd collected up the bloody evidence and stuffed it into a trash bag, including the baby itself, dumped it all into the trash can behind her apartment building, and walked away.

Devon watches the young prosecutor in his pinstripes tell his story. Watches Dom sitting beside her with hands clasped over her yellow legal pad, occasionally picking up her pen to jot something down on it. Watches the judge up front listening, his eyes trained intently on the prosecutor. Across the room, Devon watches the woman with whom Dom had spoken earlier, Ms. Gustafson; her chin is resting in the palm of her left hand. Devon watches the two women facing each other with their back-to-back computer screens, their fingers moving rhythmically over their respective keyboards. It's like a play; each person here has his own place and assigned role. Even Devon has her script—the laminated paper taped to the tabletop dictates her lines: Yes, Your Honor. No, Your Honor.

Devon wonders what her mom is thinking now, listening back there in the gallery, wearing her bright sundress. Is this the first time she's heard this story told in this way? Does she believe the prosecutor in pinstripes? Why did she wait so long to call Dom, and what did they talk about when she finally did? And why didn't her mom ever come to see her? Where had she been all this time, where did she go?

Stop thinking and focus now. She needs to concentrate on what's being said. Listen for discrepancies so she can help Dom.

"Thank you, Your Honor," Mr. Floyd says.

Devon looks up sharply. *He's finally finished?*

The prosecutor steps back behind his chair and settles himself into it. Wipes his hands on his pinstriped thighs.

Judge Saynisch turns his face toward Devon's table. He nods at Dom. "Defense?"

Dom stands slowly, pushing off the tabletop. Devon glances up at her quickly. Her face is composed, a slight smile lingering around her lips.

"Your Honor," Dom says. "I'm not going to stand here and waste your time rehearsing a litany of reasons why you should decide in favor of my client, Devon Davenport. All my client asks, Your Honor, is that you keep an open mind and weigh the evidence that's presented here today. Keep an open mind, and weigh the evidence, and I have confidence that you will arrive at the right decision. That's all I have, Your Honor."

Dom sits down.

That's it? Where's the long, persuasive speech that elicits chills or tears? Where's the drama?

Devon peeks at Dom out of the corner of her eye. Watches

her center the legal pad in front of her, pick up the pen.

Devon questions if Dom knows what she's doing after all. Devon remembers that she's never seen Dom in court, has no idea what she's capable of. The last time Devon was here she had a balding man with a dandruff-sprinkled suit who served as her attorney. He certainly wasn't impressive, but she remembers he *had* made an inspiring speech.

"Well," the judge says, "that was refreshing. A counsel who understands the meaning of the word *brevity*." He scans the courtroom. "All right, let's keep pushing ahead, shall we? Mr. Floyd, call your first witness."

Devon feels her heart pick up. Okay, these people aren't on her side, she thinks. They are here to say unflattering things, awful things, about her.

Don't react, Devon reminds herself. *Not even a little bit.*

Mr. Floyd clears his throat. "The state calls Mr. Jacob Bing-ham."

Devon consciously keeps her head down to avoid any eye contact with the man as he steps to the front of the courtroom, swearing with his right hand raised that his testimony will be the truth, and seats himself on the witness stand—a square wooden enclosure with a chair inside, situated below and to the left of the judge. She wonders what he's here to say about her, who he is. She risks a peek up at him and sees that the man is directly in front of her and sitting surprisingly close to her. In fact, other than Dom, he is sitting closer to her than any other person in the courtroom.

Their eyes meet briefly. His narrow slightly, his lips turn down with distaste.

Devon feels a cold prick inside her chest and quickly drops

her face back down to her yellow pad, her cheeks burning.

"Please state your name for the record," Mr. Floyd says.

"Jacob William Bingham. Most people call me Jake."

"Thank you. And Mr. Bingham, what were you doing the morning of March twenty-eighth?"

"I was taking my Labrador retriever, Darko, for a walk just like I do every day before going into work."

"And where do you work?"

"I work at The Job Mob, a social networking start-up in Seattle. I'm a Web developer there."

"And about what time was it that you were walking your dog?"

"About six forty-five in the morning. I'm usually out the door no later than six-thirty, but that morning I was running a little behind"—he takes a breath—"*thank God.*"

With those words, Devon can feel the man's eyes on her again, his anger and disdain directed at her. But Devon resists the urge to glance up at him again. She keeps her eyes fixed on the binding holding her yellow legal pad together.

"Yes." Mr. Floyd clears his throat uncomfortably. "And, uh, why exactly was it that you were running late that morning, Mr. Bingham?"

"I'd overslept my alarm. My sister in Chicago called me late the night before. Long story short, but our mom was recently diagnosed with second-stage breast cancer, and, well, we were just talking about the whole situation. Anyway—"

"Objection!" Dom jumps up. "Relevance."

"Yes, let's keep things focused, Mr. Floyd," Judge Saynisch says, "like a laser beam. Move your witness along."

Dom sits again, and Devon can feel Dom's tenseness beside her, can feel the heat emanating from her body.

"Mr. Bingham, you mentioned that you walk your dog every day before you go to work. Do you recall the route you took that particular morning?"

"Yes, I do, because I take the same route every day. But that day, actually, it was a little different. I took a shortcut to make up for oversleeping."

The prosecutor displays a blown-up street map of North Tacoma and asks Mr. Bingham to point out his usual route for the court to see. Then he has Mr. Bingham show the court exactly which alley he had taken as a shortcut.

"Okay, Mr. Bingham. So, when you entered the alley, did you notice anything unusual?"

"Just that Darko, my lab, started barking like crazy and straining at his leash and pulling me toward this trash can about halfway down the alley."

"What did you do then?"

"Well, I told him to be quiet because it was kind of early for a dog to be outside barking. People tend to get pretty upset that early in the morning when a dog barks like that."

"Was this behavior unusual for your dog?"

"Definitely. He hardly ever strains or barks. Never for no reason, that's for sure."

"Then what happened?"

"Well, like I said, he was pulling me toward that trash can pretty energetically. And he's a big boy, weighs like ninety-five pounds, so I just sort of went with him."

"When you arrived at the trash can, did you notice anything unusual?"

"Only that I heard this strange noise. A crying noise. A sort of squalling."

"And, Mr. Bingham, where was this noise coming from?"

"It seemed to be coming from the vicinity of the trash can."

"What did you do next?"

"Well, I tried to pull Darko away because I was in a hurry, but he refused to budge. He just wouldn't stop barking and whining. And then he did the weirdest thing—he stood up on his hind legs and tried to actually pry the lid off of that trash can—with his nose and both of his front paws. At that point, I decided to see what the big deal was and lifted off the lid myself and started pulling out the trash bags that were in it."

"How many trash bags did you pull out?"

"Well, two. The top bag was partially covering another one beneath it. When I pulled out that top one, the noise seemed to get louder. So, I dropped it on the ground, and when I picked up the second bag, which was much heavier than the first, I saw something moving around inside of it."

"What kind of movement, Mr. Bingham?"

"A sort of thrashing and squirming. And, at that point, I knew that the noise was definitely coming out of that bag I was holding."

"What did you do next?"

"Well, my first thought was that it was a cat stuck in there or something. So, I placed the bag back down on top of the other bags that were still in the trash can and ripped it open. Inside I found a white towel all covered with blood. And inside *that* was a newborn baby."

"Let's slow down for a second. Was the bag secured in any way?"

"Yes, I saw that it was tied with a knot at the top. But I didn't want to mess around with trying to untie it; that's why I ripped it open."

"Okay, so when you ripped open the bag, did you see anything in there besides that baby and the bloody towel?"

"Just some random trash. Juice containers. Grimy newspapers. That sort of thing. Feminine-type products. Tampons, I think. But I wasn't really paying close attention. When I saw that baby, I just grabbed it and shoved it, bloody towel and all, under my coat and called 911 on my cell phone."

"And how did the baby look to you?"

"It was sort of bluish white. I specifically remember its lips; they were almost entirely blue, like it had sucked on a blue lollipop or Popsicle or something. It was trembling pretty violently. And screaming for its life."

"Did you note the sex of the baby?"

"No, I just thrust it under my coat because it was pretty cold outside and starting to drizzle."

"When you called 911, what did the operator tell you to do?"

"She told me to keep the baby as warm as possible. I told her I had already put it inside my coat, and she told me that was perfect. She said that an ambulance was on its way."

"Did you do anything else?"

"Yes, after I hung up from talking to 911, I called my wife. She was going to get there right away to help me out. And then I, uh, I kind of prayed. A lot."

The prosecutor clears his throat. "Okay. About how long did it take for the ambulance to arrive?"

"About five minutes. Or less. They came pretty quick. A squad car with a police officer arrived at about the same time.

And shortly after that, my wife got there. She had just gotten out of the shower when I called her."

"Okay, and what were you doing during those five minutes while you were waiting for the ambulance to arrive?"

"I was just sort of talking to the baby, telling it that everything was going to be okay and to hold on. Rocking back and forth. Stuff like that."

"Did the baby stop crying at any point while you were holding her?"

"Yes, for a few seconds at a time, and then I would sort of jiggle it, and it would start crying all over again. I was absolutely terrified that it would die in my arms. I knew that if it was crying, it was still alive."

"And what was your dog doing all this time?"

"Just circling around me, barking. I had dropped his leash when I started pulling out the bags, but he stayed right by me the entire time."

"What were you thinking?"

Devon feels Dom move beside her.

"I was thinking, what kind of a—"

"Objection!" Dom's voice rings out as she springs to her feet. "Relevance, Your Honor—"

"—coldhearted psycho would do something like—"

"Hold it right there, Mr. Bingham!" Judge Saynisch says. He looks over at Dom. "I'm all over this, Ms. Barcellona. Be seated."

Devon jerks her eyes up toward the judge. He's glaring down at Mr. Floyd now.

"Counsel," the judge says, "you know better than that. The witness's thoughts are irrelevant here. Let's just stick strictly to the facts in my courtroom, shall we? Now, any more questions for the witness?"

Dom sits down again.

"No, Your Honor," Mr. Floyd says. "That's about all I have."

"Defense?"

"No, Your Honor."

Devon turns to look at Dom beside her. *What? She's not going to ask him any questions?*

"Then you may step down, Mr. Bingham," Judge Saynisch says. "Thank you for your testimony."

Dom's just going to let him leave? On TV, the attorneys never pass up a chance to cross-examine. Devon watches as Dom folds her hands carefully, places them on the tabletop.

Devon grabs up her own pencil and scrawls *WHY NOT???* across her legal pad and slides it in front of Dom. Dom just presses her lips together, shakes her head, keeping her eyes on the judge.

"Mr. Floyd," the judge says, "are you prepared to call your next witness?"

"Yes, Your Honor. The state calls Mr. Ron Woods."

Devon watches as another man walks up to the front of the courtroom and raises his right hand. Unlike the first, this man is somehow familiar to her. Short blond hair. Tall and muscular. His gait, Devon sees when he makes his way to the witness stand, exudes confidence and strength. He moves with an authoritative swagger, an earned one, and he's wearing a black suit and white shirt with a black tie. *Like the stereotypical FBI types on TV*, Devon thinks.

"Please state your name for the record," Mr. Floyd says.

"Ron Woods."

"And please state your current occupation, Mr. Woods."

"I am a police officer for the Tacoma Police Department, a detective within the Homicide Unit of the Criminal Investigations Division."

Devon feels a jolt. *A police officer.* Definitely not someone on her side.

"And did you hold this position on March the twenty-eighth?"

"Yes."

When the man opens his mouth to answer the questions, Devon notices his teeth, the most prominent of his features, dazzling in contrast to his tanned face. Perfectly straight and bright white. And then suddenly she remembers everything—who he is, where she'd seen him before. He's the one, the guy who'd crouched on the floor beside her while she was on the couch That Morning. He'd smiled at her, tried to shake her hand. Asked her questions, ones she couldn't—or wouldn't—answer. Devon remembers her mom, angry and embarrassed, pulling away the blanket. And Devon was left there, lying on the couch, cold and exposed.

"Yes," the detective is saying now, "I was called to the scene by the first responder, Police Sergeant Keith Cruz. Since the newborn was found in a trash can and enclosed in a plastic trash bag, requesting a detective from Homicide would be the appropriate next step. Hence, why I was called."

"When did you arrive at the scene?"

"Approximately fifteen to twenty minutes after the ambulance had come and gone. The exact time, according to my records, was seven twenty-two A.M."

The prosecutor then launches into a series of questions about what was going on at the scene when he arrived. The detective speaks confidently about how everything was running smoothly—how the area was cordoned off with police tape and the crime scene secured. How he'd instituted crowd control and ensured all witness statements were taken. How he'd organized the officers at the scene to conduct a door-to-door search within a four-block radius of the trash can. "The paramedics had estimated that the birth had occurred within the past two hours, three at the most, so time was of the essence," the detective says.

"What did you hope to find during this door-to-door search?"

"Well, obviously, the mother. But at the very least, I hoped to uncover witnesses who may have heard or seen something regarding the incident—someone seen near the trash can or in the vicinity of the alley during the early morning hours. Or perhaps ID any pregnant women, suspected or known, living in the area. Anything, really."

"Where did you begin your search?"

"I decided to concentrate first on the Kingston Manor Apartment complex."

"Why did you choose to start there?"

"Because of its proximity to the trash can. The alley runs immediately behind the complex, and the residents of that apartment building use the trash cans placed back there. The number of residents living in the complex was a factor. The complex contains thirty units, so I figured the chances of uncovering an eyewitness or any helpful information there was pretty high."

"Did you have another officer accompany you?"

"Yes, I took Police Sergeant Bruce Fowler, an officer present at the scene, with me."

"And at what time, would you say, did you begin your search, Detective?"

"According to my records, we began canvassing the area at approximately eight oh five A.M., give or take."

The prosecutor's questions continue to come, and the police officer answers them, the two male voices melding together. So tedious, every little step discussed and analyzed. Dom is attentive, though. Devon notices that her brows are creased in concentration behind her wire frames, her teeth pressing into her lipsticked lips, leaving little dents.

Devon lets her mind drift back to That Morning. She's surprised with the ease that the memories flow: the dim room, the TV flashing its morning drivel, stuff she never much cared to watch before, the sound off. How chilled and feverish she felt under the blanket, a blanket that she'd pulled from her bed at some point in the morning and dragged with her into the living room. She remembers her mom bursting into the apartment when she got home from work, then blathering seamlessly. She'd gone to answer the door later, flirted with some guys outside. The chronology is a fog, though, what happened when. And Devon, lying there on the couch under her blanket. Hiding and waiting.

Waiting? For what? For her mom to leave? For time to pass? Devon's not sure now.

"A woman in her early thirties answered the door to Apartment 213," the police detective is saying now, "and we had a brief conversation with her."

"What was this woman's name?"

"She told us that her name was Jennifer Davenport."

"And what was your conversation about?"

"Pretty standard, basic stuff. We told her that we were canvassing the area, asking residents in the vicinity whether they had seen or heard anything unusual. She mentioned that she had just gotten home from work, so she hadn't been around during those early morning hours, but that her teenaged daughter may have seen or heard something as she had stayed home from school that morning."

"Had you met Ms. Davenport prior to this conversation outside her door?"

"Well, during the course of our conversation outside her door, she reminded us that she had first spoken to me briefly in the alley earlier that morning. She'd said then that she had just stepped off the bus, coming home from work, and noticed all the police activity outside her apartment complex and had asked me a few questions about the incident. So, at that point in our conversation outside her door, yes, I did recognize that I had spoken with her earlier."

"And during this conversation, did Ms. Davenport appear to be cooperative?"

"Very much so. She seemed . . . um, how can I put it? Very eager to help us out, I guess is how I'd describe her. Very friendly and open."

"Then what did you do?"

"Well, I was interested in speaking with her daughter, so I asked Ms. Davenport if I could talk to her for a moment."

The scene replays slowly in Devon's mind now. It's all there: *Devon's mom leans closer to the man with the blond hair. Whispers something in his ear. Looks back over her shoulder, back at Devon lying on the couch. Turns again to the man. Giggles.*

The man says something to her in return. Her mom moves aside, little tiptoey steps, rearranges her hair.

"Why did you want to speak to Ms. Davenport's daughter?"

"As an investigator, I am trained to go with my gut feeling. Given the fact that an unsupervised teenaged girl had stayed home from school because she was sick, combined with her residence being in such close proximity to where a baby had been found inside a trash can that very same morning, well, my gut was sending up a little red flag. But at the very least, I was hopeful that she may have seen or heard something that could help us with our search."

"Did Ms. Davenport give you permission to enter her apartment and speak to her daughter?"

"Yes."

Her mom has that look on her face, that definite flash in her eye. That slight lift of the eyebrow, that smile playing her lips. She's in the midst of the game. He's the prey, and she's the predator, and she will catch him.

The man smiles at her, lets his eyes linger on her face for a moment, then quickly steps past her and into the apartment.

Her mom follows behind him, her eyes dropping briefly as she watches him move away from her.

Was that giving permission? Her mom wasn't thinking about permission then. No, she was thinking about *him.*

Devon looks over at Dom. Her brows furrowed behind her wire frames. Would Dom think that her mom had given him permission at that moment?

"What did you do then, Detective Woods?"

"I entered the apartment and approached the girl. She was lying on the couch under some kind of blanket."

Devon feels that prick, like when she's in class and has some unique insight to share. She feels the adrenaline pumping through her arms. Should she say something to Dom?

"How did the girl appear to you?"

Unsure of what to do, Devon only half-listens as the detective describes how he first found Devon—listless on the couch with damp hair and pale skin. How he'd introduced himself to her, crouching down so he could offer her his hand. How she'd seemed unresponsive to his questions.

"Did she appear to have understood you?" the prosecutor is asking now.

"I wasn't sure at the time. This is all detailed in my report."

"Did she seem like she wanted to get away?"

"No. She seemed barely conscious. Barely hanging on."

Devon looks over at Dom once more. Her hands are clasped over her legal pad. Devon pulls her own toward herself. Quickly scribbles: *My mom didn't really give permission to come inside. She was actually* *hitting* *on him.* Devon pushes the pad toward Dom, taps her on the elbow.

Dom turns toward Devon abruptly, annoyed. Then she notices the note, glances down, her eyes darting behind her wire frames. Suddenly her eyebrows jump up. She turns back to Devon, then back to the pad. Scribbles underneath Devon's own writing: *You remember this?* Then looks back at Devon.

Devon nods.

Writes, *You're sure?*

Devon nods again.

The prosecutor continues to question the detective. They discuss what happened after Devon's mom had pulled the blanket away. How Police Sergeant Fowler entered the apartment to get Devon's mom under control, how she'd kicked and screamed. They discuss how Devon had, in the end, passed out. How he'd radioed for an ambulance.

After the prosecutor returns to his seat, the judge looks over at Dom. "Defense?"

Dom stands. "Your Honor, I would request a short recess to conference with my client."

Judge Saynisch checks his watch, glances at the prosecutor. "Okay. Court adjourned for a ten-minute recess. Return to the courtroom at ten forty-five." He hammers his gavel, and as he departs the courtroom, the people within snap to their feet.

chapter twenty

Dom pulls Devon into the conference room outside the court-room. Drops her notebook on the round table, pulls out the folding chair farthest from the door and facing it. "Sit down, Devon. We don't have much time."

Devon takes the chair opposite Dom.

"Spill," Dom says. "Tell me everything you remember."

Devon looks down at her gnawed nails. Nothing left to pick at. She stashes her hands under her thighs. "Well, my mom's always looking for the next guy," she says finally. "That guy, that detective, was a potential candidate, I guess. When she was talking to him at the door, I remember thinking, 'Why doesn't she just take his number and make him go away?'"

Dom listens as Devon pieces together what she's remembered, how she'd watched her mom flirt with the two guys, how her mom had played with the door, opening and closing it with her foot. How she'd, most likely, only used Devon being home that morning as an excuse to get the blond guy into her apartment so she could try to work her magic on him. "I know her," Devon says softly. "She's done stuff like that so many times."

"Your mom didn't mention any of this to me." Dom's tone is doubtful.

"So, she told you stuff?" Then Devon clamps her mouth shut.

She has other questions ready to burst, like, Where was she? Why didn't she ever come? What does she think about me? But doesn't ask any of them.

"Of course," Dom snaps. "What do you think? We talked for a couple of hours. I don't call witnesses blind."

Devon nods, swallows. "Well, my mom didn't mention it because she probably didn't even realize what was going on herself. She's that clueless."

"But, apparently, *you* did. You see, this is why you tell me everything, Devon. I hate surprises, especially on the day I go to court." Dom sighs, takes off her glasses, wipes the lenses with the hem of her skirt.

"But I didn't really think about . . . didn't remember it, until I was in there hearing it."

Dom sighs again. "Fine, Devon." She peers through the lenses to make sure they're clear, then places them back on her face. "You didn't remember; I get it." She flips through a note-scrawled notebook then looks back up at Devon. "This is very important, the facts about this, what you're claiming. If we can prove that your mother had not clearly granted the detective formal entry into your apartment, and he entered anyway, then we can argue that any evidence he discovered inside should be suppressed. Which means it won't be admissible in court. Which means it can't be used against you. This is good; it may help us. A lot. So you must be absolutely clear and correct with this assertion." Dom drums her fingers on the table. "Of course, your testimony could be discounted because of your state of mind at the time. You *did* pass out."

Dom has that look on her face now, that thoughtful look.

At this moment, Devon feels a sudden surge of gratitude—how lucky she is to have Dom here with her. Always turning things over, looking at all sides. She feels tears prick at the corners of her eyes. Dom must really care about her. Right?

"Well," Dom continues, "this won't come into play until the actual trial. But I can embark on a little fishing expedition today, see if there's something to it. Test out my bait to see if it's tasty. And to discredit the detective as a witness. I can put a few dings in his seemingly flawless armor. I can make him squirm."

Dom slaps the tabletop, stands up. Her eyes are bright. "Ready?"

Devon stands up, too. Turns her head, quickly wipes at her eyes. "Sure."

"All right, then. Let's get back in there and go stir things up!"

"All rise!"

The courtroom is on its feet, and Devon watches as Judge Saynisch makes his way up to his bench. Sits down, scans the room.

"Be seated." When the room is settled, he looks over at Dom. "Defense, do you have any questions for the witness?"

"Yes, Your Honor."

"Then proceed. Let's get this show on the road."

As Dom stands, Devon feels the nervous pregame jitters spiking in her stomach. Not from dread for once, but excitement. She wonders what Dom is going to do.

Dom moves slowly around to the front of the defense table, leans against it. Crosses her arms. She faces Detective Woods, already seated back on the witness stand. "Detective Woods, during the previous examination, you stated that Ms.

Davenport, the respondent's mother, had granted permission for you to enter her apartment and question her daughter, Devon Davenport, the respondent. Is this true?"

He makes a small sneer to the question. "Yes, it is. I swore an oath to tell the complete truth."

"Well, that's admirable," Dom says. "So then, Detective, Ms. Davenport gave you *verbal* permission to enter?"

"Ms. Barcellona," Judge Saynisch says. "Watch the sarcasm. And move things along."

Dom nods. "Yes, Your Honor."

"You may answer the question, Detective," the judge says.

Detective Woods shifts in his seat, crosses his legs. "I wouldn't have entered otherwise."

"I see. So, how did this go down, exactly?"

Detective Woods frowns. "Excuse me?"

"What I'm asking, Detective Woods, is do you recall what Ms. Davenport *said* that led you to believe that you had permission to enter her apartment?"

"As I've already stated, Ms. Davenport had mentioned to me that her daughter had been home alone all morning from school because she was sick. So, I asked her something like, 'Do you mind if I talk to her?' By 'her' I meant Ms. Davenport's daughter, the respondent."

"Yes, but again, did Ms. Davenport *say* that you could enter into her apartment and speak to her daughter?"

"Objection!" The prosecutor is on his feet. "Relevance, Your Honor. This is *not* a suppression hearing, but a declination hearing."

"Good point, Counsel," the judge says. "But I'm going to let Ms. Barcellona spread her wings a little on this one." He looks over at Dom then. "I'm giving you some latitude, Ms. Barcellona. Don't abuse it."

"Yes, Your Honor."

"You may answer the question, Detective Woods."

Detective Woods clears his throat. "Ms. Davenport allowed me to enter the apartment, yes."

"*Allowed* you to enter the apartment. But you don't recall her exact words." Dom walks from one end of the table to the other, her finger trailing along its edge. Then, "Detective, you mentioned earlier"—Dom leans across the defense table, pulls her notebook toward herself. She flips through it, then looks up at the detective. "You said that Ms. Davenport was very cooperative with you and Police Sergeant Fowler. You said, and I quote, 'she seemed very eager to help us out. Very friendly and open.'" She pauses. "Would you also say that she was flirtatious?"

Detective Woods shifts around again. "I guess that could be accurate, but that's a matter of interpretation, whether someone regards another as being flirtatious or not."

"So, Detective Woods, would you say that she was *hitting* on you?"

He clears his throat. "Some might say that."

"But would *you* say it?"

"I suppose . . . yes."

"And you used that interpretation of her behavior toward you, her hitting on you, to your advantage. Didn't you, Detective? You didn't wait—did you?—for her to *formally* invite you inside the—"

"She stepped aside to let me pass."

"Also a matter of interpretation, Detective? Because didn't you make a statement to a Tacoma *News Tribune* reporter, a statement that was quoted in an article dated a day after the incident occurred?" Dom reaches behind her, snatches up a newspaper clipping lying on the defense table, an article that Devon recognizes as one that Dom had given her that first day they'd met together. "A statement referencing that once you and Police Sergeant Fowler learned—"

"Objection! Hearsay."

"I'll allow it," the judge says wearily. "Carry on, Ms. Barcellona. But quickly."

"Detective, once you had learned from Ms. Davenport that her daughter had stayed home from school, didn't you say, and I quote from the article"—Dom peers down at the article in her hands—"'That set off huge bells in my head,' Woods said. 'So, Fowler and I, we just went with it.'"

Dom looks up at the detective, waits for his reply.

Though she can't see Dom's face from her seat, Devon can imagine that eyebrow of hers, arched over her wire-framed glasses.

"Look!" The detective leans forward in his chair, his tanned face turning darker, the muscles in his neck strained. "She didn't bar my way. She didn't ask for a warrant. In fact, she followed me inside. Okay? Still talking, apologizing that . . . that her house was such a mess. I didn't construe any objection on her part to my entry. Not at all. She consented with her behavior. Is that clear?"

Dom smiles. "Just like when a rape victim hadn't screamed No!, then she must have actually consented. And therefore wasn't really raped. Hmm, Detective?"

"Objection! Argumentative, harassing the witness!"

"Ms. Barcellona," the judge says, "you've now crossed the line. Don't do it again. This is a warning."

Devon leans forward. *Yes! Dom's first yellow card!*

Dom walks toward the defense table, then turns back around. "And when was it, Detective Woods, that you actually got around to reading Devon Davenport, the respondent, her rights?"

The detective leans back in his seat, the hostility sliding from his face. Crosses his arms confidently. "Shortly after her mother removed the blanket, the one that the respondent had wrapped around herself."

"And, refresh my memory, was that before or after the respondent passed out?"

The detective licks his lips. "Before . . . I think . . . I'm sure . . ."

Dom smiles, glances up at the judge. "I have no further questions."

The rest of the morning progresses slowly. Other witnesses come and go, answering the prosecutor's questions. A police officer, Police Sergeant Keith Cruz, the first to arrive at the scene. He spoke about securing the crime scene, and Dom didn't ask him any questions. Then the prosecutor called Police Officer Bruce Fowler, who had accompanied Detective Woods in his door-to-door search. His testimony was similar to the detective's, but not as long and involved. Dom questioned him about his role in entering the apartment, but he insisted that he had stayed outside and entered only after Devon's mother had started lashing out at Detective Woods.

The prosecutor then called the pediatrician, Dr. Jyoti More, who had received the baby at the hospital; she explained that the baby's core temperature was eighty-nine degrees, that the baby arrived with the umbilical cord still attached, that the cut was ragged, not clean—an indication that the instrument used to sever the cord was blunt. That she observed the baby had sustained a small bruise on the left side of her head behind the ear, probably also the site of a mild concussion. All this testimony, she recited carefully and concisely, like she was a talking encyclopedia of medical terms. Her heavy Indian accent and funny turns of phrase were kind of cute and reminded Devon of a female version of Apu, the Kwik-E-Mart owner of *The Simpsons*.

When the prosecutor had returned to his seat, Judge Saynisch looks over at Dom. "Defense, do you have any questions for the witness?"

"Yes, Your Honor." Dom steps out from behind her chair, walks within arm's reach of the witness stand, smiles at the doctor sitting there. "Dr. More, I'd first like to concentrate on the portion of your testimony concerning the baby's bruising and concussion."

"Yes." Dr. More returns Dom's smile, her eyes bright and eager.

She seems so nice, Devon thinks. *I hope Dom isn't too mean to her.*

"Dr. More, you've stated here today that the baby had sustained an approximate three-centimeter-by-one-centimeter bruise on the left side of her head, behind the ear. Is this correct?"

"Yes, that is correct."

"And, according to your testimony today, you stated that the site of this bruise is also where the concussion was sustained. Correct?"

"Yes. I believe that the bruise and the concussion have occurred on the same time."

"And, please forgive me for being redundant, Dr. More, but you've testified today that you believe this bruising and concussion occurred *after* the baby was born, and that these injuries are consistent with head trauma due to blows to the head. Am I still on track?"

"Yes, you are. Thank you."

"And how did you come to so definitive a conclusion, Dr. More?"

"I do not think I understand the wording of this question."

"I'm sorry, Dr. More. Let me ask it a different way. You state that the bruise and concussion were consistent with head trauma due to blows to the head. But could they—the bruise and the concussion—also be consistent with an injury sustained by means other than blows to the head? Like, during the actual birth process, perhaps?"

"Perhaps. Yes."

"Could you please give me a for instance, Dr. More?"

"Objection! Calls for speculation."

"Denied," Judge Saynisch says. "She's an expert. She's speaking hypothetically here. Nothing wrong with that. You may answer the question, Dr. More."

"Yes, I am happy to. I must please think for a moment." Dr. More pauses. She frowns, places an index finger between her eyebrows, on the red dot there.

"Yes," she says after a short hesitation. "A bruise like this may be resulting from the forceps or the other birth implements. Very rare the placement, though. Usually those instruments cause bruising, sometimes even indentions, near the temples. But that is also occurring behind the ear if the doctor makes the mistake and they slip." She waves her index finger and shakes her head. "But not for the concussion. Force is required for concussion. You understand this? Also, very important, but the birth did not occur at hospital. The mother gave birth at her home, and is most certain to have not used the forceps. So, my best surmise is blows to the head by the hand of the mother. Unfortunately, this I have seen before, in my practice."

"But, Dr. More, you just said your best surmise, your best *guess*, is that the bruise was sustained due to blows to the head. So, then, you do not *know* that this is actually what happened?"

The doctor smiles. "This is true. I do not know. I was not there with her."

Dom turns around for a moment, looks down at the floor. Devon sees Dom press her lips together, take a breath. Just like she's done when she's been frustrated with Devon.

When Dom turns back around, she begins questioning the doctor about the other possibilities. The baby could have hit its head on the floor during the birth. The baby was found under two trash bags filled with garbage. Something within those bags, when tossed into the trash can, could have caused the bruise. Or the man who had discovered the baby, Mr. Bingham, could have done something unintentionally while lifting her out of the bag.

But Devon has lost track of the back-and-forth, the questions and answers.

She hears, instead, the doctor's words in her head: *Force is required for concussion . . . my best surmise is . . . blows to the head by the hand of the mother.*

Devon looks down at her own hands in her lap.

Her hands tremble. She tosses the clippers aside. They skitter across the linoleum, collide into the bathroom cabinet, spin once, and finally stop. Devon is breathing, hard and fast. The cord is cut. Sitting on the bathroom floor, a growing puddle of bloody fluids beneath her. She sees the cord dangling from her insides, the blood pulsing out of it—*whoosh, whoosh, whoosh*—matching her own heartbeat.

She pushes the length of cord back up into herself.

IT is there, too. Also between her legs, but on the floor. Pushing with ITS feet, jerking ITS knees into ITS chest, up and down like convulsions. Twisting ITS face, the squinched mouth rubbing at the floor like IT'S searching for something. And screaming.

Screaming, screaming. Like a siren, urgent.

The horrible cramping starts again, stabbing **pain** rolling across her gut. She bites down on her lip, hard. **Clutches** her stomach.

"STOP!" Devon drops her forehead to her bent **knee**s, sobs. "STOP IT! STOP IT! JUST STOP IT! *PLEASE!*"

Finally the pain fades. Devon lifts her face from her knees, panting. Swipes away the sweat that's dripped down her face. Looks around herself, at the frightening mess.

IT is still there on the floor, still screaming. Searching and squirming between her feet in its own bloody fluids. Devon reaches for the wrinkled, red thing. Her hands, two pieces of herself, grasp IT. Pull it up by where IT screams, **the** tiny face between her palms, small like a grapefruit. The legs **kicking**.

Devon pushes her hands together, ever so slightly. The small face, so fragile. So loud. She could squeeze it silent.

Instead she screams, "JUST SHUT UP!"

The mess—the blood and urine and other **liquids**, the smeared greenish black gunk, thick and sticky. **The smell**—the sweet, sickening smell. She can't leave the bathroom like this. Her mom will freak.

Devon looks up, sees the sink then. An idea forms in her mind. She holds IT around the chest and under the arms with both of her hands and scoots across the slick linoleum toward the bathroom counter.

Yes. A secure place to contain IT. She can place IT there, there in the sink's basin, while she quickly cleans things up.

She pulls herself up. Carefully lifts IT over the counter. Lowers IT down toward the basin.

But the intense cramps come again, rip across her abdomen. She cries out.

IT is slick; the slippery body slips from Devon's grasp. The body slides into the sink with a thud. The head, unsupported, snaps back. Slams into the faucet. Drops down, following the body, down into the sink.

Devon shrieks. Yanks the towels from the towel racks, the bath mat from the side of the tub, the hand towel. Throws them all on the floor to soak up the mess.

She limps out to the kitchen for a trash bag.

"Yes," the doctor is saying now, and Devon is suddenly pulled back, shaking, into the courtroom. She swallows. Sees her hands, tight fists, on her lap. "The baby may have hit the head on the floor during the birth. She may have also hit the other garbage. Yes, all of these things and others may have occurred. That is correct. But I do not believe this is what it is."

"All right, Ms. Barcellona," Judge Saynisch breaks in. "I've been very patient thus far, indulging you in this very lengthy examination. Your point is that the bruise and concussion may have been caused by some means other than blows to the head. Correct, Counsel?"

Devon reaches up to her forehead; it's damp with sweat.

"Yes, Your Honor," Devon hears Dom say. "There's a vast difference between alleging that someone had *purposefully* inflicted harm with malice aforethought and—"

"Yes, yes," the judge interrupts. "I get it. Let's move this along, Counsel."

Purposefully inflicted harm. Devon rubs at her forehead. Had she? Had she purposefully inflicted harm? *There's a vast difference between alleging that someone had* purposefully *inflicted harm and. . . .*

And . . . what? Allowing the harm through her own negligence? Her own stupid decision? Her fear?

The scene is still there, lingering in her mind. Between her hands, she'd held IT tightly. But then IT was gone, slipped from her grip. The neck limp, no strength there, can't hold the weight of the unsupported head. The head slams into the faucet, catching the rim of the sink on its way down. The sound, it echoes now in Devon's mind. The sound of something soft hitting something hard.

Devon's head had hit something hard once, too. That rainy day at practice when the dirt in front of the goal had turned to slick mud and she had dove through it.

"There haven't been any lasting effects from this alleged bump on the head," Devon hears Dom saying now. "Correct, Dr. More? In fact, the baby's doing fine."

Alleged bump on the head. Devon touches the spot where the back of her head hit the corner post. She can still remember the throb, the constant ache pulsing through her brain. It had lasted for days.

IT had felt that, too. That throb, the ache.

That small head. So tiny. Fragile.

"Yes," the doctor says, nodding. "That is correct. There are no lasting effects." The doctor smiles again. "I am very happy for this."

No lasting effects. Devon closes her eyes, lets her breath out. But, somehow, she feels little relief.

"Thank you," Dom says. "Your Honor, I have no further questions for the witness."

"Prosecution? Care to redirect?"

"No, Your Honor," the prosecutor says. "I'm good."

"Well, then, thank you for your testimony, Dr. More. You may step down."

Randomly, a line from a poem creeps into Devon's mind— *steadfast you hold/this slippery grip on life*. Where had she heard it?

Steadfast you hold/this slippery grip on life.

Devon remembers then—along Point Defiance that night, that walkway with the poetry. Holding Connor's hand. She'd thought of her mom then, thought of her slippery grip on life. And, in contrast, Devon's own tight one.

But . . . it wasn't tight enough, not That Night. She'd gripped a life in her hands then, a small life, and she'd just let it slip away. Didn't she? She'd done nothing to stop it.

"The state calls Dr. Rohit Katial."

This is the first person the prosecutor's called whose name Devon recognizes. She is still shaken from the last witness; she wishes Dom would ask for a short break.

Devon watches as the man steps up to the front, raises his right hand. When he settles into the witness stand, she notices him smooth down his tie. He turns his face then, and his eyes meet hers.

Devon feels a jolt, sucks in a hard breath. Her eyes drop to the tabletop before she can read what his say.

"Please state your name for the record."

"Rohit K. Katial."

"And what is your occupation?"

"I am a physician, a general practice physician."

"And where do you currently practice?"

The prosecutor spends a lot of time going over Dr. Katial's credentials—where he went to medical school, his professional affiliations, and where he had practiced medicine throughout his career. Then he works his way through a series of questions which, by its conclusion, draw out the story of Devon's appointment back on September twelfth.

"Do you recall the exam," the prosecutor says, "or are you relying soley on your records?"

"I do recall the exam, but I've also looked back at my records to refresh my recollection."

"And would you please tell the court what the typical sports physical exam entails?"

"These exams are essentially well-child examinations, which are biennial, occurring once every two years, generally. During these exams, I take a cursory overall look at the patient's health. In short, I work my way down the body from the head to the feet. I also rely on what the patient says about his or her own health."

"Do you routinely take blood or urine samples?"

"No, not routinely, unless the patient complains of specific symptoms that I'd like to further investigate, or during the course of the examination I hear or feel something out of the ordinary."

"So, during this particular appointment, did the respondent complain of having any symptoms?"

"Yes. Miss Davenport mentioned that she had been experiencing fatigue, which she attributed to her strenuous soccer practices. She also mentioned that she had been urinating more frequently than usual, approximately ten to twelve times each day. Specifically, she related her need to use the bathroom between classes several times throughout the school day. Also during the course of my examination, her mother, who was present in the exam room with her, stated that Miss Davenport had actually vomited that morning before coming to her appointment."

"Did the respondent concur with this statement that her mother made?"

"Yes. Miss Davenport believed she had vomited that morning because the night before she had eaten spoiled tuna salad. In addition, on the morning of the appointment, her temperature was slightly elevated to one hundred point three."

"Would you say, Dr. Katial, that the symptoms which the respondent exhibited are consistent with morning sickness, and more specifically, pregnancy?"

"Yes," Dr. Katial says, "but vomiting, fatigue, and the need to urinate are symptoms of a number of ailments, not unique to pregnancy specifically."

"At the time of the respondent's appointment, did you think pregnancy was a possibility?"

"A possibility, yes, but the patient had told me that she had started her menses—her menstrual cycle—that morning, and that she had been menstruating regularly, generally every month. Also, she stridently expressed to me that she was not sexually active. And then an additional factor that I took into consideration was the matter of her slight temperature, which could indicate an infection of some sort. Since Miss Davenport told me she had started menstruating that morning, the likelihood that she could be pregnant fell, in my mind, as less of a possibility than, say, a urinary tract infection or even juvenile diabetes."

"Did you believe the respondent when she told you that she had started her period that morning?"

"Yes. I had no reason to doubt her." Dr. Katial pauses. "I generally take my patients at their word."

Devon has kept her head down during the entire exchange. The doctor knows the end of the story now, knows why he's sitting in a witness stand answering a prosecutor's questions. He thinks that she'd lied to him.

Had she?

Devon thinks back to the morning of the appointment. *I kind of started my period today*, Devon had told her mom, *and my stomach's a little crampy from that.* Had she lied to her mom then? Because what she'd said hadn't been the truth. But was desperately hoping that something was true and then expressing that hope to someone else a *lie*? And then her mom had suggested that Devon wear a pad so the doctor would get the subtle hint that she was menstruating. Is giving a "hint" based on a hope a lie?

The doctor said he had no reason to doubt her, that he takes his patients at their word.

Devon wonders what he thinks about that practice now. Has she, Devon Davenport, made it harder for him to ever fully trust his patients again?

If she could, she'd tell him she's sorry. *I'm not having sex*, she'd yelled at him. And that statement hadn't been the whole truth, either. She didn't want to face it then, but that day she knew—buried in some deep place inside herself, but still there—that she was being dishonest. She wanted him to believe that she was still a virgin.

She wanted to believe it herself.

"To narrow down the possibilities," Dr. Katial is saying now, "the next step is to order tests. So I asked for a urine sample."

"And did the respondent give that sample to you?"

"No, she did not. Miss Davenport was unable to urinate during the appointment. She was slightly dehydrated, as she had vomited that morning, so I asked that she return a sample to my office within the next day or two. My nurse sent her home with a clean catch urine sample container and instructions on how to do it properly."

"Yes, but did the respondent return that urine sample to your office, Dr. Katial?"

"No, she never did."

Out of the corner of her eye, Devon watches the prosecutor pace in front of his table. After a moment he says, "Dr. Katial, did you have any reason to believe that the respondent was trying to deceive you?"

"I didn't at the time of the appointment, no. But knowing what I know now—"

Dom's up. "Objection!"

"I'll sustain that." Judge Saynisch turns to Dr. Katial. "Doc, you can only tell us what you've *experienced*. Not what you've learned later."

"I have no further questions, Your Honor," the prosecutor says.

Devon looks up. She watches Mr. Floyd return to his seat.

Judge Saynisch looks over at Dom. "Defense?"

Dom stands, but she doesn't move from behind the table. "Dr. Katial," she starts, "does the staff at the Urgent Care Center track whether or not its patients return specimen samples when a physician requests them?"

"Not generally, no. Hundreds of patients each week require blood work or other specimen samples, or even scheduling for follow-up appointments. To track each and every patient would necessitate several full-time personnel be dedicated to that specific task."

"So how then would you know whether or not a patient has returned a specimen sample?"

"Well, I, as a physician, see the lab results once they come in. I generally contact the patient only if the results are abnormal."

"In your experience, Dr. Katial, do all of your patients follow your advice and return specimen samples, such as urine, to your office?"

"No, not all. Most of my patients do want to get to the bottom of their medical issues, but, certainly, a small percentage are out there who just don't follow up, for whatever reason."

"Okay, Dr. Katial. Let's switch gears for a moment." Dom looks down at a notebook before her, then walks around to the front of the defense table. "Is it possible for a woman to menstruate during her pregnancy?"

"Not menstruation per se," Dr. Katial says. "It's what we call 'spotting'—basically a bloody discharge, often slightly darker in color than menstrual blood. Spotting can occur when the fertilized egg implants in the uterine wall, usually around the sixth week of pregnancy."

"Is it true, Dr. Katial, that approximately one in five women, roughly twenty to twenty-five percent, experience spotting during pregnancy?"

"I'm not familiar with the exact statistics as I'm sitting here. But, yes, that number sounds reasonable, based on my experience."

"And does spotting occur throughout the entire pregnancy?"

"Generally not. When spotting does occur, it's usually only during the first trimester."

"During the appointment on September twelfth, Devon would've been approximately five weeks pregnant, give or take. This would've been during the first trimester of her pregnancy, correct, Dr. Katial?"

"If Miss Davenport had been pregnant for approximately six weeks at the time of her appointment, then yes."

"So, as you're sitting here today, you can't say *definitively* whether Devon was or was not spotting at the time of her appointment on September twelfth, can you, Dr. Katial?"

"No, I cannot."

"And while you were examining Devon, did you notice if she was wearing any form of feminine protection, such as a sanitary napkin?"

"Yes, I did observe that she was wearing a sanitary napkin."

"So given the fact that Devon *told* you that she was menstruating and was actually wearing a sanitary napkin—and because you generally take your patients at their word—you would agree that it is likely that Devon was indeed experiencing spotting at the time. Spotting, which she could have misconstrued as menstruation. True, Dr. Katial?"

"Yes, it is possible."

"Thank you." Dom sits down. "I have no more questions for the doctor."

Judge Saynisch looks over at Mr. Floyd. "Redirect?"

"No, Your Honor," the prosecutor says. "Additionally, the state has no other evidence to present at this time."

"Then you may step down, Dr. Katial," Judge Saynisch says. "Thank you for your testimony."

Devon has no idea if the doctor glanced at her as he passed the defense table.

She's turned her face away.

AFTER

chapter twenty-one

"Defense?" The judge has his hands clasped under his chin. "Got anything for me?"

"Yes, Your Honor." Dom stands, reaches to the tabletop and opens the file folder before her. "I have documentary evidence, exhibits A through H, which I would like to present to the court."

"Present away, Ms. Barcellona."

"Yes, Your Honor. I have Exhibit A: Devon's Stadium High School transcript, which annotates her numerous honors classes and her weighted 4.15 grade point average. Exhibit B: a letter from Devon's guidance counselor at Stadium High School, a Ms. Rita Gonzales, detailing Devon's numerous extracurricular activities. Exhibit C: a letter from a Mr. Jeff Johnson, a parent of one of the youth soccer players with whom Devon conducts private goalkeeper training sessions. Exhibit D: a letter from a Miss Kaitlyn Bassett, a friend and teammate on both Devon's varsity high school and club soccer teams. Exhibit E: a letter from a Ms. Nadia Coughran, the teacher in Delta Pod here at Remann Hall. Exhibit F . . . "

All those people—her guidance counselor, Mr. Johnson— had taken the time to write nice and positive things about her?

Even after knowing everything that happened? After reading all those newspaper articles?

Even Kait? Devon thinks about the last letter Kait wrote, the one Kait had watched Devon crumple into a tight ball and toss in the trash. And still, even after being angry and hurt and drifting apart, she had written another.

Devon quickly switches her thoughts away from Kait to something else. She thinks about the time that's passed since she came to this place. Only one week and one day ago, Devon was sitting here in the courtroom for the first time. Eight subsequent nights spent lying on a rubberized mattress, staring up at the ceiling in her cinder block cell. Eight mornings waking to the bolt snapping to unlock her door. Eight showers standing naked and shivering under a low-water-pressure showerhead in the pod bathroom. Eight times pulling a black plastic comb through her wet hair afterward.

Eight days. Eight days for those other people, too. Eight days for them to hear about what she'd done. To think about it.

Her thoughts return, full circle, to Kait. Had the soccer team sat on the field before practice, discussing Devon while they strapped on their shin guards and tied up their cleats? Had they probed Kait with questions like, "So, did you know? Did she tell you anything?" And if they had asked such questions, how did it make Kait feel? Knowing that Devon, her supposed best friend, didn't trust her enough to tell her? How did it make Kait feel when she thought about what Devon did to . . . IT? Did she feel betrayed somehow? That Devon was someone very different from the person she'd always thought her to be? Did she feel like she must have *never* known Devon at all? Had she cried?

And the teachers, had they congregated in the teachers' lounge before classes started, sharing what they'd last heard, shaking their heads with disappointment and disbelief?

Had Ms. Gonzales covered her mouth with her hand when she'd first heard the story?

Did Mr. Johnson take his little daughter, Haley, aside—have her sit down—and explain to her why Devon probably won't be training with her anymore?

"Your Honor," Dom is saying now, "I have copies of each exhibit that I'd like to submit into evidence. May I approach the bench?"

Judge Saynisch shifts his gaze to the prosecutor. "Any objections, Mr. Floyd?"

"No, Your Honor," Mr. Floyd says. "The defense has previously furnished the state with copies. We have reviewed them and have no objection."

"Then by all means," the judge says, "bring 'em on."

Dom walks up to one of the women sitting behind her computer at the base of the bench, hands the stack of papers to her. The woman places little stickers on each exhibit, so that Dom is already back in her seat before the woman has even passed them up to the judge. He puts the letters aside, then looks back down at Dom expectantly.

"Your Honor," Dom says, "we also have five witnesses we'd like to call."

"Well." Judge Saynisch glances at his watch. "Before we launch into that, let's take a recess for lunch. My stomach is getting cantankerous. How does an hour sound? Any objections, Counsel?"

"No, Your Honor," Mr. Floyd says. "That's fine with me. My stomach's getting cantankerous as well."

Judge Saynisch shakes his head at that comment, then looks over at Dom. "Defense?"

"No, Your Honor."

"Then let's do it. We'll recommence at one P.M." The judge pounds his gavel and stands.

"All rise!"

Dom shuts the door to the conference room. Leans against it. "So, Devon, what do you think? Not too bad, right?"

Devon selects the folding chair with its back to the door, sits down. "It's not too much *fun*."

Dom shakes her head, moves to take the chair opposite Devon. "Stating the obvious." She drops her briefcase on the table-top and sits down. "What I'm asking is how do you think we're doing in there?"

Devon reaches up to feel her French braids. Still tight. "I have no idea, Dom."

It's actually a lot like playing soccer, Devon thinks. Passing the ball around the field, making runs, trying crosses—all to feel out the opponent's weaknesses. When you find an opening, you shoot. And if you're lucky, the ball drops between the crossbars. But in a close game, like today in court, there's that underlying tension of not knowing which team will be the winner in the end. Not until the ref blows the final whistle and the clock stops.

"Well, I think we've got in some good hits," Dom is saying. "The prosecution is trying to show that you knew exactly what you were doing—that you had a plan and then executed it. We're throwing doubt on every point they make, and I think we've managed to do that pretty effectively." Dom sighs. "But, ultimately, it doesn't matter what I think. What matters is what the *judge* thinks."

"Well, what you did to that detective, Dom. That was really good."

"Yeah." Dom smiles, nodding like she's relishing the memory. "It was, wasn't it?"

"Plus, I think the judge kind of likes you."

Dom frowns. "Meaning?"

"Oh, not in *that* way, Dom! I meant in the 'you're a good lawyer' kind of 'like.' In the 'he thinks that you totally know what you're doing' kind of way."

"Yeah?"

"Well, way more than that Floyd guy anyway. He's a complete dork most of the time."

Dom laughs. An almost giddy laugh. "Oh, yeah. You gotta love it when the opposition comes across like a dork."

A quick rap on the conference room door.

Dom shifts her eyes toward the door, at the small rectangular window there. Her expression changes. Her smile fades, her mouth forming a little O.

Devon turns her head, following Dom's gaze.

Through the rectangular window, Devon sees a familiar face crowding there. Grinning and waving.

Her mom. Devon feels her stomach drop.

Dom gives Devon a pointed look, then moves for the door. Opens it narrowly and leans out. Devon waits while Dom speaks briefly to her mom outside.

Dom softly closes the door. When she turns back around, her body's blocking Devon's view of the window. "Your mom brought lunch," Dom says. "Sandwiches from Subway."

Devon looks down at her hands. "Why?"

"She said she thought it would save us time. She was afraid we might not get a chance to eat." Dom lowers her voice to a whisper then. "And she wants to talk to you, Devon."

Devon looks up at Dom. "Now?"

"You don't have to," Dom says quickly. "I can have her go away. I'll just tell her that we are in the middle of something, which we are." She watches for Devon's reaction. "It may not be the best timing."

Devon thinks about her mom on the other side of the door, waiting for the answer. Her ear probably pressed tight against the door. Her face eager and hopeful, holding in her breath.

Devon needed her mom days ago, needed to know that her mom didn't . . . didn't what? Reject her? *Hate* her? And now? So much has happened without her. It's almost too late now.

She thinks about the awkwardness of having to sit here, the two of them finally meeting each other's eyes. Because hadn't they both wronged each other in their own way? Her mom had deserted Devon when she'd needed her most. But Devon might have done something even worse. She'd taken her mom's hopes and destroyed them. The last time she'd seen her mom, those hopes were still intact. Her mom will now be the very first person from her old life to see Devon face-to-face since that day when the image of who Devon Used To Be was irreconcilably shattered. Leaving only a splinter, a glass thorn. And sharp pain.

You didn't even give your mom the chance, Dom had said to Devon Saturday morning. *You robbed her of an opportunity to finally make a good decision for you!*

Now another opportunity presents itself. Devon can choose to push her mom away again, or allow her mom a small opening to take a step closer.

Devon takes in a breath, lets it out. This is something she must do. "No. It's okay, Dom. I'll . . . I'll see her."

"You sure? Look, I *don't* want you upset, Devon. I don't want you to lose focus." Dom sounds irritated. "You can't be all freaked out when we go back in there. Understand?" She pauses. "Actually, I don't think it's a good idea. No, you can wait to see her until after the hearing. I'll just tell her—"

"No," Devon says firmly. "I'll be fine." She looks down at her hands, softens her tone. "I think I *need* to do this. Now, Dom. Not later."

Dom shakes her head, reluctantly says, "Okay." Then she turns around, pulls the door wide.

Devon's mom steps through. A streak of color—bright sundress, golden blonde hair freshly colored. Bright red lipstick.

"Hey, Dev!" A quick and jerky smile rolls over Devon's mom's lips. "I brought some turkey subs. Provolone, extra onions and pickles and tomatoes and sweet peppers with mustard—not mayo—on honey wheat. Your favorite." She stands beside Dom awkwardly, clutches the white plastic bag tightly in her hands. "I thought that maybe you've missed them, being here. . . ." Her voice trails off.

"Well!" Dom's voice is a little too loud for the small room. She checks her watch. "I really need to hit the little girls' room, and then I've *got* to look over some notes before going back into court." She nods at Devon. "I'll just be outside. All right? The conference room next door is free. So, if you need me for *any* reason"—Dom pauses, giving Devon a significant look—"that's where you can find me. But in about twenty minutes or so, Devon, you and I will need some time alone together. Just to get on the same page again before we head back into the courtroom."

"Yes, of course." Devon's mom holds the bag out to Dom. "Oh, and I've brought a sandwich for you, too."

"Oh, no." Dom holds up a hand. "But thanks." She smiles. "Too keyed up to eat. I'll just grab some caffeine, and that should hold me." Dom grabs her briefcase from off the table and glances back at Devon once more before walking out the door, carefully closing it behind her.

Devon watches her mom from where she sits on the folding chair, and her mom watches Devon from the doorway. Neither says anything for a long moment.

Finally, her mom opens her mouth. Her voice squeaks out, "Devon!" Immediately, her eyes turn soupy. She tosses the bag of sandwiches onto the table, collapsing on the metal folding chair opposite Devon. She hides her face in her hands. "I'm sorry," she sobs. "I told myself that I wouldn't do this, be a baby like this." She looks up at the ceiling, waves a hand in front of her face, as if the small breeze she's made will dry away the tears. Presses her lips together to stop their trembling.

Devon turns her face away. Looks down at the floor, feels her throat tighten. She, Devon Davenport, has caused this. "It's okay, Mom," Devon whispers.

"Oh, yeah." Her mom laughs ruefully, then sniffs—a thick, soggy sound. "Devon, I'm sorry that I didn't come . . . before this. I just . . . couldn't. Isn't that just so *horrible?*" Her voice squeaks again, and Devon can hear her mom's losing battle against her tears. "Making you . . . go . . . through this . . . *all alone?*"

Devon feels herself start to detach now. Feels a coldness

creep in, freezing solid any feeling inside herself. Her mom, her emotions. Too much.

No, don't do this. Devon tries to push the coldness away. Seldom has anything positive ever come from detaching herself. Devon looks up.

Her mom has a hand pressed over her heart, pushing against it like she's having a hard time swallowing something. Her eyes are pleading. "I just . . . couldn't. You know? I'm not good at dealing with stuff."

Devon's eyes drop down to her mom's hand. Her nails, Devon notices, are still long, still red. No chips. The shade is perfectly matched to the color running through the pattern of her sundress. Steady hands had brushed on that polish, Devon thinks, smooth red strokes. She resents those nails, those steady hands that brushed that polish.

Those same steady hands could have pushed the buttons on her cell to make a simple phone call. They could have grasped a pen and scrawled a note.

"I was just so afraid . . . to have to talk to someone . . . especially the cops . . . about . . . you know? All those questions . . ."

Her mom's mascara is smudged. Her eyes are rimmed, red where her black eyeliner should be. Devon clears her throat, changes the subject. "So, I heard you aren't living at the apartment anymore?"

Her mom looks confused for a moment. Then, "Oh, no. How could I? Devon, the mess . . . that you . . . they put police tape across our door, you know. . . . " She clamps her mouth shut, delicately dabbing at her eyes with her fingertips. "I took a couple days for myself. I just needed to think. You know? Get away and think. Tiffany—she's been such a good friend through all this—

came by and packed up our stuff. . . . It's all in a storage unit on Sprague Avenue. I just had to get away. . . ."

A picture forms in Devon's mind. Her cleats, her gloves, her jerseys, her trophies—all dumped into a cardboard box and taped shut. Her jeans and sweatshirts and shoes, stuffed animals and CDs, posters removed from the walls and rolled, books pulled from the shelves—all crammed into trash bags and boxes. It's not a particularly difficult picture for her to imagine. She's witnessed similar scenes with her own eyes, after her mom's numerous breakups or landlord evictions. Once, a very young Devon had watched her mom pack everything they owned into brown paper bags because she didn't have suitcases, while the ex-boyfriend at the time loaded everything into the bed of his white pickup. Devon had sat in the cab of the truck between the two silent adults, looking back at their belongings through the small sliding window until the truck finally stopped in front of their new place.

"Well." Devon swallows. "Where did you go?"

Her mom shrugs. "Oh, just away. It's not important, really." She twirls a strand of hair around her finger.

"Mom! Tell me where you went! It is important." She feels her throat tighten again. "To *me*."

Her mom pulls a napkin out of the white plastic bag that's still holding the sandwiches. Blows her nose. Folds the napkin in fourths. "I went to see my mother," she finally says. "In Spokane."

"You *did*?"

"You know, it's been almost seventeen years?" Her mom shakes her head. "Time just . . . goes." She gets a distant look in her eyes. "Things really haven't changed there. So weird."

When her mom speaks again, it's much softer. So soft that Devon has to lean forward to hear her. "And then I went to see the . . . baby." She sniffs. "*Your* baby, Devon."

Devon feels a jolt. Did she hear that right? Panic surges inside her. *Why?*

Her mom must have seen the change cross Devon's face because she starts blathering. "But I . . . she wasn't there, Devon. She wasn't at the hospital anymore. They said she'd already been placed in foster care with a wonderful family. So many people wanted to take her, you know, and . . . uh, and they—the nurses, I mean—said that I wouldn't have been allowed to see the baby anyway, even if she was still there. I . . . I didn't tell them who I was or anything. I didn't leave my name. I didn't want them to know."

Why would she do that? Then, *Why would she try to see IT and . . . not come to see me?*

Suddenly, her mom snatches Devon's hand. Devon flinches. Tries to pull away, but her mom's grip is too strong.

"Why?" she wails. "Why couldn't you tell me, Devon? I'm your *mother*! Why couldn't you just tell me?"

Devon shakes her head. "Mom, stop." She feels a tear form in the corner of her eye. *Can't you see?* she wants to say. *I couldn't even tell myself.*

Her mom makes a tortured groan, a frightening sound. She drops Devon's hand then, like it's burned her, and pulls it back toward herself, rubbing it with the other.

"Am I that huge of a failure? Huh? Did I screw up *that bad*?"

Devon shakes her head again. She feels the one tear slide down her face, from the corner of her eye down to her chin. "Please, Mom. Don't. . . ."

"I mean, I was *there*. You know? I was right there, Devon! I've been pregnant and scared; don't you think I know all about that? Don't you think I know how trapped you felt? How afraid?" She pounds the table with her fist. "*Me*, Devon! Me, of all people, would know. Why couldn't you trust me?"

Devon watches all of this drama unfolding in front of her, the huge dramatic production that is her mom. It always ends the same way for Devon, the clash of conflicted emotions—feelings of guilt and annoyance, anger and sadness. Helplessness.

Devon wants to shake her mom, wants to scream: *Don't you get it, Mom? For once in your life? This isn't about you!*

An image forms in Devon's mind then—a pretty blonde girl, the girl her mom had once been, sitting in some dark room, alone. Her arms around her waist, hugging herself. A small bulge under her sweatshirt.

The realization smacks Devon hard. She sucks in her breath.

The small bulge was *her*.

That small bulge was Devon.

Devon watches as her mom takes in a wobbly breath, wipes her nose with the back of her hand. "I mean, we have a good relationship. Don't we, Devon?"

Devon lets her breath out slowly.

"We talk about things. Right? Important things?"

Devon presses her lips together.

"Please tell me that we talk about important things, Devon. *Please*."

Devon closes her eyes. She wipes away her one tear. "You asked why couldn't I tell you," Devon finally whispers. "I don't know the answer, Mom. I just don't know." She opens her eyes, looks at her mom. Devon can feel her lips quiver now. "It wasn't really you." She swallows. "It was . . . *me*."

"Oh, Devon." Her mom sounds defeated. "What could I have done differently? Huh? I keep asking myself that. Over and over and over." She rubs at her forehead. "Sitting in the courtroom all morning, listening to everything. And your attorney, that Barcellona woman, pointing out that I . . . because I let that detective into our apartment—" She starts crying again. "You don't know how hard this is for me. Because it's my fault that you're—"

She obviously hadn't heard anything that Devon said. "Mom, it's *not* your—"

"No, it is!" Devon's mom shouts. "Your attorney is right. Because you wouldn't even *be* here if it wasn't for me!"

The door opens.

Both Devon and her mom turn toward it.

Dom is standing in the doorway. She quickly surveys the scene before her.

"I knocked," Dom says. "I guess you didn't hear it." She looks closely at Devon, then at Devon's mom, and back again to Devon. "I'm very sorry to interrupt, but it's almost time to return to the courtroom. And we really have to—"

"Yes." Devon's mom quickly stands. "Yes, of course." She rummages through the Subway bag for another napkin. Blows her nose. "See you soon, hon." She tries a smile at Devon. "And eat your sandwich."

When she's gone, Dom takes the seat across from Devon. "Everything okay? Things looked pretty intense."

"Yeah," Devon says. "They kind of were."

"Yeah." Dom rests her chin on her hand, doodles on the

tabletop with a fingertip. "Well, I don't think I'm going to call your mom to testify today, after all." She pauses. "Not after what I just saw in here. I can't have her up there crying and saying unpredictable things. This hearing is too important. We can't risk it, Devon. I'm sorry."

Devon shrugs, studies the tabletop.

What could I have done differently? her mom had asked.

Could her mom have done something differently? Was she capable of being a different sort of person? A sort of person who Devon could talk to about important things, about scary things? Grown-up things, even? A person who Devon could depend upon?

But, more important, what about her? What about Devon? Could she have done something—anything—differently?

"You do understand," Dom is saying. "Don't you?"

Knowing about herself then what she knows now, would she have done anything differently?

"Devon?"

Would she?

"I hope so," Devon says. She looks up, then. Whispers, "Yes."

chapter twenty-two

"The defense calls Ms. Henrietta Apodaca."

Devon watches as Henrietta marches up to the front and raises her right hand, just like all the other witnesses have done today. She nods her head solemnly as she answers Judge Saynisch's query: Do you swear to tell the truth, the whole truth, and nothing but the truth, so help you God?

"Please state your name for the record," Dom says when Henrietta is seated on the witness stand.

"Henrietta Fernanda Apodaca."

"And, Ms. Apodaca, please state your current occupation."

Devon listens as Henrietta tells the courtroom in her crusty lilting tone all about her role as a detention officer at the Remann Hall Juvenile Detention Facility. That she's been working on the security side there for twelve years. That she's been with Unit D, currently the only female unit out of a total of eight, for just over a year. That she mainly works the night shift, but this past week, she's also worked days. "I sometimes do doubles—okay?—to help pay the bills," she says.

"Devon has been a resident at Remann Hall for the past eight days, Ms. Apodaca," Dom says. "During this relatively short time, have you had the opportunity to observe her?"

"Yes, I have. Okay?"

"And what has been your impression of her? Her behavior, her interaction with the other residents?"

"Well, first I want to say"—Henrietta shifts in her seat so that she can maintain direct eye contact with the judge—"that I was asked by that defense attorney over there"—she jerks her head in Dom's direction—"to write a letter for this hearing, but I refused. And I'll tell you why, okay? I insisted on coming in here to speak to you in person, okay? I requested it. So, know that this is a voluntary thing with me, okay?"

Henrietta *requested* to come to court and speak? Rather than write a letter? Why?

Henrietta turns back to Dom. "The second thing I want to say is that Devon is a girl who I think should stay in the juvenile system. I've been around here a long time, and I've seen a lot of different kids come in and out of this place, okay? Some in more than out."

Devon thinks of Karma then. She's one of those "in more than out" kids. And not just at Remann Hall, but other places, too. Private inpatient facilities, counseling centers, rich kid re-hab ranches, boot camps. Jenevra had cornered Devon on Saturday night when Devon was crossing the common area, coming back from her shower, and told her everything she knew. That Karma's dad got sick of spending so much money and nothing ever working. So, one day, he just decided to cut Karma off financially, and Karma's been either on the street or in detention since. Devon wonders if Karma's dad will just give up on her altogether someday. Devon hopes that he won't. Her thoughts shift then to the other people who Dom asked to appear today. Soon Devon must watch them take the witness stand. Must look into their faces and hear their voices. Devon takes a breath, lets it out slowly. She hopes that they haven't given up on her, either.

"Thank you, Ms. Apodaca," Dom says. "But could you speak specifically about Devon's behavior since she's arrived at Remann Hall?"

"Well, she has only been here just over a week, okay? And already the staff decided to bump her up to Honor status. In fact, they decided that this morning, okay? In all my time working here, I can't remember any resident who has been able to do that, okay?"

As she speaks, Devon notices that Henrietta does her head-bob nod around the courtroom, as if she's sitting there inspecting the cleanliness of everyone present, and whether they have properly aligned their pencils beside their pads of paper.

"Devon is a special sort of young lady, okay?" Henrietta says.

Someone actually thinks that she's special? Even after everything that's happened? Henrietta is a staff here. She must know, at least some of the details. And still?

Devon feels her eyes burning. Somewhere inside herself, maybe it's inside her heart, she feels a tiny drop of hope take hold.

"Has Devon had any visitors since arriving at Remann Hall?" Dom asks.

"None other than you, her attorney."

"No family members, Ms. Apodaca?"

"No. None."

Family members. No, it's family *member*, singular. Devon's one and only, her mom.

Devon thinks about what her mom had just told her in the conference room, that when she took off, she'd gone back to Spokane to see her own mother, Devon's grandmother. Devon wonders how that scene went down. Did she just walk up the steps to the house where she grew up and knock? Or did she call first? Agree to meet at a neutral place, like the nearest IHOP? When they first saw each other, was the conversation stilted? Or did they just hug each other and cry?

And that visit to Spokane and whatever happened there, is that what had prompted her mom to try to see IT? The . . . baby? Did she feel guilty, was that what inspired her? Because her own mother in Spokane never got the chance to see *her* baby? Never got to see Devon?

Then in Devon's mind, the dots connect.

You wouldn't even be *here if it wasn't for me!*

Her mom had screamed that fact in the conference room. Dom had entered then, disrupting the trajectory, and Devon hadn't had the chance to fully digest it.

Her mom had meant to lift some of Devon's culpability, that's why she'd said it.

You wouldn't even be *here if it wasn't for me!*

Devon wouldn't *be* here. In a rush, she grasps the significance.

Her mom intended to take some of the blame, but what she'd done instead was add to it.

Not "here" as in the courtroom, but *here.* Period.

Devon covers her mouth with her hand. Bites down. If she doesn't, she might scream.

Dom is still up there, questioning Henrietta. They're discussing the self-paced program the staff would like to implement for Devon, so she won't fall behind in her academics.

Dom wouldn't be happy, seeing Devon like this. She'd expect her to stay composed.

Devon tries to shove the distracting thoughts away, but they stubbornly remain.

For so long, Devon realizes, she had lived trying not to be her mom. Anytime she would recognize some "Mom" trait in her own life, Devon would immediately squelch it. But as immature and insecure, as man-crazy and self-centered as her mom could be, she had at least kept Devon. She'd run away from Spokane and the life she knew, but at least she'd changed Devon's diapers, had fed her bottles. Zipped her into pajamas at night, woke in the wee hours when Devon had cried and maybe even tried to comfort her, sing her back to sleep. Her mom would have had to, or Devon would never have survived.

Her mom had left Devon sometimes, frightened and alone in the apartment, while she'd partied or hooked up with some loser guy. But her mom hadn't scooped Devon into a trash bag and dumped her in a container full of garbage. She hadn't wished that Devon was dead.

Is that what Devon had wanted? For the baby that came out of her to die?

The picture comes back—the round little face, blood sprinkled. The opened mouth, screaming. The flailing arms and legs. The billowing black trash bag.

Oh, God. Is Mr. Floyd right about That Night?

Devon turns around, looks behind her at the gallery. Scans the row of people. Finally, she finds her, there on the end near the exit to the courtroom. She's examining the nails of her left hand. With the other, she's twirling a strand of blonde hair.

Her mom. She should've told her, Devon knows this now. Her mom is imperfect and mostly ridiculous and totally self-absorbed, but she's the only mom Devon has. Dom was so right;

Devon never once gave her mom the chance to step up, to finally be the sort of person she always should've been.

When Devon turns back around, Dom's walking back to their table. An expression of concern crosses Dom's face, an eyebrow raised in question.

Devon quickly pulls her hand from her mouth, shakily places it in her lap. How could she have blown it so badly?

Dom whispers, "What's wrong?" as she slips into her chair.

Devon shakes her head. "Nothing."

"Okay," Dom whispers back. "Stay focused. I'm counting on you."

Mr. Floyd is telling the judge that he has no questions for the witness.

Devon pulls her yellow legal pad toward herself. Writes, *Just thinking about my mom.* Slides it over to Dom. Waits while she reads it.

Think about your mom later, is Dom's response.

"The defense calls Mr. Mark Dougherty."

Devon stares down at the tabletop while her coach moves to the front of the courtroom and raises his right hand. Sweat pricks down her spine, under her arms. She can feel his eyes on her, that sensation of being watched. She can't raise her eyes though, can't muster up the courage to look at him.

When *was* the last time that she'd seen him? She closes her eyes, thinks back.

It was a day shortly after the opening weekend of State Cup, Devon remembers. Her team had lost one of the three games in pool play and so probably wouldn't make it to the quarter finals, a huge disappointment, considering they'd played in the finals just last year, losing only 0–1. The goal scored against Devon had been a fluke, hitting her net in the last minutes of the game.

Coach Mark had spotted Devon as she was standing outside her lit class before fourth period. She'd ducked into the classroom, hoping to avoid him, but he'd followed her into the classroom anyway.

"Hey, Dev!" He slapped her on the back, winked. "You haven't been hiding from me, have you?" He was smiling, but his eyes held a mix of worry and hurt.

Devon squinted up at him, laughed one of those fake, nervous laughs. "Of course not, Coach!" She'd kept her eyes locked on his eyebrows so she wouldn't have to meet his eyes. "No, I've just been really busy. You know, getting ready to come back and everything."

"Kait mentioned she saw you running over the weekend. Down on Ruston Way."

"Yeah, I've been running a lot. . . ."

"And the physical therapy? Still going okay?"

Devon had felt a small twinge then. There was no physical therapy. "Sure. Great." Then she added quickly, "I'm . . . I mean, *they're* thinking that maybe I'll be able to come back and practice soon. Maybe even next week. Limited at first, but still . . ."

"Great! *Great* news, Dev." Coach Mark paused, and his face turned serious for a flash. "Really missed you at State Cup. I'm sure you've heard—"

"Yeah, I'm really sorry, Coach. I—"

He put up his hand, stopping her. "Don't worry. State Cup's not the end of the world. There'll be other years, lots of them. We don't want you back until you're one hundred percent." Then his face brightened. "Hey, why don't you just come by and watch practice this week? Maybe end your run at the field. I've been working on some new drills; you can tell me what you think. Sound good?"

"Okay." Devon smiled big, locking it in place. "Yeah, I'll do that, Coach. Definitely."

"Okay, then." He'd winked at her again, gave her a thumbs-up. "I'll be looking for you."

"Okay, Coach."

Devon watched him round the classroom door just as the bell rang. When he was gone, Devon's smile fell. Taking her seat in class, she realized that her face actually hurt. As if the muscles in her cheeks and around her eyes weren't strong enough any-more to hold something as heavy as a smile.

She knew she wouldn't be jogging by practice, not that week. Not ever.

Dom is talking now, asking Coach Mark where he works. Devon opens her eyes.

"I'm a history teacher at Stadium High School," he says. "Here in Tacoma."

"And in what capacity do you know Devon Davenport?"

Coach Mark clears his throat. "I'm her soccer coach. At Stadium High School each fall, I coach the varsity girls' soccer team, where she's played as my starting goalkeeper for two seasons. I also happen to be Devon's club soccer coach at the Washington Premier Football Club, which pretty much runs all through the rest of the year with a few weeks off here and there in the winter and summer. I've been her club coach ever since she started competitive soccer at age eleven, in fact, so that'll make it"—he pauses to think—"a total of five years that I've known her now."

"So, Mr. Dougherty, after coaching Devon over those five years, could you please describe to the court what kind of person you have known her to be?"

Devon knows that Dom wouldn't have asked him to speak today if he was going to say something negative. But still, she can't help but feel tense listening. She bites her lower lip, holds her breath.

"Devon's a great kid," Coach Mark says. "She really is. The kind of kid that would do anything that you ask her to do; she's what I call a 'go to' player. She's reliable, always shows up for practices on time. Even on the varsity team where she's one of the youngest players, she takes a leadership role. She does extra practices, often with the boys her age, and the other players see this. So, she's a great role model in that area. Unmatched work ethic. And that crosses over to her academics as well. She's a top student in honors classes, from what I understand. Just an overall fantastic kid."

Devon feels that swelling in her throat again, that awful ache. He doesn't really mean all those things. How can he? Not after what he knows about her now.

"And what do you think of her potential as a soccer player?"

"Unlimited. And I don't say that about many of my players. If she had continued on the curve she was on, there's no question that she'd be playing soccer on a college scholarship at a D One—excuse me, a *Division* One—school someday."

"According to your observations over the past five years, do you believe that Devon has had a lot of support at home for her sport?"

"If you mean by 'support,' were Devon's soccer fees paid on time? Yes, they were, generally. Did she show up with the correct equipment—cleats, goalie gloves, uniforms? Always. But if you're talking emotional support, from my perspective, Devon's mother wasn't much involved in Devon's soccer career. And let me say that it's understandable, given her work schedule. From what I've gleaned about Devon's home life, her dad's completely out of the picture. And Devon's mom, trying to make ends meet as a single parent, keeps two jobs. I imagine her mom's stretched pretty thin most of the time."

"Did Devon's mother often attend the games?"

"No, not much. She came pretty regularly when Devon was younger, but her attendance really dropped off as Devon entered middle school. I mean, to the point that I started checking the sidelines while the game was going on to see if she was out there."

"And why did you do that, Mr. Dougherty?"

"You know, I feel sorry for my players whose parents run their lives—micromanaging their kids' soccer careers or living vicariously through their successes or failures. But I also felt sorry for Devon, who was on the opposite side of the spectrum. Nobody seemed to be a part of her life, nobody seemed to *care*, at least about her soccer, and yet she pushed herself so hard. Was so hard on *herself*. Was so driven. And I couldn't see the source of it. It must have been coming from somewhere inside, from a need to prove something to herself."

"You say that Devon is very hard on herself. What is it like being her coach? Does she take constructive criticism well, for instance?"

"Yes, she does. She's very coachable. Whenever I point out

mistakes any of my players make, I also give them ideas of how they can fix them or do things differently. Devon's the kind of player who, when a similar situation pops up again, she'll make the correction. It's almost like she's looking for the opportunity to put the advice into practice."

"Okay, but when you said Devon's 'hard on herself,' what did you mean, exactly?"

"She hates to make mistakes. She doesn't cut herself any slack. Absolutely none."

"And how does she demonstrate this lack of 'cutting herself slack'?"

Coach Mark doesn't say anything for a moment. Then, "She gets very quiet. Very broody. During a game, if she gives up a goal, for example, because she made what she'd perceived as a mistake in judgment or timing, she doesn't seem to allow it to affect her play while the game's on. It just sort of rolls off of her. But afterward, when the game's over, she'll go off by herself. And you get the impression that she doesn't want to be disturbed, that you should just leave her alone for a while."

"Thank you, Mr. Dougherty." Dom steps back to her seat. "I have no further questions."

Mr. Floyd leaps to his feet.

"I take it, Mr. Floyd," Judge Saynisch says, "that the State wants to examine this witness?"

"Yes, Your Honor."

"Then proceed."

"Mr. Dougherty," the prosecutor starts, "you've spoken very admiringly about the respondent—what leadership she's dem-onstrated, what a team player she is. How driven. How smart. How reliable. You've praised her work ethic, but have said nothing of her *ethics.* Her trustworthiness. Her proclivity to tell the truth. Do you have an opinion to offer on that issue?"

"Yes," Coach Mark says. "I've never known Devon to be untrustworthy."

"Oh?" The prosecutor paces in front of the witness stand. "So you feel that someone who has deceitfully hidden her pregnancy from everyone around her, has conceived a plot to murder—"

"Objection! Your Honor—"

"No, Ms. Barcellona," the judge says, "I'd like to hear Mr. Dougherty's response."

Coach Mark rubs the back of his neck. "I don't believe that's been proven yet."

"Fair enough. Then let's go back for a moment to January of this year, Mr. Dougherty. Did the respondent injure herself during a practice session?"

"Yes, she hit her head on the goalpost and injured her shoulder."

"And, subsequently, did the respondent tell you that she had visited a doctor who had diagnosed these injuries and outlined a treatment plan?"

"Yes, she did."

"What did the respondent tell you that diagnosis was?"

"A concussion and a subluxed shoulder."

"And what did the respondent tell you about the treatment for these injuries?"

Coach Mark takes in a breath. "Because of the concussion, Devon told me that she wouldn't be able to practice for at least four weeks. And she'd need to visit a physical therapist three times a week, I think it was, for about six weeks for her shoulder."

"Did the respondent bring you a note from her doctor? A written excuse of some sort?"

"No, but I've been around soccer long enough to know that concussions aren't anything to mess around with. What Devon told me sounded exactly right."

"What would you say, Mr. Dougherty, if I told you that the respondent's medical files contain no record of a doctor's diagnosis for any injuries during that time period? That there exists no referral for a physical therapist?"

"Then I would say that perhaps Devon's medical files are incomplete."

"Let me get this straight, Mr. Dougherty. You mean to tell me that you believe these records were somehow misplaced? Or not included?"

"Not at all." Coach Mark sits forward in his seat. "What I'm saying is this—in the five years that I've coached Devon, I have *never* known her to skip practice without a valid reason. In fact, I can't think of a time that she's missed training for *any* reason. She has come to my practices coughing and sneezing. She's jammed her fingers so badly that she was unable to practice in the goal, but she'd come anyway to work out with the field players or just shag balls, if that's all she could do. I don't need a doctor's excuse, and I don't need medical records. If Devon said she had to miss practice for a couple of weeks, then I believe she had a good reason for it. No matter what explanation she actually gave me."

"If the respondent had told you that she was pregnant, you would've helped her out. Correct, Mr. Dougherty?"

"Man." Coach Mark sits back in his seat. He shakes his head slightly. "If Devon had trusted me enough to confide that fact to me," he says softly, "yes. I would've done anything and every-thing I could think of to help her."

Devon looks up at him. Their eyes meet.

Devon sees so much hurt there, so much regret.

Still holding Devon's eyes, Coach Mark says, "I would've told her that I was one hundred percent there for her. She wouldn't have had to try to fix her problem alone."

Devon feels chills shoot up her spine. She drops her eyes to her lap.

"But she didn't give you that opportunity. Did she, Mr. Dougherty?"

Coach Mark sighs sadly. "No," he says, barely audible. "No, she did not."

"I have no further questions."

After Coach Mark leaves the courtroom, Dom leans over, places her hand on top of Devon's, whispers in her ear. "You doing okay?"

Devon shrugs. She squeezes her eyes shut.

"We can ask for a short break if you need it."

"No, I'll be okay."

Dom pats Devon's hand, then stands. "Your Honor, the De-fense calls Ms. Deborah Evans."

The woman steps up to the front, raises her right hand. When she's seated in the witness stand, she catches Devon's eye. Gives her a small smile.

Devon bites her lip. She can't return the smile.

Dom begins her battery of questions. In response, Debbie tells her that her full name is Deborah Lynn Evans. That she's worked for more than ten years as the copresident and escrow manager at the Puget Sound Title Company in University Place. And that she knows Devon because Devon had babysat for her family on and off over the past two years. "But last summer," she says "from the middle of June up until the middle of August, Devon babysat full-time during the day while I was at work. Every day from about eight A.M. until around five P.M."

Dom nods. "And how many children do you have, Ms. Evans?"

"Two. A set of fraternal twins, a boy and a girl. Their names are Dayton and Danica."

"And how old were the twins during the time that Devon was watching them?"

"They were three years old. Just turned three in April."

Dom paces in front of the witness stand. "Toddler twins. Wow. That's a huge job, Ms. Evans. And you believed that Devon, at age fifteen, could handle this sort of responsibility?"

"Of course." Debbie frowns. "I would never have hired Devon otherwise. The previous summer, I had hired a college student attending the University of Puget Sound to be our nanny. Let me just put it this way—without going into detail—Devon exhibited much more common sense and maturity, let alone fortitude under stress, at age fifteen than that other girl did at age twenty." Debbie smiles then. "Plus, the twins absolutely love her."

"Ms. Evans, you say the twins 'absolutely love her.' Based on your observations of Devon with your children, how did she treat them?"

"She was just a lot of fun. She played games with them, whatever they wanted to play. She read books to them, put them in their double stroller and pushed them to the library for story hour or just to hang out there. She took them to the pool—we're members of the Tacoma Swim Club, only a few blocks from our house. Fed them lunch. I'd come home after work, and on the refrigerator or the kitchen table, there'd be art projects they did together. Devon was just wonderful with them."

"Did Devon ever harm them in any way?"

"No, never."

"Did she ever lose her patience and yell at them or even hit them?"

"No."

"Did you ever notice any evidence of neglect? Such as her failing to change their diapers or feed them? Such as leaving them in front of the TV for long periods of time? Or leaving them inside their beds or room unsupervised?"

"No. She actually helped potty train the twins, since she was with them so much during the day, and that takes a lot of determination, let me tell you!"

Dom nods. "Did Devon ever bring male visitors into your home, Ms. Evans?"

"Absolutely not. She never even talked on her cell phone while she was watching the twins, unless she was talking to me, of course. No, she took her job very seriously. We even discussed it once or twice. She told me that she had plenty of time for her friends when she wasn't at work. That if she had any other job— at a restaurant or in the mall or at a grocery store—she wouldn't be able to talk on the phone, so she shouldn't do it while she's watching the twins, either."

"Ms. Evans, are you aware of Devon's charges? That shortly after giving birth eleven days ago, Devon allegedly attempted to murder her newborn child when she threw her in the trash can behind her apartment complex?"

"Unfortunately." Debbie shakes her head, looks down at her hands. "Yes, I am."

"So, Ms. Evans, knowing this information, would you ever have Devon babysit your children again?"

Debbie looks up at Dom. Then she scans the courtroom, her eyes finally finding Devon's. For once, Devon doesn't drop her eyes. Not only does Devon want to hear what Debbie has to say, she wants to *see* her say it, too.

"Yes, I would," Debbie says finally. "And I mean it. Many people, those who know that Devon had watched the twins this summer, have asked me that very same question. And I tell them that if Devon really did what she's accused of doing—dumping her own baby in the trash—something very terrible and desperate must have happened for her to resort to that. I've never witnessed Devon in a crisis situation, but that morning must have been it. You know, I've been sitting here in the courtroom most of the day today, and I've heard what's been said, and it may be inappropriate for me to say this, but I'm going to do it anyway: I do not believe that Devon had planned on hurting that baby. It's just not in her. She may be an aggressive soccer player, but she'd never *ever* intentionally hurt anybody, and absolutely never someone as defenseless as a child. So, yes, I would have no reservations whatsoever about asking Devon to babysit my twins again."

The courtroom is silent. Devon's eyes are still connected to Debbie's.

"In fact," she says, "if she were available next week, I'd make a point to call her. That's how strongly I feel about it."

She's talking to me, Devon thinks. *Directly to me*. Devon feels something deep inside herself crack. A feeling, warm and nervous, moves through her. Melting what's been cold.

"Thank you," Dom says. As she turns around, she glances over at the prosecutor. "I have no further questions."

Dom walks back to her seat behind the defense table.

Judge Saynisch clears his throat. "State? Care to examine the witness?"

"No, Your Honor," Mr. Floyd says. "I do not."

"All right, then," the judge says. "You may now step down, Ms. Evans. Thank you for your testimony."

"You're very welcome," Debbie says.

As Debbie steps away from the witness stand, Dom leans over to Devon. "Still hanging in there?"

Devon turns to Dom. She shakes her head, whispers, "No . . ."

That coldness inside her had melted too fast.

These people—Coach Mark, Debbie, Henrietta, Kait, even her mom—they don't hate her.

And Devon starts to cry.

chapter twenty–three

"The defense calls Dr. Nicole Bacon."

It takes Devon a moment to recognize the woman whom Judge Saynisch swears in, because she doesn't resemble the Dr. Bacon that Devon knows from Remann Hall. A tight bun and charcoal suit replace the long graying braid and earthy skirts she's worn before. Instead of the hemp mocs, she's wearing stiff professional-looking black shoes, pointed at the toes.

"Please state your name for the record," Dom says.

"Nicole Alexis Bacon."

"And what is your occupation?"

As Dom goes through Dr. Bacon's credentials and employment history, and why she's qualified to testify as an expert witness, Devon allows herself a moment to tune out. She's so entirely wiped. Her jaw hurts; she must have been clenching her teeth the entire day.

So much like being in the goal, she thinks. Moments of intense boredom as the battle is being waged up the field in the offensive half, or moments of extreme stress, when the ball's in her box and chaos is all around. Players pushing and scrambling to get a foot on the ball. Or, in Devon's case, a hand. Exhausting not just physically, but also mentally.

That is what sitting in court feels like. But much, much

worse. And so much more is riding on it than the outcome of a soccer game.

"Denial is a defense mechanism," Dr. Bacon is saying now. "In simple terms, it's the mind's ability to *not* acknowledge something that is truly happening. It's the mind's way of keeping unpleasant things in check so that we don't become distressed all the time. Dr. Benjamin B. Wolman, in his classic work, the *Handbook of Clinical Psychology*, defines *denial* as, quote, 'a defense against the perception of a painful reality.' So, in Devon's case, that 'painful reality' from which she was protecting herself was her pregnancy. Actually"—Dr. Bacon puts her hand up— "we'd need to first acknowledge her *primary* painful reality. This is what triggered everything that followed."

"Please explain," Dom says.

Dr. Bacon nods. "Of course. Devon's primary painful reality— or the event that triggered everything else that followed— occurred when she first engaged in sexual activity. When she denied this fact to herself—the fact that she ever had sex at all— then the natural extension of this primary denial was avoiding the subsequent reality. This subsequent reality was the resulting pregnancy from that one sexual encounter."

"But, Dr. Bacon, in today's society, teen sexual activity is rather rampant. TV, movies, and popular music generally portray sex as something positive, an experience to strive for. So why would Devon feel so negatively about having engaged in sexual activity herself?"

"I believe shame played a major role," Dr. Bacon says. "When you hide something, or deny that something occurred, it's generally because you are ashamed."

"Yes, but what would Devon have been ashamed of?"

"During my sessions with Devon, I learned that Devon had viewed herself in a very particular—very *rigid*—way. She desperately needed to see herself as someone diametrically different from her mother."

"But isn't it common for teenage girls to have issues with their mothers? To want to be different from them? Sometimes to the extreme?"

"Yes. It's very common in adolescence to define oneself in terms distinct from one's same-sex parent. It's an important component of the identity's development process. But Devon was extremely strict in her definition of self. She had constructed some stringent rules for herself with not much wiggle room."

"And what were these rules, Dr. Bacon?"

"Devon's mother had been a teen parent herself; she had Devon when she herself was sixteen. And as Devon grew up, her mother entered into relationship after relationship with a variety of men. She paraded her sexuality in front of Devon in a manner that Devon both resented and feared. She watched her mother struggle financially. She witnessed firsthand the result of forgoing an education; her mom had earned her G.E.D. eventually, but never attended college. Devon was terrified of repeating this family history. So, she came up with Rule Number One for herself—avoid any sexual activity altogether. When Devon succumbed to it—broke her own rule—in her mind she had failed beyond forgiveness. She was so ashamed that she completely blocked out the memory of it. If she couldn't remember it, then therefore, in her mind, it never happened."

"Was Devon aware of the various forms of contraception?"

"Yes, we briefly discussed that. She'd learned a lot about birth control over the years during sex education classes at school and from her classmates. And also from her mother, incidentally. Devon's mother was generally very open about sexuality."

"Then why didn't Devon use it?"

"Well, if she had used a form of birth control, such as taking the pill or purchasing condoms, then this would be admitting to herself and others that she *planned* to have intercourse. Her self-imposed rule would never have allowed that."

"Okay, so just to quickly recap, Dr. Bacon, in your opinion, Devon's mind kicked into denial mode because she couldn't deal with the fact that she had had sex. Because she had convinced herself that the sexual relationship never occurred, she could then rationalize away the possibility that she might be pregnant."

"Exactly." Dr. Bacon nods. "And to throw another factor in the pregnancy denial equation, an interesting phenomenon that occurs in most of these cases is this: the pregnant woman's family and friends also deny the existence of a pregnancy. They don't want to see it, either, for their own reasons. So they are complicit in the denial; they reinforce it. In Devon's case, *nobody* confronted her with her pregnancy. Not her mother. And not one of Devon's peers confronted her—no teammate or teacher or classmate or coach. If anyone suspected a pregnancy, they certainly didn't step forward."

"What about the physical changes that occur during a pregnancy? The weight gain, the missed periods, the fatigue and vomiting. And as the pregnancy progresses, the enlarged abdomen that's unique to pregnancy. How do these women maintain the denial at that point?"

Dr. Bacon shrugs. "It's pretty simple, actually. Don't we all try to hide the extra ten pounds we've packed on over the Thanksgiving to New Year holiday season? We put on the bulky sweatshirt and looser jeans. It's the same with these women; they attribute their changing bodies to weight gain." Dr. Bacon pauses. "The issue of a missed period is reasonable, too. It's common for teenaged girls to experience irregular periods anyway. In Devon's case, she's a girl who's very athletic and exercises at an exceptionally intense level. A female athlete often experiences a disruption in the menstrual cycle; this is a menstrual disorder called amenorrhea. It's usually due to an imbalance of caloric intake. Not enough calories taken in to compensate for the calories burned during exercise. So when Devon started missing her monthly period, she really wasn't anxious about it. It had happened before."

"So Devon denied engaging in any sexual activity. And she denied the possibility of pregnancy. But Devon was pregnant all along, Dr. Bacon."

"That's right."

"So, in your expert opinion, what happened when the time came for her to finally give birth?"

"All right, think of it this way: if anybody sitting in this room, let's say the Honorable Judge Saynisch, for instance, suddenly had a baby burst from his body—"

"Objection!"

Judge Saynisch shakes his head disparagingly. "Have a sense of humor, Mr. Floyd. I, myself, am intrigued by the proposition. Continue, Dr. Bacon."

Dr. Bacon nods. "Thank you. Now, if Judge Saynisch suddenly gave birth to a baby, it would be an extremely shocking, not to mention emotionally wrenching, situation. Wouldn't it? Remember, for eight or nine long months, no pregnancy existed in Devon's mind. For the average woman, during that same nine-month period, she'd be thinking about her baby—what will its sex be? What will it look like? What should I name it? But for Devon, there *was* no baby. She formed no bond with that unborn child. So, when the baby finally arrived, this 'thing' she'd been hiding from everybody, including from herself, is inexplicably there. To her, it's not a living being. It's something she must continue to hide. So, she placed it in a garbage bag and threw it away. And, *voilà*, the denial continues. Out of sight, out of mind."

Devon is staring at Dr. Bacon. Listening to this is like looking in a mirror. Like staring at her own reflection. But how does the doctor know all this? Devon hadn't told her most of those things. She'd told Dr. Bacon about her mom, about growing up. About her middle name, Sky, and how it made her feel. She'd answered Dr. Bacon's questions as fully as she could. But she's never told anyone, not even Dom, what she'd experienced That Night.

"For most of the women who have abandoned their newborn babies shortly after giving birth and leaving them to die," Dr. Bacon is saying, "the reality that they've carefully constructed for themselves comes crashing down around them. The moment of birth is the moment they realize everything they've believed to be true about themselves was a lie. It's not a matter of *planning* to kill their newborns, it's a matter of panic—"

For the women who have abandoned their newborn babies . . .

Others have done this? How did Devon not know that?

A small relief sweeps through her.

She's not the only one.

*   *   *

Dr. Bacon was on the stand for over an hour, answering both Dom's and Mr. Floyd's intricate questions. When she stepped down, Judge Saynisch asked for the probation officer's risk assessment. The woman sitting over on the far side of the courtroom stands up and carries a thick file over to one of the women at the base of the judge's bench. And, as with Dom's exhibits, the woman places a sticker on it and hands it up to Judge Saynisch.

"Thank you, Ms. Gustafson," the judge says. "You may be seated."

Devon watches as the probation officer returns to her seat at the far table. Devon pulls her legal pad toward herself, picks up her pencil. Writes, *She didn't even say anything! Why no ?'s*

Dom scribbles back: *All in her report. No need. The J will read it.*

"All right," the judge says. "We're seeing the light at the end of the tunnel here. You've got any closing comments there, Mr. Floyd?"

"Yes, Your Honor."

Judge Saynisch glances at his watch. "It's currently three thirty-seven, Counsel. Unless there are no objections out there, I'd like to carry on." He looks around the courtroom wearily. "Object now or forever hold your peace."

"No, Your Honor," the prosecutor says. "I have no objection."

"Neither do I, Your Honor," Dom says.

"Very well. Mr. Floyd, keep it *very* brief. Note the emphasis on the word *very*. Drive on."

Mr. Floyd adjusts his bright blue tie, then stands.

"A child began her life in a garbage bag, Your Honor," Mr. Floyd says. "And her mother put her there. Her graveyard was to be a landfill in Graham, Washington." He pauses. "The baby's destiny was for a Tacoma Waste Management truck to pick up and take her to the Tacoma Landfill in South Tacoma. There, she was to join the other residential trash, be put through a compactor, and weighed. Just a mere six pounds, ten ounces, Your Honor, of the two hundred fifty-thousand *tons* of trash that crosses the scales at the Tacoma Landfill annually. After that, a tractor trailer was to haul her away to the Graham Landfill, where she would've found her final resting place." He pauses again. "But instead, Your Honor, fate intervened. You've heard today from Mr. Jacob Bingham and his Labrador retriever, Darko, who found the baby. . . ."

Mr. Floyd continues his speech, but Devon is stuck with the image he'd created in her mind—that tiny baby, the one who was lying on the bathroom floor between her legs, being crushed by a trash compactor within a black plastic bag. The tiny face, the miniature hands and feet. The small mouth.

Had she really meant for that to happen?

Standing in the doorway, the cramps start. She grips the doorframe with her left hand, leans against it. In her right hand is the trash bag.

IT's out, she thinks. *Why does it still hurt so much?*

She glances over at the sink.

There IT is. Slumped inside the basin like a rubber baby doll.

Devon slowly steps toward it, her breath ragged. The pain is subsiding again.

She looks down.

IT is still. The eyes half-opened. Blood smeared along one

side of the white porcelain basin, where the tiny body had slid.

The pale skin is covered with something. White goop, like cream cheese.

Devon feels the puke rising in her throat, turns, and heaves.

She collapses onto her hands and knees. Grabs the towels she'd already tossed on the floor. Sops up the blood and puke and urine and whatever else has pooled on the linoleum.

The pain comes again.

"Oh, GOD!" she sobs. She clenches her teeth. "Please! Please make it stop!"

She lies down on the towels, soaked with the filth, clutching her stomach and groaning until the pain finally fades again.

She glances up at the sink, panting; the small limbs motionless. Then she thinks she detects movement. Yes, a little foot appears, kicks up then back down and out of sight.

Then she hears a wail.

"OhgodOhgodOhgod!" She frantically seizes the garbage bag, starts shoving soiled towels into it. She picks up the cleanest towel, a white one.

That white towel she holds twisted in her hands.

Then she stands, leaves the bag at her feet. Approaches the sink.

Peers into it.

IT is there. The legs moving. The hands. The mouth opened and howling.

She hesitates a moment, watching.

Then drops the towel over IT.

She holds her breath and pulls the towel upward, scooping with both hands, IT snug inside.

Looks down at the open black trash bag, bends at the waist, and places the bundle into it.

Grabs the wastebasket beside the toilet. Dumps it. The stripped toilet paper roll and tampons she'd used to try to stop the blood from running down her legs, they tumble into the bag, too.

She lugs the bag into the kitchen, pulls out the trash container under the sink. Upends it, too. Not much is there. The frozen concentrate orange juice container, the Tim's chips bag, the crumpled newspaper pages.

She ties the bag shut.

She doesn't hear anything, doesn't feel anything, doesn't think anything. She picks up the bulky black bag, hauls it out of the kitchen. Across the living room past the ratty recliner. Opens the door, leaving it ajar. Takes the steps down to the parking lot and into the alley.

She finds the trash can, the same one she finds every morning when taking out the trash.

Yanks up the lid.

Other trash bags are already stuffed inside—black and brown and gray ones.

She closes her eyes, drops her bag in with the others.

Places the lid back.

And quickly turns away.

She looks up at the sky; it's started to drizzle.

"You've also heard today, Your Honor," Mr. Floyd is still pontificating, "from the respondent's coach and from her employer. You've read the letters that the Defense has submitted. Again, more people who described their distress over the respondent's refusal to reach out for their help—help they would've freely given had the respondent simply asked for it. You've learned from her primary care physician, Dr. Katial, that when faced with an opportunity to seek medical care, the respondent instead refused it. She attempted to deceive her doctor when she told him that she had started her menstrual cycle that morning, even going so far as to wear a sanitary napkin in her underwear for emphasis. She hid her pregnant body in oversized clothing. She misled her coach, describing in detail two injuries she supposedly sustained and their fictionalized treatment plan. All these facts point to one central theme: that the respondent had a plan to deliberately hide her pregnancy and then, after the baby was born, to dispose of its body in the trash can behind her apartment complex. At any point, the respondent could have changed her own course. At any time she could have relinquished her plan. But she didn't, Your Honor, and that's why we are here today."

Mr. Floyd continues to talk, but Devon doesn't follow his words anymore.

Because what he'd just said strikes her as the complete truth. *At any time she could have changed her own course*, he'd said.

"Thank you, Your Honor," Mr. Floyd finally says, and returns to his seat.

At any time . . .

When Mr. Floyd is seated, Devon notices him make a quick gesture under the table. He draws his fist toward himself and mouths the word, *"Yes!"*

Judge Saynisch nods at Dom. "Defense? You may commence."

Devon hears the prosecutor chuckle.

Dom stands. "A plan, Your Honor. That's what I've been

hearing this entire day from the state. That Devon Davenport had this *nefarious plan* to murder her baby. But where does the evidence point? It doesn't point to a nefarious plan, Your Honor. If anything it points to a *lack* of a plan. I'm not going to rehash everything that went on in this courtroom today. But you've heard Dr. Bacon testify about the role of denial in abandonment cases such as this one. You're heard Dr. Bacon describe the basis for Devon's denial—her shame, the fear of following in her mother's footsteps. And how Devon tried to protect herself by constructing strict rules for herself. The primary rule, Your Honor, was never to allow herself to engage in any sexual activity. Earlier today, Devon's soccer coach, Mr. Dougherty, testified how very hard Devon is on herself, that she hates to make mistakes and doesn't cut herself any slack. The evidence, Your Honor, doesn't paint Devon as a cold, calculating premeditating murderer, but as a panicked child who couldn't allow herself to fall short of her self-imposed, rigid standard."

Dom paces in front of the defense table. "I'm not going to lecture you about the *Kent* factors, Your Honor; you are well aware that these factors must be considered when deciding matters regarding where a juvenile should be tried. But I would like to quickly highlight those few that are particularly relevant to my client's case."

Dom goes on to discuss Devon's rehabilitative potential, based on the probation officer's evaluation in her risk assessment report. Dom emphasizes Devon's home life, which created an atmosphere that would breed Devon's brand of denial. Dom reminds the judge about Devon's academic and athletic achievements, her potential as a Division I soccer player. She talks about Devon's nonexistent criminal record prior to the incident.

"One of the main *Kent* factors that pertains to my client, Your Honor, is the calculus between societal protection *from* the respondent versus rehabilitation services *for* the respondent. The adult system has limited resources for rehabilitating its inmates. In contrast, the juvenile detention system was designed for it. The adult prison system does not offer its inmates therapeutic or psychiatric care, but the juvenile detention system does. Defendants within the adult criminal system are sentenced to prison, in part, to protect society. But how will society be protected if Devon is eventually placed there? Society actually stands to *gain* from someone as bright and determined as Devon *if* she is given the opportunity for therapy. Devon will go on to lead a productive life. Devon will go on to be a more effective adult. But she needs therapy, Your Honor. Give her a future. Allow her to remain under the jurisdiction of the juvenile court system. Thank you, Your Honor."

Dom returns to her seat.

Judge Saynisch clasps his hands under his chin. He surveys the courtroom. "I have looked at all the evidence presented to me today, and I've heard the witness testimony. And I am happy to announce that I have arrived at a decision."

Devon's heart picks up. *Already?* No recess for him to think about it? Devon feels Dom shift in her seat. Devon glances sidelong at her; Dom's face is calm, but she's gripping her pen so hard that her fingertips are white.

Devon peeks over at Mr. Floyd behind his table in the center of the room. He's wiping his hands on his pinstriped pants. One foot jiggles up and down.

Judge Saynisch looks down at a paper in his hands. "Pierce County's Juvenile Court will"—he glances around the courtroom again for dramatic effect—"*retain* jurisdiction of the respondent, Devon Davenport, in the case of *State versus Davenport*. The respondent will remain in custody here at the Remann Hall Juvenile Detention Center until trial."

Dom's expression doesn't change behind the wire-framed glasses, but Devon notices a puff of air escape between her lips.

The prosecutor clenches his jaw.

"I'll get with my clerks," Judge Saynisch says, "and we'll set a trial date. This court is adjourned."

The gavel bangs through the courtroom.

"All rise!"

Dom and Devon and the rest of the courtroom jump to their feet. Judge Saynisch collects his papers and slowly descends from his bench, exits the side door of the courtroom.

Dom turns to shake Mr. Floyd's hand. They converse for a moment. As they're talking, Mr. Floyd replaces his Bluetooth to the side of his head, and pulls his BlackBerry out of its holster.

Devon stares up at Judge Saynisch's empty bench.

When he'd announced his decision, Devon didn't feel as relieved or exhilarated as she imagined she would. And she doesn't understand why.

She's exhausted; that's the most prominent feeling Devon's aware of. Maybe she's too tired to feel relief.

Dom turns to Devon. Her smile is huge. She holds out her hand.

Devon looks down at it. She remembers the first time Dom had offered her hand for Devon to shake. That first time in the conference room. Devon had ignored it that day. Not a good way to kick off a relationship.

"We won!" Dom says. "Congratulations, Devon."

Devon reaches for Dom's hand. They shake, then high-five.

"No, congrats to *you*, Dom. You totally did everything." Devon tries to return Dom's smile, but she doesn't feel much like smiling.

"Hey, guys!"

Devon's mom's voice. Both Devon and Dom turn around to look for her.

She's rushing up from the gallery, pushing past the few people lingering between them. "That was amazing!" Devon's mom says. "You were so *awesome*, Ms. Barcellona." She giggles. "You should be on TV. Like that Judge Judy. You're that good."

Dom laughs. "I'll take that as a compliment, Jennifer. And please call me Dom."

Dom turns to Devon, squeezes her shoulder. "We *won*, Devon," she whispers. "We won."

Devon nods. "I know."

Then why does she feel like she's lost?

chapter twenty-four

"Let's pop into a conference room," Dom says as they exit the courtroom. "Just for a sec."

Dom, Devon, and her mom file into the nearest empty room. Dom drops her briefcase on the tabletop. Pulls out one of the folding chairs.

"Anyone want a soda?" Dom asks. "My mouth is a desert."

"Sure." Devon pulls out a chair, oriented in the customary position—directly across the table from Dom. "Maybe a Mountain Dew?"

"I'll get them," Devon's mom says.

"That would be great." Dom rummages in her briefcase for her wallet. "Diet Pepsi, if they have it. Diet Coke if they don't." She hands Devon's mom a handful of change. "Thanks so much, Jennifer."

When Devon and Dom are alone, Dom says quickly, "I know you're totally exhausted, Devon, and the last thing you want to talk about right now is law stuff, but you mind if we just take a few minutes to go over what went on in there?"

"Sure, Dom. That's fine."

"Okay, good. So the verdict. Now you do understand that the judge's decision to retain your case in the juvenile court system is great for you. But his decision makes no statement whatsoever about your guilt or innocence. All right? The hearing wasn't about guilt or innocence, but about in which system your guilt or innocence will be ultimately determined."

Devon yawns; she's so tired. How can Dom still be so energized? "Yes, Dom. I understand that."

"Okay. So, we're not off the hook. But I've been doing some thinking while we were in there."

Devon shakes her head. "Dom—"

"Yeah, I know. I'm totally obsessed, right? That's one reason why I'm still single at the moment."

"Who's single?" Devon's mom says.

Devon and Dom turn to look at her, standing in the doorway, already back from the soda machine.

"I am," Dom says.

Devon's mom hands out the cans. "Oh, well, you're not the only one—I definitely feel your pain. But, on the bright side, they had Diet Pepsi, so you're in luck. Or *still* in luck. Or your luck is continuing. Or, this is your lucky day. Or—"

"Mom."

"Oh, I'm so happy!" Devon's mom says. "This is *such* a good day. Isn't it?"

Dom smiles. "Definitely." She pops her Diet Pepsi and takes a sip. "So, I was just about to tell Devon that I think there's a slight chance that this thing could go away."

"What thing?" Devon's mom's face shifts to anxious. "The jurisdiction thing that was decided today? Please say no."

"No, not that."

"They can't reverse it, can they?"

"No, Jennifer. I really doubt the State would request an appeal. No, what I'm talking about is the slight possibility that we could get rid of the most serious charges. The attempted murder charge, specifically."

Devon feels something prick inside herself. She looks at Dom closely. "Why?"

"Well, because of that issue you brought up, Devon, about the detective and your mom not granting him entrance into—"

"Oh, God," Devon's mom says. "*That*. Don't remind me. That labeled me permanently as the courthouse slut."

"Mom," Devon says. "Please. Dom's trying to talk."

"Okay, hon." Devon's mom winks. "Sorry." She makes a motion of zipping her lips.

Devon shakes her head, sighs. She glances down at her Mountain Dew can. Condensation is forming on it causing tiny rivulets, like tears, to flow down its sides.

Dom takes another sip of her Diet Pepsi. "The reason why this issue is so serious is because what happened that morning with the detective may have been an illegal search. Searches and seizures are Fourth Amendment issues, very big deals. Anyway, if we can show that Detective Woods didn't have your permission to enter"—she nods at Devon's mom—"or that he didn't have probable cause to believe that he would find evidence of a crime inside your apartment—"

"Well, didn't he have probable cause?" Devon brings her thumbnail up to her mouth, chews on it. "Maybe?"

"For what?" Dom sounds annoyed now. "To find a teenaged girl staying home from school? Hundreds of kids do that every day in Tacoma." She sighs. "Look, if the police have neither permission nor probable cause, then they can't *legally* enter a person's home. Period. And we can argue that since they had neither, they in fact entered *illegally*. And if they entered illegally, then any evidence that they found inside the apartment because of it—like you, Devon, covered in blood and lying under a blanket, for example—"

The words send a jolt through Devon. Again. When will these ugly facts about her finally lose their sting?

"—then that evidence would not be admissible in court. At all."

But still . . . it should be admissible, Devon thinks. *Shouldn't it?*

"I'm sorry, Dom," Devon's mom says. "I know that I'm probably being very dumb about this legal stuff. But what does that all mean?"

Dom takes off her wire frames, polishes them on the hem of her skirt. "Look, a case is built on evidence, right? So, if we can block the evidence from coming into the trial, there's no case. Understand?"

Devon's mom's face brightens. "Are you kidding? No case? That would be great! We should definitely go for it."

"So, if we got rid of the search," Dom says, putting her glasses back on, "then the only charge that might stick is the assault charge against the doctor in the emergency room. And even with that one, we can make a pretty good argument against it. That crime is only a misdemeanor anyway."

"I still can't believe you did that, Dev," Devon's mom says. "Kicking that doctor when she was only trying to help you."

Neither can I. Devon traces one of the Mountain Dew can's tears with a fingertip. She opens her mouth, and before she realizes what she's doing, she says it. "No."

Dom turns to Devon, frowns. "What's 'no,' Devon?"

Devon can't take it back now. She clears her throat. "No, as in I don't think I want to do that, Dom."

Dom frowns. "Do what?"

Devon sighs. "You know . . . whatever it is you're talking about. Saying that the detective came into our apartment illegally. It just doesn't feel right . . . or something."

"Why not? Look, it might not even fly. We'd have to file a suppression motion, have a hearing on it, and there's a fair chance that we'd lose. Just based on your mom's body language alone, which arguably could convey tacit permission, not to mention the doctrine of discovery." She pauses. "At the very least, we could use the search as a bargaining chip. Get the state to knock the murder charge down to manslaughter, or even off the table altogether, and just keep the criminal mistreatment and abandonment charges." Dom's eyes are bright with the possibilities.

Devon can't believe that Dom is saying this. Where was all the tough talk she'd fired at Devon over the past week? Threatening that Devon could end up in jail for life, insinuating that she'd probably deserve it, too, if it ended up that way.

Was Dom so intoxicated with her victory that she couldn't see things straight anymore?

The day had been excruciating, something Devon would never ever want to go through again. But she had learned so many things . . . about herself.

She looks at her mom over on the opposite side of the table. She's digging in her purse now, searching for lipstick and the tiny mirror she always keeps inside. She'd dug around for a baby bottle once. She'd carried diapers, too.

Devon looks over at Dom. Dom doesn't know. She *thinks* she knows, but she doesn't. Not the details of That Night. Only Devon knows them. Only Devon and that little baby, and, thankfully, she'd never even remember it.

But Devon, she will *always* remember it.

Devon closes her eyes. She sees that tiny body again, lying in the sink, the limbs momentarily lifeless.

Devon had hoped, hadn't she? She feels the resistance, but her brain pushes through it. Yes. She had stood outside her bathroom door, the trash bag limp in her right hand. She had stared across the bathroom at the thing slumped in the sink. And at that moment, she had hoped that IT was dead.

But she saw it move again. She knew it was alive.

No, Dom has never seen the nightmare in the bathroom. The gore spread across the bathroom floor and splattered up the walls. How could Devon ever explain it to her? She bites her lip at the memory. No words exist to adequately describe that particular glimpse of hell.

I think there's a slight chance that this thing could go away, Dom had said.

This thing could go away.

How would that help, exactly? It wouldn't take away the memories. It wouldn't change the truth.

Devon feels moisture slipping down her cheeks. She wipes it away.

When you commit a foul, you have to take the penalty. In the game of soccer, it's not an option. Sometimes it's a kick, and sometimes it's a red card, sending you off the field to sit the bench for the rest of the game.

Devon had earned the penalty against her.

She must face it.

"What's the matter, hon?" her mom says suddenly. "You're not crying?"

Devon opens her eyes. She looks at her mom's face. She looks at Dom's.

"Oh, she's just so happy." Her mom sniffles then, and smiles. "It's been such a good day. Those are joy tears."

"Devon?" Dom asks, her tone concerned. "Are you okay?"

"Actually, I think I am," Devon says. "Because I know what I want to do, Dom."

Dom narrows her eyes, asks warily, "What?"

"I—" Devon takes a breath. "I want to plead Guilty."

Dom studies Devon quietly. Then, "Devon, you're tired." She starts gathering her things. "We don't need to make the decision now. There's no hurry. We'll get you back to your unit, give you a couple of days to rest up. And talk about this later." She looks up from her briefcase, over at Devon. "I should've just waited to discuss all this—"

Devon shakes her head firmly *no*.

"Why, Devon?" Dom stops packing her briefcase, places her hands on her hips. "Why in the world would you want to plead Guilty at this point? We have a strong case here. Even if the suppression motion fails. They can't sentence you beyond the age of twenty-one, and I think I can certainly do better than that—"

Devon shakes her head again. "*No*. I want to plead Guilty, Dom."

"But, again. Why?" Dom squints at Devon. "Because you think you'll get less time? Is that it?"

Devon swallows. The words are right there, waiting for her lips to form them, her tongue to force them out.

"Because you think that you'll get out of detention quicker that way? What?"

"No, Dom," Devon says, louder. "I want to plead Guilty because . . . I *am* guilty."

Devon's mom gasps.

Dom presses her lips together. Crosses her arms. "Look, you need to think this over, Devon. Very carefully. As I said before, there's no hurry. We'll talk about it tomorrow. The pros and the cons."

"No." Devon keeps her eyes focused on Dom. She doesn't blink. Not even once. "I've already thought this over very carefully, Dom. I'm not going to change my mind. Not tomorrow. Not ever."

Dom and Devon stand like that for a long moment, each watching the other.

There's a battle going on there, behind Dom's wire frames. Devon sees Dom's lips move. She has something more she wants to say.

Dom lets her breath out slowly. And nods.

"Okay, Devon." Dom drops her arms down to her sides. "Okay. I'll work hard to get you the best deal that I can." She shrugs. "I don't know if I agree with your decision, but the decision has to be yours." She shakes her head, sighs. "Not mine."

Devon throws her head back, smiles up at the ceiling.

She's never felt so free from something in her life.

She'd won.

author's note

The "Dumpster baby" phenomenon is an invisible American tragedy, poorly understood, and rarely acknowledged.

Though most people would consider the behavior inexplicable and unusual, its occurrence is disturbingly common. Approximately one baby is abandoned to a trash can every day in the United States, and when an American child is slain by a parent, 45 percent of those killings occur within twenty-four hours of birth.[1] After conducting a study of the issue over the nine-year period between 1989 and 1998, the Center for Disease Control and Prevention has concluded that "the homicide rate on the first day of life was at least 10 times greater than the rate during any other time of life."[2]

This may be just the tip of the iceberg. Experts believe that the vast majority of discarded babies are never found. No statistic exists for those babies. They lie in the unmarked graves of numerous municipal garbage dumps across the country.

I first became interested in "Dumpster babies" while living in Philadelphia in the mid-nineties. My husband was a law student at the University of Pennsylvania at the time, and my third child, Arianna, was about five months old. A few days before Christmas 1995, I was listening to public radio when I learned that earlier that morning an off-duty Philadelphia police officer had found a baby in the trash. He had been out walking his pit bull when the dog started barking and straining toward a trash bag set out at the curb near a couple of garbage cans. Inside the bag, the baby was still alive. The emergency room nurses nicknamed the newborn "Baby Nick" because he was miraculously rescued in "the nick of time" during the holiday season. Given the twenty-two-degree temperature that morning, had he been discovered even fifteen minutes later, Baby Nick would've undoubtedly died. This story strongly affected me. I had three little children of my own at the time, and though money was very tight for us in those days, I couldn't fathom what desperation would lead a woman to throw away her helpless infant.

Other stories started popping up in the news after that, and I took notice: the infamous Amy Grossberg/Brian Peterson story where two young unmarried—but economically privileged—college students killed their newborn son upon his birth, and the shocking story of Melissa Drexler, whom the media dubbed "Prom Mom." The New Jersey teen gave birth in the bathroom stall during her high school prom, returning to the dance floor shortly after dumping the baby's dead body in the restroom's trash can.

Then, when I was pregnant with my fifth child and my husband was an Army prosecutor in Washington State, I truly grew intrigued with the issue. My husband was assigned a "Dumpster baby" case to try. In that case, a soldier secretly gave birth in the barracks, placed the newborn in a trash bag, and tossed the bag into a Dumpster behind the barracks. Fortunately, another soldier passing by heard a cry and discovered the baby alive. I was amazed that a soldier living within the stringent military environment could successfully conceal her pregnancy.

As my husband began to pull the case together, many interesting facts came to light. He discovered that several members of the soldier's unit, including her superior officers, had suspected she was pregnant during the last few weeks of her pregnancy, but they were afraid to approach her. They didn't want to offend her if they were mistaken, and they didn't want to intrude on the female soldier's private life.

Beginning then, I started researching the issue for myself and discovered that baby dumping has a long history. In England during the Middle Ages, neonaticide (the killing of a newborn by its parent during the first twenty-four hours of life)[3] was such a problem that the *Stuart Bastard Infanticide Act of 1624* was enacted. This law mandated that any woman having concealed her pregnancy and childbirth must provide proof that the child was stillborn or be guilty of murder, often with the penalty of death. In Colonial America, lawmakers similarly passed statutes whose aim was to punish "lewd and dissolute women" who produced "bastard children" but lacked enough "natural affection to keep them alive."[4] By the time of the Reformation, children were being abandoned at such a high rate that governments in Northern Italy, France, Spain, and Portugal created foundling homes, often in cooperation with the Catholic Church, in order to help eradicate the problem.

Fast forwarding to contemporary times and the United States, in an attempt to alleviate the growing problem and give pregnant women a way to anonymously abandon their babies without fear of prosecution, Texas was the first state to enact what would later be termed "safe haven" legislation. That was in 1999, and since then, all forty-nine other states have passed similar legislation. Yet news outlets all over the United States are still reporting these "Dumpster baby" stories with alarming regularity. So why is this still happening? *After* attempts to answer that question.

---

[1] Kaye, Neil S. (1991). Abstract of Kaye, N., Borenstein, N., Donnelly, M.: Families, Murder, and Insanity: A Psychiatric Review of Paternal Neonaticide. Clinical Digest Series.

[2] Riley, Laura. (2005). Neonaticide: A Grounded Theory Study. *Journal of Human Behavior in the Social Environment,* Vol. 12 (4), 3.

[3] Dr. Phillip Resnick, forensic psychiatrist, was the first to coin the term "neonaticide," differentiating it from infanticide and filicide in his 1970 groundbreaking study on the issue (published in his classic article, "Murder of the newborn: A psychiatric review of neonaticide," in the *American Journal of Psychiatry,* Volume 126, 1970.)

4 Schwartz, Lita Linzer, and Isser, Natalie K. (2000). Endangered Children: Neonaticide, Infanticide, and Filicide. New York: CRC Press, 36–37.

acknowledgments

This may seem cliché, but it's nevertheless true: writing is a lot like being pregnant. First there's a conception. Then comes what feels like an endless period of development. And, finally, the birth. The hard work of labor is finally over, and everybody celebrates and gushes, "How beautiful!" and "You must be so proud!" You hold this new, exciting thing in your hands and somehow forget the pain it took to put it there.

Also, like a pregnant woman, a writer needs tons of support. *After* would never have entered the world had the following people not been there for me. I owe you all huge thank-yous! To Jo Anne Martin for letting me be a fly on the wall of your classroom in Remann Hall—if only every kid could have a teacher with as big a heart as yours. To Detention Manager Gerald Murphy and Remann Hall Administrator Daniel Erker for giving me access to the girls. To Dr. Phillip Resnick, forensic psychiatrist and pioneer in the field of neonaticide, for taking the time to provide me with feedback on an early draft of my book. To Brad Poole for allowing me to pick away at your brain about Washington State juvenile defense, and to Robert C. Gottlieb for your legal expertise with cases like Devon's. To Todd Kelley for showing me around Tacoma General, and to Laird Pisto for providing answers to my legal questions relating to hospital procedure. To Dr. Rohit Katial for all the time you spent thoroughly answering my many questions, and to the rest of my medical experts—Dr. Nicki Bacon, Dr. Barbara Echo, and Nan Gilette—for your willingness to impart your knowledge. To Susan Pollock for helping me to understand how Child Protective Services handles abandoned baby cases, and to Yael Ben-Ari for providing a social worker's perspective. To Virginia Pfalzer and Joan Dedman of Safe Place for Newborns of Washington for making me smart on "safe haven" legislation. To Mark Dougherty for checking that my "soccer mom" descriptions of "the beautiful game" made sense. To Alix Reid for believing in Devon's story from the very beginning and focusing her voice. To my fab "Wild Folk" critique group for all the insightful constructive criticism and "inciteful" debate. To my agent, Amy Berkower, for firmly believing in this book and finding it the perfect home at Viking. To Regina Hayes for firmly believing in this book and *offering* it the perfect home at Viking. To my wonderful editor, Joy Peskin, for your incredible enthusiasm and polishing rag in the form of a pen—your seemingly innocuous suggestions prompted me to work harder and stay up later than I ever thought I would. Fingers crossed, we will do it again! To Sara Gustafson, Vivian Gembara, and my little sis, Bonnie Etnyre, for reading early drafts and suggesting great improvements. To Connie K. Walle for granting me permission to use the poems that were once sandblasted into concrete on the Promenade at Point Defiance but have since washed away—at least they are commemorated here! To my mom, Elizabeth Moudry, for being a total "mom," nagging me nonstop to finish this book. To my long-suffering kids—Alix, Anastasia, Ari, Andrew, and Kat—for putting up with all those cold cereal and tuna melt/tomato soup dinners, that cluttered kitchen table, and often all-over-the-map ADD mom. This seven-year project was always present and demanding of my time and attention, almost like another sibling. To God through Whom all inspiration is given. And, of course, to Andy—words are inadequate to express my gratitude.